THE
DARK
INHERITANCE

AN INVESTIGATION DUO NOVEL

LIANE CARMEN

ISBN: 978-0-9984247-4-3 (paperback)

ISBN: 978-0-9984247-3-6 (e-book)

Cover design by 100 covers.

Author photo by Bill Ziady.

(www.matchframeproductions.com)

*To Mark and Ben, for understanding
just how much time it takes to write a book.*

CHAPTER ONE

SHE DIDN'T CARE that he was dead. It sounded harsh, but as far as Donna was concerned, her father had died long before the day he succumbed to cancer. She had lost her father the same terrible day her mother died during childbirth. A delivery that came early and went horribly wrong. In a split second, the life Donna had was gone.

She never even knew if she would have had a sister or a brother. Her father refused to talk about the baby or her mother. He just simply shut down. Donna tried to remember a time when her father hadn't been distant and cold, but those memories had faded a long time ago.

Donna looked over at Jay, still sleeping with one leg outside the covers. He was a hulking sort of man with dark hair and a goatee starting to show a little gray. Jay was 6'4" and the kind of man you wanted on your side in a barroom brawl. He'd been in a few of those and had the scars to prove it.

She nudged him on the shoulder. "Come on, baby, it's payday."

Jay uttered what sounded like an aggravated grunt and rolled over to bury his face in the pillow.

Donna threw the covers back and trotted off into the bathroom. Placing her hands on the vanity, she leaned in to take in her reflection in the mirror. Her red curls were in a tangled mess on top of her head, and her blue eyes sparkled with an excitement she hadn't seen in a long time. It was like her birthday and a winning lottery ticket all in one.

She stepped into the shower and let the hot water run over her. Everything would be different after today. No more shitty apartment. No more dead-end job.

She held up her left hand and imagined a larger diamond sparkling on her ring finger, an upgrade to something nice. Right before her dad died, Jay had finally proposed with the modest diamond she had now. They hadn't gotten around to the actual ceremony yet. Maybe now they'd fly somewhere exotic and have a destination wedding. Tahiti sounded nice.

Her father wouldn't be there to see his only daughter get married. Not that he would have cared, even if he was still alive. He hadn't been there for her first wedding either.

When she finished showering, she toweled off and attempted to tame her curls before accepting defeat with a sigh. As she stood looking in the mirror, putting the finishing touches on her makeup, Jay filled the doorway and then made his way into the small bathroom.

He smacked her on the butt. "Out." Jay was a man of few words.

Donna padded to the closet and pulled out the dress she'd bought for this day. She'd decided black would be most appropriate. It was wildly expensive, and it would have been something she couldn't afford in the past. But now, the world was about to become her kingdom. After today, never again would she have to worry about credit card balances or rent checks bouncing.

Donna dropped her towel and slid into the designer dress. She bit her bottom lip and slipped on the new black heels, which had cost even more than the dress. She stepped back and admired her reflection in the mirror. Perfect. Precisely the way someone who was about to be rich should look.

As she sat at the kitchen table finishing her coffee, Jay strolled into the kitchen. He chugged some orange juice right from the carton and wiped his mouth with the back of his hand.

"Ready?" he asked.

Donna frowned and tried to keep the dismay from her voice. "Is that what you're wearing?"

Jay was dressed in jeans, worn work boots, and a T-shirt from one of the construction companies he had worked at the year before. Donna was always nagging him to try to get his general contractor's license. He was too smart to be wasting his time in the Florida heat banging nails for someone else, but he always said he was just fine the way he was. His 'just fine' also meant time off when he was between jobs.

Jay glanced down at himself and scowled as he brought his gaze back up. "What's wrong with what I'm wearing?" He eyed Donna's dress. "And what are you wearing? Are we going to a fashion show, or are we going to pick up a big check?"

It wasn't worth fighting about. "You're right. It doesn't matter."

Donna didn't want Jay to change his mind about going with her. She just wanted to get this over with so she could start her new life.

* * *

The entrance to the lawyer's office was richly decorated and positively reeked of expensive furnishings and old money. Donna gave the receptionist her name and lowered herself into the chair next to Jay, perching on the edge, her heart thumping in her chest.

After a few minutes, she got up and paced in the reception area. As Donna's heels clicked rhythmically on the lobby floor, the girl behind the desk watched her with a hard stare.

Jay grabbed the bottom of her arm and pulled her back down into the chair. "Sit the hell down, would you?"

Donna was feeling too anxious to sit but did what Jay told her to. She had played the part, said the right things, cried on cue at the funeral. Today had been her goal. When her father was alive, he had never given her anything.

She'd left home as soon as she turned eighteen, determined to make it on her own. But how could she? If she hadn't needed someone, anyone, to take care of her, she would have never married Nick.

She could still hear her father's voice when she graduated high school, moved out, got divorced. "I could buy you a new car, a new house, but what would that teach you, Donna? You'd become entitled and unappreciative." That was a joke. He had never given her a single thing to be appreciative of, not his time or his money, and certainly not the affection a daughter deserved from her dad.

But now, there was no one to leave his wealth to. Donna was it. She'd never been a priority for him, but it wasn't like he could take his money with him.

Finally, after what seemed like an insufferable amount of time, a thin blonde woman in a skin-tight business suit pushed open the offices' doors. She glanced around the waiting room. Who was she looking for? They were the only ones sitting there.

The secretary's gaze froze momentarily on Jay and finally fixed on Donna. "Norman will see you now."

The woman waited for Donna and Jay to stand. She led them across the perfectly polished floor, through the glass doors, and into an office. Two chairs were placed in front of the most enormous mahogany desk Donna had ever seen.

4

She and Jay took their seats after shaking hands with Norman, her father's attorney.

The lawyer looked uncomfortable as he glanced in Jay's direction. "Donna, I expected you would come alone. Is this your husband? I was under the impression you weren't married."

Donna dismissed his concerns. "We'll be married soon enough. I have no problems with him hearing anything you have to say."

Jay leaned back in his chair, his lips set in a firm line, arms crossed in front of his chest. Clearly, he wanted Norman to know he had only come because Donna wanted him there.

Donna settled into the big brown leather chair in front of the lawyer's desk, crossed her legs, and flicked her expensive shoes in anticipation.

"Okay, then. As I told you on the phone," Norman said, "your father nominated me in his will to be the personal representative for his estate." That news hadn't surprised Donna. Her father didn't need family. He paid people to care about him and meet his needs. "I have filed the original last will and testament with the probate court, but there are some ... some special circumstances. I thought it would be best for you to come in so I could go through them with you."

Donna stole a glance at Jay. She had no idea what kind of special circumstances could arise from a will, but she reminded herself it would all be over soon.

"It's never an easy thing to lose a parent, but we're here today to discuss your father's final wishes."

Norman opened a legal-sized folder that had Donna's father's name typed on the label. He seemed to study the contents and then brought his gaze back up to Donna. A flicker of something crossed his face. Was it pity? Donna's heartbeat ramped up.

"I knew your dad for many years. I'm not under the

mistaken impression he was the father any little girl deserved. I do know that losing your mother hurt him more than he would ever admit, and maybe that changed him." Norman paused as if he wanted to say more and then removed what appeared to be a letter from the file.

Donna caught her breath and shifted in her seat.

"I'm going to read you a letter written by your father with the request to read it after his death. It was written not long before he died."

Donna's stomach twisted. Was this the old man's way of screwing her even after he was gone? Oh my god, what had he done?

CHAPTER TWO

NORMAN PERCHED a pair of glasses on his nose, cleared his throat, and began to read:

Dear Donna,

By the time this letter is read to you, I will be gone. As I prepare to meet my maker, I have had no choice but to reflect on the life I have led. It's times like this that all the business success in life really doesn't matter. You can't take the money with you, and you can't get the time back you should have spent living differently. I won't lie and tell you I'm not disappointed in myself as a father. I know you deserved better.

No shit, she did. Donna involuntary let out a sound and flicked her shoe impatiently. She wished the attorney would just get to the point.

Norman paused and seemed to wait to see if Donna would interrupt. Her lips were pressed together, her anxiety reflected by her bouncing shoe. He looked down and continued reading.

I wasn't a good father to you, and I was an even worse father to your sister.

Donna narrowed her eyes as she leaned forward in her chair. Had she misheard the attorney? "Um, I'm sorry," she interrupted. "But I don't have a sister."

Norman held up his hand. "Let me continue, and I'm sure it will start to make sense soon." The attorney turned his attention back to the letter, found his place, and continued to read.

Yes, that's right, your sister. Somewhere in the world, I have another daughter. I'm ashamed to say I never acknowledged her. When your mother died, I fell into a deep depression that I didn't know if I could ever get out of. I couldn't even be a father to you. I certainly couldn't handle being a father to another child, especially since I barely knew her mother.

Her mother and I met at the airport about a year after your mom died. I was on a business trip to New York and trying to get home before the bad weather set in. As I sat at the airport bar waiting for my flight, a pretty, young girl named Molly sat next to me. We started chatting. It was never my intention that anything would happen between us, but it began to snow, and all the flights were delayed. We were sitting at the bar, having one drink after another. Finally, the weather got so bad, they announced all flights were canceled for the night, and we should come back the next day. We decided to share a cab back into the city to find hotel rooms, and you can imagine what happened next. She was a sweet girl, and I was so very lonely without your mother.

The next day, we headed back to the airport, boarded our respective flights, and went our separate ways. This was not a relationship in the making. She was much younger than me, I'm ashamed to say, and while it was definitely consensual, I'm sure the alcohol played a big part. I certainly should have known better, but I was a lonely man, and ultimately, as you are more aware than most, a selfish man as well.

A couple of months later, she called my office, and I had no idea who she was. Apparently, I had given her a pen from my firm to write down her flight information, and she had used it to find me when she discovered she was pregnant. Was I even supposed to believe her that it was mine? I knew I couldn't have anything to do with this baby. I couldn't even handle the way you looked at me after your mom died. You were so needy, and you looked at me with your big blue eyes wanting me to make sense of it all. How could I explain it to you when I didn't understand it myself?

I couldn't handle another emotional attachment, so I bailed. Molly called several more times, and I finally told Ella to stop putting through her calls. I acted like a selfish bastard and refused to acknowledge her or my responsibility to my unborn child. I left her to deal with it on her own and turned my back on them both, much the way I emotionally abandoned you. She tried to bring your sister to see me once when she was a toddler. One look at her and I knew she had been telling the truth, but I called her a liar and told her to never come back.

As I prepare to die, I can't go without making it right by taking care of both my daughters. For that reason, I have designated that she should receive a portion of my estate. Until you have located my other child, your half-sister, Norman has been instructed that he cannot disburse your share of the inheritance.

I never thought much about trying to locate her until recently. I have tested my DNA and left my results and account information with Norman to pass along. See the article enclosed. It sounds like these two women have found that DNA can find almost anyone, and they've opened a detective agency to help others. Maybe they can help you. As this method may not be accepted legally, I have also left a sample with a local lab for final confirmation.

I don't know much about your sister or her mother except for the few details I remember from so long ago. Your sister was born when you were about five years old, and if I had to guess, her mother, Molly, was in her mid-twenties. She mentioned taking some time off after high school to travel. She was in New York for her first big job interview after graduating from college, though she never told me where she went to school. She was leaving to go back to Orlando, where she was from and was disappointed when the flight got canceled. She was missing her niece's first birthday party. She mentioned Bella, the baby, had been sick at Christmas, so she hadn't gotten to see her, and she knew her brother and his wife would be upset she wasn't going to be back in time. Apparently, she came from a large family, and it was to be quite the gathering with lots of relatives.

I wish I could tell you more that might help you. There's so much I'm sorry for, and I'm not even sure I'm brave enough to tell you everything that's on my mind. Please understand I have so much to make right, not only with you. I hope in time, you'll be able to forgive me and get the life you have always deserved.

Dad

Norman placed the letter in a folder. He added the newspaper article, a second sheet of paper, and a photocopy of the will. He slid the file across the desk until it was in front of Donna.

Paralyzed, she looked helplessly at Jay and then at Norman. "So, I'm not sure I quite understand this. Are you telling me I don't get my inheritance from my father because of some girl who may or may not be his child? What if I find her and she isn't his?"

Norman nodded. "According to the terms of your father's will, you'll need a positive DNA test between your sister and your father before I can distribute the funds from his estate to either of you. Though I can't verify his means, your father was firmly convinced she's his child."

While Donna was shocked, she saw Jay's hands balled up into fists. Clearly, he was pissed at the turn of events and seemed to be figuring out who he could punch to fix it.

Donna raked her fingers through her hair and let out a deep breath. "Okay, so my father split his estate between the two of us?"

Norman pursed his lips. "Not exactly."

Was there more? It was like her father had reached out from the grave to give her the middle finger. Donna hung her head and rubbed her temples. Finally, she glanced back up at Norman and nodded that she was ready for him to continue.

"Your father was very efficient about tidying up his affairs before he died. He dissolved his law firm, paid all his outstanding debt, and sold the house."

Donna let out a sarcastic chuckle. So much for ditching the apartment and moving to the house she'd grown up in. The only place where there were any memories, however distant, of her mother. He couldn't even leave her that. She shook her head and fixed her gaze on the design of the carpet under her chair.

Jay nudged her. "When we get your money, I'll build a great house. Better than anything he ever had."

Donna gave the attorney a hard stare. "Exactly how much are we talking about?"

Norman pulled a piece of paper from the folder and slid it across the desk in front of her.

Jay leaned over and whistled. "That's a lot of commas."

"So, this is my portion—half of his estate?" Donna asked. "My sister gets the same amount?"

Norman cleared his throat. "That is your portion, but his entire estate was divided into three equal parts."

Donna's eyes widened as she leaped from her chair. "Three?"

The attorney nodded. "One-third is to go to you, one-third to your sister, and the last third was left to …" With his finger, Norman scrolled through the document and flipped pages until he found what he was looking for. "The other beneficiary is Robert Taylor."

Donna's throat tightened and her eyes welled up. The word came out as a strangled whisper as she placed her hands on the attorney's desk and leaned over it. "Who?" She swayed woozily on her heels and lowered herself back down to collapse into her chair. "Who the *hell* is Robert Taylor? Is there also a brother he didn't mention in that stupid letter?"

Norman offered Donna a sympathetic shrug as his gaze shifted for a moment to the oversized man ready to explode next to her. It was clear he didn't know quite what to expect from Jay, whose face had grown crimson with anger. "I don't know who this person was to your father or why he included him in his will. I wasn't privy to his reasoning. I can only tell you what's in the document." His face softened. "I'm sorry, Donna, very sorry. I know this probably wasn't what you were expecting."

Donna let out a snort. "No, it—" She suddenly had a thought. "What about a life insurance policy? That wouldn't fall under these silly conditions. Surely my father had life insurance."

Norman sat for a moment before responding. "That doesn't fall under my responsibility. Any payout would be handled directly by the insurance company. It would be up to the beneficiary to contact the life insurance company directly."

Donna scowled. "But how would I even know who to—"
She faltered when she saw that look flicker across Norman's
face again. It said she was not going to like the answer he had.
"Let me guess. I'm not the beneficiary of his life insurance,
am I?"

Norman hesitated, then shook his head slightly. "I'm not at
liberty to discuss anything your father may have told me."

Jay spoke through clenched teeth. "Just give us the name of
the insurance company. We'll call them ourselves and find out
the truth."

Norman flinched and sat back in his chair, almost as if he
was afraid Jay might come over the desk. "I don't have that
information. I can tell you that the beneficiary is not something
they'll share, and it's not part of any public record like the
will is."

Jay elbowed Donna. "Don't worry. His will is bullshit. You
can just contest it."

Norman's gaze traveled from Jay to Donna as he shook his
head. He pulled out his copy of the will and started flipping
through the pages. "If you refer to Article VII, you will see
your father has included a no-contest clause. If you contest the
validity in any way, all benefits will be revoked as if you had
failed to survive him."

Donna's shoulders sagged. Her father had screwed her
even in the end. "So, what's my next step?"

"Let me explain the provisions left by your father."
Norman took a sip of coffee from the cup on his desk as if he
was buying time. "You have one year to find your half-sister.
The relationship must be proven by DNA. If she's unable to
take the test, we can also use an original birth certificate so
long as it lists your father. Once you have that, I can disburse
your portion to you."

"And what happens if I don't find her?"

Norman hesitated as if he knew his words would not be

received well. "If you do not find her within the one-year time-frame, your money will then be placed in a trust to be released to you upon your retirement at the age of sixty-five."

Donna's eyes widened in horror. She smashed her fist on the desk. "Sixty-five?" she shouted. "Are you kidding me?" Nausea overwhelmed her.

"I'm afraid I'm not."

Donna clutched her stomach. "And what about my half-sister's portion?"

"Your sister's money will be donated to The American Cancer Society, as will yours if you don't survive to the age when the trust terminates."

Now, all of a sudden, her father felt charitable. He admitted he hadn't been a good father. Was this how he asked for Donna's forgiveness? Hadn't he always told her that nothing could be appreciated unless you were willing to work for it?

Donna glared at the attorney. "I have no intention of waiting until I'm sixty-five. I'll just need to find her as soon as possible, that's all there is to it. She should give me a portion of her money just for putting in the effort to find her."

"No kidding," Jay muttered.

Norman's gaze bounced to Jay and then settled back on Donna. "Within the year, if you find your sister has prede-ceased your father or she passes away before she can collect, her portion will be divided between you and the other benefi-ciary, Mr. Taylor."

Donna pounded on the desk again, winced, and then rubbed the heel of her hand as it throbbed. "What? So, I have to do all the work, and he just sits back and does nothing but collect money? This is unbelievable. And if she's dead, am I supposed to have her dug up? What the hell was my father thinking?"

Norman seemed unsure how to respond, almost as if he

agreed with Donna. He removed his reading glasses and laid them on the desk. "I know this is a lot to absorb. You've lost your father and gained the knowledge of a sister in a short amount of time. I'm sure your father had his reasons for what he did."

"He needed to atone," Donna muttered. "He was afraid he'd end up in Hell."

Norman ignored her comment and gestured at the folder. "He included the information about his DNA kit and sample and has also included an article about a detective agency that may be able to help you. They were written up in the newspaper about using DNA to find family members. They've started an agency to help others solve family mysteries, so maybe they can help you."

Donna didn't have money to pay a detective agency. She also didn't have a choice. She stared down at her expensive shoes, furious her dad made her look like a fool once again. Now she regretted not just tucking in the tags so she could at least return the dress.

"Not sure how I'm supposed to pay this agency to find my sister so I can actually get what I deserve. It seems ridiculous that I have to find someone who didn't even know my daddy existed, and then I have to dump half his money on her—wait, I'm sorry, a *third* of his money. I'm the one who put up with his shit all these years." Donna's voice cracked. "I'm the one who was ignored while his secretary celebrated my birthday. The only reason I had anyone to celebrate the holidays with was because she invited me to her house. It's not fair."

"I understand," Norman said. "I wish I could do more, but I'm bound to simply administer his wishes. I can't change anything about how it's written. None of us can." He picked up the file from the desk to hand to Donna. "A copy of the will is in the folder as well. All the details about the stipulations around the other beneficiaries are very carefully detailed."

Donna snatched the file from his hand and stood. "I guess when I find this mystery sister of mine, we'll be back."

Norman held up his hand. "One more thing. Several boxes have your father's effects. I can have them sent to your apartment in the next day or so."

Donna snorted. "At least he left me boxes of his crap to throw away. How generous of him."

"Maybe if you go through them, you'll start to understand him a little better. It might help you grieve and forgive."

Donna fixed an icy gaze on the attorney. "There's nothing to grieve. The father I loved died a long time ago, and nothing he's done since would allow me to forgive him." She turned to Jay. "Let's go. I need some air."

Donna's heels clicked as she raced out across the polished marble. She couldn't escape that oppressive office fast enough. Anger burned her insides.

God, she hated her father. And now she had a new half-sister to hate, too.

CHAPTER THREE

THERE WAS A TENTATIVE KNOCK, then their office door creaked as it was pushed open. A woman with a mop of red curls peered around the door and inquisitively glanced inside. "Are you open?"

Jules and Becky both raced toward the door.

"Yes, yes," Becky said. "We're open. Come on in." She didn't want to tell this woman she was their first official visitor.

The woman's gaze fixed on the empty receptionist desk and then swept around the sparsely decorated office. A frown crossed her face as if she wasn't sure she was in the right place.

Becky tried to reassure her. "We just secured this space, so we're still getting situated." She gestured toward an open door. "Why don't you come into our office so we can find out how we can help you." Becky aimed a celebratory smile at Jules. They had a potential new client.

The women had been best friends since they were little girls. When Jules decided she wanted to slow down her photography business and open the agency, Becky didn't think twice.

The boutique she had owned with her business partner, Tonya, had been her happy place. And then it wasn't. Even though she knew none of it was Tonya's fault, it could never be the same. Becky sold her share to one of the employees who was thrilled to get it and went to work with Jules.

Every part of Becky had expected she'd be getting ready to have a baby. She'd desperately needed something to distract her and take her mind off the reality that the pregnancy hadn't happened.

Jules directed the woman to the chair in front of her desk, and Becky rolled her chair over.

Jules made introductions. "So, my name is Jules." She gestured at the chair next to her. "And this is my partner, Becky. Your name?"

The woman shifted in her seat. "I'm Donna. Donna Thomas."

"Hi, Donna. So, what brings you in today?"

The woman let out a huge sigh, and Becky noticed her eyes glaze over. "I'm not sure where to even start. Apparently, I have a sister I didn't know about. Well, a half-sister."

Becky raised her eyebrows and shot Jules a knowing look.

"Did you find her through DNA testing?" Becky asked. "It's not as uncommon as you might think to find something unexpected like that in your results."

Donna shook her head. "My father died. He told me in a letter and stipulated in his will that I can't get my inheritance until I find her." She gritted her teeth. "She's also due a nice chunk of change thanks to his guilty conscience."

"Well, that's a new twist I've never heard of," Jules said.

Donna slid a folder out of her bag and placed it on the desk. "This is everything he left me. Apparently, my father also did a DNA test."

Jules pulled the contents from the folder and placed them on the desk in front of them.

"Hey." A glimmer of recognition crossed Becky's face. "That's the news article about our agency." What happened to

Becky was big news in their town. The local media had all covered it.

They weren't licensed investigators just yet, but Jonas—Jules's half-brother was a cop—had pulled a few strings and backed them so they could get the doors opened. Technically, they were training under him, but he was mostly a silent partner. Besides, they specialized in DNA reunions, and it wasn't like they carried guns.

"It was my father's suggestion to see if you could help me. Apparently, he saw the article and saved it. I glanced through it. That was *quite* a story." Donna's eyes met Becky's. "I'm glad you're okay."

Becky dipped her head in acknowledgment. "Thank you. It taught me a lot about the power of DNA." She gestured at Jules. "My partner was adopted and used DNA to find her birth mother."

"And a half-brother who's fabulous. We wanted to be able to help others. It's what inspired us to open the agency." Jules pulled the letter out of the folder. "Are you okay if we read this?"

Donna shrugged. "Sure. I don't have anything to hide. My father was an asshole as you'll soon see for yourself."

Jules laid it on the desk between her and Becky. Donna sat silently as their eyes traveled down the page.

"I can see why you'd be upset," Becky said when she finished reading and glanced up.

Donna answered with a dismissive wave. "She gets the money without ever having to know what a bastard her father was. She dodged a bullet as far as I'm concerned."

Jules scanned the rest of the contents in the folder. "From what I can see, your father left his DNA sample with a local company. That can be used to legally confirm paternity, but you'll need a sample from your half-sister. He also left his account information and password for a DNA test he took with one of the companies that utilize autosomal testing."

"Autosomal?" Donna asked.

Becky answered. "DNA is passed down from generation to generation. An autosomal DNA test looks at the segments of your chromosomes which contain DNA that's shared with everyone you're related to. The test provides matches with your genetic relatives and tells you how many centimorgans of DNA you share. Based on that cM number, we can come close to figuring out how you might be related."

Donna let out a breath. "So, you could use this test to find my half-sister?"

Jules leaned back in her chair. "Those tests are a great resource for finding unknown family members. However, here's the problem with your situation. The only way to use DNA to find your half-sister is if she tested or a descendent of hers tested. Otherwise, you both share all the same matches to your father's side of the family."

"And since we want to look everywhere possible for that match, we need to consider all the sites where your half-sister might have tested," Becky added. "Your dad tested at only one of the possible sites. We'd need you to take a few tests, too. Don't worry. Your half-sister will match you just as easily as she matches your father. Less DNA, of course."

Becky pulled a few boxes from her desk drawer and placed them in front of Donna. "They're simple. Just a little saliva and we send it in."

"But it sounds like I'm looking for a needle in a haystack." An aggravated moan escaped Donna's lips. "My father had to know this wouldn't be easy. He didn't even leave me any information I can use in that letter."

A smile crept across Jules's face. "That's not necessarily true." She glanced over at Becky. "Will you take some notes on the whiteboard?"

Jules picked up the letter as Becky got a marker and stood poised to write. "Your father actually told us more than you might think. We know the woman he met is named Molly. We know she has a brother who has a child named Bella. Maybe her given name is Isabella or Annabella."

Donna's brow wrinkled as Becky wrote on the board. "What would you be able to do with that?"

"It's a piece of the puzzle," Jules said. "From this, we also know she got pregnant in the winter in New York. It's a big snowstorm. But we also know it was after Christmas since Molly said she hadn't seen her niece for the holidays. So, now we have that night at the airport narrowed down to January through March unless we can find an unusually late winter storm in April of that year. Figure nine months or so from then is your sister's birthday." Jules paused. "I'm very sorry about your mother. How old were you when she died?"

"I was almost four." A flicker of pain crossed Donna's face. "She was pregnant. There were complications during childbirth. Both she and the baby died."

"Oh, I'm so sorry." Jules waited to see if Donna would say more. "Do you need a minute?"

"No, I'm okay." Donna wiped at the wetness that had formed under her eyes. "It was so long ago, but it still hurts. I basically lost my whole family when it happened."

"I can't even imagine," Jules said. "Well, your father thought you were about five when your half-sister was born. And he says when he met Molly it had been over a year since your mother had died, so that lines up. When were you born?"

"February 18, 1990."

Becky scribbled the date on the board. "And when did your mother die?" she asked gently.

"January 2, 1994." Donna winced. "It was—it was right after Christmas. I remember the tree stayed up for so long. Finally, it was surrounded by a circle of pine needles, and the ornaments were hanging on bare branches." She shrugged. "Somebody eventually took it down." Donna glanced down at her hands in her lap. "My mom was the one who always decorated the tree. We never really had a tree after that."

Becky spun around. "That must have been so hard for a little girl."

Donna's eyes welled up again. "It was." Her voice took on an edge. "It would have been nice if my father had tried to make it easier, but he pretty much checked out after that. He didn't have a way to officially back out of fatherhood with me, but he was smarter with the next one. He accepted no responsibility, and then there was nothing to escape."

Jules shook her head and hesitated.

"I'm sorry," Donna said. "Keep going. Really. It's okay."

Jules glanced up at the notes Becky had taken. "So, that means you were almost four when your mom died in January of 1994. Your dad met Molly about a year later, and we know it was during the winter, but after Christmas, so we're looking at the early part of 1995. If that's the case, your sister—"

"Half-sister," Donna said, stressing the first word.

"Sorry, half-sister," Jules corrected herself. "She must have been born in late 1995. And from what your father's letter said, her mother was from Orlando. So, we know most likely, your half-sister was born in October, November, or December of 1995 in Orlando, Florida, to a mother with the first name Molly. We'll start searching for records to see if we can find anything while we wait for your test results."

Becky added. "If we find anyone that seems to match, we can also start researching and building family trees, looking to see if they have a brother and a niece named Bella. Your dad also guessed she was in her mid-twenties in early 1995." She wrote on the board. *Molly born 1970?* "We'll start looking in Orlando and hope she grew up there. It's all just a matter of putting the puzzle pieces into place until they all fit."

"I'm amazed you figured out all of that." Donna's eyes scanned the whiteboard. "I thought that letter was useless."

Becky was still impressed by how good Jules was at all of this, but after spending so much time training with Mimi Morris, a seasoned genealogist, they'd both come a long way. The private investigator training they'd gone through had only given them more ways of uncovering information.

"You just have to look at all the clues." Becky capped the marker and went back to her chair. "Leave no stone unturned. Of course, there are a few things to consider if we start searching this route. Most likely, Molly got married and changed her last name. There's also the possibility she gave the baby up for adoption. We could find Molly and discover she has no idea where her daughter is now."

Donna's shoulders dropped, and she sighed. "Wait." She leaned forward in her chair. "The letter mentioned bringing my half-sister to see my dad when she was a toddler. That means Molly didn't give her up for adoption, at least not as an infant."

Becky and Jules nodded in unison.

"Great catch," Becky said. "You're probably right. That makes the search much easier."

"My dad left me a few boxes of stuff," Donna said. "I have no idea what's in them, but I can have his lawyer send them to you." She shrugged. "If you want to sort through them."

"It can't hurt. So, are you thinking you want to hire us?" Becky pulled out a piece of paper with their rates on it and slid it across the desk. So far, they had solved several adoption cases, even before they had the office space, but this case was much different. This could be solved through DNA, but it sounded like they would have to do some old-fashioned detective work, too.

Donna glanced down at the paper and frowned. "The quicker you find her, the less it costs me?"

Becky nodded. "Pretty much."

Donna pursed her lips as she folded the piece of paper and placed it in her purse. "If you find anything in those boxes related to a life insurance policy, you'll let me know?"

"Of course." Jules slid two business cards across the table. "Here's our cards so you'll know how to reach us."

Donna eyed the cards on the desk before she picked them up. "Investigation Duo. Cute."

"We'll figure this out, don't worry," Becky said. "Any other questions?"

Donna reached for her purse. "Will you take a credit card?"

After Donna had given samples for the DNA tests and filled out paperwork, she shook hands with Becky and Jules and turned to leave.

"Hey," Becky said as she grabbed the folder off the desk. "Don't forget your file. We made a copy of everything, so we have a set here, too."

Donna took the file, but as she got near the front door, she spun around. "Finding my half-sister is my priority, but there's someone else who stole part of my inheritance. I need to figure out who got the rest of my father's money. I definitely want to have a chat with a certain Robert Taylor."

CHAPTER FOUR

Surrounded by Donna's boxes, Jules grunted as she attempted to lift one of them. "What could be in here? Feels like bricks."

"Need help?" Becky asked after she dropped her stuff on the receptionist's desk.

Jules pushed her long wavy hair off her face. "From you?" Becky's petite frame couldn't weigh much over a hundred pounds soaking wet. She'd never exactly been the muscle in their friendship.

Becky smirked as she strolled past Jules. When she returned, she was wheeling a hand truck behind her.

Jules let the box fall back to the floor. "Okay, I need help."

"I forgot Bryan left this here when we moved in some of the file cabinets. Kind of glad now."

The women systematically worked together until all four of the large boxes were in their office.

"I'm guessing these are the boxes Donna mentioned." Becky took a pair of scissors out of the desk drawer and handed them to Jules.

"Yeah, I caught the courier from the law office dropping

them off." Jules rolled her eyes. "He wouldn't even consider bringing them back here. Said he was only paid to get them inside the front door."

Jules cut the tape and lifted the flaps on the first box. "No wonder it was so heavy. It's filled with file folders." She pulled out the first folder and opened it. "Well, I guess this explains how he made his money. He was a corporate attorney." Jules removed the next couple of files. "Looks like his job was to make sure they didn't have to pay out if they got sued. I'm sure they compensated him well."

Becky grabbed a handful of files and studied the typed labels. "Hey, Donna's last name is Thomas, right?" She tilted her head. "Why does the name McDermott sound familiar?"

"It's probably her maiden name. That was her dad's last name on the will."

"Oh, right. Well, this one is labeled Ava McDermott."

Jules scooted her chair closer to Becky. "You think that's Donna's mother?"

"Maybe." Becky started skimming through the folder. Her shoulders sagged. "Oh, this is so sad."

"Why? What does it say?"

"It looks like Donna's father was a plaintiff himself. He sued the hospital for negligence and wrongful death." Becky glanced at the date. "May of 1994."

"So, four months after she died."

"Yeah …" Becky's voice drifted off as she kept reading. "It says she was admitted when she was thirty-two weeks pregnant. Complained of a bad headache but had a history of migraines. They gave her a prescription for some Tylenol with codeine and sent her on her way."

"Uh, oh."

"Yeah, 'uh oh' is right. Ava collapsed in the parking lot before they even got to the car. It says she was unconscious and unresponsive." Becky flipped the page. "She had a weak pulse when they finally got her back inside. She wasn't breathing, so they intubated her and took her in for an emergency C-section."

"Thirty-two weeks. Is that too early?"

Becky tilted her head and considered the question. "Well, two months early, and this was about twenty-five years ago. Nowadays, the survival rate would probably be pretty high at that point." Becky continued to read. "The infant needed to be intubated as well and rushed to the NICU. It says Ava never regained consciousness." Becky gasped as her hand flew up to cover her mouth.

"What? What else does it say?" Jules asked urgently.

Becky's eyes were filled with tears. "It says Ava had been without oxygen too long, which impacted the baby." There was an uncomfortable silence, and finally, Becky choked out the words. "They were both brain dead. Donna's dad had to make the decision to take them both off life support."

Jules let out a whoosh of air. They were both silent as the painful story of Donna's family hung in the air around them.

"I can only imagine how crushing that was for him." Jules paused. "Not that I'm excusing the way he treated Donna, but you can understand how someone might not recover from something like that. I wonder if Donna knows this. She said her mother died during childbirth."

"The hospital settled out of court. Not even that much money considering." Becky flipped to the next page. "Oh, wait —the autopsy showed a blood vessel burst in her brain. Apparently, it wasn't anything anyone did or could have prevented. It was a congenital abnormality." Becky looked up. "I guess maybe the hospital settled just to make the case go away."

"That's so sad. Was it a boy or a girl?" Jules gave a small shrug. "Not sure how this could be related to Robert Taylor, but you never know."

Becky located a page near the back. "Here's Ava's death

certificate. It lists the aneurysm as the cause." She turned to the next page. "And here's the baby's." Becky scrunched up her face. "It was a boy. Jerome James McDermott, the third." Her brow wrinkled. "So, he named his son after him, even though he knew he wouldn't make it?"

"Seems that way."

Becky closed the file. "I wonder if Donna would want to see this."

Jules fished around in her drawer and pulled out a tote bag. "Let's put everything in here we think she might want."

Becky scanned the next few folders. She held one up for Jules to see. "Look at this. In December of 1994, his letterhead now says Jerome McDermott, Personal Injury Attorney."

"So, after his own case, he wanted to help others."

"These other files are all cases where he fought for the plaintiffs who were injured." Becky glanced over the first page. "I sort of remember this one. A ten-year-old girl injured on the ride at the fair over in Parkland Springs."

"I remember that. Our parents refused to let us ride any of the rides because someone had gotten hurt. Did he win?"

Becky nodded. "Oh, yes, he did. Big. Almost a million dollars. And that was a long time ago."

Jules's mouth dropped open. "Geez."

Becky flipped through the remaining files in her lap. "More of the same."

"I doubt there's much in these that could help us. It's not like he represented Molly. Maybe he wanted Donna to see that he tried to help people."

"Just not his own daughter." Becky stuffed the files back in the front of the box. "I mean, I feel sorry for him. What happened was just awful, but she was a little girl. She needed him."

"I can see now why she's so eager to get her inheritance. It must be substantial. Did you upload the father's DNA to the other sites?"

"Yesterday. So far, no parent/child match."

Jules dragged the file box toward the closet. "Well, we knew it would be a long shot. We still have the other sites when Donna's results come in. They'll have bigger databases anyway."

"That could take a few weeks. Maybe we should see if we can figure out anything about Molly."

"Let's make a plan of attack." Jules went to the whiteboard. "You see if you can find anyone named Molly born in or around 1970 in Orlando." She tapped the end of the marker against her lips. "Molly said she was heading home for her niece's first birthday. So, if it was the winter of '95 in New York, she would have a brother with a child born sometime in January, February, or March of 1994, the previous year." She made notes on the board and called out over her shoulder as she wrote. "Maybe go into April of '94. Just in case."

Jules turned back around. "You might also see if you can find any weather reports from that year that talk about a big storm. Maybe we can figure out when it was."

Becky nodded in agreement and took a photo of the white-board with her cell phone.

Jules wrote her name on the board and underlined it. She started adding bulleted items.

"I'll see if I can find birth records. Some of them are online, but if not, maybe there's another way. Jerry did say Molly came from a large family. Maybe they were Catholic, and the baby was baptized. Might also explain why she decided to have the baby, although I'm sure being unwed didn't thrill her parents. If we need to, we could check out some of the churches in Orlando." Jules capped the marker and leaned against Becky's desk. "Remember, I'm out on Monday."

"Photography job?" Becky asked.

"Nope." Jules bit her bottom lip. "Lunch with Barb. She's been good about texting and emailing. Even a call every so often. I guess she's finally ready to meet in person." Jules had used DNA to successfully find her birth mother, but at the time, Barb hadn't been ready to see her. Now that the plans had been made, Jules was more nervous than she wanted to admit.

"Oh, Jules, I'm so happy for you. I know the last six months have been hard waiting."

Jules put her hand on Becky's shoulder. "It's nothing compared to what you've been through."

Becky and swallowed hard. "Let's see what's in here." She leaned down to open another box, a signal she wasn't going to talk about the failed IVF. "This one seems to have desk stuff in it. Like maybe when he cleaned out his office." Becky reached for a framed picture of a woman pushing a swing that held a toddler with wild red hair. She laughed. "This *has* to be Donna and her mother."

Jules pulled out several more. "There's a few of Donna's mother and look, their wedding photo. If he still had these up in his office all these years later, that must say something about how strongly he felt about losing her and their son. I'm sure Donna would want these."

Jules placed the frames in the tote bag and then grabbed a large envelope from the box. She undid the clasp and slid the contents into the palm of her hand. More pictures but without the frames.

Becky leaned over Jules's shoulder to see. School portraits of Donna. A graduation picture. "See, he did care. He just didn't show it." There were photos of a family, and on the back, someone had written, *Jerry at ten*. There was a shot of a young Jerry grinning while he displayed a large fish he had caught. The next photo was a toddler-aged Donna, two other small children, and two women. Jules studied it for a moment. "Well, that's Ava. I wonder who the other woman was." She flipped over the photo. *Summer vacation with Kathy and family, 1993.* "Maybe Ava had a sister named Kathy."

"Maybe. Let's ask Donna when we see her next. Summer of '93. Ava would have probably just found out she was pregnant." Becky reached for the picture and wrinkled her nose. "She looked so happy."

Jules added the photo to the pile of pictures they had already looked at. There were two more photos. Jules caught her breath. The first was a hospital picture of a tiny baby with a tube down his throat and wires everywhere. The tag said, *Baby McDermott.*

"Oh wow, that must be Donna's brother. This must have been when he was first delivered."

"The death certificate said he died three days later." Becky shrugged awkwardly. "I guess Donna's dad waited a few days before making the decision."

"I'm sure she'll want this. It didn't sound like she even knew whether it was a boy or a girl. This is probably the only picture of him that exists."

Becky gave the last picture a quizzical stare. "Who do you think this is? It doesn't look like it's Donna." She held it up.

Jules shook her head after looking at it. "It's definitely not Donna. Is there anything on the back?"

Becky flipped it over and read what was written. "*Jerry, this is your daughter, Ally. She's 6 months old. How can you not even want to meet her?* She signed it Molly. Damn. No last name."

"That's okay." A grin spread across Jules's face. "At least now we know Donna's sister's name is Ally."

CHAPTER FIVE

Donna nodded toward the boxes. "I see they got delivered. Find anything in those boxes of crap?"

"We haven't finished going through them all," Jules said. "But we have found some things that are fairly interesting."

"Oh, yeah? Like what?"

"Your father became a personal injury lawyer after your mother died. He went from defending big corporations to helping victims. He worked on some big cases. Did you know that?"

Donna snorted. "He didn't talk to me about work. He never said much to me at all."

"Well," Becky said. "I think maybe he wanted you to know how he fought for others so they would be compensated if something terrible happened."

"Hmmph. I doubt that was my father's logic. So, it was all a bunch of case files? That's a waste."

"The first box was, for the most part." Becky pulled the tote bag from beside her desk. "And we found a file about your mother. Your father filed a wrongful death suit. I suppose it was also on behalf of your brother."

Donna's mouth opened, then she closed it slowly. "So, you're saying it was—it was a boy? I would have had a brother?"

"Yes, it was a boy." Becky pulled a file from the bag and pushed it across the desk toward Donna. "I'm not sure if you know all the details. There are things in here that may be painful to read. You might want to wait until you're home with your husband."

"We're actually not married yet," Donna said. "My fiancé, Jay, wasn't a big fan of my dad's. I can't believe after all these years I finally get to learn what happened. My father wouldn't talk about it. It was taboo to even mention her or the baby in his presence. When she died, he cut off her side of the family. Aunts, uncles, cousins—poof, just gone."

"Did your mother have a sister named Kathy?" Jules asked.

Donna smiled. "She did. My Aunt Katherine. She was my mother's older sister. We spent a summer with her and my cousins at the beach." She offered a small shrug. "I don't even know where they are anymore."

"There were some other things we found as well. Pictures. I'm sure you'd want them." Becky pulled out the framed prints and put them in front of Donna.

Donna picked up one of the pictures of Ava. She ran her finger across it and then wiped the dust on her pants. "My mom was beautiful. I knew she would be, but I couldn't even remember what she looked like. I've never even seen this picture." Donna stared at her parents' wedding picture. "They looked happy. I'm sure they didn't know on that day how wrong it would all go."

Next, she picked up the photo of her with her mother and smiled as she blew off a layer of dust. "This was the swing set in our backyard."

Her father had never pushed her in the swing or down the slide. It had sat unused for years after her mother died.

Donna tossed the frame back on the desk. "He must have only kept this one because my mother was also in it. There were never any pictures of me after she died."

"That's not exactly true." Becky handed the large envelope to Donna. "These are pictures, too."

Donna unclasped the envelope and slid the contents onto the desk. A small smile of recognition crossed her face. "This is my father's family." She pointed at the older couple. "Those are my grandparents. The guy in the wheelchair was my grandfather." She gazed off as if she were reciting a story. "He was injured in some sort of work accident and paralyzed. My father was only twelve when he had to start working to help out the family."

Donna recalled all the times her father had reminded her. *I had to work for everything I had. No one had anything to hand me.* It was true, but she never understood why he hadn't wanted to make her life easier if his had been so hard.

"My grandfather died when I was little and my grandmother—she didn't drive. So, unless my dad took me to see her, which wasn't often, I didn't get to spend time with her. She lived in an assisted living home and died when I was a teenager."

Donna flipped through the next few pictures. "These are all my school portraits." She held up a photo of herself in a cap and gown. "This was my high school graduation."

Jules reached for the photo to look more closely. "Who's that woman with you? Is that your aunt on your father's side?"

Ella, her father's secretary, had brought flowers to her high school graduation. For many years, she handled everything in her dad's life. Including Donna.

Donna pressed her lips together and looked up. "My dad didn't have any siblings. This was his secretary. She stood in for him when he couldn't make it." *Big case, Donna. I have to be in court. Sorry, I can't make it, but Ella will be there.* How many times had he said that to her over the years?

Donna's expression turned wistful. "I was surprised she wasn't at the funeral, but someone told me she broke her leg. Ella was wonderful to me. On holidays, I was always invited to her house. She even invited people from her church who had no place to go."

"She sounds like a lovely woman," Becky said.

Donna nodded. "There's room for everyone she always said. Ella only had one son, but her siblings had kids and she invited people over all the time. There were always kids to play with. Mostly boys, but occasionally there were a couple of girls. The older one was a bit of a tomboy." A smile crept across Donna's face. "I loved to play mother with the other one. Dress her up, style her hair. You know, that kind of thing." Her expression turned melancholy. "I guess I thought I could replace the baby my mother didn't have." She squeezed her eyes shut for a moment. "Of course, I never knew it was a boy." Donna shuffled the photos in a pile and grabbed the envelope.

Becky leaned forward in her chair. "There's a couple you missed."

"More of my father fishing? I can't even fathom him having the patience to fish."

Becky shook her head. "No. I think you'll want to see the last two pictures at the bottom."

Donna shuffled the majority of the photos out of the way. She slowly brought her hand up to cover her mouth while staring at the one of the infant. "Is that—"

"Looks like he was given your father's name," Jules said.

"It was tradition to pass it down," Donna said mindlessly. But then confusion flooded her. The story her father told her contradicted what she held in her hand. "Wait, he lived? I thought he died the same day my mother did."

"According to the death certificates, they both actually died three days later. I also found the order form for her headstone." Becky passed a yellowed piece of paper to Donna. "It appears they were buried together."

Donna sniffled and fought back tears. "Where is she? She's not in the plot with my father."

"She's not far," Becky said gently. "The address is on the order form."

Donna noted where the cemetery was located. All this time and her mother was ten minutes away. One more thing her father had stolen from her—the ability to sit by her mother and brother's grave and grieve.

"There's one more picture," Jules said.

Donna turned back to the pile and moved the picture of her brother aside. She scrutinized the final photo and shook her head. "That's not me."

"Read the back." Jules picked it up and handed it to Donna.

She pursed her lips as she read and then flipped it back over to study it closer. "So, this is her. Little did Ally know when this picture was taken that my father would make her a millionaire one day." Donna clenched her jaw. "It's not fair. It's not fair at all."

CHAPTER SIX

MEETING JONAS, her half-brother, had given Jules a feeling of completion she'd never had. A biological connection. It had been tempered when he revealed Barb, Jules's birth mother, needed time to reconcile the fact she'd been found. That stung like hell.

The previous week she'd had dinner with Jonas and his fiancée, Erin. Afterward, Jonas had leaned in, hugged her goodbye, and whispered in her ear, "Mom wants to meet you." For months, Jonas had told Barb it would be okay. He reassured her that Jules's adoptive parents had been good to her, and Jules wasn't angry with her. Her birth mother had finally come around.

The plan was for Barb to come to Jules's townhouse. Jonas had offered to join her, but Barb wanted to meet her daughter alone. She insisted. Jules had been wandering impatiently around the first level of her townhouse, the area set up as an office and studio for her photography. She stared at the time on her phone, and her heart thumped wildly in her chest. What if Barb changed her mind?

Jules didn't think she could stand waiting much longer. She

glanced at the bouquet of pink tea roses. They were Jules's favorite, and she hoped Barb liked them, but flowers were the least of her worries.

Jules's cell phone rang, and her heart sank. This was it. It had to be her calling to cancel. She exhaled when she saw her boyfriend Tim's name on the caller ID. They had rekindled their relationship just after she found her birth mother. He had been Jules's voice of reason as she waited for this day.

"Hey, honey," Tim said when she answered. "What time is Barb coming?"

"She should be here any minute. I'm so nervous. Even though I've talked to her a few times, this feels so different."

"You'll be okay. Barb will love you. How can she not? Probably not for the same reasons I love you." He laughed. "I mean, for me, you're just sexy as hell."

A smile crept across Jules's face, and some of the tension lifted from her shoulders. "Is that the only reason you love me?"

"Of course not. You also give great foot massages, and the way you reheat takeout food makes me positively swoon."

"You're nuts, you know— Oh, I think I hear her knocking. Love you. Gotta go."

The knock had been hesitant and not very loud. Jules was glad she hadn't been upstairs on the second level, or she wasn't sure she would have heard it. She took a deep breath to calm herself, unlocked the deadbolt, and opened the door. Jules reeled back slightly and stifled a small gasp. It was uncanny how much the women looked alike.

Barb stood in front of the door holding a gift bag, her lower lip quivering. Jules swept her into a hug, and the two women wept while they held each other.

"I don't know if I can let you go," Barb whimpered into Jules's ear.

Finally, they separated, and with the initial moment past

them, Jules laughed. "I guess I should let you come in."

She closed the door behind Barb, and they hugged again.

"Oh, my goodness." Barb stared at Jules. "You're all grown up. I still think of you as that little baby in the hospital. Jonas keeps telling me I need to stop doing that."

Jules grabbed the flowers and handed them to Barb.

She inhaled deeply from the bouquet. "Did Jonas tell you? These are my favorite flowers."

"He didn't tell me. They're mine, too." Both women smiled, and Jules showed her the stairs. "Down here is my office and photography studio, but the living room and kitchen are upstairs. C'mon, let's go up and get comfortable. I think we have a lot to talk about."

At the top of the stairs, Barb caught her breath.

"I know." Jules laughed. "It's the only workout I get some days, but it's a good one. There's another set leading to the third floor, which is where my bedroom is." She led Barb into the kitchen and opened the refrigerator. "Can I get you something to drink?"

"Do you have a Diet Coke?"

Jules laughed again. "It's my one addiction, and sometimes it's the only thing in my refrigerator."

She poured a glass for each of them and motioned toward the living room couch for Barb to have a seat.

Her birth mother placed the gift bag on the table and sunk into the cushions of the couch. "Oh, this is so comfortable. I just hope I can get out of it when I'm ready to go."

Jules couldn't help but think wistfully of her mom, who always made the same comment when she sat in that spot. It seemed surreal to see Barb seated in the same place her mother usually occupied.

Jules tried to wipe the guilt from her mind. After dreaming of meeting her for so long, it felt unbelievable Barb was now sitting in her living room. Jules was no longer nervous.

Both women started to speak at once, and they laughed. Jules went first. "I'm not sure what to call you. Barb? Mom?"

Barb hesitated. "I know I gave birth to you, but I'm not sure I've earned the title. Your mother who raised you is still your mom. She was there when you were sick, all your graduations—" Barb's eyes welled up with tears.

Jules went over and hugged her. "It's okay. You're here now, and that's what matters."

"I've just missed so much of your life."

"This is a new beginning for us. Yes, my mom is still my mom, but she couldn't have been there for me if you hadn't given birth to me. How about for now I'll call you Barb, and we'll take it from there?"

Through her tears, Barb nodded. "I need you to know. I didn't want to give you up. I guess it's kind of weird now, but I named you Jessica on your birth certificate."

Jules only had her amended certificate, so she had no idea that had been her birth name. She definitely didn't *feel* like a Jessica. "Did I have my father's last name or Bennett on my birth certificate?"

Barb paused as if she hadn't considered she'd have to tell Jules about her birth father, or maybe that's why she'd been so hesitant to meet.

Jules patted her arm. "It's okay, Barb. You can tell me anything. I've come this far, and I can handle it. Though I'll admit, I was a bit devastated when Jonas told me you weren't ready to meet me at first."

"Oh, Jess—Jules, I'm so sorry. Oh, the panic I went into when I got that call from my sister, Bonnie. I've always imagined you were bitter about me giving you up. I worried if you'd been placed with parents who would love you as their own. Every time I heard a horror story about an adoption gone wrong, I worried about you. Every birthday I hoped you were having cake and a party, and I cried you were growing up without me." Barb blinked hard and then turned away while she wiped tears from her face.

Jules got up, went into the small bathroom, and emerged with a box of tissues. "We're going to need these, I think."

As she handed Barb a tissue, Jules steered the conversation back to her birth father. "So, what *did* you put on my birth certificate?"

Barb shifted uncomfortably in her seat. "Naturally, you'd want to know about him." She closed her eyes searching for the right words. "It's painful to remember. Nobody knew I was pregnant, not even my family. I was ... ashamed." She let out a sigh as if she was releasing all those memories. "You were listed as Jessica Bennett on the birth certificate, but ..."

Jules reached out for her hand. "You can tell me the truth."

Barb searched Jules's face and winced as she spoke. "Your birth father didn't want to be listed. As you can imagine, he wasn't thrilled about the situation. He was worried sick his wife was going to find out he had an affair and I was pregnant."

Jules pinched her lips shut and nodded. "So, did he want you to have an abortion?"

Barb hesitated as the tears continued to fall. "He did, but I refused. The affair was over when I found out I was pregnant, but I just couldn't do it. You were this wonderful life growing inside me, and I couldn't extinguish that. But I knew I couldn't keep you. I wanted you to have everything I couldn't give you." She wiped her nose. "I'm sorry."

Jules handed her a fresh tissue. "There's nothing to be sorry about. I appreciate that you carried me even though I'm sure it must have been tough to handle all of it by yourself."

"He did offer to help once he knew I was steadfast in my decision to continue the pregnancy. I had quit working for him when the affair ended, so he helped me pay my rent and gave me some money until you were born." Barb looked down as her hands crumpled the tissues she held. "I told my parents I had gotten a job in another city. I couldn't go home since they didn't know I was pregnant. Thanksgiving. Christmas. I was alone and only twenty minutes away. My parents didn't understand why my job wouldn't let me come home for the holidays. I hated lying to them." Barb shrugged sadly. "Looking back, I wish I had told them. Maybe they would have offered to help me so I could keep you."

It pained Jules to see how agonizing it had been for Barb. "I'm so sorry you had to go through that."

"Oh, honey, this is not your fault. None of this is your fault, so don't for one second think it was. You were the result of something that probably just shouldn't have happened."

Jules cringed, even though she knew Barb meant the affair and not necessarily her.

"I do believe things turn out the way they are meant to. I believe we all have lessons to learn in our lifetime, and this was a lesson for all of us. Me, you, your adopted parents, even your birth father." She focused her gaze on Jules. "I'm not going to say I wasn't broken inside about giving you up. It was like I handed over a piece of my heart that day in the hospital. But I don't regret the decision to give you life, and I thank God for giving you two good parents who loved you."

Jules's lips curved into a small smile. "My adopted parents really are wonderful. They never treated me like I wasn't theirs —" The smile disappeared, and she bit her lower lip. "I can't lie and say I didn't wonder about you. I obsessed about why you gave me up. I thought maybe—maybe you just didn't want me."

"Oh, Jules, no!" Barb reached out and drew Jules into a hug. "I always wanted you."

When they pulled apart, Jules continued. "It's the not knowing that's so hard. And for you, too. You had no idea where I went or even if I was okay. That's not right either."

"No." Barb shook her head. "No, it isn't."

"Do you think my birth father ever wonders about me?"

Barb gazed off almost as if she was considering what to say. Jules hoped Barb wasn't trying to protect her feelings again. She really did want to know the answer.

"He came to the hospital when you were born. I'm not sure what he told his wife, but he was there. I caught him. Staring at you in the nursery." Barb offered Jules a wistful smile. "I think there was a moment he wished it had all been different, too. I checked in on him a few times over the years. He was still married, probably cheating, and he had three of his own kids. So, you have a few more half-siblings in addition to Jonas."

Jules caught her breath. "Wow. After Jonas told me what happened, I had ruled out ever wanting to meet him, but three half-siblings make me think twice."

"I honestly don't remember if they were girls or boys. I think he had one before you were born, and then the other two came after that."

"I hope I never tried to date any of them. Can you imagine?" Jules's face grew serious. The last thing she wanted to do now was hurt Barb. But she had siblings, and Jonas had been a wonderful addition to her life. "I'm not sure what I want to do, but how would you feel if I tried to find him or his children?"

Barb blinked hard and let out a deep sigh. "Jules, my actions have dictated your life for a long time. You're an adult. It's not my place to tell you who you can and can't talk to. I will tell you his wife probably won't take kindly to you. It will be obvious by your age that he cheated on her while they were married. But it's your decision. Those kids are your family, too, just like Jonas, and maybe they grew up to be great people." She laughed. "Though not as great as Jonas, obviously."

"Oh, he is fabulous. I can't tell you how much I adore him."

"He told me you opened an agency to help other people. You'll need to show me one day how you figured this all out.

All this DNA stuff is incredible. I honestly never thought I would get the chance to meet you."

Jules made lunch for the two of them, and they sat and chatted for several hours. As Barb prepared to finally head out, she confirmed what Jonas had mentioned about a big family gathering so Jules could meet her cousins, aunts, uncles. "Everyone can't wait to meet you." She looked hesitantly at Jules. "How do your parents feel about this new family invading your life?"

Jules looked away and then shrugged. "I haven't told them yet. They were concerned when I told them I was going to look for you."

"I can understand how scared they'd be. Will you tell them?" Barb gave Jules a pointed stare. "Secrets aren't a good thing. Take it from me."

"I guess I've been just looking for the right moment, and of course, I wanted to be able to meet you first and see how this went." She nodded with a small smile. "Yeah, I'm going to tell them."

Barb hugged her. "I hope they understand we're not trying to steal you away. You're family, and so are they now. Please let them know how much I would love to meet them and say thank you for giving you such a good life."

Jules wasn't sure how her parents would feel about that. "I will. It would make me so happy if everyone got along, and I didn't have to feel guilty for being so incredibly happy that I found you."

Barb handed Jules a folded piece of paper. "Honey, this is for you to decide what you want to do with it."

Jules unfolded the piece of paper. *Lee Cantrell, Birth Father.* She brought her gaze back up to Barb and dipped her head in gratitude. "Thank you."

"He was thirty-two when you were born. Last I heard, he was in Smyrna, Georgia. Oh, I almost forgot, I brought you something." Barb pulled the gift bag off the table. "I paint sometimes."

Jules waved her hands at the photos she had taken that lined the walls. "I knew I got my artistic ability from someplace. Jonas told me it was your therapy."

Barb gripped the handles of the bag. "I've saved this for a long time. I knew if I ever found you, I wouldn't be able to tell you how it really felt to give you up. I put my emotions on this canvas, and I've kept it in case I was ever lucky enough to meet you." She pulled the painting from the bag.

It wasn't huge—about eleven by seventeen, and Jules took in a deep breath when she saw the picture. She took it from Barb's hands and held it up so she could study it.

The painting was a contrast of two worlds, like a summer storm that leaves one side of the street gray and dismal while the sun shines on the other. In the lower right corner, bathed in foreboding darkness, was the silhouette of a young girl. She was on her knees, her arms outstretched as if she was reaching for something just outside her grasp. Even without seeing her face, you could sense the deep longing and heartbreak for what she could no longer hold.

As the dark turned to light in the painting, the image depicted a couple bathed in sunshine, holding a baby and walking away from the young girl. In the upper left corner, a faint rainbow encircled the family.

Jules's eyes welled up, and she swallowed past the lump in her throat. "Oh, Barb, this is amazing. I can't tell you how much I appreciate you saving this for me."

They hugged goodbye at the door. Jules marveled that only a few hours had passed since she had opened the door to find Barb standing there, lip quivering, tears rolling down her face. It seemed like a lifetime ago. Now it felt like they had known each other forever.

CHAPTER SEVEN

BECKY PULLED up to the curb in front of a modest, one-story house. She checked the address she had against the black numbers that ran down the column to the right of the door. They matched.

"Here goes nothing," she muttered as she stepped out of the car.

Jules would have insisted on more research before reaching out. Becky knew she'd been slightly impulsive but imagine if she was right about this. It would be the fastest case they'd ever solved.

She rang the doorbell. After a moment, the door opened, and a slender woman in her fifties smiled at her. There was the strawberry blond hair Becky had seen in her Facebook profile.

The woman gestured with her hand. "Come on in."

Becky followed her to the kitchen, where she had two glasses of lemonade waiting, the condensation dripping down the side of the glass. The woman handed one to Becky.

"It's just so hot. I mean, really, it's October. I'm ready for some relief from this heat and humidity, aren't you?" She gestured at the kitchen table where she plunked into a chair.

Becky took a sip of her drink and lowered into the chair across from her.

"I'm glad you sent me the link to that newspaper article," the woman said. "When you first left me a message, I thought for sure someone was scamming me. I mean, really, a big inheritance. Who would believe that's for real?"

"I'm sure." Becky reached into her purse for the notebook she had brought. She fished around for a pen and placed them both on the table. "So, Susan, I'm doing some research for a client, and I came across some information I wanted to ask you about."

"Please, call me Sue. No one calls me Susan. Well, except my mother when I was in trouble."

"Okay then, Sue it is." Becky opened the notebook. She clicked the pen and held it poised to write. "Your parents are Margaret and Ed Ryan, right? You have four brothers and one sister. Is that right?"

She nodded and laughed. "You *are* a good detective. That's all correct."

"And your sister's name is Molly. She was born in 1970, and she has a daughter named Allison, who's about twenty-five, right?"

"Sounds about right."

"It said in the article your sister graduated from Rollins. Did you remember what year that was?"

Sue tapped her index finger to her lips. "Well, let's see. I was younger than her, but she didn't go to college right away. She decided to work and save up some money. She was a freshman when I was a sophomore. Of course, I went across I-4 to USF."

"So, when would she have graduated?"

"Well, I was the class of '93. She would have graduated the following year. Oh, wait, I do remember she was short a couple of credits. She enjoyed college a little too much if you know what I mean. My parents were mad that she had to go the extra semester and couldn't walk with the rest of her class."

"So, did she go over the summer, or did she finish up in the fall?"

"I'm pretty sure she finished up in the fall. There was no one to party with at school in the summer." Sue laughed. "Besides, my parents had her working to pay for the missing credits. Molly wasn't happy at all about that."

If she met Jerry in early 1995 for her first big job interview, this would all line up. It had almost been too easy. Becky's pulse quickened as she leaned in. "I have to ask, so I'm sorry if this is too personal. Did Molly have Ally as an unwed mother?"

Sue shook her head vigorously. "Oh, no. She married her college boyfriend right after they graduated. To tell the truth, I think she was trying to get away from our parents." Sue sipped her lemonade. "We always said Allison was a honeymoon baby. They were so young and then to have a new baby ..." She left the thought unfinished. "It didn't last. They divorced after about three or four years."

"Oh, I'm so sorry."

"Nice guy, but just not the one for her. She remarried a great guy when Allison was about eight, and they moved to North Carolina. Steve—that's his name—always treated Allison like she was his. I keep begging her to move back, but she says she's had enough of this heat and the traffic."

Becky pressed her lips together, but she wasn't ready to give up. Everything else fit. "I know I'm prying and asking you to speculate, but is it possible her husband wasn't the father? I'm just doublechecking because if she's the right person, as I told you on the phone, there's a sizable inheritance for her daughter."

Sue considered it for a moment. "I guess it's possible. Molly was always a little wild, and she was a stunner. Still is. Men used to stare at her all the time. I think she liked the attention. I can ask her, discreetly, of course. I'm sure she'd want Allison to be financially secure, even if it means admitting she lied about who her father was."

Becky nodded and closed her notebook. "I think that's everything I needed. I really appreciate you chatting with me. Let me know what you find out from your sister." She took a final swig from her glass. "And thanks for the lemonade."

Susan showed Becky out, and as she walked to her car, Becky heard a car start from across the street. When she glanced over, it appeared as if the driver in the silver car ducked down in their seat. Becky's pulse quickened. She knew she was just being paranoid after being stalked six months earlier. Peyton was in prison now. She wouldn't be getting out for a long time.

Becky gripped her keys, and after a quick glance around her, she slid into the driver's seat and locked the door. Sue's sister wouldn't have advertised Allison wasn't her husband's baby. Maybe Sue just didn't know. Jules would never believe with one random newspaper article Becky had found Molly.

She dug around in her purse for her cell phone. No messages. Becky hoped that meant Jules's lunch with Barb was going well.

She'd considered going to the library in Orlando to look up birth announcements on microfilm. Now she didn't really think she needed to. The pieces seemed to be lining up, and Becky had a good feeling about it.

She'd told Bryan she'd be home by dinner, but it would be much earlier. A romantic night could definitely be on the agenda. Becky pushed down the idea of getting pregnant. So far it hadn't happened naturally, and even after six months, the failed IVF still hurt too much. She would have been approaching her final trimester had it worked out the way she planned. The way it should have if—she had to stop thinking about what could have been.

There was comfort in knowing she still had two frozen embryos, but her insides ached for the one that had been lost. She'd relentlessly considered the other option but eventually accepted the conclusion that anything else would have been unthinkable. It didn't make it any easier. Dr. Levine had offered to help them try again. It was the least he could do, but right now, her heart simply wasn't ready.

She plugged in her phone and hit play on the audiobook she'd been listening to. Becky turned up the volume, looked around, and eased her car out of its parking spot. As she hit the gas, she stole a quick glance in her rearview mirror.

The silver car across the street had pulled out, too.

CHAPTER EIGHT

"I STILL CAN'T BELIEVE you drove to Orlando and left after a thirty-minute conversation," Jules said as she unlocked the office door.

"Bryan said the same thing. If we found Molly, I didn't see any reason to spend the afternoon surrounded by microfilm at the library. When the ages and the names matched up in that article, I had a good feeling. It felt awkward to ask Sue over the phone if her sister had a one-night stand and got pregnant. I needed to soften it by going in person."

Jules dropped her bag on her desk. "But you said her sister Molly was already married when she would have met Jerry."

"Yes, but Sue also said her sister was a little on the wild side. Who knows? Susan actually left me a voicemail last night. I was—" Becky paused. "Well, let's just say I was busy with Bryan when she called."

Jules spun around. "I'm glad to see you haven't given up completely on having a baby."

Becky shrugged, but she was smiling. "I'm not trying to, and I'm not trying not to. We're just going back to being us, without a schedule or ovulation charts or all those shots. It's nice. Anyway, I figured we could listen to the voicemail together."

Becky laid her cell phone on Jules's desk. When she pressed play, they heard Susan's voice. *Hey, Becky. I talked to my sister Molly last night. She swears up and down Allison is her first husband's kid. Even when I told her about the money. I don't think she'd have a reason to lie. It's not like they're even married anymore, and you know, Allison is all grown up. Anyway, sorry to be a dead end. I hope you find whoever really inherited that money. It was nice to meet you yesterday.*

Becky deleted the message and frowned. "Well, damn. When I found that newspaper article that mentioned Molly and her daughter, Allison, who lived in Orlando, it seemed like a sure thing. The ages matched up and everything. Even the year Molly graduated from college seemed to line up." Becky's cheeks flushed. "Impulsive, I know. I ignored the fact that I didn't find a niece named Bella." She shrugged sheepishly. "I just figured there was a chance Donna's father didn't remember the name correctly. I mean, it was a long time ago—"

"Do you think she could be lying?" Jules asked.

"Who, Susan?"

"No, Molly." Jules pressed her lips together and pushed her index finger against them. "Maybe she's too embarrassed to tell her sister the truth."

Becky tilted her head and considered it. "I guess it's possible."

"Call Susan back and see if maybe she'll give us her sister's number. If we call and tell her exactly how much money is sitting on the table, maybe she'll sing a different tune."

"It's worth a shot." Becky picked up her phone and dialed the number from the voicemail.

Jules tapped her fingers on the desk as she waited.

Becky's eyebrows knit in confusion when the phone was answered. "Um, is this Susan?"

She paused for the response.

"My name is Becky Morgan. I came and met with her yesterday."

Jules leaned forward in her chair and tucked her leg underneath her. Apparently, Susan had someone to screen her calls. She was frustrated Becky hadn't called on speakerphone.

When Becky glanced over, Jules mouthed, *who answered?* Becky shrugged in response.

"Well, we have a client looking for her sister," Becky said into the phone. "Turns out I had the wrong person, but Susan was very helpful. I was actually calling to see if she had a phone number she could share with me for her sister Molly."

Becky turned to Jules as her eyes grew wide. "Oh, this *is* Molly? Wow. I thought you lived in North Carolina."

Jules stood and went around her desk. She nudged Becky's arm. "Well, that was meant to be," she whispered. "Put her on speakerphone. Let's both talk to her."

Becky swatted Jules away and held up a finger. "You drove all night? Did Susan know you were coming? She must have been so excited."

Jules winced. Maybe the conversation between the sisters had sparked something. It had to be something big if Molly drove all night to get to Sue's house. Maybe Molly wouldn't want to talk to them at all about her daughter.

Becky's hand flew up to cover her mouth. "Oh, no, I am *so* sorry. That's terrible. Who could do something like that?" She wobbled on her feet and grabbed the edge of Jules's desk.

Jules fixed her eyes on Becky, her face etched in confusion.

When Becky finished the call, she tossed the phone on the desk. She sunk into the guest chair, her hands wrapped around her head as she stared at the floor.

Jules gave her a moment, but then anticipation won out. "You're killing me," she said, probably a bit too dramatically.

"Why was Molly answering Sue's phone? Why didn't you ask if we could both talk to her?"

Becky lifted her head and stared off at the ceiling. Jules tried to read her expression. Was it shock? Disbelief?

Becky swallowed hard. "Apparently, Susan goes for a three-mile walk every night. Last night—last night, someone's car jumped the curb." Becky sucked in a deep breath as she met Jules's demanding stare. "Susan's dead. She was struck and killed by a hit and run driver."

CHAPTER NINE

"Stop mooning over the old man," Jay said as he walked by her sitting at the kitchen table surrounded by her father's things. "I'm going out."

Donna glanced up and couldn't hide her annoyance. "Where?" she asked sharply.

"I'm meeting my brother for a couple of beers." He caught the look Donna gave him. "Yes, again. I won't be late this time, I promise."

She pursed her lips and shook her head. "I hope not."

"What can I say? He's trying. We're trying. You know he's all I have."

Donna had no one either. Except a very expensive half-sister she wanted nothing to do with.

Jay and his brother Kevin had been estranged since their mother died. His father was never in the picture, and the two boys had disagreed on how to split their mother's things when she passed. They had a big blow-up and went their separate ways. Jay started working in construction. According to mutual friends who called Jay, his brother always seemed to find himself in trouble. Nothing major. Bar fights, petty theft.

Kevin had called looking to reconcile and hadn't been back in Jay's life for long. Two weeks. Donna hadn't met him yet, which she found odd, but Jay said he wanted to make sure his brother would stick around first. Donna didn't trust him. She worried Jay would get his hopes up that the brothers would finally have a decent relationship. He acted tough, but he'd be hurt if his brother really hadn't changed.

"Are you going to be okay here while I'm gone, or will you still be looking for missing meaning in your father's stuff?" Jay hadn't liked her dad. He never had his father in his life and claimed it didn't bother him. Donna knew deep-down it must have, but Jay just refused to admit it. After all, she'd accepted her father didn't care about her, but it still hurt like hell.

"I'm just a little surprised my father saved all this. And the file about my mom …" Donna's voice drifted off. Jules and Becky had given her back the folder from Norman, but it still sat in her car. That made her angry, but this stuff they'd found gave her pause as to how her dad really felt. Donna had been stunned to read that he had to make the decision to let her mother and brother go. She hadn't even told Jay. It felt like information she had to sit with emotionally before she could share it.

Jay dismissed her with a wave of his hand. "It was a long time ago. Nothing you or your father can do about it now."

Donna dipped her head slightly. "I know, you're right." Why hadn't her father told her what really happened? It might have made him easier to understand. She still would have wanted her dad, but as she got older, she might have had a little more sympathy for what he had been through.

Jay pulled open the pantry door and rummaged through it, looking for something to eat. "Where did you get all that stuff anyway?" he asked over his shoulder. "I didn't see those boxes from the lawyer. Did you move them down to the garage your-self?" They had a garage that went with the apartment, but it was in a separate building. Dark and creepy. "I know I haven't started building those shelves yet," he said in a sheepish tone that acknowledged he'd promised and not delivered for far too long.

"I had Norman's office send them to Jules and Becky at the detective agency."

Jay spun around, a bag of chips in his hand. "You did? Why?"

"I didn't think there'd be much of anything in them. Besides, if they're willing to go through them looking for clues about my half-sister, I'm all for it."

Jay sighed. "There could be important papers in there, Donna."

"I told them if they saw anything about a life insurance policy to let me know. So far, they haven't found anything. Besides, you saw Norman's face when I asked about it. He knows who the beneficiary is, and he knows it's not me." Donna banged her fist on the table. "But seriously, who the hell could he have left that money to?"

Jay dropped into the kitchen chair across from her. "Do you think it's possible he left that to this Robert Taylor, too?"

Donna shrugged. "I guess anything's possible. I've been thinking about that nonstop. How could my father leave so much money to someone I don't know anything about? This guy must know who I am, and yet I have no clue about him."

Jay stood and kissed her on the top of her head. "You'll get your fair share. Don't worry about it. It will all work out in the end."

Donna glanced down at her left hand. She wouldn't mention yet that she had considered the idea of upgrading her diamond. "You know, I was thinking … when I finally get my money, let's do a destination wedding. Someplace amazing. What do you think?"

Jay cocked his head as he considered it. "Sounds complicated. Let's just get married here, and then do a kick-ass honeymoon when you get your inheritance. I'll teach you how to scuba dive." He leaned over and kissed her. "You've had your asshole ex's last name long enough. I'm ready to marry you right now. We'll go to the courthouse."

Donna frowned as she looked up at him. "Can't we at least do something nicer? Maybe a ceremony at the beach?"

Jay dipped his head. "Sure, if that's what you want. You make the arrangements and tell me where to be. How about next weekend?"

Donna's brows lifted in surprise that he wanted to do it so quickly. "Okay, let me see what I can pull together. I wish I had my money now so we could just jet off afterwards. I suppose I could ask Becky about her trip to Orlando. She thought she had a lead that might help find my half-sister's mother."

Jay lifted his eyebrows and handed Donna her cell phone. "Maybe she found something. Call her."

Donna dialed and put in on speakerphone. "Hi, Becky, it's Donna," she said when the phone was answered. "I was just wondering how it went in Orlando. Did you find Molly?"

Becky paused for a moment. "It was—it was fine. She actually wasn't who I hoped she would be. I actually thought she was Molly's sister, but it doesn't look like she is."

Donna glanced up at Jay, but he was busy getting his cell phone off the charger and checking messages. "Oh, I didn't realize you were going to see the sister. Well, that's disappointing. Were you able to find out anything at the library?"

"Um, no, I actually didn't go, but Jules and I are planning another trip on Friday. We have a few things we want to check out."

Jay turned around. "Ask about the life insurance," he whispered.

Donna nodded at him. "Anything else interesting in the boxes? Any life insurance information?"

"We haven't been back in them, but we'll get to it soon. Don't worry, Donna. These things take time. We'll find her."

Jay shook his head and expelled a puff of air. "Of course, it takes time. That's how they rack the bill up. And what about Robert Taylor?"

Donna shushed him with a wave of her hand. "Sorry, that's just Jay in the background. Any leads on Robert Taylor and who he might be?"

"He's a little harder because we don't know the first thing about him—his age, where he lives. We may start searching locally. We'll make a list and just cold call to see if we can find anyone with a connection to your dad."

That sounded like another needle in a haystack. "He'll be the one at the bank with the big check." Donna's tone was bitter.

"I know you're frustrated, but I'll keep you posted on what we find. Like I said, we're going to Orlando on Friday. Also, Jules had a good point. With a big family, maybe she was Catholic. We considered that maybe she was baptized. We're going to the library, but if it comes down to it, we can check out some of the churches."

"I appreciate the update. If you could just keep me in the loop every step of the way, I'd appreciate it."

"Absolutely. I'll call you after our trip Friday and let you know what we find."

Donna hung up and turned to Jay. "It doesn't sound like they've made much progress."

Jay sat back down at the table and stuck his hand in the bag of chips. "I wish we could figure this out without them. I mean, you have all the same information they do, right?"

Donna reached over for a chip. "They have access to all sorts of stuff I would never know how to get. I'm just hoping when my DNA results come in, that half-sister of mine is at the top of the list."

Jay shoveled a handful of chips in his mouth and nodded. "That would make this much easier, that's for sure." He shoved a few more chips in his mouth, closed the bag, and pushed himself away from the table. "I'm out of here. I'll see you later. Not too late, I promise." He wiped crumbs from his lips, leaned down, and kissed her goodbye.

Donna stared at the bag he'd left behind and brushed the potato chip crumbs into a pile with her hand. "Don't let your brother drink too much. Stay out of trouble."

As she heard the front door slam, Donna turned back to the pictures in front of her. Jay was a little gruff sometimes, but she knew it was because he didn't like to see her hurt.

He obviously loved her if he wanted to marry her as soon as possible. Soon she'd be Mrs. Jay Kittsmiller. Why *had* she kept her ex-husband's last name since her divorce? Maybe it was because she didn't necessarily want her dad's name either.

She and Nick had been married for seven miserable years. She had no frame of reference for what a good marriage looked like, but she knew hers wasn't it. Donna always blamed her father. If he had helped her even a little, she would have had options other than Nick and his shitty little house next to the train tracks.

When Donna finally had enough, she waited until her husband ran out to get beer one night. Her bag had been packed, hidden, and just waiting for the right opportunity. Nick was livid when he discovered she'd left him. She didn't care and filed for divorce.

Eventually, she'd gotten him to agree the marriage wasn't working and was grateful when he got a lawyer to handle it for both of them, quick and painless. They didn't have any kids, and she had no money to fight him. Her dad had been going through treatment for lung cancer at the time, but was he so sick he couldn't write his daughter a check? Help her out even a little? Donna had walked away when it was over and didn't want to ever look back.

This time would be different. Jay wasn't Nick. So why was she so nervous about getting married again?

CHAPTER TEN

"Can you make a couple of extra burgers?" Becky smiled sweetly at her husband.

Bryan turned from the counter and raised an eyebrow. "Extra hungry today, are you?"

"Not exactly." Just then, the doorbell chimed. She offered him a sheepish grin.

"Something tells me you might know who's at the door." Bryan reached into the refrigerator and grabbed more hamburger meat.

"It's Jules and Tim. Since I left early to see my mother, I have something to go over with her, and you boys can talk sports." The men were used to being second fiddle when the two women were together.

"Come in," Becky called out as she headed for the door.

Jules entered with Tim following. "Hey, Sherlock." Becky's orange cat glanced up, leaped off the couch, and hurried to the safety of Becky's room. "I think he's finally warming up to me," Jules told Becky with a trace of sarcasm.

Becky's socially awkward orange cat wasn't one for company. Going missing for a couple of weeks earlier that year had made him even more suspicious about anyone but Becky.

After greetings were had, the women disappeared to the porch. Becky sank into the oversized club chair and gestured for Jules to take the other.

"How was your mom?" Jules asked.

Becky shrugged sadly. "The same. It feels like she's deteriorating so fast. I mentioned something to her nurse at the Memory Care Center, and she said it happens. Something could have triggered it, or the dementia is just progressing."

"I'm sorry. I guess she's still claiming not to remember anything from your childhood?"

"I stopped asking. If my mom really does remember, it doesn't seem like she'll share anything with me. I just have to take what Ros told me and have that be enough. I'm lucky that her best friend is still around to tell me what really happened." She offered a small shrug. "I'm moving past it. It's not like I have a choice."

Becky knew Jules wouldn't ask about Peyton. That name was taboo. Peyton wasn't allowed to call Becky from prison or write or have contact in any way. She had agreed to plead guilty, so there would be no trial. As far as Becky was concerned, she had just ceased to exist.

Nothing was tying the two of them together, and Becky had come to terms with that. She'd get her baby somehow. For now, she had let the obsession go to focus on her marriage and new business with Jules.

"So, after I left you this afternoon, I had a couple of interesting calls," Becky said as she slipped off her flip-flops and tucked her feet underneath her.

Jules leaned forward in her chair. "Do tell."

Just then, Bryan walked out and handed a glass of wine to each of them.

"Aw, honey, you're the best." Becky lifted the glass to her

lips, took a sip, and then placed it on the small table next to her. They'd run into a rough patch while she went through IVF, but after Peyton, they had found their way back to the closeness they used to have. "So, the first call I got was from a detective at the police station. The Orlando police station to be exact."

Jules arched an eyebrow. "The police called you? Why? Was it about Susan?"

"Yup. Since I was the last call she made, they wanted to know how I knew her, everything we talked about. Obviously, I didn't have much to offer since I just met her yesterday."

Jules crossed her legs and made circles in the air with her sandal. "You were already home when the hit and run happened. It's not like you could have had anything to do with it."

Becky nodded. "I know. It doesn't seem like they think it was an accident. They have a witness who said the car sped up and seemed to be aiming right for her."

Jules frowned. "Who would do that?"

"No idea. She seemed nice enough. Definitely not a woman who would be on someone's hit list."

"Is she going through a messy divorce or anything like that?"

Becky picked up her wine glass and swirled the contents thoughtfully. "I don't think so. I saw pictures around the house of her and her husband."

"Did the detective believe you when you said you didn't know anything about it?"

Becky slowly nodded. "Yeah, I think so. And then I got another call. This one was from Molly."

"Molly, Susan's sister? Wow. Was she trying to blame you or something?"

"No. She wanted to get a little more information about the inheritance for Donna's half-sister."

Jules leaned forward and jabbed her finger in the air. "See, I told you she was lying."

Becky shook her head. "Actually, she wasn't. I think she thought maybe she could scam her way into it. I told her we needed a positive DNA test to Jerry. That stopped her dead in her tracks. Apparently, she *was* messing with some guy before she got married, but her new husband made her get a paternity test. Allison was his. She's never heard of Jerry. Never been to New York. No niece named Bella."

Bryan and Tim stumbled through the opening of the sliding glass door onto the porch. Bryan had a beer in one hand and a plate of burgers in the other. "Just passing through." He elbowed Tim and laughed. "Don't worry, girls. We're bonding over beer and a hot grill. Manly stuff."

Becky shook her head and smiled. "I love that they get along so well. Oh, with everything that happened with Susan, I forgot to ask, how was your time with Barb?"

"It was nice. Really nice." Jules paused and took a long swallow from her wine glass. "She gave me the name of my birth father."

Becky studied her friend. "Are you going to try to find him?"

Jules leaned her head back and gazed upward. "I'm not really sure. I don't see how it could go well. He was married at the time. But it does seem I have three more half-siblings."

"Oh, wow. That's got to be tempting to want to know about them." Becky sipped her wine and tried to read her friend's expression. She knew how great Jonas had been for Jules.

"That does intrigue me for sure. But right now, I feel like I want to continue to work on the relationship with Barb and her side. She's actually setting up a barbeque at her sister Bonnie's next weekend." Jules's cheeks turned pink. "The whole family wants to meet me. She even invited Tim."

"And how *are* things with Tim? You both look pretty happy."

Jules leaned in toward Becky. "I think I'm finally getting this relationship thing right. He keeps talking about our future, and I'm not even freaking out." She held out her left hand, pointed toward her fourth finger, and grinned. "I think he might be thinking about putting a ring on it."

Becky stifled a squeal, which caused Jules to burst out laughing.

"Hey," Tim called out from where he stood next to Bryan in the backyard. "What are you two girls up to?"

"Nothing," they said in unison and then broke into laughter all over again.

Jules dismissed him with a wave. "I'm sure he knows we're talking about him. Oh, I almost forgot. I opened up one of those other boxes, and it was full of date books. You know, the kind with calendars and to-do lists. I brought it with me in case we wanted to split them up after dinner."

"How many are there?"

Jules widened her eyes. "Tons. I'm going to guess they go back to when he first became a lawyer. The quality got a bit nicer as the years went on. Tim can get the box out of the car when we're done with dinner."

"That's pretty amazing Jerry saved them all. There's got to be something about Molly in one of them, don't you think? Maybe we can even find a flight to New York around the time he and Molly met or figure out who Robert Taylor is."

Jules crossed her fingers and nodded. "Let's hope."

Bryan pushed open the screen door, and the smell of freshly cooked burgers wafted through the air. "Okay, ladies, your gourmet dinner is served."

As the two couples sat around the table, a comfortable banter ensued. When dinner was over, Tim went out to his car, brought back the box with the datebooks, and placed it on the table for them.

Becky grabbed two shopping bags with handles from the laundry room and sat down next to Jules. She handed her one of the bags. "Let's just divvy them up, and then I'll toss the box. Do you want to organize them by year?"

Jules started removing the datebooks from the box. "Nah. We can figure it out. Just take half of them, and we can reconvene on them tomorrow. If you find anything interesting, just set it aside."

After they said their goodbyes, Becky changed into pajamas and plopped down at the kitchen table. She peered at the covers of the books and tried to organize them by year. Some were so old the dates had been rubbed off the front, forcing her to look inside.

Bryan's gaze drifted from his wife to the stack of books on the table. "Let me guess. You're planning to read a little in bed."

"Just while you watch the baseball playoffs." Becky offered him a coy smile. "And then I'm all yours."

He raised an eyebrow, a mischievous smile on his face. "Well, let's get going then." He grabbed her hand to pull her toward the bedroom.

She pulled back. "Wait one minute …" Becky scoured the pile of books on the table and grabbed the one she was looking for. "1995. Let's hope Donna's dad was organized that year."

Sherlock snuggled next to Becky as she settled into bed and flipped through the pages. Lots of handwritten notes. Meetings, court times, client leads. There was a phone number here and there, but none that seemed related to Molly. She scanned through January and then February, but there didn't seem to be anything relevant.

"Are you done yet?" Bryan asked as he leaned over and planted small soft kisses down her neck.

"Nope. Just give me——" she giggled as his breath tickled her skin. "I just need a few more minutes." She was already up to the first week of March. Still nothing. She flipped the page and sat straight up in the bed. "Bingo."

Bryan sat up, too. "What's bingo?" He picked up her arm and started trailing his lips up toward her shoulder. "Am I bingo?" he asked and met her eyes hopefully.

"You're always my bingo, babe. But tonight's bingo means I found the trip where Jerry met Molly." She showed Bryan the book as he groaned softly. "Look here." She pointed at March fifteenth. "See the address? He had a meeting at 2:00 p.m. with somebody at a New York City address. There's his flight information from Jacksonville to JFK in the morning. He had flight information that night for his return home but see, it's crossed out, and there's a new flight written in on the morning of the sixteenth. This had to be when he met Molly. It matches the story he wrote in the letter. Wait until I tell Jules."

Bryan expelled a prolonged sigh and fell back onto the bed. "Naturally, this can't wait until tomorrow."

Becky leaned over and kissed him. "Of course not, but I promise I won't take long." As she picked up her phone from the nightstand, it rang in her hand. She glanced over at Bryan when she saw Jules's name pop up. "See, she was calling me anyway."

Becky started to spew information as soon as she answered the phone. "Hey, you're never going to believe what I found in the 1995 journal. Jerry met Molly on March fifteenth. He was in New York City for a meeting. He had a flight out that night, but he took a different flight home the next morning."

"Good work," Jules said enthusiastically. "Well, I found something interesting, too. In the 1996 calendar. Stuck in the back was an envelope. Jerry probably put it back there and then thought he threw it out. It was the envelope Molly must have sent the picture of the baby in."

"Oh, wow, that's great. Did it have a return address?"

"Sure did. And an Orlando postmark." Jules paused. "Our job just got a little easier."

"She included her name?" Becky held her breath while she waited for an answer.

"Yup. It looks like her last name was Middlebrook."

CHAPTER ELEVEN

"Do you want to go to the library first?" Jules glanced at the clock on the dashboard. They'd spent the week searching online records and still hadn't had any luck finding Molly, even with the last name they'd found.

Becky nodded. "I think that's the best plan. We can see if they have any old yearbooks from the schools around here. I can also search for newspaper articles and see if I can find anything."

Jules arched an eyebrow as she shot her a look.

Becky put up her hand. "I know, I know. I won't be quite as impulsive this time." She googled the Orange County Library System and plugged an address into the GPS.

Fifteen minutes later, they were standing in front of one of the librarians. Though she did have a pair of reading glasses hanging on a chain around her neck, she didn't look anything like the ones Jules remembered when she was in school. This woman was friendly and eager to help.

"Yearbooks, huh?" She came out from behind the desk. "Follow me." She led them through the library, past the stacks of books and students on computers, until she reached the reference section. She swept her hand past shelves of multi-colored spines. "We don't have every single high school here, and we are missing some years for the ones we do have. But you're welcome to see if you can find what you're looking for." She gestured at a table. "Feel free to use this. Just stack the ones you pull out over here so I can put them back where they belong."

Jules leaned in to read dates on the spines of the books on the shelf. "This is great."

"I was also interested in seeing newspaper articles from the nineties," Becky said.

The librarian nodded. "Okay, those would be on microfilm. Come with me, and I'll get you set up."

Becky gave a quick wave to Jules. "Let's meet up in an hour and compare notes. I'll come back here."

Jules went through the shelves until she got to the years she was looking for. There were considerably less than for recent years.

"Born in 1970 should make her a senior in about 1988," she muttered to herself.

But what if they had her age wrong? Mid-twenties when she met Jerry was just a guess. Jules sighed as she pulled out a book. She had to start somewhere.

After she stacked the first batch of heavy books in her arms, Jules brought them to the table. This could take all day.

She lifted the top book off the pile. Colonial High School. These were the Grenadiers of 1988. Jules's forehead wrinkled. She didn't even know what a grenadier was, but she opened the book.

"C'mon, Molly, come out, come out, wherever you are."

Jules flipped to the senior class and searched the last names that started with the letter M. She ran her finger down the list.

Marsh, Mayo, McCracken, McCrohan, Mebane, Milam. Jules scowled, closed the book, and put it off to the right. She pulled the next book off the pile. These kids were the Knights. Still nothing.

She glanced at her watch, hoping Becky was having better luck in the microfilm room.

She was about to pull some of the 1987 yearbooks as Becky approached. Jules dropped them on the table, and they landed with a resounding thud. She winced as the people around her stared.

"That good, huh?" Becky asked in a low voice.

"This seemed like a good idea, but do you have any idea how many high schools are in Orlando?"

Becky's eyes scanned the table. "Um, a lot?"

"Too many. I haven't found anything. You?"

Becky grinned and sat down. "I think I found some good stuff." She placed a pile of printed pages in front of her. "I started looking for a birth announcement for Ally. Since we know they met in March, I looked in December of 1995 and even into January of 1996. Nothing."

"Which wouldn't be that odd considering Molly was probably unmarried."

"Right. So, I started looking for *Molly's* birth announcement. There were a few candidates." She handed the papers to Jules.

Jules peered down at the first paper. "So, this one had her born in 1971. That isn't too far from what we thought. She would have been twenty-four." She flipped to the second page. "This one had her born in 1969. That would have made her twenty-six. Still possible." Jules turned to the last page and frowned. "1974? I kind of hate to think she was twenty-one. I mean, Jerry was what—in his mid-thirties at the time?"

"Thirty-six."

Jules curled her lip. "Yuck. Though, I guess stranger things have happened. What else did you find?"

"Well, Molly Ann Middlebrook, the one who would have been twenty-four when Ally was born, was also mentioned in her grandmother's obituary. So, I had her parents' names. I hopped on a computer and did a little searching. Her parents are Douglas and Melanie." She handed the piece of paper to Jules. "The same Douglas and Melanie who own a little restaurant a few blocks away." Becky smiled. "You hungry?"

* * *

After Jules and Becky were ushered to a booth and handed menus, Becky scanned the restaurant. "Do you think they're even here?"

"I don't know too many restaurant owners that don't need to be there to make sure everything goes well." Jules peered over her menu. "Maybe that's her. By the cash register."

Becky nonchalantly glanced around until her gaze landed on the woman Jules mentioned. "The age looks about right."

A young blonde woman with her hair in a ponytail approached the table. "Hi, welcome to Tucker's. Do you know what you want, or can I get you something to drink?"

They placed their order, and as the waitress turned to walk away, Jules called out after her. "Excuse me."

She spun around. "Did you forget something you wanted to order?"

Jules shook her head. "No. We were wondering if you could tell us if the Middlebrooks are working today."

"Doug's here. He's manning the grill in the back and Melanie …" The waitress's gaze roved through the restaurant, and then she nodded toward the register. "She's ringing up takeout orders. Do you want me to tell her you're looking for her?"

Jules smiled. "That would be great. No rush, obviously."

The waitress returned a few minutes later and delivered their Diet Cokes but didn't mention that she had spoken to Melanie.

"If we have the right family, they must know they have a grandchild." Becky ripped the paper off her straw, stuck it in her glass, and took a long sip. "I think Donna was right when she said it didn't seem like Molly put her up for adoption, especially if she brought Ally to see Jerry when she was three or four."

After a short time, their lunches arrived, and Jules grabbed her fork and dug into her salad. "I'm starving."

Becky gave the woman behind the register another glance. She didn't seem to be aware of them. She let out a sigh and picked up her sandwich.

They had almost finished eating when Melanie approached their table. She was wiping her hands on a rag tucked into an apron around her waist.

"Sorry that took so long. Busy lunch rush today. I'm getting a little too old for it to be this busy." She laughed and whipped out a small order pad. "So, you're interested in a catering order?"

Jules shook her head. "Not exactly." She scooted over in the booth. "Would you like to sit?"

Melanie's brow wrinkled only slightly, but she didn't turn down the chance to take a seat. "So, what can I do for you?"

Since she was sitting across from Melanie, Becky answered, "We have some questions about your daughter."

Melanie furrowed her brow. "Nancy? Or Molly?"

"Molly."

Melanie flinched. "Is she in some sort of trouble?"

"No, no." Becky tried to reassure her. "She's not in any trouble. We've been hired by a client who is looking for someone named Molly Middlebrook. She apparently lived in Orlando. So, we're just checking out all potential leads."

Melanie's guard appeared to go up. "Why is someone looking for her?"

"It's actually about a very generous inheritance," Becky said.

The older woman narrowed her eyes slightly. "Who would she inherit money from that I don't know?" It was clear she thought they were scamming her.

Becky slid her business card across the table.

"I promise you," Jules said. "This is a legitimate case."

Melanie turned to face Jules. She hesitated, studied the card, and then nodded. "Okay."

"Does your daughter Molly have kids?" Jules asked.

Melanie nodded. "Yes, two. A son and a daughter."

"Her daughter's name is …" Becky hoped Melanie would finish the sentence with her granddaughter's name.

"Renee."

Becky tried to mask her disappointment. "Well, thank you. She's not the Molly we're looking for."

There was still a deep furrow between Melanie's brows as her gaze drifted between Becky and Jules. "I'm still a little uncomfortable with this conversation. Can't you give me any more information?"

Becky glanced at Jules, who responded with a small shrug followed by a nod. They could tell Melanie the basics without giving too much away.

"We can't tell you much, except we are looking for a woman named Molly Middlebrook who had a little girl in 1995," Becky said. "The inheritance is actually for the daughter."

Melanie nodded. "I see. Renee is Molly's youngest child. She wasn't born until 1999. I'm sorry I couldn't help." She slid out of the booth and stood by the table.

Becky scooted across the bench on her side of the booth and stepped out. "We appreciate your time. If you think of anything that might help, you have my card. Just give us a call."

Jules stood as well and grabbed her purse. "Do we pay you at the register, or does the waitress take it?"

Melanie gestured at them to follow her. "I'll take it for you."

"Well, that didn't go the way I hoped," Becky said as they strolled toward the car. "This is going to be harder than I thought."

"I'm starting to think the same th—" Jules stopped and turned to Becky. "Did you leave a tip?"

"I paid the check. I thought you left a tip."

Jules let out a groan. "I'll be right back." She turned and jogged back toward the restaurant.

Becky held her hand over her eyes, shielding them from the sun as she waited for Jules to return. A man in a worn baseball hat stood next to the entrance of Tucker's. He could have been waiting for someone, but Becky noticed his gaze had followed Jules as she went back to the restaurant. Now he seemed to be peering at her through the window. Jules was beautiful. She always had men staring at her, but despite the warm day, this one sent a shiver through Becky. She thought about the silver car that had pulled out behind her the last time she was in Orlando. And now Susan was dead.

After a few moments, Becky shook her head and chastised herself for being so paranoid. She had to stop thinking people were lurking in the shadows, or in this case, a sidewalk in broad daylight. But when Jules came out of Tucker's, the man's eyes tracked her until she reached Becky in the parking lot.

"C'mon, let's go," Jules said as she strolled in the direction of the car.

Becky fell in step beside her, but after a few seconds, she spun back around. The man was still staring in their direction. When he saw Becky turn, he pulled open the door to the restaurant and disappeared inside.

CHAPTER TWELVE

AFTER THE DISAPPOINTING trip to Orlando, Becky felt like they were back at square one. She'd convinced herself the man at the restaurant was just ogling Jules. He wasn't the first one.

She'd done some digging on the other two potential women she'd found. Now that she had their dates of birth, she was able to do more research. It didn't seem either of them had a daughter named Ally, so that was that. A big bust.

Maybe Jules had found something over the weekend. She had called earlier about being a little late but teased that she had a surprise for Becky. A big surprise. Maybe she was bringing Ally. That would be a big surprise—a fantastic one.

Becky was just getting ready to start digging through Jerry's boxes when she heard the office door open. A blur of enthusiastic golden fur bolted toward her, a leash dangling from his collar.

"Gene," Jules called after him. "We talked about this. You have to be a good boy."

Becky asked the dog to sit. He did and offered his paw. "Aww. You're too cute." His long pink tongue hung out of his mouth, and she could have sworn he was smiling. "Uh, Jules, whose dog is this?"

"He's sort of mine." Jules shrugged her bag off onto her desk, tossed a dog bed on the floor, and sat down next to him to give him a hug. "Well, mine and Tim's. We're sharing custody. For now." She held up her left hand, pointed at her bare ring finger, and grinned.

Becky cocked her head as she tried to make sense of Jules's pantomime. "So, you got a dog instead of a ring?"

"We went to the party at my Aunt Bonnie's this weekend. It was amazing. I met my aunts and uncles and all my cousins. Barb and I watched the Georgia game together. How cool is that?" She let out a woof. "Go Dawgs. Oh, and she loved my red and black boots. Everyone was so welcoming—"

Becky clapped her hands in front of Jules's face. "That sounds great, and we can go back to all of that, but for now, can you fast-forward to the part where you got a dog."

"Oh, okay. My Aunt Bonnie and Uncle Jeff live on a great piece of property—where the party was held—and she volunteers for the golden retriever rescue. They have two of their own, and three she's fostering while they look for homes. Including my buddy, Gene, right here." Jules kissed him on his snout. "They rescued him from Puerto Rico after the earthquake. Flew him up and got him healthy. Luckily for me, they've been teaching him commands in English. Isn't he a doll?"

Becky gave Jules a quizzical look. "So, how did you know his name was Gene?"

"Oh, I gave that to him. I figured he could be our little DNA mascot." Jules dismissed Becky's concerns with a flick of her wrist. "Don't worry. He won't be here all the time, and he'll be calm once he settles in. Tim's taking him tonight."

Becky lifted her eyebrows. "So, now you two sort of have a kid together."

"Yup." A wide smile broke out across Jules's face. "You know what comes after the dog." Jules pointed to her ring finger and started humming, *Here Comes the Bride*.

Becky let out a chuckle at how enthusiastic Jules was now that she was finally on board with the idea of getting married. "I'm not sure the dog isn't supposed to come second, but I'm glad to hear the family outing was a success. I'm assuming your parents weren't among the attendees."

Jules stared at the floor and then brought her gaze back up to meet Becky's eyes. "No, but it all went so well. I'm going to tell them soon. Really. I just want them both without feeling guilty, you know?"

"I think you're doing the right thing telling them. They'll come around, I'm sure of it."

"Well, aside from bonding with Gene here this weekend, I went through all the rest of Jerry's datebooks. I couldn't find anything that was related to Molly or her daughter or even Robert Taylor. It's all court times and case numbers and addresses. It was actually pretty boring stuff."

"I went through mine, too. Nothing. I also did a little homework on the other two potential Molly candidates I found at the library. No luck there either." Becky sighed. "I feel like we're missing something. I was just about to finish going through these boxes when you and Gene bounded in."

The dog had already curled up on the bed Jules had brought him and was fast asleep.

"See, he's a good boy." Jules walked over to the boxes. She dragged the heavy one off to the side. "We already know this has case files in it." She pointed at the last box that hadn't been opened and nudged it with her foot. "Should we open this one? I'm dying to know what's inside. It's not heavy at all."

Becky handed Jules a pair of scissors. "I'll give you the honors."

Jules cut through the packing tape and peered inside.

"What is it?" Becky knelt on the other side of the box and checked out the contents.

"It seems to be a quilt," Jules said as she removed it from the box and spread it on the floor so they could look at it. It consisted of small squares made from different fabrics. "Look, this square is Tigger from Winnie the Pooh."

"Jules, look at this." Becky pointed at the center square made from a photo of Ava with Donna as a baby.

"Do you think Donna's mother made this for her?"

Becky glanced back inside the box, and there was a yellowed slip of paper with a photo paper-clipped to it. "Looks like it was ordered from a quilting place. But it's Ava's name at the top. It says patchwork quilt with squares made from baby and maternity clothes provided. Photo to be duplicated and stitched as the center panel."

Jules ran her fingers across it, studying each square. "This is an awesome idea. I wonder if this was Donna's."

Becky handed her the paper. "Look at the date. Ava dropped it off on November 15, 1993. Look at the date it was due back to her. January 21st, 1994.

"But she died before it was done."

"Right. Look at the signature at the bottom when it was picked up."

Jules's eyes drifted to the bottom of the receipt. "So, Donna's dad picked it up after Ava died. It looks brand new. Do you think he just never gave it to Donna?"

"I guess we'll need to ask her. I'm thinking Ava wanted this done before the new baby came, but she died before it was finished. Maybe they called and asked why it wasn't picked up. Jerry went and got it, but maybe he figured it was too painful to give Donna right then, so he put it away and ultimately forgot about it."

"That makes sense." Jules folded it and put it back into the box. "I hope Donna treasures this as much as I think Ava hoped she would."

Becky laid the receipt back on top of the quilt. "So that was it for this box."

"What about the box that had the pictures?" Jules asked as she pushed her hair off her face. "What else is in there?"

Becky rooted through the box and then started removing items. Jerry's framed law degree and diplomas. Some awards he received. Several bags of canceled checks all made out to the same company, M&A Enterprises, Inc. One of the bags had a Post-it with a question mark on it. Becky pulled out a business-sized envelope and opened it.

"It's a flash drive." She turned the envelope over and examined both sides. "No password."

"Maybe it's not protected," Jules said as she crossed her fingers.

"Let's see." Becky got up off the floor and went to her desk, where she inserted the drive into her computer. "I hope it's not some sort of virus. Can you imagine if it's a trick of some kind?" The request for a password blinked on her screen, and Becky wrinkled her nose. "So much for that. Maybe it's just a copy of his will or the letter he wrote Donna."

"Maybe. I guess we can see if Donna has any guesses for a password. Is there anything else in the box?"

"Just this." Becky took out a hardcover book.

"A book?"

Becky frowned and turned the book around so Jules could see. "Odd choice."

Jules shrugged. "Maybe he was a Superman fan. Or maybe he enjoyed inspirational autobiographies."

There was a knock at the front office door, and Gene hopped up to go investigate.

"He's very friendly," Jules called out as she got up to see who it was.

She came back with a letter in her hand and a scowl on her face.

"Jules, what is it?"

"It's a cease and desist letter."

"Cease and desist what?" Becky asked as her forehead wrinkled.

Jules glanced up from the paper and put her hand on her hip. "Any further conversation with Melanie or Doug Middlebrook."

CHAPTER THIRTEEN

"I MEAN, WHAT THE HELL," Jules said as she tossed the letter onto the desk in front of Becky. "This makes no sense. We've already talked to her. She knows her daughter isn't the person we're looking for."

Becky picked up the paper and skimmed it. "She did sound like maybe she didn't trust us."

"Do you think she has something to hide? I mean, she hired a law firm to scare us away." Jules rubbed her temples as she tried to figure out what possible motive there could be. "Maybe she was lying about her granddaughter's name. I think I'll do some research and see if it backs up her story. Can you work on trying to put together a list of the Robert Taylors you can find? Maybe we'll take a little break from Molly."

"Sure. Should I start local first?"

"I would think so. Focus on the closest ones and then spread north and south a little bit. It's a pretty common name. Let's see what that nets us. I'll check all of Jerry's matches, too, just to see if anything's changed."

After taking Gene for a quick walk, Jules logged in to her

laptop. All the DNA profiles they managed were in one account. There were new rules that each kit needed its own login, but from there, they could transfer the rights to view all their client's matches in their own account. It was much easier to work this way. She cast a glance in Becky's direction. "Do you want me to check your matches while I'm in here?"

"No, thank you." Becky's answer was firm. "I don't think I'm ready for that just yet."

She wasn't sure Becky would ever be ready. But Jules had offered to check, and that's more than she had done last time.

Before she went to Jerry's matches, she pulled up her own. Sitting right at the top was Sasha, the first cousin who led her to Barb. Below Sasha was Lucy16. Jules had been obsessed with her when she'd first gotten her DNA results and started searching. Thinking Lucy had all the answers, Jules practically stalked her when she didn't respond. Lucy had finally admitted she'd been devastated when DNA uncovered the dad who raised her was not her biological father. She had no idea who was.

Jules went to Lucy's match and pulled up the messaging feature. She began to type. *Hi, again! I've found my birth mother, and she gave me the name of my birth father. Since I know we're not related on my maternal side, I thought this might help you in your search. My birth father's name is Lee Cantrell, and last my bio mom knew, he was in Smyrna, Georgia.* Jules paused with her fingers on the keyboard. Barb had told her Lee was thirty-two when she was born. Jules did some quick math and typed. *He was probably born around 1957.*

Lucy matched her with 528 cMs of DNA. That meant most likely she was a half-great-aunt, a first cousin once removed or a half-first cousin. When she found out that Lucy didn't have any idea who her father was, Jules had moved on. At that point, neither one of them had information that could help the other. Jules hadn't really tried to figure out how they were related, but her age might be a clue. She added one last sentence. *By the way, how old are you?* She hit send.

Several hours later, Becky glanced over to find Jules intently staring at her computer. "How's it going?"

Jules looked up from her computer and rubbed her eyes. "It looks like Melanie told us the truth about her daughter and granddaughters. Which makes me even more confused why she sent that cease and desist. But if there's nothing here, we'll have no problem following it. I also sent Lucy a note."

Becky leaned back in her chair. "The mystery cousin? What did it say?"

"I gave her the information Barb gave me about my birth father. We're related on that side, so maybe it will help her search. She seemed like she wanted to find her biological father. Once she got past the initial shock, that is."

"What about you?" Becky asked.

"I think I need to figure out my relationship with Barb first." Jules held up her hand. "And tell my parents. How are you doing with the Robert Taylor list?"

Becky stood and grabbed the papers from the printer in between their desks. "I have three pages of them to start. It's a pretty popular name, so this could be a long shot to find him. I've got a page of local candidates, and then I searched about a fifty-mile radius. It gives us plenty to start with."

Jules glanced at the time on her phone, yawned, and stretched at her desk. "Let's leave the cold calling until tomorrow. I have to go by Tim's to drop off Gene."

"Oh, Donna also left me a voicemail."

"Me too. I guess we should call her back. Ask her to come in tomorrow so we can give her that quilt. She's probably also wondering what we found in Orlando."

Donna sounded aggravated when she answered. Jules

wondered if she had called at a bad time. She put the phone on speaker. "Hi, Donna, it's Jules and Becky."

"I called both of you earlier, but I guess you were both too busy to call me back." Apparently, her aggravation *was* aimed at them.

"I'm sorry. It was a bit of a crazy day. But we wanted to see if you could come to the office tomorrow. We'll give you an update, and we found something in one of the boxes you might want."

"I'll come when I can get a break from work. Does that work?" She sounded less annoyed now that she knew there was an update.

"Sure. See you tomorrow."

Becky waited until she was sure Jules had disconnected the call. "She sounds frustrated that we haven't found her sister yet, but we told her it would take time. We don't even have her DNA results yet."

Jules dismissed Donna's call with a flick of her wrist. "She'll be fine when she sees the quilt." She stood and rolled her neck in a circle. She'd been sitting staring at her computer for too long. "Let's get out of here."

"Sounds good. Bryan just texted that he was getting ready to start dinner. A *romantic* dinner." Becky clasped her hands together over her chest.

"A man that cooks …" Jules shook her head. "Exactly what makes it a romantic dinner?"

Becky smiled mischievously. "The *dessert*." She giggled.

Jules rolled her eyes. "I'm glad y'all worked things out, but now you're like two high school kids in heat."

Becky gave a small, unapologetic shrug. "For so many years, all we worried about was trying to get pregnant. It's nice to let all that go for now."

She organized her desk and left the printout with the list of names on top of her computer.

"I get it." Jules unplugged her laptop and inserted it into her leather computer bag. "Tim's got another set of things for Gene at his house, so I think I'll just leave his stuff here for now." She threw the strap of her bag over her shoulder and clipped the leash to Gene's collar. "C'mon, Tim's expecting you."

"I hate this time of year," Becky said as they got to the bottom of the stairs and started walking toward the parking lot. "It starts to get dark so early and—"

The leash Jules held loosely tugged in her hand. "Hey, Gene, stop."

She tightened her grip before he could yank it free. A low growl vibrated from him as he pulled the leash taut, straining to go farther. His attention was laser-focused and fixed on something on the side of the building. His hackles were up.

Becky followed Gene's gaze and squinted into the darkness.

Jules reined the dog in. She reached down to pat the side of his head and reassured him. "Gene, what's up? It's okay." She glanced at Becky and frowned. "That's an odd place for someone to hang out. It's too late for the landscapers."

"It looked like there was someone there, but I don't see them anymore," Becky said, still peering off into the darkness.

Jules patted the dog on his side to get his attention. "You're okay. They're gone."

Gene remained frozen. His growl, which had started low in his throat, grew louder and more intense. The sound of a warning.

Jules's eyes widened. "This is a side of him I've never seen. Gene, c'mon." Jules tugged at the leash until he finally broke his statuesque stance, and then like nothing had happened, he trotted after her.

"That was really odd," Jules said as they reached their cars. "Wonder what that was all about."

Becky hit her key fob to unlock her car, the beep echoing

loudly. With a quick glance around, she pulled on the handle and then turned back toward Jules.

"One thing seems pretty clear. Gene saw *someone* over there. Whoever it was, they're lucky you didn't turn him loose. They might have found out the hard way just how much he didn't like them."

CHAPTER FOURTEEN

"So, how was your romantic dinner last night?" Jules asked as they trudged up the set of stairs that led to their office.

Becky couldn't help but smile. "I would never kiss and tell."

Jules threw her head back and laughed. "Sure, you wouldn't."

"Well, if you're sure you want the gory details—" Becky's feet froze at the top of the stairs.

The lock on their office door was broken, and the doorknob hung loose. There were gouges in the wooden frame where it looked like someone had tried to pry the door open.

She spun around to face Jules, her eyes round. "Someone broke into our office."

Jules grabbed Becky's arm. "Don't go in there. Let me call Jonas and see what we should do."

A few moments later, Jules hung up and reported back. "Jonas is off today, so he's on his way over. He said to stay outside and call 911 to report it."

Becky reached for her phone, her hands shaking as she unzipped her purse.

Jules put her hand on Becky's shoulder. "I'll call it in." After providing the address for their office, Jules confirmed the police were on their way.

Becky leaned against the wall for support. "What could anybody possibly want in our office, Jules? We don't have cash or valuables."

"Well, they don't know that. I wonder if anyone else got broken into." Jules walked hesitantly down the row of doors and then made her way back to Becky. "The rest of the offices seem fine."

"So, just us?" Becky's legs wobbled, and her eyes drifted toward the stairs. "I need to sit." Since the entrance to their office was accessible from the outside, they could keep watch for the police car or Jonas.

As Jules sat on the step next to Becky, her phone buzzed. "I guess I won't tell Tim I called Jonas before I called him. His man feelings will be hurt."

Becky nodded. "I guess I should call Bryan, too."

After offering assurances that not only were they both fine, but Jonas and the police were on their way, the men let them go.

Becky glanced nervously over her shoulder. "You don't think someone could still be in there, do you?"

"Doubtful, but that's probably why Jonas said not to go in. Also, I guess maybe they can dust for fingerprints."

"What about Gene growling last night?" Becky gestured toward the side of the building. "I know I saw someone over there. Do you think they had anything to do with this? Like maybe they were waiting for us to leave so they could break in?"

Jules lifted a shoulder. "I guess it's possible, but again, why target us?" She stared down at the concrete step below them.

Becky elbowed her. "The cops are here."

The police car had driven up without any sirens or lights

and parked at the curb. Jules waved over the railing. "We're up here," she called out. "Suite #204."

After a quick glance around the parking lot, the police officer made his way up the flight of stairs. "You reported a break-in?" he asked when he reached them.

Jules nodded. "When we got here this morning, it was clear someone broke the lock and forced the door open. We haven't gone inside yet. My brother's a cop. He told me to wait until you got here."

"Good advice." The officer held up his hand. "Stay here. Let me just make sure no one is still on the premises."

They watched as he drew his gun and slowly pushed their office door open.

Becky let out a deep breath. "I really hope he doesn't need that gun."

A few minutes later, he was back. "Come on in, but don't touch anything. Let me know what's missing."

It was a strange feeling to know someone else had been in their office. Becky felt violated. The reception area appeared untouched. A quick look confirmed the box with the quilt for Donna still sat underneath the desk.

Jules glanced at Becky and nodded as together they made their way to their office.

Becky let out a gasp as her eyes drifted around the room. The filing cabinets had been yanked open and everything pulled out. The floor around their desks was littered with the contents.

"Thanks for making a mess, asshole," Jules muttered under her breath.

Becky's gaze landed on her desk. "Oh, crap." She glanced at the police officer and then at Jules and groaned. "My laptop's gone."

"Are you sure you didn't bring it home last night?" Jules asked.

"I'm positive. I left it with the list of numbers to call today sitting on top. I didn't bring it home because—because I had dinner plans with Bryan." Her voice grew softer. "I knew I wouldn't need it, so I left it."

"Anything else missing?" the officer asked.

Jules glanced around. Their little kitchen area was untouched. Microwave, coffee pot, kitchen supplies. Exactly how they left them.

"I don't think so. We haven't been in this office long, so there's not much here."

The officer nodded. "So, it looks like just the laptop was taken. That's a pretty common thing to grab. No cash in the office. A safe?"

Jules shook her head. "Neither."

"It looks like a simple break-in. Probably looking for money. My guess is they got aggravated when they didn't find any and wrecked your office on the way out as a way of letting you know."

Becky cleared her throat. "Last night, we had a dog here. When we walked out, he was growling. I mean, *really* growling. It was dark out, but we thought we saw someone at the side of the building. Maybe it's related." Even as she said it, Becky knew the cop would dismiss it. It wasn't proof of anything.

He affirmed her belief. "Probably nothing. Here's what I'll do. I'll look around and see if there are any surveillance cameras, but I wouldn't hold my breath. Just be thankful you didn't lose more, and you should get that lock fixed as soon as possible. If you think of anything else, I'll be in my squad car writing up the report." He handed his card to Jules. "I'll let you ladies clean up."

Becky heard him talking to someone by the front door. "They're here. In the back."

A moment later, Donna peered into their office and looked around. "What the hell happened? Why are the police here?"

Becky stooped down to start gathering papers from the floor. "We had a break-in."

"Oh, that's horrible." Donna's gaze scanned the floor. "They certainly made a big mess. I hope they didn't get much."

"Just my laptop," Becky said with a pout.

"Hey, Jules." Jonas's booming voice sounded throughout the office.

"In here," she called out. "My brother," Jules explained to Donna. "He's sort of our silent partner. Plus, he's a cop, so I called him. He's actually off-duty now."

Donna pursed her lips. "Your brother's a cop?"

Jules didn't go into details. "Yeah, it comes in handy some-times." She marched toward Jonas, and he enveloped her in a hug.

"You okay?" he asked.

"Yeah, more freaked out than anything." She gestured toward Donna. "Jonas, this is Donna, one of our clients."

Jonas stuck out his hand. Donna hesitated, then shook it.

"Hey, Becky." Jonas bent at the waist and turned his head sideways to address her as she crawled on the floor.

She raised a hand, her fist clutching a stack of papers. "Hi, Jonas. I wish you were visiting under better circumstances."

He bobbed his head. "Me too."

"Donna, do you want to take a seat by my desk?" Jules asked. "Let us get a little organized."

Donna glanced at the time on her phone. "Sure, but I don't have that much time. I have to get back to work."

Jules put her hand on Jonas's arm. "You good for a little bit?"

When he nodded, she went out to the reception area. When she came back, she put the box with the quilt on her desk.

"This is one of your father's boxes," she said to Donna. "We found something in it we think you'll want."

Donna's brow wrinkled. "What is it?" she asked as Jules helped her unfold it over the desktop.

"It looks like your mom had a quilt made. The squares are made from your baby clothes and your mom's maternity clothes." Jules gestured toward the photo. "And in the middle, she put a picture of the two of you."

Donna swallowed hard. She stared at it without saying anything.

"You've never seen this?" Jules asked.

She shook her head silently and then finally said, "No. Never."

"It looks like your mom ordered it to be made while—while she was pregnant with your brother," Jules said gently. "Your father picked it up after she passed away." When Donna turned her head quickly, eyes narrowed, Jules added, "He signed the receipt."

Donna shook her head on the verge of tears. "He picked it up and hid it away."

Jules put her hand over Donna's. "She clearly meant for you to have this, and I'm sorry you didn't have it to comfort you when you were a little girl."

Donna bit her bottom lip and nodded. "Can you help me fold it back up?"

"Sure. Do you need a hand putting the box in your car? Jonas can help you."

Donna glanced in his direction and shook her head. "No, I got it. You both have things to do here. Why don't I call you later, and you can update me by phone?"

Becky glanced up. Donna wanted to find out what was going on with her case, but now she was so quick to leave? Maybe the quilt had taken an emotional toll.

"Okay, sure," Jules said with a quick nod. "We can do that. We'll get this cleaned up and be good as new."

After Donna left the office, Jules gestured for Jonas to sit in the seat she vacated.

"Finished," Becky said as she pointed at the piles of paper now on her desk. "We may have to spend some time putting the files back together, but at least they're off the floor." She rolled her seat over to Jules and Jonas and sat down.

"So, I talked to the cop," Jonas said. "It doesn't look like they're going to be able to do much. And to be honest, I doubt they'd have the manpower to expend any significant effort over the theft of a single laptop. My station would probably be the same way."

"I figured that would be the case," Jules said.

"I also took a look at the door. I can help you fix it." Jonas glanced at Becky. "And you're probably going to need to get a new computer."

Becky rolled her eyes and let out a heavy sigh. "Yup, and the sooner, the better. I've got work to do."

"Jonas, do you find it odd that no one else had a break-in on our floor?" Jules asked.

"Maybe they had better locks. Hard to know."

Becky nudged Jules. "Tell him about Gene."

Jonas's curious gaze traveled between the two women. "Who's Gene?"

"That's what I named the dog I got from Aunt Bonnie."

Jonas chuckled. "I knew it. Once you and Tim started playing Frisbee with him, I figured you'd have a hard time leaving the party without him." He gestured toward the kitchen area. "That explains the dog bed and water bowl."

"Well, Tim and I are sharing custody. For now." Jules shot a glance at Becky and then brought her gaze back to Jonas. "I had him here yesterday with us. When we left, something caught his attention at the side of the building. He wouldn't stop growling."

Jonas lifted an eyebrow in surprise. "Really? From what I saw at the party, I wouldn't have figured him for a growler. Is that something he's been doing?"

Jules raised her shoulders. "Well, I've never seen him do it before, but you know, I've only had him a few days. He's normally very friendly."

Jonas cocked his head to the side. "I'm not sure what to make of that. Maybe it's something, maybe it's not."

Becky spoke up. "There's something else. Something I haven't even told Jules."

Jules put her elbow on the desk and rested her chin in the palm of her hand. "Oh, really?"

"I know I have a tendency to be a little paranoid," Becky said sheepishly.

"Who, you?" Jules asked with a trace of sarcasm.

Jonas swatted playfully at Jules across the desk. "Ignore her. After Peyton, you have a right to be a little paranoid."

Becky bowed her head in his direction. "Thank you, Jonas. When I went to Orlando—the first time when I went by myself —I saw something that didn't seem right."

Jonas frowned. "All the way in Orlando?"

"I know. That's why I didn't say anything. I went to meet this woman I thought might be relevant to Donna's case. This car was parked across the street, and I swear I saw somebody in the driver's seat duck down when I came out of her house." Becky stole a glance in Jules's direction to determine her reaction. "When I left, the car pulled out right behind me."

"Could be a coincidence," Jonas said.

Jules leaned forward. "Tell him the rest, Beck."

Becky dipped her head and continued. "That night, the woman left me a voicemail, which confirmed she wasn't the person I'd been looking for. I tried to call her back the next day, and her sister answered her phone. The woman I went to meet was out walking that night and was killed by a hit and run driver."

Jonas rubbed his chin thoughtfully. "Could still just be a coincidence."

"There's more," Becky said insistently. "When Jules and I went to Orlando together, we ate lunch at this restaurant." She turned to Jules. "Remember when you went back to leave a tip on the table?"

Jules's eyes narrowed. "Yeah?"

"This guy was waiting outside the restaurant. It seemed like he was watching you through the window, and then he seemed fixated on you as you walked back toward the parking lot. I just figured it was the usual, you know, a guy checking you out because you're so pretty." Becky shook her head. "But now, I'm not so sure."

Jules raised an eyebrow. "Not sure I'm so pretty or that he had another motive for checking me out?"

Becky's mouth was set in a firm line. "Jules, I'm serious."

Jonas raised his hand. "So, what are you saying, Becky? You think someone's been following you in Orlando, and now they're here, and they're the person who broke into your office?"

"I know it sounds crazy, but—"

Becky's phone rang, and she rolled in her chair over to her desk to see who it was. "It's a four-oh-seven area code number. Orlando." She answered the phone. "This is Becky Morgan." Her eyes widened. "Oh, hi, Melanie." She put her hands out in a what do I do now gesture.

"We're not allowed to talk to her," Jules whispered urgently.

Becky put her phone on speaker and then muted it. "She's calling *me*. What do I do?"

"I guess we can always claim we didn't know it was her."

Jules threw a quick glance at Jonas. "You didn't hear any of that."

He shrugged. "That's fine. I don't understand any of it."

Melanie's voice came through the phone. "So, as I was saying, I was talking to my daughter, and she reminded me of something interesting—"

"As much as I would like to hear what you have to say, I'm a little confused," Becky cut in. "You sent us a cease and desist letter. Your lawyer was very clear you wanted no further contact with us."

"Cease and desist?" Melanie sounded perplexed. "I'm not sure I know what you're talking about. I didn't contact any lawyer. In fact, I told the gentleman that came in after you that I was sorry I couldn't be more help."

Becky whipped her head around to give Jules a hard stare. "Gentleman?"

"Yes, right after you left, a man came in and said he had just missed you, but he told me you all worked together."

Becky muted the phone and jabbed her finger in the air. "See, I'm *not* so crazy." She took the phone off mute and tried to respond casually. "Oh, our partner. Right. I'm sorry. I didn't realize he came in as well. I must be thinking of another case with the cease and desist." Becky laughed and then cringed at how fake it sounded.

"Oh, okay. As I said, I was talking to my daughter. She reminded me about another girl named Molly. Her name was Molly Middlebrooks, with an S on the end. My daughter sometimes got mail that didn't make any sense, and she finally figured out it was for this other girl. My daughter called around last night to a mutual friend. Turns out, she does have a daughter."

Becky held her breath. "What's her daughter's name?"

"I'm not sure what it's short for, but the friend said they call her Ally."

Becky shot Jules a wide-eyed stare. They might get to wrap this up. "Does the friend know where Molly is now?"

"Well, that's the problem. She moved out of Orlando to North Florida somewhere, and they lost touch. The friend thinks she heard she got married and moved out of state, but she didn't know where."

Jules wrinkled her nose in disappointment. "Ask if we can talk to the friend?" she whispered.

"Do you think your daughter's friend would be willing to talk to us?" Becky asked.

"I'm not sure what else she'd have to tell you, but I'll call her," Melanie said. "If she's willing, I'll give her your number."

Becky disconnected the call, smiled, and raised her fist in victory.

CHAPTER FIFTEEN

Jules put the brakes on the premature celebration. "There's a lot to dissect here, Beck."

"Where's the envelope from Molly?" Becky asked, full of excitement.

Jules dug into her computer bag, pulled it out, and placed it on the desk.

Becky squinted at it. "That could definitely be an S at the end."

Jules held it in her hand and scrutinized it. Finally, she bobbed her head in agreement. "I thought it was the way the pen blotted at the end, but now that I'm looking at it again, her last name could definitely be Middlebrooks."

"I'm lost here," Jonas said, a befuddled expression on his face. "We went from Becky thinking someone was traveling up I-95 stalking the two of you to some sort of celebration?"

"Okay, let me explain from the beginning," Jules said. "Disregard the last name drama. The woman that just called. We got a cease and desist letter that she didn't want us to talk to her. We spoke to her once. It was no big deal, and we didn't think we'd ever need her again, but now, as you just heard, she says she didn't send it."

"Well, first of all, a cease and desist letter usually means you're doing something illegal, which clearly doesn't apply here. Where's the letter?"

Becky gestured toward the mess of papers on her desk. "Somewhere in those piles, I would assume."

Jonas rolled his eyes. "Yeah, that's going to take a while to sort out."

"But Jonas," Jules said. "Isn't the point that not only did she not know what we were talking about—"

"The letter actually referenced her *and* her husband," Becky interrupted. "It could be she talked to the husband about our conversation and he had it sent without telling her."

"I guess that's possible," Jules said with a lift of her shoulders. "But who was the guy who came in and said he was working with us? It had to be the guy you saw outside the restaurant." Jules turned to Jonas. "Maybe Becky isn't so paranoid after all."

Jonas dipped his head in agreement. "Something's not right, I agree." He passed a stern gaze between Jules and Becky. "You two need to be careful until we figure out what's going on. Here and on your road trips."

"At least it doesn't seem like she gave the information she had to this mystery man," Becky said hopefully. "Don't you think we're on the right track? This Molly even moved to North Florida. Maybe she moved to be near Donna's dad."

Jules considered it. "I guess it's possible, but if Molly was watching him, it doesn't seem as if Jerry ever knew." She stood and pulled a marker from the ledge beneath the whiteboard.

She started to write something and then froze with the marker in her hand. Jules wheeled around. "Do you think whoever broke in was looking for information about Donna's case?" She studied the writing on the whiteboard. "All of this was written up here for anyone to see."

Becky let out a groan. "You're probably right."

Jules turned back around, and her eyes scanned the board. "Let's see. We haven't updated it since the first day. We didn't even add her last name. With or without the S at the end. All they're going to know is what we knew in the beginning."

"We haven't figured it out yet, and we have way more information than what's here," Becky pointed out. "I have a picture of what was up there on my phone if we need it."

"Let's not use this anymore." Jules took the eraser and wiped off the writing until the whiteboard was blank.

Jonas cleared his throat as if perhaps they had forgotten he was there. "I know I'm supposed to be a silent partner, but you two seemed to have stepped over the 'let's use DNA to solve adoptions' line. Are we talking about an inheritance with a large amount of money at stake?"

Jules and Becky exchanged a glance, and then Jules nodded. "Donna's dad died."

"Maybe someone knows he was well off, and they heard he passed away. They could just assume Donna's about to come into some money. They've been following her to see if she goes to a bank or a car dealership for some expensive purchase. It's kind of like the lottery ticket winners. One day they're on the news with the big check, and the next thing they know every creep out there is following him to try to scam them out of their money."

Becky cocked her head to the side as she considered it. "I guess it's possible. Maybe they're trying to figure out what we have to do with her and potentially her inheritance."

Jonas wagged his finger at them. "As I said, you two need to be very careful until we figure this out. First order of business, you need to get the lock fixed." He turned to Jules. "Can Tim come to stay with you while I run to the hardware store? I'm not comfortable leaving you both here alone. At least not until the door is fixed."

"I can call Bryan, too," Becky said as she glanced at Jules. "If Tim can't get away from work."

"Okay, let's see who can take the ride over, but I'm not leaving until one of them is here with you both," Jonas said, a deep-set frown on his face. "Something's going on, and I don't like it one bit."

CHAPTER SIXTEEN

DONNA GROANED as she glanced down at the light glowing on her gas gauge. Jay was always warning her not to let it get so close to empty.

She was exhausted and had already stopped at the grocery store. Mentally she weighed her options before finally letting out a sigh and pulling into the gas station across the street from the apartment complex. She knew herself well. The last thing she'd want to do on her way to work in the morning would be to stop for gas.

After she scanned her credit card, she inserted the nozzle into her gas tank and watched the numbers begin to roll as the tank filled. Letting out a yawn, she glanced mindlessly around the parking lot, cringed, and quickly turned her head.

Living in the same town, she'd seen him a few times while she was out and about, but mostly she'd been able to dodge him over the years. Maybe he hadn't seen her. She waited hopefully for a few moments, but then heard his voice.

"Donna?" He sounded like he was right behind her.

Damn her red hair. It was a dead giveaway. She tried not to

visibly grimace as she slowly turned back toward him. There was no escaping him this time.

His lips curved upward in a smile, but it was warm and genuine, and not the cocky grin she remembered. It was what had drawn her to him in the first place.

"Hey, stranger," he said. "It's been a while, huh?" He laughed as if running into his ex-wife was no big deal.

Donna was sure he could see her pulse throbbing in her neck. "Nick," she said in acknowledgment as she swayed slightly. She felt betrayed by her emotions that she still felt anything at seeing him.

"I was actually going to reach out to you. Crazy timing. Do you have time for a quick chat?"

What could he possibly want to talk to her about?

"I only need a few minutes," Nick said when she hesitated. "It's kind of important."

Donna glanced around nervously. "You mean now?"

"Well, we're both here now," Nick said with a shrug and a hesitant smile. "Unless you want to go grab a bite to eat or a cup of coffee."

Donna placed her palm on the roof of her car to steady herself. She wouldn't be going anywhere with him.

When she didn't respond, he threw up his hands. "I come in peace, I swear."

Donna leaned against her car and took in a deep breath. "Fine."

"I appreciate it. I just need a few minutes."

Donna decided to head off any idea he might have about a reconciliation. After clearing her throat, she licked her lips nervously. "I'm getting married, Nick."

He smiled. "That's great. I'm happy for you. Really."

"Oh." His sincerity caught her off guard. "His name is Jay."

"Well, he's a lucky guy. Congratulations to both of you. How's everything else in your world?"

Donna narrowed her eyes. Nick had never been this easy to talk to. Her shoulders relaxed. "Still have the same crappy job." She paused. "Not sure if you heard, my dad died."

Nick's face fell. "Oh, man. You okay? When we were together—well, I know when he was diagnosed, you had a hard time with that."

She shrugged. "It actually wasn't the lung cancer that killed him. He got through that, but then he got pancreatic cancer. It happened fast this time."

"I'm sorry. If there's anything I can do to help …"

She opened her mouth and then closed it. Was she falling for a new and improved Nick? Donna blinked hard and broke the spell that seemed to have fallen over her. "I have Jay to help me now. We're about to be married. You need to let go."

"I have let go. I swear. The reason I wanted to see you was to actually thank you for leaving me."

Nick had begged her to reconsider when she left. Pleaded with her to call off the divorce. Her eyebrows lifted in disbelief as she stared at him. "Thank me?"

Nick nodded. "I know that sounds odd, but it took you leaving for me to turn my life around. I finally went to AA. I got help."

Donna couldn't help but glare at him. "Really? How many times did I ask you to go when we were married?"

"I know, I know. What can I say? I hit rock bottom without you." His eyes pleaded with her. "I'm five months sober. Allow me the chance to apologize and make amends. It's important for my recovery. I hurt you more than anyone."

Donna crossed her arms over her chest and studied him. He seemed calmer, less agitated. He was certainly in better shape now than he was then.

"I have a steady job now. I'm hoping I can even move out

of that house you hated so much." Nick gave her a smile. "No more annoying train whistle twice a day."

Donna felt an unfamiliar twinge. She had prayed so many times that Nick would get his act together. Now the Nick she'd always wanted was standing right in front of her. Across the street from the apartment complex where she and *Jay* lived.

"I'm happy for you, really I am. I wish it hadn't taken so long, but I'm glad you finally got your shit together." Donna paused as she considered his motive for telling her. "You do know that doesn't change anything, right? I'm not coming back, Nick."

He shifted his weight from one foot to the other. "Of course. We've both moved on. You're getting married and I have an amazing girlfriend. She's been good for me."

The words hit Donna in a way she hadn't expected. What did this girl have that she didn't? She'd obviously been able to convince her ex-husband to change.

Nick touched Donna's arm. She flinched, and he pulled his hand back. "I just wanted to say I'm sorry for the way I treated you when we were married. You deserved better, and I don't blame you for leaving. That's all. I'm not looking to cause you any trouble with your new guy."

"His name is Jay." She'd already told him that. "And he's not new. We've been together for a few years."

At the mention of his name, Donna's heart thumped harder in her chest. She needed to get home.

The sound of a ringing phone interrupted her thoughts. Nick reached into his back pocket and silenced it as he glanced at the screen. "I gotta go. Are we good?"

Donna stared at him for a moment, then nodded. Maybe this had been the closure she needed with him. "We are. I accept your apology."

"Thank you, Donna. I really mean that." He leaned forward and hugged her, much longer than felt comfortable.

Finally, she pulled back. "I have to go. Bye, Nick."

As she drove into the apartment parking lot a few minutes later, she breathed a sigh of relief. Jay's spot was still empty.

And then it wasn't. She watched with dread as Jay swung his car into the space next to hers. If he was just getting home, had he noticed her across the street with Nick?

"Hey, hon, you're home," she said, popping the trunk to take out the groceries.

"You're running late." Jay eyed her curiously as he stepped out of the car and took several of the grocery bags off her arm. "I brought my brother over so you two could meet."

A man got out of the passenger side and offered a wave.

"Hi, Kevin, I'm Donna. It's nice to finally meet you." She glanced at Jay and then his brother. "Come on up. I just got back from the store." She reached into the trunk, grabbed the 12-pack of beer, and held it up. "I've got cold beer." At least she hoped it was still cold.

Jay pursed his lips as he stared at her. Was guilt seeping through her pores? She made an effort to control her breathing, act naturally. She reminded herself she hadn't done anything wrong.

"So," Donna said over her shoulder as she ascended the stairs. "I'm glad you and Jay have patched stuff up. It's nice for him to have you nearby now."

She was sure he would notice her ragged breathing. "I'm a little out of breath," she acknowledged. He didn't need to know the real cause was anxiety over whether Jay had seen her with her ex-husband. She shrugged and offered a sheepish smile. "The stairs. Jay's always after me to start working out. We have a gym at the clubhouse here. I'm thinking it's time to start getting in shape."

"That's great you have a gym here you can use," Kevin said. "Me, I gotta pay to work out. I'm hoping to move to this side of town soon. The place I'm in now is kind of a dump. Who knows, maybe I can rent here."

Donna ignored the implication that they might be neighbors. She held her breath as she turned the knob and pushed open the door.

"Let me get you both a beer." She hurried toward the kitchen and exhaled a deep breath as she grabbed two beers from the 12-pack and put the rest in the refrigerator. She handed one to each man. "Here you go."

Kevin popped the can and took a swig. "Nice place."

Donna scowled. "Ugh, it's really not. We'll be moving soon enough. I'm sure Jay told you about my dad dying."

He bobbed his head. "Yeah, he did. Condolences."

Jay placed his can of beer on the kitchen table but didn't open it. Donna tried not to panic, but that wasn't like him.

Jay looked her firmly in the eye. "Donna, could I speak to you privately? In the bedroom."

Donna swallowed hard. "Sure, hon."

He grabbed her arm and led her to their bedroom. When they got there, Jay pulled her in and shut the door behind them.

"Everything okay?" Donna could feel a flush growing across her cheeks. They felt hot.

Jay sat on the bed and rubbed his goatee. His cold eyes met hers. "You tell me."

Donna offered what she hoped was a carefree shrug. "Everything's fine. I'm glad you brought your brother over so I could finally meet him. The store was crowded which is why I was late tonight, but maybe I can run back out and get something nice we can make for dinner. I saw Publix has steak on sale—"

"Just stop it," Jay whispered tersely as he bent over and put his head in his hands. He looked like he was trying to gain control of himself, but when he brought his gaze back up, it was clear his strategy hadn't worked. He shook his head as he gritted his teeth.

Donna swallowed hard when she saw his hands were balled into fists at his sides.

"Baby, are you okay?" She hoped her question sounded like she was concerned and not fearful she was the reason for his anger. If only she had gone for gas in the morning, none of this would have happened.

Jay let out a snort. "I am definitely *not* okay." He fixed a steely stare on her. "Maybe you can answer a question for me."

"Sure," Donna stammered. Her heart thudded in her chest. Holding her breath, she waited.

Jay pressed his lips together and pinned her with his icy stare. "Just what the hell were you doing with your ex-husband?"

CHAPTER SEVENTEEN

DONNA'S EYES WIDENED, and her chest deflated when she exhaled. She rushed to Jay's side and put her hand on his arm. He yanked it away.

"Jay, I swear, nothing's going on. I just ran into him at the gas station. That's it."

A darkness crossed his face. "Don't lie to me," he said through clenched teeth. "I saw you both. He had his arms wrapped around you."

"It's not what you think," she said insistently. "He's been going to Alcoholics Anonymous. He's supposed to make amends for the people he's hurt. I swear that's all it was. I accepted his apology and he hugged me goodbye."

Jay hung his head and stayed silent.

Donna leaned into him. "I love you. I would never do anything to jeopardize our relationship. Especially with Nick. You know that."

His eyes fixed on hers. "Then why didn't you just tell me you ran into him?" He studied her. "You weren't going to tell me, were you?"

Donna shrugged and shook her head. "I was worried you'd

jump to the wrong conclusion. I know how you feel about him. I was afraid it would come to blows. The last thing we need is for someone to call the police on you." She offered a half-hearted smile. "You're much bigger than him. You could do some real damage. Nick's not worth it."

Jay pressed his lips together and gazed off as if he were considering this. "I hate that you feel like you can't tell me something."

"There's nothing to tell. I swear," Donna said insistently. "It was nothing."

Jay ran his hand over his face and then looked Donna straight in the eye. "Listen, you know I'm not very good at expressing my feelings, but I love you and I don't want to lose you. To anyone, but *especially* him."

Donna rubbed his arm. "I know, honey. I swear, we're fine. I'm ready to plan our wedding." She leaned over and kissed him. "Your brother probably thinks we came in here for a quickie. Maybe we should get back out there." She smiled at him and tried to break the tension. "Unless, of course, you did have a quickie in mind …"

"I'll take a raincheck. But seriously, Donna, next time—" Jay's stare was as cold and unrelenting as his tone. "If I catch him near you again, next time I swear I'll kill him."

Donna stood and pulled on his arm. "There won't be a next time. C'mon, your beer's getting warm."

"I was starting to worry about you two," Kevin said as they made their way back into the kitchen, where he still sat at the table. He took a long swallow of his beer. "Everything okay?"

Donna glanced at Jay and nodded. "Everything's fine. How about if I see what I can find for dinner. Are you two hungry?"

While the men went into the living room and turned on the television, Donna busied herself in the kitchen, trying to pull together a meal. She heard the murmur of voices but couldn't hear what they were saying.

"Hey, you two," she called out after she had the table set and dinner ready. "Ready to eat?"

"Smells good, Donna," Kevin said as he took a seat.

"Nothing fancy, really. Spaghetti with meat sauce and garlic bread." She'd already portioned it out onto the plates. "Oh, and some salad." She grabbed the salad bowl and handed it to Jay. "Can you put this on the table, please?"

He took the bowl from her and placed it in the center of the table.

She pulled three beers out of the refrigerator and brought them to the table.

She popped the top of hers. "Dig in."

She took a swallow of her beer while Jay started dishing out the salad.

"So, Jay tells me you have a sister you never knew about," Kevin said as he speared a tomato. It was a statement rather than a question.

"A half-sister, actually." Donna shrugged. "Apparently, my dad wasn't too keen on claiming her while he was alive."

"I'm sure she won't mind. She's coming along in time to cash in. That's probably all she'll care about," Kevin said with a laugh. "Once you find her, I mean."

Just how much had Jay told him? Kevin had been nothing but appropriate so far, but Donna still wasn't sure she trusted him. "Yeah, well, I hired some detectives to track her down. It's not like I have time to do it."

"And who cares how much it costs, right? By the time you get the bill, you'll have your inheritance, and you two will be packing for easy street. I want to be invited to your new place. Man, that's gonna be somethin', huh?"

"Kevin, enough," Jay said as he swirled spaghetti onto his fork.

"What? I'm just sayin'—"

"You're forgetting that in all this, Donna lost her dad. Have a little respect."

Jay was protecting her. He knew how she felt about her dad, but at the same time, he wanted to make sure his brother respected her. That had to mean the issue with Nick was forgotten.

Kevin's cheeks turned crimson. "I'm sorry, Donna. I didn't mean no disrespect. It must be hard to lose your dad and then find out you have a sister you didn't know about. And isn't there some other guy in the will? Did you figure out who he is? Maybe you have a brother, too. Wouldn't that be wi—"

Jay held up his hand. "As Donna told you, she's hired detectives to figure this all out for her. When they do, we'll know more, but for right now, we're all having a dinner that I would like to enjoy."

"Is it okay to talk about the wedding?" Kevin asked cautiously. "Though I'm not sure why you wouldn't wait until you get Donna's money. You could have something ridiculous. You know, like those ones the celebrities have. Caviar and lobster—"

"Kevin, eat your dinner," Jay said as he rolled his eyes. "Or we might not even invite you to the wedding."

Donna was taken aback that Jay had told his brother so much. She wasn't sure how she felt about it. It seemed clear Kevin planned to ride his brother's coattails when they finally got her inheritance. She hoped Jay had been smart enough to not tell him just how much money was at stake.

CHAPTER EIGHTEEN

"ARE you nervous about coming back to the office?" Jules asked when Becky told her she was going to work from home. "The locks are changed, and Tim even installed the camera outside the front door. If anyone tries to break in, we'll know."

"No. I'm fine. Really. My new computer's even all set up. The AC started having problems last night. Bryan had an early meeting, so I'm waiting on the repair guy. Besides, I'm going through that list of Robert Taylors, and I can just as easily do it from here."

"Hopefully, they get it fixed." Jules glanced down at the dog, sleeping by her feet. "How about I stay home with you today?" she asked when his brown eyes gazed up at her. His tail thumped enthusiastically against the floor in response. "Well, that's settled. Gene approves."

Jules sighed. "I guess I could invite my parents over. Gene can help soften the blow. I'll have to explain where he came from, which will lead me right to Barb and the rest of the family. Do you need help going through the Robert Taylor list?"

"Maybe. I'll let you know if I do."

After hanging up with Becky, Jules made plans for her parents to come over for dinner. Her stomach would be in knots all day.

She logged in to her email, and there was already a response from Lucy. Now that Jules had information to share that might help her figure out who her birth father was, Lucy was quick with a reply.

Hi, Jules, Wow! I can't believe you figured out who your birth mother is. That's amazing! I'm sure that information has given you a lot of answers and peace. I've started to do a little digging with the information you gave me. Thank you so much for sharing. I'll let you know what I find. BTW, I'm 36 years old. Lucy

Jules typed back a response. *I'm 31, so based on the amount of DNA we share, my best guess is that we are half-first cousins on our fathers' sides. Our bio dads must have been half-siblings. It could be our bio grandfather had two wives (or mistresses ... or one of each!) and had sons with both. Or I guess they could also share our bio grandmother but have different fathers—either through marriage, infidelity, or before she was married. I was the result of an affair on my birth dad's side with my unmarried birth mother. Maybe the cheating apple didn't fall far from the cheating tree. Ha!*

If you need any help, let me know. We've solved a few adoptions but now have a big case on our desk we're trying to solve. Let's keep in touch, cuz! Jules

Jules hesitated and then went back and added her phone number. She hit send.

After she sent the email, she thought about her birth father. Wouldn't she certainly be rejected if she was the result of an affair? He would be bitter at his secret being revealed, and his wife would hate her. What would their children—her half-siblings—think? They were adults. Would they be able to make a decision about Jules on their own? Maybe they would realize she was just an innocent baby when this started. None of this was her fault.

Her eyes drifted downward. "What do you think, Gene? Think they'd reject me?" The dog got to his feet and whipped his tail back and forth. Jules leaned down to hug him. "If only people were as accepting as dogs. Can you imagine what kind of world we'd have?"

She looked out the window—beautiful crystal blue sky. A distraction before tonight was just what she needed. She pulled herself out of her chair. "C'mon, let's go to the dog park."

After a couple of hours and a stop to pick up lunch, Jules was back at her computer. Gene was worn out and snoring by her feet.

She didn't expect that Lucy would have answered her email yet, but she checked anyway. No response. She stared at the screen for a moment and wondered what Lucy would find. Obviously, Jules had been given up for adoption, but in Lucy's case, one man had given her life, only to let another man raise her as his own. It didn't sound like Lucy or her father had any idea. Would Lucy's dad feel betrayed like her parents did if Lucy searched and found her biological father?

But Jules had her birth father's name. With a few keystrokes, she could probably have an address, a phone number. But it wasn't *just* her biological father she could find. It was an entire side of her family tree. Jules still wasn't sure she was ready to know him, but Barb had said there were half-siblings. Probably aunts and uncles, cousins.

Curiosity got the better of her. Jules pulled up her match with Lucy and clicked on shared matches. If these people all matched Lucy and Jules, they were paternal relatives. Jules created a new tree, labeled it Cantrell, and made it private, so she was the only one who could see it. Jules added her name to the bottom. She hesitated and then winced as she added Lee Cantrell as her father.

Using records and her shared matches, Jules lost herself in her ancestry. She found her grandparents and great-grandparents quickly and found herself wondering about the kind of people they were. This wasn't unlike what she did for her clients, but this time it was different. This was *her* past. Her history. Adoption couldn't simply erase where she had come from.

When the doorbell chimed, Jules glanced at the clock and was shocked it was so late. She'd lost track of time entirely and hadn't even gone to the store. She closed the screen with her family tree, a guilty heat on her cheeks as if she'd been caught doing something awful.

She lifted herself from her chair just as her parents started knocking. Gene raised his head and zeroed in on the sound. He got to his feet and barked as he made his way down the stairs.

As Jules opened the front door, her mother peered in. "Is that a dog I hear—"

The answer jumped up to greet her, tail wagging furiously, his tongue hanging from the side of his mouth. Jules tried not to laugh at her mother's reaction. Shocked but already scratching him behind the ears.

"Gene. C'mon, you know we don't jump on people." Jules coaxed him down off her mother. "Sit, and they'll say hello to you." She gave the motion for him to sit and turned to her parents. "He's usually better, but he's excited to see you both." Gene followed her direction and sat, but it was as if his paws were made of springs that could bring him back up at any moment.

"Hey, buddy," her dad said as he knelt to say hello. Gene picked up his paw and offered it to her father, who shook it and laughed. "Nice to meet you, too."

Jules's mother leaned in and kissed Jules on the cheek. "Hi, sweetie."

"Hey, Ma. Glad you could come over."

"You said we had things to talk about. I guess we can start with where the dog came from. He's charming."

"I'm working on the training," Jules said as she started up the stairs with her parents following and Gene bringing up the rear. "By the way," she called over her shoulder, "I lost track of time, so we're going to have to order in something to eat."

As they made it to the top, her mother took a deep breath. "Those stairs are killer. I need a drink." She fluffed her short gray hair with her fingers and then trotted into the kitchen. "Honey, you want something?" she called out to Jules's dad as she pulled open the fridge.

As her father went to check out his meager beverage options, Jules's phone buzzed in her back pocket. It was a text from Becky.

Melanie's daughter's friend left me a message. She wants to see if she can help. Also, I think I found Robert Taylor, but I have more proof that something VERY strange is going on. Call me.

CHAPTER NINETEEN

"Hey," Becky said when Jules answered the phone. "You didn't call me last night. Everything okay?"

"My parents came over. I told them about Barb." Jules let out an audible yawn.

"Oh, how'd that go?" Becky pulled into a parking spot at the office.

"Not sure yet."

Becky laughed as Jules's car pulled into the spot right next to her. She waved and disconnected the call. Grabbing her latte, she then pushed open the car door.

"I guess we're both running late this morning." Becky winced when Jules got out of her car. "You look exhausted. I stopped for a latte. I should have gotten you something." She held out her cup to Jules. "You look like you need this more than me."

"Keep it. I was planning to make some when we get inside. I'm going to need a whole pot today."

They trudged up the concrete stairs together toward the second floor. Becky waited to see if Jules would say more, but she seemed to be lost in thought.

When they got to the landing, Becky reached over and pulled Jules into a hug. "It will be okay. Do you want to talk about it?"

She pulled back and nodded. "Yeah, let me get some coffee in me first. And I didn't forget your text. I want to hear all about what you found yesterday."

"It's not good, Jules. Something is definitely off, and it has to be related to Donna's case."

Ten minutes later, Jules had a large mug of coffee in her hand. She sat in the guest chair in front of Becky's desk. "Okay, ready."

Becky took a long swallow of her latte and wrinkled her nose. Lukewarm. "Do you want to go first, or do you want me to?"

"I'll go. Mine won't take long."

Becky leaned over the desk. "So, your parents didn't take the news of Barb well?"

Jules took a sip from her cup. "Not at first. I did what we said. Gene met them at the door." Her lips lifted in a small smile. "At least they loved him. My dad, especially."

"Who wouldn't love Gene? By the way, where is he today?"

"Tim stopped by this morning to check on me, which is why I was running behind. He has the day off, so he took him. Apparently, Gene's going jogging this morning." Jules took a deep breath. "So, of course, my parents asked where I got him."

"And you told them?"

"Yup. I had them sit down, so they knew it was something serious. I told them I found Barb six months ago." Jules stared into her coffee mug. "I think that's what bothered my mother the most. That I waited so long to tell them."

"But did you tell her you just met her in person for the first time?"

Jules rested her elbows on the desk as if she needed the

support. "I did. I told them about Jonas, about Barb, about meeting the whole family at my aunt's. I told my parents everyone wants to meet them, too."

"How did that go over?" Becky asked, even though she already knew the answer.

Jules let out a snort. "Like a lead balloon. At first, anyway. I tried to reassure them they weren't losing me. I told them what Barb said about wanting to thank them. I thought it might make my mom feel better. I even told her what Barb said about not wanting me to call her mom."

"Did that help?"

Jules sipped her coffee and gave a shrug that said she wasn't optimistic. "Maybe. She said she needed some time to adjust to the idea."

Becky offered an encouraging nod. "Okay, so she'll come around."

"I just hate feeling guilty. I've got this great family that wants to welcome me with open arms. I don't want to leave my parents for them. I just want them to be part of it."

"What about your dad?" Becky asked as she slugged down the last of her tepid latte.

"When he hugged me goodbye, he told me not to worry. Said he would get my mom to understand how important this was to me."

"Okay, at least you have him on your side. He'll get through to your mom. By Christmas, you'll all be spending the holidays together."

Jules rolled her eyes. "I can only hope. It would be the best present any of them could give me. Okay, now you. What did you find out?"

"It seems Melanie Middlebrook followed through and asked her daughter's friend if she'd be willing to talk to us. She must have said okay because she left me a message yesterday."

"So, what's weird about that?"

123

Becky shook her head. "That's not what I was talking about in the text I sent you. Yesterday I reprinted the list of Robert Taylors and started making calls."

Becky reached into her computer bag and pulled out a pile of papers stapled together. Names were highlighted and crossed out. Some had notes in Becky's handwriting.

"So, I got a ton of voicemails. Mostly I just left messages that we were looking for someone named Robert Taylor who knew Jerry McDermott. Very generic, you know?" Becky flipped through the pages and then pushed them toward Jules. "The one with the star next to it."

Jules scanned the list and found the one Becky was referring to. "Yeah? Did he know Donna's father?"

"I didn't actually talk to him. The number I had was a landline at his house. I didn't even know anybody still had one of those. Anyway, his wife answered."

Jules motioned with her hand for Becky to get to the point of the story. "And ..."

"Her husband has an office in the same building where Jerry had his office. Jerry was on the first floor, and her husband's CPA office was on the third floor."

"So, there's our connection." Jules gazed off thoughtfully. "I'm still not sure why Jerry would have left him all that money. Did his wife say they knew each other or what the relationship between the two of them might have been?"

"Here's the interesting part." Becky tucked her leg underneath her and leaned over the desk toward Jules. "She said the men were friendly. Went to grab lunch sometimes. Robert had mentioned to his wife that he felt bad when Jerry got sick and needed to close down his practice." Becky tapped her finger on the desk. "Robert and his wife actually went to the funeral."

"There's *got* to be something here," Jules said as she gestured wildly and nearly knocked over her coffee cup. "I guess you didn't ask if her husband had recently inherited a pile of money. We should go see him in person." Jules pushed back her chair, stood, and gave Becky an expectant look. "Let's go. I'm ready."

Becky held up her hand. "We can go, but there's more. Here's the creepy part." She took a deep breath. "After she told me all of this, she said, and I quote, 'I told all of this to the guy who called yesterday. He was asking the same questions.'"

Jules's mouth fell open. "You think it's the same mystery man from Orlando?"

"I don't know what to think. Obviously, someone is looking for the same guy we are and asking if he has a connection to Jerry. And someone in Orlando was talking to Melanie Middlebrook and asking about her daughter, Molly. That's too much of a coincidence, Jules. Donna's case and Jerry's will are the common denominators."

Jules nodded with her hands on her hips. "Do we know where Jerry's office was? I think we need some tax advice."

CHAPTER TWENTY

JULES SCANNED the directory on the first floor and found the listing for Robert's CPA office. She pointed to the empty slot for suite 101. "This must have been Jerry's office. I guess they haven't rented it out yet."

She glanced around at the suite numbers and found the right door. A bright square of paint contained four holes where the screws had held Jerry's nameplate in place. The wall around it was in desperate need of an updated coat of paint.

A voice from behind startled them. Jules and Becky wheeled around to find a casually dressed older man carrying a toolbox. "Excuse me. I'm the building manager. Are you interested in renting office space?" He gestured at Jerry's office. "That suite is available."

Jules gave Becky a sideward glance and then nodded at the man. Maybe seeing Jerry's office would help them figure something out. "We are. Could we take a look?"

"Sure." The man pulled out an oversized keyring, inserted a key, and unlocked the door. "I'll give you a few minutes. We've got plans to give it a fresh coat of paint. The previous tenant was here for a long time, and he did leave some furniture. You're welcome to it if you have a use. Otherwise, we can get rid of it before you move in. I need to go meet an electrician on the second floor. Let me know if you need anything."

"Okay, thanks." Jules pushed open the door.

Becky hung back. "I feel kind of weird. Like there's a ghost here or something."

"Don't be silly," Jules said as she looked around.

The office space wasn't large. There was a desk off to the left with two large windows behind it that looked out into the parking lot.

Jules ran her palm along the desktop. "This was probably where his secretary sat."

"Look." Becky walked over to the windowsill behind the desk. She picked up something to show to Jules. *Jerome McDermott, Attorney-at-Law.* "This must have been the sign outside the door."

Jules grabbed the sign and slipped it in her purse.

Becky's eyes widened. "What are you doing?"

"I'm taking it. C'mon, nobody else needs it. You never know, eventually Donna may want it. If we leave it, someone will just throw it in the trash."

"I guess you're right." Becky pulled open the desk drawers and found a small notepad with *From the Desk of Ella McBride* embossed on the pages. "Nothing in here except this," she said as she tossed the pad on the desk. "Ella was Jerry's secretary. The one Donna told us was so good to her."

"Yup. Jerry mentioned her in his letter," Jules said as her eyes drifted around the space.

Off to the right, she saw the kitchenette area, similar to what they had at their office, and an empty supply closet. The walls that led to the large office were lined with file cabinets. Jules pulled open the drawers one by one. All that remained were a few empty hanging folders. She wandered into Jerry's office.

Becky followed Jules in. "That's some desk. No wonder he left it behind. I can't imagine how he got it in, much less how he would have gotten it out."

"Can't you just imagine him sitting there calling out to his secretary? I guess he couldn't have been *too* bad. Sounds like Ella worked for him a long time."

A large hutch with shelves still sat behind the oversized desk. "You can see the dust from where those pictures were displayed," Becky said as she dragged a finger across one of the shelves.

Jules checked the drawers in the hutch, but they were empty. She pulled open the desk drawers and found nothing except a small box half-filled with his business cards.

"I guess he figured he wouldn't need these anymore." She pulled out a few cards and threw them in her bag. Jules shrugged. "For Donna."

"I'm kind of surprised he didn't have a nicer office space," Becky said. "It's not like he couldn't afford it. But maybe that's how he kept so much of his money."

"He didn't really need it. His reputation spoke for itself." Jules gave one last glance around the office. "There's nothing for us here. Let's go upstairs and see what our friend the CPA has to say."

As they pulled the door closed, Jules was relieved the building manager wasn't around so they could take the elevator to the third floor without any questions. "Do you remember what suite number he was in?"

"Suite 305," Becky said, just as the elevator dinged and announced their floor.

As they exited the elevator, Jules glanced around and found a sign with an arrow directing them down a hallway to suites 305-310. "This way."

Robert Taylor, Certified Public Accountant, was on the sign prominently placed next to the door. Becky tried the knob and frowned. "The door's locked."

"Knock. Maybe Robert doesn't leave the door unlocked while he's working."

Becky rapped swiftly on the door. "But what if he has clients coming to see him?" She pressed her ear against the door and listened for movement or someone on a phone call inside. She knocked again, more intently, and waited. After a moment, she turned to face Jules and lifted a shoulder. "Nothing."

"Google him, and let's get an office number."

When Becky called, it was evident the phone was ringing from inside the office. "Voicemail. Should I leave a message?" Becky asked. "I already left one with his wife."

"Can't hurt."

"Hi, Mr. Taylor. My name is Becky Morgan, and I was hoping to speak to you about a personal matter. Could you give me a call?" Becky recited her number and hung up. "Maybe he takes off when he's not in the thick of tax season."

"That certainly sounded like a cell phone ringing inside. Do you have Robert's home address?"

"I only pulled phone numbers, but we should be able to figure it out from his landline. Becky scrolled through her call history. "There were a ton of numbers from yesterday, but he was the last call I made. 4:00 p.m. Here it is. Can you look it up on your phone?"

Becky read the number out loud, and a minute later, Jules looked up and smiled. "Got an address. Let's head over there."

As they got off the elevator, the building manager was waiting for them. "Were you looking for something on a different floor? How did you like the space?"

"We liked it, but we're going to give it some thought," Jules said. "I was actually looking for an accountant and saw there was one in the building. We went up to his office, but it doesn't seem like he's in. The door was locked, and his voicemail is picking up."

"Rob Taylor? On the third floor? That's odd. I saw him early this morning. He never keeps the door locked."

"Well, he does today, I guess. Thank you so much for your help." Jules offered a breezy smile, and the man's face grew flushed.

"No problem." He cleared his throat. "You ladies have a nice day."

As they exited the building and headed to the car, Becky laughed. "He told us both to have a nice day, but did you notice he never took his eyes off you? I should be used to it after all these years, but still."

Jules dismissed her friend's comment with a shake of her head. She stared down at her phone. "Okay, it looks like our friend Rob lives ten minutes from here." She handed the phone to Becky. "You navigate."

"Something feels off," Becky said in between dictating directions. "Don't you think?"

"I'm not sure what I think. I still can't understand why Jerry would have left him so much money." Jules squinted at the street sign. "Is this my turn?"

Becky stared down at the directions on the phone. "Oh, sorry. Yeah, make a right here and then a left on 44th Way. He's house number one-twenty-one. I don't like the fact that someone seems to be on the same trail as us, though. Talking to the same people we're talking to. Do you think Donna hired another agency? You know, she didn't trust us, so she found a backup to see who could figure it out first?"

"I guess it's possible—" Jules tapped the brakes as dread pooled over her. "Um, I think something's going on that's much bigger than Donna hiring another agency. Much bigger."

Becky glanced up from the phone. "What do you mean?"

Jules lifted her hand from the steering wheel and pointed at the white house with the blooms of colorful impatiens filling the front flower beds. "That's the house we're looking for, and clearly, we're not the only ones looking for Rob Taylor."

Up ahead, lined along the curb in front of the white house, were three police cars.

CHAPTER TWENTY-ONE

"WHAT DID JONAS SAY?" Becky asked the moment Jules said goodbye.

"Appears it's a missing persons case. Rob's wife called it in. Apparently, she was on the phone with him, and he told her to hold on a minute. She heard what sounded like a struggle, and then the phone went dead. Her husband hasn't answered since. He was on his cell, so she's not entirely sure where he was when this happened."

The news hit Becky squarely in the chest as she realized this case was starting to spin outside the acceptable realm of coincidences. "Robert Taylor is missing?" Becky asked, her voice high and tight. "First Sue and the hit and run, and now the other person we're looking for goes off the grid? I'm not paranoid." She shook her head vigorously. "Something is definitely not right."

"That's a possibility," Jules said in a measured voice. "But Rob could also have a lady friend his wife doesn't know about. Or maybe he got his huge check and left town with the money."

Becky knew Jules was trying to suggest scenarios that

weren't quite as sinister as the one she had written in her head. Her shoulders sagged under the frustration. They'd been so close to figuring him out, but now she couldn't even fathom what this new development meant.

"If Rob left town, then it was after the building manager saw him this morning," Becky pointed out. "And the wife said she heard a struggle. Was his lady friend roughing him up?"

Jules pressed her lips together but didn't respond.

They were pulled over several houses down from the last police car. As they stared at the house, it became apparent there would be nothing to see. Clearly, the action and the officers were inside.

Finally, Jules put the car in gear. "Let's go back to the office. There's no chance we'll get to talk to his wife, and I don't think we want to be caught lurking here."

As they drove, silence filled the car. The enormity of Rob going missing was not lost on either of them. Becky knew she was right. Something *was* off.

"So, I think I figured out how Lucy and I are related," Jules said eventually.

Becky was relieved for the distraction. "Lucy? Your mystery match?"

"Yeah, I found out she's thirty-six, so the most reasonable relationship is half-first cousins. Her father and my birth father had to have been half-siblings. I still don't know if our fathers shared a mother or a father, but I guess she's working on figuring it all out." Jules stared at the road, her face expressionless. "I did start a family tree. You know, just to see what I could find."

"Did you change your mind about wanting to find him?" Becky asked softly.

Jules offered a small shrug. "I'm still not sure. Knowing I have half-siblings is a big draw. But if he's still married to the wife he cheated on with my mom, I can't imagine how it could go well. Besides, I still need to work through the issues with my parents ..." Jules didn't finish the thought.

Becky didn't push her, and after a moment, she turned up the radio to try to fill the silence. It couldn't compete with the noise in her head.

They had just gotten back to the office and sat down at their desks when a man's voice echoed through the office from the reception area. "Hello, is anyone here?"

Becky turned to Jules. "Any idea?"

The man was dressed in a suit he clearly wished he wasn't wearing. Florida was too hot for a jacket most days, and Becky could see a light sheen of sweat on his forehead.

"Hi, can we help you with something?" Jules asked.

The man nodded and wicked the sweat from his forehead. "I'm looking for Becky Morgan."

"That's me," Becky said, and raised her hand slightly.

"I'm Detective Feeley. I was wondering if you had a few moments to answer a few questions about a case we're investigating."

Becky felt her cheeks grow warm as she studied the ID he flashed her. It looked legitimate. "Um, sure. Do you want to come back to my office?"

The detective's gaze traveled to Jules, who had turned to head back as well. "Would it be okay if we had a little privacy?"

"Oh, sure, I'll stay out here. Use the office so you can close the door."

Becky threw a wide-eyed gaze in Jules's direction and followed the detective. She shut the door behind them and took a seat at her desk. She started to sweat and subtly wiped her palms on her pant legs.

The detective slid into her guest chair and pulled out a small notebook. "We're investigating a homicide, and it seems your number called his house yesterday asking about the victim. Are you familiar with a man named Robert Taylor?"

Becky sat in stunned silence. "I don't know him personally," she finally choked out. The detective had said *homicide* as in Robert Taylor was *dead*. Becky took a deep breath and tried to pull herself together. "We have an active case that has us looking for a man named Robert Taylor. I've been cold calling men with that name in the area who might be the person we're looking for." Becky's hand drifted up to cover her neck. It was probably red and splotchy, her tell that she was nervous. "He was one of the names on a list of about a hundred men named Robert Taylor that I called yesterday."

"Okay, I see." The detective scribbled notes into a pocket-sized spiral notebook. "And was he the one related to your case?"

Becky hesitated. "I'm not sure since I wasn't able to speak to him."

The detective lifted his eyes from his notebook. "Mr. Taylor's wife mentioned a man also called the day before you asking similar questions. Would you happen to know who that was?"

Becky shook her head. "I don't." She didn't know if it was reasonable to ask, but it couldn't hurt. She wanted to know who this guy was probably more than the police did. "I'd be interested to know who he is as well. Would you be able to share that information when you track his phone number?" Obviously if they had found her, they could locate him, too.

"Looks like it was one of those pre-paid phones." The expression on Detective Feeley's face told her he wouldn't be sharing any more than that.

"Oh, okay." Becky's stomach twisted. This man was deliberately trying to hide.

The detective leaned back in his chair and clicked the top of his pen. "We're still trying to figure out if this is business-related or personal. It will be public knowledge soon, but he was found in his office. My men are there now processing the scene."

The same office where they had just been. Becky's neck felt like it was on fire. "Our case revolves around an inheritance. If Mr. Taylor collected a significant amount of money, isn't it possible that might be a motive? Someone following him?"

The detective gave a shrug that said he didn't place much merit in Becky's theory.

"Could be. His wife didn't mention anything, but I'll certainly look into it." He pulled out his business card and handed it to her. "If you think of anything else that could be helpful, you have my number. I may have more questions. If so, I'll be in touch."

"I'll do anything I can to help." Becky held his gaze for a moment and hoped she seemed sincere.

Jules grabbed Becky's arm and hustled her back to their office as soon as the door shut behind him. She whispered as if she thought the detective could still hear them. "Was that about Rob's disappearance?"

Becky's eyes, filled with equal parts horror and disbelief, told the story. "It's no longer a disappearance. It's a *murder,* Jules. I'm really getting tired of being in the cops' crosshairs when someone gets killed. Can you imagine if the Deerfield police talk to the Orlando police?"

Jules's eyes rounded. "Rob's *dead?* What happened?"

Becky let out a moan and held her head in her hands. "He was found in his office. Did I mention he was *murdered?*" She repeated the word in an attempt to let it sink in. "It happened this morning." Her eyes searched Jules's for reassurance. "How long do you think it takes before the building manager remembers us looking for him? He'll remember you for sure."

"Did the detective say how he was killed?"

Becky held her stomach as it churned. "No. He said they're still processing the scene."

"We must have just missed the police at his office if they've already found you."

Becky sank down into the chair in front of her desk and raked her fingers through her hair. "They were probably looking for me when he went missing, and his wife told him about my call." It still felt surreal to consider Robert was most likely dead in his office while they stood in the hallway knocking on his door.

"I'm sure they're just following up because it seemed like such a random call you made yesterday." Jules leaned against the desk in front of Becky. "We didn't do anything to him, and we weren't in his office. We even told the building manager he hadn't answered the door. Clearly, when he saw us, we weren't disheveled or covered in blood."

Becky struggled to breathe as her chest tightened. "I did leave that voicemail with my name and number. I said it was a personal matter. Maybe they'll think I left it as a way of trying to cover my tracks."

"I think you're being paranoid. The police know you called Rob's house," Jules said matter-of-factly. "You never heard back. It's not a stretch you'd call his office and leave another message. It doesn't mean you were there."

"Except that my fingerprints are all over the doorknob to his office."

They heard the sound of the front door opening, followed by a deep voice. "Hey, get ready cause here he comes."

Gene came galloping into the office, his ears flopping up and down as he raced toward Jules. "Hey, buddy, how was your run?" Jules moved to greet him and scratched behind his ears.

Tim was right behind the dog. "He's got to be tired. He kept up with me pretty well." He stood over Jules. "How about me? Do I get a little love, too?"

Jules wrapped her arms around him. "You bet you do." She gave him a kiss, and he plopped down into the chair in front of her desk.

"Who was that guy I just saw leaving your office? New client? He looked official."

Jules sat behind her desk. "I'll fill you in later. Are you leaving our boy with me?"

Tim nodded. "If it's okay. I've got some errands, and I figured since you're in the office, he'd rather be here with you than sitting at my house all alone. Besides, I'm not sure I can afford another sneaker loss. Your boy is quite the chewer."

Becky let out a snort. "So, he's Jules's boy when he's bad. I see how this works."

Tim glanced in Gene's direction. "Nah, I love him naughty or nice."

"You say the same thing to me," Jules said with a coy smile. "We actually just got back. It's been quite the day so far."

Tim's curious gaze drifted between Jules and Becky. "Oh, really?"

"Too long of a story to start now," Jules said with a shake of her head. "But the guy who just left is part of it. I'll tell you tonight over dinner, and by then, there could even be some new developments."

Becky rolled her eyes. "Let's just hope one of them isn't me in jail."

Tim raised his eyebrows as he stood. "That does sound like quite the morning." He leaned over Jules's desk and gave her another kiss. "Okay, hon, I'll see you later." He winked at Becky. "Try to keep yourself out of the slammer, would ya."

Becky gestured with her chin in Jules's direction. "Your girlfriend was with me. We might be in a cell for two."

Tim glanced quizzically back at Jules. She shot Becky a look and shook her head. "I'll see you later, don't worry."

Becky craned her neck to make sure Tim was gone. "Do you think they really could suspect us? Or me?"

Jules moved to the sink to refill Gene's bowl. "What would either one of us have to gain by killing this guy?" she asked as she ran the faucet. "Whoever the man was that talked to Robert's wife could have made the leap, the same as you did, that he was the right guy. It also could have nothing to do with Donna and just be a big coincidence."

Jules put the water bowl down on the floor. Gene lapped it up greedily, and with water dripping off his chin, he trotted to his bed.

The sound of Jules's phone vibrating buzzed against her desk.

"Your phone's ringing," Becky called out.

"Who is it?" Jules asked as she poured herself a new cup of coffee.

Becky looked at the ID screen. "It's Jonas again."

"Get it. At this point, you may know more than he does."

Becky answered the call, laid the phone back on Jules's desk, and pressed the speaker button. "Hey, it's Becky. Jules is getting coffee."

Jules shuffled back to her desk as fast as her cup would allow without spilling. "I'm here now, too."

"Hey, I found out some information about the guy you asked me about," Jonas said. "Turns out he's not missing anymore. Robert Taylor's dead. He was a CPA, and someone killed him in his office. Probably early this morning."

Jules took a sip of her coffee. "We actually know. A detective came to see Becky."

"Becky? Why?"

Jules glanced at Becky to make sure she was okay with telling Jonas. Becky nodded and whispered, "We need to fill him in if we want him to help."

"Here's the short version," Jules said. "Our client Donna—

the one you met in the office the day of the break-in—has a half-sister she didn't know about. Her father wrote her into his will. That's who we were writing about on the whiteboard. Donna can't get her inheritance until she finds the sister, which is why she hired us."

"Okay, so she has to split it all with the unknown sister. Where does the murdered guy come in?"

"It's actually not split. The estate's divided into thirds," Jules explained. "Donna and her sister each get a third, but there's another person named in the will. Donna has no clue who he is, but his name is Robert Taylor."

"Oh," Jonas said as air escaped him like a deflating balloon.

"Right. Becky compiled a list of all the Robert Taylors within a fifty-mile radius."

"I started cold-calling," Becky said, "to see if I could find one of them that had a connection to Donna's dad. I called this guy yesterday, but it was a home number. I got his wife. She told me her husband's office was in the same building as Donna's dad's office."

"So, could he be the right one," Jonas said.

"He could be, or it could just be a coincidence. The name's pretty common. Becky found tons for her list."

"So, the detective questioned Becky because they found her number had called his house asking about him. That's a pretty reasonable action."

"Right." Jules hesitated. "But there's more."

A beat. Then Jonas said, "Go ahead, I'm listening."

"The wife said a man had called before Becky, asking the same questions."

"A man? Any idea who?"

"Becky and I think it has to be the same man who went into the restaurant and asked Melanie Middlebrook about her daughter."

"The lady in Orlando? With the cease and desist?"

"Right," Jules said.

Jonas was silent for a moment. "I might agree," he said finally. "It does seem possible someone's on the same trail as the two of you."

Becky spoke up. "At first, we thought maybe Donna hired a second set of detectives just to see which one of us could solve her case first."

"I guess that's a possibility. Becky, did you tell the detective all of this?"

"Not all of it. I told him why I called Robert's house, but I called about a hundred potential numbers yesterday. I asked him if they were going to track the man who called." Becky wrinkled her nose. "It was a pre-paid phone."

Jonas gave a soft whistle. "Yeah, that doesn't seem like another detective agency. Somebody's trying to conceal their identity. But don't worry, the police aren't going to come after you simply because you called him. They'd need more evidence than that. They're just starting the investigation and covering all the bases."

"Well ..." Becky stammered.

Jonas let out a groan. "Oh, geez, there's more?"

Becky gave Jules a sideward glance and winced before admitting the truth to Jonas. "We were at the office building where he was killed. This morning. Before we knew he was missing or murdered. Before we went to his house and saw the cop cars and Jules called you."

"Okay ..." Jonas said slowly, as if he knew there was more coming.

Jules leaned closer to the phone and picked up the story. "We wanted to ask him some questions, but while we were there, we wanted to check out Donna's father's office. It's still empty. They're trying to rent it, so the building manager let us check it out. He had a key."

Jonas exhaled loudly. "So, you were seen by someone in the building. Continue."

"After that, we went to Robert's office to talk to him, but he didn't answer the door. Becky called while we were standing in the hallway. We heard the phone ringing inside, but he didn't answer."

"What time was that?"

"Maybe eleven this morning." Jules glanced over at Becky for confirmation.

Becky scrolled through her phone history. "I left him a message at 11:13 this morning."

"So, you were there, just past eleven. You knocked on the door, but he wasn't there. And you didn't see anyone coming or going that might have seemed suspicious?"

Jules shook her head. "No one, and the door didn't seem like anyone had tried to force their way in."

"It just looked ... normal," Becky added.

"Well, again, a phone message isn't proof of anything, but the fact that you were in the building the morning he was killed certainly won't help your case. Anything else you two want to share?"

Jules cringed in Becky's direction. "When we went up to the office, we didn't realize at first that the door was locked."

Becky swallowed hard. "Jonas, my—my fingerprints are on the doorknob."

"Did you mention that when you talked to the detective?"

"Not exactly." Becky felt her neck get hot again. "I was— frazzled. He asked me about the phone call to Robert's house, so that's what I answered."

"It'll be okay. If you've never been arrested, the police won't be able to identify your fingerprints unless they're specifically looking for you. And they can already place you in the building. I'm assuming you two didn't have anything to do with the murder?"

"Of course not," Becky and Jules said in unison.

"I don't like any of this. You two need to be careful." Jonas's tone was stern. "You know, when you talked about this agency, you were supposed to be staring at family trees on your computer, not trying to figure out murders. You need to lock the front door to the office when you're there, especially if you're not expecting anyone."

Becky got up, bolted the door, and was back a moment later.

"Becky's already done it," Jules said. "Besides, Gene's here to protect us."

Jonas let out a snort. "Right. I've met that dog. He's not exactly a guard dog."

Jules glanced over. Gene was sound asleep with his legs pointed up in the air. "Well, I told you he did growl at someone the other day. I'm sure he would wake up in a hurry if we were in trouble."

"I'm serious. Keep in touch. Let me know if anything else happens."

"I will." Jules said goodbye and turned to Becky. "Now what?"

"I guess I won't be calling any more Robert Taylors. That seems to have found me a load of trouble."

"Hey, we were so preoccupied with Robert this morning, we never went back to the message you got from the woman Melanie Middlebrook asked to call us. The daughter's friend. She leave a number?"

"Yup." Becky scrolled through her voicemails and found the number the woman had called from.

"What did she say her name was?" Jules asked as the phone started ringing.

"Darla."

As if on cue, a voice answered. "Hi, this is Darla."

"Hi, Darla, this is Becky Morgan. You left me a message yesterday about trying to help us find Molly Middlebrooks."

"Oh, hi. I would love to help you if I can. I'm actually just getting ready to leave a meeting. Could I call you when I get in the car?"

"Of course. Are you in Orlando?"

"I actually moved. I live near Jacksonville now, but my meeting is in Parkland Springs."

"You're actually not far from us."

"I'm starving," Jules whispered. "You?"

Becky's stomach had finally settled after talking to Jonas. She nodded vigorously. "Darla, do you want to meet my partner, Jules, and me for a late lunch? We can come to where you are."

"That would be great. My meeting ran late, and I haven't had anything to eat all day. Text me the address, and I'll meet you there."

CHAPTER TWENTY-TWO

"THAT HAS TO BE HER," Becky said as they slammed the car doors and made their way across the restaurant parking lot.

As they approached, the woman was on her phone. She glanced up, smiled, and held up a finger. "I gotta go, but the meeting went great. I'm getting back on the road after lunch, and I'll call you then."

She stood. "I'm hoping one of you is Becky."

Becky extended her hand. "I am, and this is my partner, Jules."

Jules reached out to shake Darla's hand and then pulled open the front door to the restaurant. "I hope this was okay. They have the best pizza in town."

Darla nodded with a smile. "Who doesn't love pizza?"

After they had ordered salads and a pie for the table, Darla sat back and sipped her iced tea. "I told Mrs. Middlebrook—Melanie—everything I could remember. I'm still good friends with her daughter. We met in grade school and have been friends ever since."

"So, you're friends with her daughter, Molly?" Jules asked.

"Right. The other Molly I met at a waitressing job when I

was a junior in high school. I had no idea what her last name was. You know, she had a name tag that said Molly, and why would I ever ask? I didn't know that she had almost the same last name as my best friend for a long time. She was a year older than me, but we became friendly. My poor mom. She'd answer the phone and have no idea which one was calling. Eventually, she started calling them blond Molly and brunette Molly."

They all paused while the waitress dropped small salads at the table.

Becky picked up a fork. "And which was which?" she asked before taking a bite.

"My childhood friend was brunette Molly," Darla said. "You're looking for blond Molly. We only worked together for about six months. She graduated high school, and even though she got accepted to FSU, she decided she wasn't ready. She took a year off and went to Europe. She was kind of a free spirit."

Becky and Jules exchanged a glance while Darla started on her salad. This had promise. It matched the story Jerry had told in his letter.

"Her parents were less than thrilled," Darla said. "She was the baby in the family. The youngest of five, but she came from a strict Catholic family. Anyway, we stayed in touch. Molly decided to stay local, and we both ended up at UCF. I would see her occasionally on campus, and we'd grab a cup of coffee or a bite to eat. One summer, we both went back to the restaurant and waited tables again. She ended up graduating the same year as me."

Jules sipped her soda. "You said she was a year older than you?"

Darla nodded while she speared lettuce on her fork.

"And you're how old now?"

"I just turned forty-eight. I didn't see Molly much once

college was over, but every so often, I'd go back to the restaurant, and someone would fill me in. The summer after we graduated, I went in for dinner with my boyfriend. Someone told me she was pregnant. She wasn't married, and it seemed her parents weren't very supportive."

The waitress arrived with their pizza and placed it on the stand in the middle of the table. Jules slid a slice onto a plate and handed it to Darla. She and Becky got their own. Jules moved the remains of her salad off to the side.

Darla lifted the slice and carefully took a bite. She let out a happy moan. "It's hot but so good." She placed it back on the plate to cool. "I ran into Molly and her little girl at the mall once." She smiled at the memory. "Her daughter looked just like a little doll. That's when Molly told me they were moving to North Florida. She'd found someone who was helping her, and she needed the support. I heard through the grapevine a few years later that she'd gotten married and moved out of state."

"Do you know where?" Becky asked.

Darla shook her head. "If someone told me, I don't remember."

Jules folded her pizza and took a bite. "Do you know if Molly had a niece named Bella?"

"Oh yeah, that was her brother Billy's little girl. She actually had both girls with her that day at the mall."

Jules exchanged a glance with Becky. "So far, this all lines up with the information we've been given."

"And Melanie said there was a big inheritance for her?"

"Actually, it's for Molly's daughter," Becky said. "Her biological father passed away and named her in his will."

Darla bit into her pizza and looked confused. "He didn't know where she was?"

Becky shook her head. "He never—he never really played a part in her life."

"Oh, that's sad. But now the father wants to make up for that by leaving Ally money?"

"It would seem that way."

Darla sat silent for a moment as she seemed to process Molly's story. "I wish I knew where she was now. I can ask around to see if I can find any old friends from the restaurant, but it's been twenty-five years. The other Molly and I keep in touch, but she's about the only one from back then."

"Do you remember her parents' names?" Jules asked. "Anything about her family?"

Darla tilted her head while she tried to remember. "Molly's mother never worked. I think I heard her dad call her Fran. I never knew his name. She had three brothers, Billy, Brian, and Bret, and a sister named Mary." Darla laughed. "Her parents were into naming them with the same letters. The boys were all B's, and the girls were M's."

Jules popped the last bit of pizza crust into her mouth and wiped her lips with a napkin. "That might help us track her down. If we can trace her family, we might find a marriage certificate or a family obituary that would tell us Molly's last name. It sure sounds like your friend is the one we're looking for. Blond Molly, that is."

After they all finished up, Jules paid the check.

"I know you've got to get on the road, but you've been a huge help." She handed Darla her business card. "I know you have Becky's number, but here's mine, too. If you find out anything else, will you give one of us a call?"

"Sure, of course." Darla stood, and they all made their way to the door.

As she and Jules slipped into their car, Becky let out a squeal. "I can't believe it. We found her." She reached behind her for her seatbelt. "I mean, I'm not being impulsive again, right? You agree this is our Molly? It has to be."

Jules started up the car. "It certainly seems that way, but we haven't found her just yet. Let's go back to the office and see what we can find with the information she gave us about Molly's family."

As they pushed open the office door, Gene bounded to greet them. "Okay, okay, I know, we're back," Jules said as he wagged his tail and wiggled his whole body with happiness at seeing her again. "C'mon, let me take you out."

"I'll take him," Becky said, and she grabbed his leash from Jules's desk. "Do you want to start seeing what you can find?"

Jules flipped open her laptop. "I'll start a tree for Molly and add the siblings' names and approximate dates of birth. We know she's about forty-nine now, and we know she was the youngest of the five."

As soon as Becky opened the door, Gene was tugging on the leash. "We're going, don't worry." As she headed with him down the concrete stairs, she had a fleeting regret about not locking the door as she left. Jonas's words were starting to get under her skin.

In a flash, the reality of what had happened that morning came flooding back over her, and Becky shuddered. A man was dead. Was he connected to the will, or did he just have the unfortunate luck of having the same name as the man who was? She wanted to believe the Robert Taylor who'd been killed had no connection to their case, but it was getting harder to believe that was true.

Despite the sunshine, Becky felt a cold chill on her neck when it occurred to her they hadn't given a thought to their surroundings when they met Darla. Had someone been watching them? Anxiety tightened her chest when she considered they could have put Darla in danger.

Becky pulled on Gene's leash. He had led her across the grass toward the trees that bordered the parking lot. It was broad daylight, but someone could be lurking in the trees, hiding. She stared at the line of trees but saw nothing suspicious. Would she always feel like someone was watching her? She turned toward the building.

"C'mon, Gene, let's go back up."

Becky unclipped Gene's leash as they headed into the office. She shut the door behind her and then doubled back to turn the lock. "Okay, Gene should be good for a while, and I'm ready to—"

Jules was sitting with her chin resting in her hand while she stared at the computer, her lips turned up in a satisfied smile. "Finally, something is going right today."

Becky's lips pushed forward into a pout. "I've been gone five minutes, and you figured it out already? You found her?"

Jules gestured at the seat in front of her desk and spun her laptop around so Becky could see.

Becky squinted at the screen. "What am I looking—are these Donna's matches? That was quick."

"Yup, one set of her results just came in. Do you see the match that's sitting at the top?"

Becky leaned in. "Is that what I think it is?"

"Her top match is female," Jules said. "1875 cMs of shared DNA. You know what that means?"

Becky leaned back and her lips curved upward. "She's right in half-sibling range."

Jules grinned, her oversized smile lighting up her face. "She sure is."

CHAPTER TWENTY-THREE

Donna had just plopped down on the couch and turned on the television when Jay and his brother came through the front door. So much for leaving work early and thinking she could relax.

"Hey, babe," Jay said and planted a kiss on the top of her head.

Donna watched as Kevin made his way to the kitchen and pulled open the refrigerator. She scowled. "Does he live here now?"

Jay glanced toward the kitchen and shrugged half-heartedly. "Don't worry, I'll reel him in."

Donna reached over the back of the couch and grabbed Jay's arm as he started to walk away. "Hey," she said, her voice a hiss of aggravation. "Did you give him your favorite Lightning hat? I got you that for Christmas. Wasn't cheap, you know."

He waved his hand dismissively. "He just borrowed it. Don't worry, I'll get it back."

Kevin came back into the living room, a cold beer in his hand. "Hey, Donna. How's it going?" He plopped down at the other end of the couch, leaned back, and put his feet up on the coffee table.

Donna grimaced as she stared at the dirty sneakers propped up in front of her. "It's going," she said. She fixed her gaze on the bottle in his hand. "Was that the last beer in the fridge?"

"This one?" Kevin said and held out the bottle as if he wasn't the only one with a beer in his hand. "Yeah, sorry 'bout that, but Jay said you left work early. I figure you're probably going to the store soon anyway. I mean, what could you really do with one beer, right?" He smiled at her as if he made all the sense in the world.

Donna glared at him but said nothing.

Kevin flinched at the look aimed at him and glanced over at his brother. Donna was glad to see Jay wasn't defending him.

"Hey," Kevin said. "I'd run and get some, but I have a job interview to get to. Cross your fingers. One of those big clubs is looking for a bartender. I could make a fortune in tips. Not like the kind of fortune you two will have, but you know …"

Donna bit the inside of her cheek to keep from saying anything.

"Gotta run. Jay, I'll call you later. Let you know how it goes." He slugged down the rest of his beer and slammed the bottle on the coffee table like he'd just won a drinking bet.

As he turned to leave, Jay called out, "Hey, Kev …"

Donna tried to hide her smirk of appreciation. Leave his bottle on the table in front of her like she's some kind of maid. How dare he? At least Jay was going to say something.

When his brother turned around, Jay raised his chin. "Leave my Bolts hat, would ya."

"Sure, big brother, no problem. Kevin took the hat off and tossed it like a Frisbee until it landed on the couch next to Donna. "See ya."

When the door was closed behind him, Donna let out an aggravated groan.

Jay turned to her, confused. "What's the matter?"

"What's the *matter*? You're spending entirely too much time with him. He feels far too comfortable here, and why does he keep talking about my inheritance like he thinks he's gonna get cut in? I don't trust him."

Jay came around and sat next to her. "I get it. He's a little … unpolished. I'm working on it."

Donna shook her head. "I don't know why you had to tell him so much about the money. Maybe that's the only reason he's hanging around." She gave him a pointed look. "Did you ever consider that?"

Jay flinched as if she had hit him. She grabbed his arm. "I'm sorry. I'm not saying he isn't happy you've patched things up. You're an awesome brother, so why wouldn't he be? I'm just saying, be careful. It's been a long time since you've been in his life. You don't know much about what he's done all these years."

Jay hesitated and then dipped his head in agreement. "You're right. I'll talk to him and maybe slow things down a little. Hopefully, he'll get this new job and have someplace to go at night. All-Star Construction called and said they're getting ready to start on a new office complex and they want me back. I went to check out the job site this morning. It's huge."

"I hope he gets the job, too, so I get you back at night with me." Donna reached for his hand. "What'd you do to your finger?" She intertwined her fingers with his and nodded toward the Band-Aid.

"Nothing really. I was working on those shelves you wanted in the garage. That picture you hated—the one of the dogs playing poker—it fell over and the glass shattered. Sliced my finger cleaning it up. The whole thing's in the dumpster now."

She smiled. "Can't say I'm disappointed."

"I didn't think you would be." He leaned over and kissed her. "I am looking forward to life going back to normal with a little less Kevin." His eyes narrowed. "You haven't seen Nick again, have you?"

Donna shook her head. "Nope. I told you that was just a one-time—"

A video on the evening news caught her attention. It looked like the building where her father had his office, so she reached for the remote and turned up the volume.

... a local man was found murdered this morning in his Deerfield accounting office. Police are following up on all leads. If you have any information, call the tip line you see on the screen.

Donna hit the pause button. "Do you think—"

"Think what?" Jay asked. "That the world's becoming a dangerous place? Yes, I do. Now about dinner. What do you say we—"

"Look at the name, Jay. Under the picture. *Robert Taylor.* Could it be the same guy we've been looking for? He was killed in his office, which just happens to be in the same building where my dad had his office."

"If he's dead, we'll probably never know the connection now. Maybe he got iced for having so much of your father's money." Jay got up off the couch and headed toward the kitchen. "How do you feel about barbeque chicken?"

Donna kept her attention on the TV while she tapped two fingers against her lips. How could she find out if this was the same man from the will? He had an office in the same building as her dad. That had to mean something. Not that the name wasn't fairly common, but still, what were the odds? Donna glanced around and felt in between the couch cushions for her cell phone. Maybe Jules and Becky knew something.

Just as she was about to dial, there was an insistent rapping on the door. She let out an aggravated sigh. Jay's brother probably realized he needed gas money to get to his interview, but at least he was knocking and not walking right in.

Donna got up off the couch, strode to the door, and pulled it open. "Yeah, now——"

Two men flashed badges at her, and her breath caught in her throat.

"Hello, ma'am. We're detectives with the Deerfield police department. Is there a Jay Kittsmiller that lives here?"

CHAPTER TWENTY-FOUR

"Donna, slow down." Jules put her phone on the desk and hit the speaker button. "We're both here. Tell us what happened."

Becky scooted her chair over.

"I saw something on the news that someone named Robert Taylor was murdered. It happened in my father's office building, so I thought maybe, just maybe, there was a connection and he was the person in the will. I mean, I don't know for sure that he was, but then the police showed up. They took Jay down to the station for questioning."

It was the exact knock on the door Becky had worried about getting herself. "Why did they want to talk to him?" she asked.

"I have no idea," Donna said breathlessly. "They can't think he had anything to do with it. I mean, why would he? Robert already got his money. It's not like we'd get it back if he died. Jules, can you call your brother and see if he can find out anything?"

There was a lot Donna didn't know. Jules wasn't ready to share any of it with her right now, especially if there was a chance Jay was involved.

"Let me see what I can find out, but if he didn't do anything, you should have nothing to worry about."

After they hung up, Jules leaned back in her chair. "This is an interesting twist."

"Donna's right. Why would he do it? It's not like they can get Robert's money back."

"Think about the will, Beck. If Donna's half-sister isn't found alive, who gets her money? Donna and Robert have to split it. But if Robert's dead, too, wouldn't that mean Donna gets the entire portion that was her sister's? That's what it said, right?" She glanced toward the file cabinets. "Where's the will?"

Jules rolled in her chair over to the filing cabinet. She rifled through the hanging folders and then glanced back at Becky. "Donna's folder's not here. Did you put everything back after the break-in?"

"Everything I had. I thought maybe you had it."

Jules tore into her computer bag, and then her shoulders dropped. "It's not here. I guess now we know why someone broke into our office."

"Well, that wouldn't make sense if it was Jay. Donna has her own copy of everything that was in the folder. Why would he need to break into our office?"

Jules shook her head. "I don't know. Maybe to keep us from having the information? Slow us down?"

There was a knock at the front door, and Jules rose from her chair.

"Check before you open it," Becky called out.

Jules peeked through the window and saw Jonas standing there.

"Just stopped by to make sure you're both okay," he said after she swung open the door. "I'm glad to see you're taking my advice and using the lock." He leaned over and grabbed a chewed-up cooler bag next to the reception desk. "Did someone want this, or did you donate it to Gene as a chew toy?"

Jules grabbed the bag. As they entered her office, she held it up for Gene to see. "Did you do this?" she asked in an accusatory tone.

Gene stood, his tail wagging in short spurts. Jules could tell he wanted to greet Jonas but knew he was in trouble. His brown eyes drifted to the cooler bag Jules held in her hand. Finally, he dipped his head and slunk back to his bed.

Jonas went over and patted him on the head. "It's okay, Gene. I still love you."

Jules tossed the bag on Becky's desk and winced. "Sorry. I'll get you a new one."

Becky moved the bag from her desk to her trash can. "I guess we can blame it on Gene when we ask Donna to bring her file back in so we can copy it again."

"Poor Gene, always getting thrown under the bus," Jules said with a pout.

Becky gestured at her trash can. "Sometimes he earns it."

Jonas had taken the seat at Jules's desk. "What happened to Donna's file?"

"We just realized someone took it during the break-in."

"And they took Becky's laptop." Jonas shot her a look. "But that was password-protected, right?"

Becky averted her gaze. "The new one is …"

Jules opened her mouth to say something and then closed it. If it was Jay that had taken the laptop, he'd know everything they told Donna. Besides, all the websites they used were pass-word-protected.

She turned to Jonas. "We just found out the police took our client's fiancé in for questioning."

Jonas let out a whistle. "The fiancé, huh?"

"I just can't figure out why he'd need to break in to steal

information Donna already has," Jules said. "It doesn't make sense."

Jonas got up and strolled to their small refrigerator. "What would he have to gain?" he asked while he grabbed a bottle of water. "You said Donna didn't know anything about the guy in the will."

"She didn't," Jules said. "But there's a stipulation in the will that if Donna's sister is deceased before she collects, her portion of the estate is split between Donna *and* Robert——"

Jonas narrowed his eyes. "So, what happens if Donna's sister and Robert aren't alive to collect? Does Donna get the whole third?"

Jules slowly nodded. "We think so."

Jonas took a long swig of his water while he considered this news. "So, it would be to his benefit because Donna would inherit two-thirds of the entire estate if they were both out of the picture. They get married and now he's got access to it."

"Right," Jules said while she studied his expression. She could tell he was working through something in his head.

Jonas rubbed his chin thoughtfully. "There's something else you may not have thought about. Say Donna inherits all that money, and something happens to her, who gets it? Does she have anyone but him? Any other family?"

Becky gulped. "We didn't think about that, but other than this half-sister, she has no one that we know of. So, you think Donna could be in danger?"

Jonas leaned back in his chair and let out a deep breath. "If her husband-to-be is behind this, she could be. Not immediately, obviously, but one thing does seem very clear."

"What's that?" Becky asked nervously.

"Someone else is out there looking for Donna's sister. We need to figure out if it's the same person that killed Robert Taylor." A warning gleamed in Jonas's eyes as they drifted between Jules and Becky. "If it is, you need to find Donna's sister first. If you don't, there's a good chance you won't find her alive."

CHAPTER TWENTY-FIVE

"So, the guy you called yesterday is dead now?" Bryan was standing at the counter, dicing garlic with a sharp knife.

"Well, I didn't actually talk to him." Becky unpacked her new laptop and laid it on the kitchen table. "I spoke to his wife. She said some guy had already called the house asking the same questions. The detective said that call came from a pre-paid phone." She plopped into a chair.

Bryan scraped the garlic off the cutting board into the pan and spun around, a frown on his face. "That seems suspicious. You think that could be the guy who killed the accountant?"

"I don't know, but—" Becky closed her eyes and inhaled deeply. "That smells amazing. It's a good thing you like to cook. If I was in charge of dinner, we'd be eating takeout again." She rubbed the back of her neck. "It was a long day."

"I got you." Bryan came up behind her and massaged her shoulders. "So, this guy, you think maybe it's the same guy you saw at the restaurant in Orlando checking out Jules?"

The massage felt heavenly. Becky's head fell forward, and she let out a soft moan. "I do. And I'm starting to think he had something to do with the hit and run, too. I just can't figure out what someone would have to gain. Unless, of course, it's Donna's fiancé, Jay." She hesitated. "Or Donna, I guess."

Bryan kissed the back of her neck. "No one's heard from her again?" he asked over his shoulder as he went back to stir his garlic and add the shrimp.

"I haven't, but she only called a couple of hours ago." Becky opened her laptop and turned it on. "We split up the search for Donna's half-sister. Jules is doing research based on the information from the woman we had lunch with, and I'm working off the match we got today. Our research should overlap and land right on her."

"What about Donna's father? Wouldn't this mystery woman just match him as a parent/child?"

Becky smiled. Her husband had learned so much of this to keep up with her. "It isn't the same site Jerry tested at. This is why we always have our clients test at all the major sites. You just never know where someone's going to show up."

"Oh, so it's a good thing Donna did her tests, too." Bryan squeezed both halves of a lemon and poured some white wine into the pan. He gestured with the bottle. "Want some?"

Bryan was already reaching into the cupboard before Becky nodded. He knew her well.

"Yeah, I'm just a little confused," she said as she reached for the glass. "We know the half-sister is named Ally, but the ID for this match is J Salter."

Bryan poured a second glass of wine for himself. "Does she have a tree attached?"

Becky shook her head. "She doesn't."

"Can't you send her a message?"

Becky sipped her wine thoughtfully. "I could, but I want to see what we can figure out first. The last thing I want to do is spook her." She glanced up as he turned off the burner under the pasta.

"You'll figure it out. You and Jules always do. I mean, it has to be her, right?"

Becky stood so she could set the table. "She definitely has the right amount of DNA to be Donna's half-sister. I mean, technically it's also the range for an aunt, a grandmother, or a double first cousin." She reached into the cupboard and pulled out two plates. "Donna said her father didn't have a sister." She put her arms on either side of Bryan.

He grabbed them and spun around and kissed her. "Don't you want to eat first?" he teased.

Becky smiled. "You're actually blocking the silverware drawer."

He swung back around and opened the drawer. When he faced Becky again, he had a handful of cutlery.

He lifted his eyebrows up and down and grinned. "So, you *do* wanna fork."

She laughed despite the bad joke. "First dinner, then we fork." She slid her laptop to the end of the table and laid down the plates and silverware. "I guess there's always the chance her father had another child out there he never knew about. If there's anything I've learned through DNA testing, anything is possible."

The sound of the doorbell rang into the kitchen, and Becky looked quizzically at her husband. "Expecting someone?"

"I'll get it. Maybe it's Mrs. Ritter. She was over before asking to borrow a couple of eggs."

Becky loved their neighbor across the street but wasn't up to small talk. She was starving.

Bryan was followed by a man in a suit when he returned. "Uh, Beck ..."

She felt her face grow warm. Now what?

The man introduced himself. "Detective Stephens. You spoke to my partner earlier. Would you mind if I asked you a few more questions?"

Becky's heart thumped wildly in her chest. She hoped nervousness and guilt didn't look the same. "Of course not." She had nothing to hide except that she'd been in the building where the murder took place.

Her apologetic gaze drifted to Bryan and his dinner.

Her husband caught her eye. "Don't worry. I'll keep it warm until you're ready."

Becky gestured to a chair at the table. "Will this work, or do you want to go into the other room?" She glanced longingly at her wine.

"The other room. If I stay here, I might start drooling." The detective glanced at Bryan. "I don't know what you're making, but it smells amazing."

"My husband's a great cook. His shrimp scampi is delicious." It felt good to talk about dinner. Something mundane that gave Becky a minute to collect herself.

Detective Stephens took a seat in the armchair in the living room, and Becky settled into the loveseat. He pulled out a small spiral notebook.

"So, Becky, you told Detective Feeley something about calling Mr. Taylor about an inheritance."

"I didn't know for sure that Mr. Taylor, um, the one you're asking about, was the right person, but we were looking for someone with that name that had recently inherited some money."

"Okay." He flipped back through his notebook. "You work for an investigations agency. Investigation Duo?"

Becky nodded. "Right. We're working on a case."

"So, you were merely cold-calling men with that name to see if they were the person named in the will?"

"That's correct."

"Mr. Taylor's wife said you asked specifically whether her husband knew a man named ..." Detective Stephens consulted his notes and then glanced back up. "You asked if her husband knew a man named Jerry McDermott."

Becky cleared her throat. She hadn't taken her wine, but she wished she had at least taken some water. "I did. I asked all the men I called."

He nodded. "I see. And she told you that Jerry McDermott had an office in the same building as her husband."

Becky felt her forehead dampen. She reached up to subtly wipe it. "She did."

The detective read from his notes. "Mrs. Taylor told me that Mr. McDermott was an attorney, had been in that building for years. Jerry and her husband were friendly and used to grab lunch occasionally." He looked up. "She also told me he passed away recently."

"He did." It wasn't like Becky was telling the detective anything that Rob Taylor's wife hadn't already told him.

Detective Stephens leaned back in his chair. "So, I'm going to make the leap that Jerry McDermott's will left some money to someone named Robert Taylor. You're now wondering if those lunches netted my victim an inheritance. Did you find anyone else named Robert Taylor with a connection to Mr. McDermott? You know, while you were cold calling?"

Becky lifted her hand to cover her neck. "I didn't."

Detective Stephens pinned Becky with his gaze. "Wills are an ugly business sometimes. People don't agree with what's in them, and next thing you know, families are fighting. Was there someone that wasn't happy about money that was left to Robert Taylor? Sounds like they didn't know who he was if you're trying to figure him out." He shrugged with a small knowing smile on his face. "That would certainly piss me off if someone outside the family inherited money, and I didn't know who they were."

Her breath hitched in her throat. Donna had been angry, but Becky certainly wasn't going to incriminate her client. "It's still an active investigation. I'm really not at liberty to say more."

He narrowed his eyes and nodded. "Sounds to me like maybe I need to take a look at Mr. McDermott's will and see what's in it. It's public record, so it'll be easy enough to get my hands on it." He cocked his head as he was about to write something in his notebook. "Unless you have a copy you want to share?"

Becky took in a deep breath. "We did, but someone took it."

Detective Stephens bit the end of his pen and frowned. "Took it. You mean stole it?"

Becky nodded. "Our office was broken into a couple of weeks ago. The file went missing."

"They take anything else?"

"My laptop. They threw our files all over the office. We thought they were just trying to be obnoxious—you know, messing up the place. After I put all the files back together, the file with the will wasn't there anymore."

"You file a police report on the break-in?"

"We did."

"Interesting." Detective Stephens scribbled in his notebook. "I'll see it for myself soon enough, but is there anything in the will that would give someone a reason to want Mr. Taylor dead?" He looked Becky firmly in the eye. "There was nothing in there that said if Robert Taylor died, someone else would get his money. Nothing like that, right?"

Becky swallowed past the lump in her throat. "No, but—" He was going to see the will anyway, and she didn't want the detective to think she lied to him. "There are certain stipula-tions." She lifted a shoulder uncomfortably. "It's complicated."

The detective's eyebrows lifted as if this information was what he'd been waiting for. "Sounds like I have some fascinating reading ahead of me." He tapped his pen against his lips. "Ever meet anyone named Jay Kittsmiller?"

Becky was sure the detective could see her pulse throbbing in her temple. "No." That was the truth. She hadn't ever met Donna's fiancé.

"I see." He scribbled something and then glanced back up at Becky. "So, we know that you called Mr. Taylor's house, but you also called his office this morning." He flipped through his notes. "Around 11:15 a.m."

"I did." It wouldn't take the building manager long to report they'd been there looking for Robert. She might as well admit it. "We were actually in the building. We went to talk to him since he hadn't called back from the day before. But he didn't answer the door. So, I called to see if he was in there."

The detective looked up from his notepad. "And you didn't hear anything in his office?"

"We heard the phone ringing, but that was it."

"You were in the building at the time you made the call?"

She nodded. "Yes, right outside his door."

He leaned forward with his forearms on his knees. "And you weren't in the building any earlier than that?"

Becky's forehead creased in confusion. "Earlier? No. I mean, we got to the building and the office on the first floor—Jerry's office space—hadn't been rented. The building manager asked if we wanted to see it, and he let us in. We just wanted to see if there was anything in there that would help our investigation."

"And was there?"

"No. Nothing. When we were done, we went to the third floor to look for Mr. Taylor, and well, you know what happened there. After that, we left."

"So, that was the only time today you were in the building?"

"Correct."

"And how long did you spend in Donna's father's old office?"

Becky shrugged. "Ten minutes, maybe."

"And where were you this morning before that?"

"I was … here." Becky gestured toward the kitchen. "With my husband until about 9:30 or so. Then I left to go to the office." She paused as she ran through her morning. It seemed like a lifetime ago. Then she remembered. "Oh, I did stop for gas and at the coffee shop. Then I got to the office and pulled in right at the same time my partner did."

"Any chance you have receipts for the gas and the coffee?"

Becky flinched that she needed proof of an alibi. "I'm sure I do. I throw everything in my purse."

She got up from the loveseat and grabbed her purse off the end table where she had dumped it when she got home earlier. Digging nervously through it, she let out a deep breath as she pulled out her wallet. Stuck in between two folded up dollar bills was the receipt for her latte.

"My change from this morning," Becky said. She unfolded the bills, pulled out the proof of her purchase, and handed it to the detective.

He pulled out a pair of reading glasses and scanned the small piece of paper. He put it down on the coffee table in front of him and made several notes.

Becky had also unearthed the gas receipt. She laid it on the table and sat back down.

The detective reached for it, wrote something in his notebook, and then took off his glasses. "Okay, those match up. Could you ask your husband to come in here?"

"Hey, Bryan," Becky called out. They didn't have a large house. She was sure he'd been able to hear most of their conversation. When he poked his head out of the kitchen, she waved him over.

"Would you be able to verify that your wife was here with you this morning?" Detective Stephens asked.

Bryan nodded. "She was."

"Until what time?"

"We left the house together around 9:30. We both went to work."

The detective scribbled one final note and then shut his notebook. "I appreciate your time, and I'm sorry I held up your dinner."

Becky stood when he did and shook his hand. "Can I ask you a question before you go?"

"You can." He offered her a small smile. "I'll let you know if it's something I can answer."

"Were you able to find out if Robert Taylor had recently come into a large sum of money?"

Detective Stephens pressed his lips together and shook his head. "My partner asked his wife. She didn't know anything about an inheritance, and we haven't found any indication that he's come into any money whatsoever. Either it's unrelated—" He paused and met Becky's probing gaze. "Or maybe someone killed the wrong Robert Taylor."

CHAPTER TWENTY-SIX

"WHAT COULD they possibly have had to say to you for so long?" Donna asked as she pulled away from the police station. It was after midnight.

"They claim to have something, but it's bullshit," Jay said testily. "I didn't do anything, so there's nothing to pin on me. I didn't even know who the guy was."

"That's why I don't understand why they even wanted to talk to you."

"They found part of an envelope in the parking lot. It had this guy's address and suite number on the back and my name on the front."

"So what? Anybody could have picked up a piece of your mail. Sometimes when I go to the box, I dump all the junk mail right there in the can by the mailboxes. Why do they think *you* dropped it or that it's even related? Maybe someone from our building needed an accountant."

Jay stared straight ahead. "It had blood on it. They're testing it now to see if it's from the guy who was killed."

"Oh." Donna gulped. "It still doesn't prove you were the one who dropped it there."

"That's what I told them." He turned his head toward her. "They asked a ton of questions about your dad's will. Looks like someone told them this guy inherited a pile of money from your father." He gave her a hard stare. "Maybe your two little detectives."

Donna's cheeks grew hot. Were they the reason the police were looking at Jay? From now on, she'd need to be careful about what she shared. "I mentioned the police wanted to question you, but they didn't say anything about the police coming to see them. And besides, what does my dad's will have to do with anything? Isn't it possible it just could be a burglary gone wrong?"

"They didn't make it seem like anything was stolen, but who knows? They could be feeding me a line of crap for all I know. You know, try to get me to confess to something I didn't do." He held up his hand to block the headlights of someone turning in front of them and then pulled down the visor. "What's this?" he asked when a folder fell into his lap.

Donna glanced over. "The papers from Norman."

"Damn, Donna. These are important." He tucked the file between the seat and the center console. "Don't leave them sitting in the car. Apparently, a will is an incriminating thing," he said in a bitter tone. "Even if you're not named in it."

"That's true. Why wouldn't the police question me? I live at the same mail address you do."

"Apparently some guy called this accountant guy's house asking his wife a ton of questions. It was a man. When they tried to track the number, it was a pre-paid phone. They're going to get the records on the phone and see if it pinged anywhere near where I was this morning. Check out all the stores around here to see if they can catch me buying it. They're getting my phone records, too, to see if my phone backs up where I said I was."

"Exactly where were you this morning?" Donna tried not

to make it sound accusatory but knew any form of the question would come across that way. She was right.

He whipped his head in her direction. "Are you saying you think I had something to do with this?"

"No—no, not at all." Donna tried to backpedal. "I'm just thinking if you had someone who could give you an alibi, they'd have to leave you alone."

"I already told you," he said slowly, enunciating every word to make his point. "I went to check out the new construction site. I wanted to see how big it was, you know, how long the job might take." He threw up his hands. "No one else was there."

She couldn't help herself. "And you didn't stop, get coffee, anything?"

Jay let out a small growl. "No, Donna, I didn't." His voice was clipped. "I made a cup before I left the house. You were sleeping, and when I got back, you had gone to work."

Donna pulled into the entrance of their apartment complex. As she made the right turn to head to their parking lot, she noticed a car parked next to Jay's with its headlights on. "Who the hell is that next to your car?"

"Probably my brother. I called to tell him what happened."

Donna let out a deep sigh. "Seriously? It's late. Couldn't it have waited until tomorrow?" She knew she sounded irritated, but she didn't care. The last thing she wanted right now was to deal with Kevin.

"It could have, but he was up, and he wanted to come over. Is that a problem?" Jay's eyes met hers and dared her to say it was. "I'm so wound up, it's not like I'm going to sleep anytime soon."

"Speak for yourself. I've been an anxious mess since you left. I'm exhausted."

Donna watched as Jay's brother extinguished the lights, turned off the car, and stepped out.

"Hey, Kev," Jay said. He shot a look over his shoulder at

Donna and then slapped his brother on the back. "Come on up." The two men walked toward the stairs to the apartment.

Donna lingered behind them, and by the time she got into the kitchen, Kevin was already pulling open the refrigerator. "Man, Jay, you hit the jackpot with that wife of yours. Donna's already restocked the beer for us."

"Yeah, well, I needed something to do while I was waiting to hear from this one." She nodded in Jay's direction.

Kevin handed a bottle to Jay, twisted the top on his, and plopped down into one of the kitchen chairs. "So, what the hell did the police want?" He took a long swallow of his beer.

Jay leaned up against the kitchen counter. He took a swig from his bottle and wiped his mouth with the back of his hand. "Apparently, they wanted to ask me about a guy that got murdered this morning."

"Murder?" Kevin let out a whoop. "Man, that's the big time there. Why the hell would they think you murdered someone?" His face grew serious. "They got anything on you?"

Jay snorted as he dug into the pantry for a snack to go with his beer. "A crock of BS, that's what they have."

"They're just grasping at straws, huh? Did you even know the guy?"

Jay poured some nuts into a bowl and shrugged. "Nope, but it looks like maybe he's the guy from Donna's father's will."

"The unknown guy? What was his name?" Kevin drummed his fingers on the kitchen table and then glanced up. "Robert Taylor, right?"

Jay tossed back a handful of nuts and left the bowl on the table. "Yeah. That was the name of the guy who was killed. He had an office in the same building as Donna's dad."

Kevin whistled. "So, that had to be the guy, right? Why did they think you did it? Didn't he already get his money?"

"I guess. But there's also Donna's sister's portion."

Half-sister, Donna said silently in her head.

"I guess they figure if something happens to the sister and this guy, Donna gets the sister's portion, too." Jay didn't even glance in her direction.

"Oh," Kevin said as he bobbed his head. "Because you're about to be the husband, they figure you have an interest because you'd get the money, too?"

"I guess so. I mean, the detective had a copy of the will there."

"So, they're serious it could be a motive. I guess it is a lot of money. You two need to think about writing up wills when you get all that money." Kevin turned his gaze to Donna. "You don't have one already, do you? A will?"

Donna glared at Jay. All she wanted to do was go to bed. Not sit and listen to Kevin ask a bunch of questions about stuff he shouldn't even know about. "No. Jay's going to be my husband. He would get everything. Who else would I leave it to?"

Kevin's eyes widened, and he shrugged as if he was under attack. "I don't know, I'm just saying, it's a lot of money. You need to be smart about it."

Donna didn't respond.

After a moment of awkward silence, Kevin turned to his brother. "So, how'd they leave things?"

Jay emptied his bottle and let out a belch. "They told me they had some further investigating to do. Don't leave town, that kind of shit."

"What about the murder weapon? They find it?"

Jay shrugged. "They didn't say."

"Do you even own a gun?" Kevin asked.

"Nah. I lost my concealed carry permit a few years ago. But according to the cops, he wasn't shot."

Kevin reeled back slightly in his chair. "No?"

Jay shook his head. "Nope, stabbed to death." He lifted a shoulder. "And who doesn't have access to a knife, right?"

CHAPTER TWENTY-SEVEN

"DONNA LEFT ME A MESSAGE, but they didn't let Jay go until midnight." Jules marched toward the small kitchenette with one thing on her mind. "I didn't see her voicemail until this morning."

Becky meandered over and watched as Jules made coffee. "Do you think he really had anything to do with the murder?"

"I would hope not, but I guess anything's possible. Money's a big motivator."

Becky leaned against the small counter. "Well, I didn't get much done on Donna's match last night. I had a surprise visitor."

Jules frowned as she watched the coffee brew. "I'm afraid to ask. You were home, I guess."

"Just about to enjoy Bryan's shrimp scampi when the doorbell rang."

Jules's eyes lit up. "Oh, I love when he makes that. Did you bring me any leftovers for lunch?"

Becky snapped her fingers. "Focus, Jules. It was the partner of the detective who came to the office. More questions."

"Like what?"

"He asked me where I was yesterday morning."

Jules poured the coffee in a mug and pulled the creamer from the refrigerator. "You mean like, did you have an alibi?"

"I guess. I told him I was home with Bryan until I left for the office."

Jules wrapped her hands around the mug and took a sip. "And I'm sure Bryan backed you up."

Becky shrugged. "For what it's worth. He's my husband, so not sure his word isn't taken with a grain of salt. But luckily, yesterday I stopped for gas and coffee. I had receipts in my purse." She gave a small chuckle. "Sometimes it pays to never throw anything away. And then I told him I came here and pulled in at the same time as you."

"Well, you know I can vouch for you." Jules headed back to her desk.

Becky plopped down in the chair across from her. "I guess if he didn't believe me, he'll be stopping by today."

"Why didn't you call me last night?"

Becky shrugged. "I knew you were having dinner with Tim. I figured as long as they didn't cart me off to jail, it could wait. Did you go to the new place by the bookstore?"

"We did. Food was great, and so was the company." A slow smile spread across Jules's face.

Becky couldn't help but smile back. "So, is this it? You and Tim?"

Jules sipped her coffee. "Yeah. I don't know what I was so scared of last time we were together. If we hadn't wasted almost a year apart, we'd probably be married now."

"Things work out the way they're meant to, Jules. You had some stuff you needed to deal with. And now you've found Barb, met that side of the family."

Jules stared off as she considered Becky's comment. "I guess I always felt like if my birth mother didn't want me, why would anyone else. Once I found out Barb wanted to keep me, it was like a weight was lifted." She wrapped both hands around her coffee cup and lifted it to her mouth, peering at Becky over the top. "He talks about our future, and I don't even sweat it anymore."

"You *deserve* to be happy. And Tim really is perfect for you."

Jules felt a little guilty. She'd gotten the answers about her adoption and was back with Tim. Becky wanted a baby more than anything and still didn't have one.

"So," Jules said, changing the subject. "I looked at Donna's match last night when I got home. That ID is just throwing me. J Salter. Even if her mother got married and changed her last name, where does the J come in? We know her name is Ally."

Becky nodded. "Bryan and I talked about it last night, too. What are the chances there's another child Jerry didn't even know about?"

"Anything's possible." Jules sipped her coffee. "Listen, I was thinking about Donna last night. I think we should play things close to the vest until we're sure what's going on." She scrunched up her face. "If it's the right Robert Taylor, we could have played a part in leading the killer to him. Who—"

"I can't believe I forgot to tell you the most important part," Becky interrupted her. "The detective said there's no indication that the guy who was killed had just inherited anything. His wife had no idea about any money. No big deposits or purchases. Nothing."

"So, it could have nothing to do with Donna ..."

Becky finished the sentence for her. "Or someone killed the wrong man."

Jules shook her head thoughtfully. "That's not good if someone's killing first and asking questions later."

"I think we need to assume someone's after the same information as us. I agree we need to be careful with Donna. If Jay's involved at all—"

"We need to not hand him Ally on a silver platter." Jules

was already worried Sue and Robert Taylor were dead because of them. "What happens if the murderer realizes he killed the wrong guy?"

"I'm going to leave that one alone for now," Becky said. "Let's work on the stuff Darla told us, and Donna's match."

"Let's call Donna back first and see what happened with Jay." Jules dialed the phone and put it on speaker.

A sleepy voice answered.

"Hey, Donna. It's Jules and Becky. Just calling you back. Did we wake you?"

She let out a soft moan. "A little. It was a late night. I actually called out from work today. Let them fire me."

"Is everything okay?" Becky asked. "Why did the police want to question Jay?"

Donna seemed to hesitate. "It was nothing. They didn't have anything on him, obviously. Just a wasted night. Did the police reach out to either of you?"

Jules exchanged a glance with Becky. Why was she asking if the police had contacted them? "Careful," Jules mouthed.

"No, they didn't." Becky cringed as she told the lie. "Did they think the murder was related to your case?"

"No, not really. I was just wondering. Anyway, I'm glad it's over. I'm just tired."

"I can imagine." Becky gave Jules a pointed look and added, "Hey, Donna."

"Yeah?"

"Did you know Jules got a new dog?"

"I didn't know he was new, but I saw the dog bed in the office. The day of the break-in." Donna sounded confused about why Becky was talking about the dog.

"Jules is embarrassed, but she's trying to train him. He's a real chewer."

"I am trying, Donna, I swear," Jules called out in the background.

"I'm not sure what that has to do with me. I'm not a dog trainer."

Becky let out a forced laugh. "No, of course not. It's just Jules had your file on her desk. We had to run to a meeting, and he got to it. Shredded some of the papers inside. Dropped them in his water bowl. It was a mess."

"Maybe you shouldn't have a dog in the office." Based on Donna's tone, Jules could just picture her scowling on the other end.

"You're so right," Becky agreed to appease her. "Anyway, when you get a chance, can you bring your copies of everything back to the office? We'll scan it and file it in the computer. No more paper for him to chew this time."

The sigh Donna let out sounded like she was aggravated. "Fine. I'm not going in to work today, but it will take me a little while to get moving."

"That's no problem," Jules said. "And again, I'm sorry for the inconvenience. It won't happen again."

After they hung up, Jules put her head in her hands and let out a groan. "Poor Gene keeps getting blamed for everything."

"At least she's bringing it in."

"Did you get the feeling she wasn't telling us everything?"

Becky leaned forward with her forearms on Jules's desk. "Yeah, I did," she said as if she was glad Jules had thought the same thing. "And what about asking if anyone questioned us? Maybe she thinks they brought Jay in because of something we said."

Jules reached into her computer case and pulled out her laptop. "If he didn't do it, nothing you said will make a difference." She tapped on the power button. "I'm getting to work on this match of Donna's to see what else I can figure out."

Becky pulled herself to her feet. "Okay, then I'll start a tree for Molly based on the information Darla gave us. If I can figure out the parents and the grandparents, maybe I can find her in an obituary with her married name."

Jules was already engrossed in something on her screen. "That's a great idea." She lifted her head quickly. "Oh. If you find the last name Salter anywhere, holler."

* * *

After a few hours, Jules leaned back in her chair and stretched. "See, if you'd brought leftovers, we'd have something delicious for lunch right about now."

"Should we go out and grab something?" Becky asked with a yawn. "I need food."

"What if Donna comes by with the file and we're both gone?"

"Oh, right," Becky said as she stood. "I'll go."

After Jules had written her very specific sandwich instructions on a Post-it, Becky grabbed her purse and headed toward the front door of the office.

"Hey, lock it when you leave, okay?"

Jules rested her head in her hand and turned her attention back to her computer. She'd gotten so good at this DNA stuff that it frustrated her when something didn't make sense. Like now. She'd been working with J Salter's shared matches and wasn't finding the McDermott name at all. Even if Jerry had another child he didn't know about, his ancestors would still be part of this person's tree.

"I'm missing something," she said out loud as she squinted at her screen. She glanced up when she heard persistent knocking.

Jules slipped out of her chair and went to peer through the small window at the front. "Hey, Donna," she said as she opened the door. "Sorry, Becky's out, and we lock it when it's only one of us here."

"Oh, okay. I brought you that folder. Jay just yelled at me last night that it's been in my car ever since the lawyer gave it to me." Donna expelled a puff of air. "I mean, where should I put it? In a cabinet filed under *Secrets My Father Kept From Me?*"

Jules reached for the folder, but the news that Donna had the folder in her car this whole time hung in the air. Jay had just found it there. Maybe when he couldn't find it, he had decided to break into their office instead.

Jules gestured with her chin. "Come on back. I'll scan it all."

As Jules fed pages into their small office scanner, she attempted to get Donna to talk about the interrogation, but she wouldn't say much.

When she was done scanning everything, Jules stapled the will back together and put everything back in the folder. She handed it to Donna across her desk and spoke in a soft voice. "Are you enjoying the quilt your mother made for you?"

Donna's guard collapsed, and a smile warmed her face. "I have it on the living room couch for now. In a way, I feel my mom close to me when I use it."

"Have you been able to visit your mother and brother's grave? I know that was important to you."

Donna's smile fell away as she bowed her head. "I haven't yet. I guess I'm afraid."

Jules's forehead wrinkled. "What are you afraid of?"

Donna hesitated, and Jules could tell she probably didn't talk about her mom much, if ever. She reached across the desk for Donna's hand and gave it a squeeze.

Donna raised her head and blinked quickly. "It's just—my dad cut off my mom's side of the family when she died. I guess I'm worried that maybe she's not the only one buried there." She pressed her lips together. "My dad isn't buried with her, and now I know she's in a different cemetery. I'm worried there's a Campbell family plot."

"Campbell? Is that your mother's maiden name?"

"Yeah." Donna's eyes welled up. "What if that thing that killed my mother ran in the family? I'm not sure I'm ready to find out my Aunt Katherine and Aunt Jone are gone, too."

"I understand." Jules came around the desk and wrapped Donna in a hug. "If you need someone to go with you, let me know."

Donna ran her finger under her eyes and wiped away her tears. "Thanks. I'll think about it." She reached for her folder and pushed herself up off the chair.

Jules rubbed her arm. "I'll walk you out."

Just as she opened the door, Becky appeared on the other side with lunch.

"Oh, hi, Donna, I guess you came by with the folder."

Jules nodded and hoped Donna didn't plan to linger. "She did. Everything's scanned this time. Nothing for Gene to sink his teeth into." She tapped the side of her leg until Becky shot her a look.

As soon as the door shut behind Donna, Jules hurried back to her desk.

"What's up with you?" Becky asked as she unpacked the bag with the sandwiches. "I got you a Diet Coke and some chips, too."

Jules put her finger up. "I think I'm on to something. Hang on."

"On to something about what?" Becky asked as she twisted the cap on her soda and took a sip.

Jules didn't respond. She narrowed her eyes, staring at the screen. She bit her bottom lip as she typed in what she was looking for. Several clicks, and there it was.

Becky placed Jules's lunch on her desk. "You look like the cat that ate the canary. What are you up to?"

Jules sat back in her chair and allowed herself a satisfied

grin. "Something Donna said gave me an idea. And I was right."

Becky looked interested as she sat back at her own desk and pulled her sandwich out of the bag. "Okay, tell me."

Jules swiveled in her chair to face Becky. "Donna's match?" Jules shook her head. "That's not Ally."

"No?" Becky tilted her head in curiosity. "So, Jerry *did* have another child?"

"Nope," Jules said emphatically as her lips curved upward. "It's not on Jerry's side at all. Donna's match isn't a half-sister." She leaned toward Becky. "It's an *aunt*. Her mother had a sister named Katherine, but she had another sister named Jone. Maiden name Campbell. Just found her marriage certificate."

Jules clasped her hands behind her head and beamed at Becky. "And wouldn't you know it. Her married name is Salter."

CHAPTER TWENTY-EIGHT

BECKY LET OUT A GROAN. "How did we not even think about that? I guess we've been so focused on Jerry's side, we forgot about Ava. Not to mention, I was praying it was Donna's half-sister, so this would all be over."

"If Jerry had tested on this site, we would have been able to see right away that Jone didn't match him. That would have been an easy clue we needed to look on Ava's side."

Becky took a bite of her sandwich. "Did you say anything to Donna?"

"I didn't know for sure until after she left. She mentioned her mom's maiden name, and Campbell was a surname I kept seeing in her matches. When she mentioned one of her mother's sisters was named Jone, I had a hunch. That amount of DNA they share is enough to be half-siblings, but an aunt is in the same range." Jules unwrapped her sandwich, inspected the contents, and took a bite.

"Yeah, I mentioned that same possibility to Bryan last night, but for some reason, I was still stuck on it being a sibling of Jerry's." Becky gritted her teeth. "I feel so stupid. How do you think Donna will feel about finding her aunt?"

While she ate, Jules recounted the conversation she had with Donna. "At least something good came out of this for her. Maybe the aunt's been looking for her."

"That would be great. Getting her mom's side of the family back after all this time. After lunch, let's see if we can track her down."

Jules stuck her hand in her bag of chips. "Should be pretty easy, I would think. But it puts us back to square one on Molly and Robert."

"Not exactly," Becky said with a small smile. "I feel pretty confident Darla's got the Molly we're looking for."

Jules raised an eyebrow. "Really? Were you able to find anything on her family? Parents? Grandparents?"

Becky popped the last piece of her sandwich in her mouth and nodded. "I found three of the sibling names in one Middlebrooks family with a mom named, Francis, maiden name Moore. Francis Lee Moore married George W. Middlebrooks, and I found his parents. That's as far as I've gotten. I haven't been able to find any obituaries."

"That's still progress. Let's put it on hold and see what we can find out about Donna's aunts. We know Ava had two sisters. Do we know the age order?"

Becky tapped her finger against her lip and tried to think. "When we found the vacation picture at the beach, Donna mentioned Katherine was her mom's older sister."

"And Ava would be how old now?"

Becky thought for a second and went to her computer. "I scanned some of the stuff in Ava's file before we gave it to Donna."

"Sure, *that* file you scanned," Jules said with a trace of sarcasm.

"Well, I also had it in the cloud, or I might have lost it with my stolen computer. Okay, so according to Ava's death certificate, she died in 1994, and her date of birth was July 12,

1963." Becky scrunched up her face. "She was almost thirty-one. That's too young to die."

"No, kidding. I'm thirty-one," Jules said. "Okay, so she'd be about fifty-seven now. Let's figure that Jone's the youngest, so let's see if we can find her in her mid-fifties."

They both turned their attention to their laptops and studied their screens while their fingers typed. Searching. Clicking.

"I found one in North Carolina, but I don't think the age is right," Becky said. "Seems too young. Late forties."

"I guess it's possible." Jules moved to look over Becky's shoulder at her screen. "Oh, definitely not the right one. She spells it J-o-n-e."

Becky narrowed her eyes and gave Jules a low growl. "Well, that would have been good information to have."

Jules sat back down at her computer. Two minutes later, her eyes lit up. "Got her."

"You found her?" Becky hustled over to Jules's desk and checked out her screen. "Age fifty-three. Looks good so far. Click on the relatives."

Jules read from the screen. "Looks like she's married to a man named, Alfred. That matches the marriage certificate I found. These must be her kids, Colleen and Kolin." Jules scrolled down a little farther. "Margaret Campbell, age seventy-nine. I'll bet that's her mom."

"There." Becky pointed. "Katherine Mulligan, age fifty-nine. That has to be the Aunt Kathy from the picture. Mulligan must be her married name. Click on the, *may also be known as* button."

"There you go," Jules said with a smile, as the name Katherine Campbell showed up.

Becky lifted herself up to sit on the edge of Jules's desk. "This has to be her. Where did you say Jone lived?"

Jules hit the back button several times. "Nashville, Tennessee."

"Let's also check Katherine."

When the address popped up on the screen, Jules let out a chuckle. "I know exactly where that is. Donna's aunt only lives about twenty minutes from here."

CHAPTER TWENTY-NINE

JULES LET out moan when the first number they had for Jone was disconnected.

"Try the next number," Becky urged impatiently.

"I am," Jules said as she punched in the number. Her eyes widened with anticipation when someone picked up, and she put the phone on speaker so Becky could hear, too.

"Hello?" the voice said again.

"Hi, is this Jone Salter?"

"It is," she said, her tone suspicious as if she regretted picking up the phone.

"Hi, Jone, my name is Jules Dalton, and I'm here with my partner Becky Morgan. We own a small detective agency in Florida."

"Okay ..." Jone dragged out the word. "What exactly can I do for you ladies?"

"One of the things we specialize in is family reunions that are made through DNA matches. Have you submitted an at-home DNA test?"

Jone seemed to hesitate for a moment and Jules held her breath. "Yes—yes, I did," she said finally.

Jules gave Becky a thumbs-up. "We're currently working on a case for our client, Donna Thomas. Your match to her is somewhat unrelated to the person we were hired to look for, but we wanted to reach out all the same to see if you would be interested in finding out more."

"Donna Thomas? Is that her married name?" Jone asked breathlessly. "I did the DNA test, hoping to find my niece, Donna McDermott. I haven't seen her in over twenty-five years."

Jules's shoulders relaxed, relieved for Donna's sake that her aunt was looking for her. "Well, then we have good news for you. Donna Thomas is your niece, ma'am."

Jone let out a squeal. "Oh, I have to tell my sister Kathy. She told me I'd never find her with a DNA test. But I thought maybe, if there was any chance at all, it would be worth trying."

"Your sister Kathy, does she live in Fairfield, FL?"

"She does," Jone confirmed.

"She's only about twenty minutes from where we are. Would you prefer we talk to both of you together?" She gave Becky a small questioning shrug. It wasn't far.

"I don't know. Oh, maybe. I just can't even believe this." Jone was clearly flustered. "Can I reach out to my sister and call you back?"

"Sure." Jules laughed. Jone's excitement was contagious. "Can you see my number on your caller ID?"

"I can. I'm going to save you right now. What did you say your name was?"

"Jules. My name is Jules."

"Okay, Jules, you've made me so happy. I'll call you back."

Jules turned to Becky, who was welling up. "I can't help it," she said as she wiped her eyes. "I just love this part."

"And this isn't even what Donna hired us for," Jules reminded her.

Becky's face grew serious. "Do you think we should have given the number to Donna and let her make the call?"

With adoption cases, they'd always been told the adoptee should make the first call if at all possible. Just in case there was no second chance.

"I considered that, but it's not like Jone's a birth mother who may decide to never talk to Donna. These are her aunts who seem excited to have found her. I just feel like we should give them a little background, so they know what they're walking into."

Jules's phone started ringing. That didn't take long. "Hi, Jone."

"My sister Kathy is beyond excited. I live in Tennessee, but if my sister is only twenty minutes from you, would you go to her? We have a way to video chat, and then we can both hear everything at the same time."

"Sure. When would be convenient for both of you?"

"Um, now?" Jone laughed. "We're ready as soon as you are." She gave Jules her sister's address, not knowing it was already sitting on Jules's computer screen.

"Okay, we're on our way." Jules hung up and threw her hands in the air. "Let's go."

Becky hesitated a moment and then winced. "I can't go now. I have something—an appointment. I can't really miss it."

Jules frowned. Couldn't it wait? "What kind of appointment?"

Becky stared down at the floor and nibbled on her thumbnail. "Just something personal. I'd rather not talk about it."

Jules flinched. They told each other everything. Then it dawned on her. Maybe Becky was considering doing IVF again and wasn't up to talking about it yet. The least Jules could do is give her privacy until she was ready to share

"No problem. I can go by myself, and I'll let you know

what happens." Jules grabbed her purse. "I'll lock the door behind me."

When she got in the car, Jules punched the address Jone had given her into her GPS. As she pulled out of the parking lot, a car parked at the very end of the lot pulled forward. They'd been backed into a spot at the other end of the lot surrounded by empty spaces. Jules kept an eye on it as it eased onto the main road several cars behind her.

She put her phone on hands-free and called Tim, excited to tell him she had figured out the mystery match.

"Hey, honey," he said when he answered. "I'm running out the door. Is it okay if I call you back?"

Jules let out an exaggerated groan. "Oh, all right. I have big news about Donna's match, but I'm heading to meet with someone. Call me later."

As her thoughts drifted to curiosity about Becky's mysterious appointment, Jules realized she'd forgotten about the car from the parking lot. Her eyes flicked back to the rearview mirror as she pulled onto the highway. There was no silver car. Jules let out a breath and turned up the radio.

Twenty minutes later, she pulled off the exit and stopped at the traffic light. She glanced in her rearview mirror. Four cars behind her was a silver car. She leaned forward in her seat and squinted to try to see it better. Was it the same one?

When the light changed, she turned left and noted the silver car made a left, too. There were no cars between them, but he was keeping his distance. It seemed deliberate. She came to an intersection, and without signaling, she made a sharp right. The silver car turned right, too. Her heartbeat quickened.

Jules lifted her foot off the gas to see if the silver car would catch up and pass her. He seemed to decrease his speed as well, and the distance between them didn't lessen any.

Jules had to know if her imagination was starting to run

wild. She made a last-minute swerve into a gas station. If the silver car was really following her, he would have to turn in, too. Jules pinned her gaze on the road and let out a deep breath as the car went past her. She was as paranoid as Becky now.

Jules slowly drove toward the exit but then slammed on the brakes. The silver car had taken the turn into the fast-food restaurant directly next to the gas station. Jules bit her lip as she considered her options. There was no way she could get back onto the road without him seeing her.

Her chest tightened. She pulled around to the other side of the station, hoping he'd pulled into the drive-through line, and she could scoot out unnoticed. She inched her car toward the exit and then floored it onto the road. Jules was speeding, but she didn't care. Whatever it took to lose him. If a cop pulled her over, she'd explain someone was chasing her.

She didn't even watch to see if he pulled out behind her, just focused on the road and stomped down on the gas pedal. At the first intersection she yanked the steering wheel hard to the right. Her tires squealed as she took the turn. Next street, left. No signals. Just random turns wherever she had the chance. Sweat was pooling on her upper lip and forehead. She punched the button for the air conditioning and relished in the relief as it spilled cold air onto her face.

Eventually, Jules pulled over and tried to catch her breath. She turned in her seat and glanced around at the road behind her. Then she peered out her side window, worried the person following her would pop up beside her car like some sort of boogeyman. She placed her palm on her chest, her heart thumping wildly underneath it, and exhaled. If he'd been following her, she'd succeeded in losing him. For an instant, she couldn't help but wonder if she'd just imagined being pursued. The case was getting to her.

Jules checked the GPS and scowled when she realized she'd

added fifteen minutes to the drive to Kathy's house. She headed to the next traffic light to go back in the direction she had just come from. When she got the green arrow, she made a U-turn. She felt her breathing returning to normal until she glanced in her rearview mirror. A fresh wave of panic washed over her. The silver car had returned, and he was taking the same turn she had just taken.

Should she go to Kathy's house now? She punched in Becky's number. "Hi, you've reached Becky—"

"Where are you?" Jules wailed into the phone. She was usually the calm, stable partner, but that was before people were getting murdered.

She dialed Tim's number next. "Hey, it's Tim, you know what to—" Jules let out a frustrated groan and hung up. Where the hell did he go? She needed him.

Helpless frustration made her eyes well up. Kathy and Jone were waiting for her, but she couldn't go there now. There was no way she could lead someone right to Kathy.

Jules crushed the gas pedal and raced through the next intersection just as the light turned yellow. The silver car was still more than a few car lengths behind her. He'd have to blatantly run the red light if he intended to keep up with her.

Jules's stomach lurched when she heard a horrific screech of tires behind her. Car horns blared loudly. She winced as she prepared for the crunching sound of metal on metal, but it never came.

When she looked in the rearview mirror, she pounded her fist on the steering wheel. He'd made it through the intersection, but not without causing road rage in another driver or two with his recklessness. This was definitely not her imagination.

Fear stuck in her throat. It wasn't like her to fold like this, but she had no idea what this person was capable of doing. She couldn't lead them to Kathy's house. Could she even go home?

She needed Tim, and he wasn't there for her. For an instant, the little voice inside her head taunted her. *This is why you can't depend on anyone.* She blinked hard and forced the idea from her mind.

She had another option. Jules dialed, and her voice shook when he answered. "Jonas, I'm scared, and I don't know what to do. Someone's following me, and I'm terrified of what he might do if he catches me."

CHAPTER THIRTY

"HEY, ARE YOU OKAY?" Becky asked when Jules picked up the phone. It was late, but she had just heard her voicemail, and her friend sounded frantic.

"No, not really." Jules took a deep breath. "Beck, this case is messed up."

"Why, what else happened? Are you back from Kathy's house?"

"I didn't go. Well, I went, but I never made it there."

"I don't understand." Becky sucked in air. "You didn't get into an accident, did you?"

"No. I left the office, and someone followed me. They pulled out of the lot right after me."

Becky felt her shoulders relax with the news that Jules wasn't hurt. "That could just be a coincidence."

Jules let out a snort. "Oh, it was *not* a coincidence. They were still following me when I got off the exit for Fairfield."

Becky's brow creased. "You're sure it was the same car?"

"Absolutely. Trust me, I deliberately tried to lose him, and I couldn't. He even ran a red light to keep up with me. Almost caused a huge accident."

Becky started pacing. "It was a him? Did you see the person?"

"No, I guess it could have been a her," Jules admitted. "They never got close enough for me to see. I just assumed it was a man because that's who seems to be on the same path as us."

Becky placed a hand on her forehead. "So, what did you do?"

"I didn't know what to do. I called you, and then I tried Tim. Neither of you picked up. I was freaking out."

Becky felt a twinge of guilt. She couldn't tell Jules where she'd been. What were the odds Jules would be looking for her and Tim at the same time? "I'm sorry I wasn't there when you needed me. What did you do? You're home now, right?"

"I called Jonas. He told me to GPS to the nearest police station. He called ahead, and an officer came out and met me at the car."

Becky raked her nervous fingers through her hair. "Were you able to file a police report?"

"No, I had nothing—no license plate. I couldn't even see the make and model of the car. Silver sedan. Not very specific. Jonas just figured—"

"The car was silver?" Becky felt a chill come over her.

"Yeah. Why?"

"The car I saw in Orlando by Sue's house. That car was silver, too."

There was silence as Jules seemed to be considering the insinuation Becky was making. Finally, she said, "Well, I had no plans to end up like Sue. Jonas thought whoever was following me would take off if he thought I was going to the cops."

Becky leaned on the kitchen table. "He's probably right."

"It seemed that way, but I couldn't take a chance. I couldn't lead him right to Kathy's house. After what happened to Robert ..." Jules didn't finish the thought. She didn't need to.

"The police officer followed me in a patrol car back to the highway. I came home, but believe me, I circled my area several times until I was positive no one followed me. I *finally* got Tim on the phone and demanded he gets over here."

There was something in Jules's voice when she mentioned Tim that had Becky concerned. This wasn't the time to be overly curious, so instead, she asked, "Did you call Jone?"

"I did. I apologized and said I had car trouble. Finally, when I got home, I kept one eye out the window and got them both on a call. They're thrilled they found Donna. They've been looking for years."

"Did they say what happened?"

"Not too much. It sounds like there was a disagreement between Ava's family and Jerry about taking Ava and the baby off life support. Jerry had the final say as her husband. After the funeral, he stopped returning their phone calls, and he changed his number. They figured he didn't want Donna to know what happened and worried someone in Ava's family would tell her the truth."

"He was probably right," Becky said. "But sad that he kept Ava's family from Donna, who needed them more than ever."

"They said it took time, but eventually they understood why he made the decision. By then, they didn't have a phone number for him, and they weren't sure if he was still in the same house he shared with Ava."

Becky was confused about why the aunts had given up so easily. "It seems they could have just searched Jerry's name. He covered some pretty notable cases. They could have found him if they really wanted to."

"I thought the same thing," Jules admitted. "It sounded like they didn't want to go through Jerry, and they didn't want to bring it all back for Donna until she was an adult. They started looking for her sometime after she turned eighteen but never had any luck. Hey, let me call you back. It's Jonas on the other line. He was trying to see if he could find any updates."

Becky disconnected the call and glanced at Bryan. "Did you get any of that?"

He leaned against the kitchen counter. "Sounds like someone was following Jules."

"Yeah. She was pretty freaked out. She tried to call Tim and me, and neither one of us picked up. At least she finally called Jonas." Becky hung her head. "I feel terrible."

Bryan came over and wrapped his arms around her. "You had no way of knowing that was going to happen. It was just bad timing."

"I know, but she asked me where I was going. I said I had an appointment. Babe, I tell her everything. It feels so strange to be keeping this from her."

"C'mon." He put his finger under her chin and tipped it up so she was looking him in the eyes. "You didn't do anything bad. When she finds out where you were, it will all be fine."

Becky nodded somberly. "I guess you're right."

"I know I'm right." His gaze lingered on her, and his lips were set in a firm line. "But we need to talk about you backing off this case. It's getting entirely too dangerous."

Becky bit her bottom lip. "I don't know what to think, but we can't quit now. I think we're close to figuring out who Donna's sister is. We just need to figure out her married name, and we'll be able to find her. Then that's the end of it."

He narrowed his eyes as he studied her face. "Do you promise?"

She held up two fingers. "I do. Donna wants to know about Robert, but if we don't figure him out, so be it. And whoever got the life insurance doesn't matter. It doesn't change anything for Donna. Except maybe it would make her mad. We'll just find the sister, and we'll be careful."

Worry lined his forehead as Bryan wagged his finger at her. "No more trips to Orlando without Tim or me. I'm not kidding, Beck. And if you're going to meet someone, I need to know about it. Where you're going. Who you're going to see. You need to stay in contact with me." He put his arms around her. "I almost lost you once already this year. I can't go through that again. No way."

She leaned up on her toes and kissed him. "Trust me, I have no desire to ever go through anything like that again."

"You and Jules may have bitten off more than you can chew with this. This is not your usual adoptee looking for their birth family. Who knows what would have happened if Jonas hadn't helped Jules." He put his hands on her shoulders. "People are getting *killed* here."

"We don't know this is all related to Donna's case." But deep down, Becky did know. All the things that had happened. There was no other explanation.

"It's Jules again," she said as her phone rang.

Her husband gave her a stern stare as he walked away.

"Hey," Becky said when she answered. "Did you find out anything from Jonas?"

"The only thing they would tell him is that they're serving a search warrant right now."

Becky exhaled loudly. "Well, that means they must have something on someone. At least I'm off the hook." She turned to Bryan and ran her fingers across her forehead as a sign of relief. "They have an idea of who might have done this. That's great. Was he able to find out where the search is?"

"He was. They just got—"

"They just got where?" Becky cut her off in anticipation. "This has to be the guy that was following you, that's been making the calls. They must finally have him. This is great news. Did he tell you where the search was?"

"He did, but I'm not sure I'd consider it great news."

Becky tilted her head in confusion. "Why not?"

"It's Donna, Beck. They're getting ready to search Jay and Donna's apartment."

CHAPTER THIRTY-ONE

THEY KNOCKED ON THE DOOR, flashed some official documents, and told her they had the right to search the apartment. A balding guy in a suit and two uniformed officers. No warning they were coming. Just a knock and they expected to be let inside.

"My fiancé isn't home now," Donna said through the half-opened door. "I'm not sure I'm entirely comfort—"

The man extended his hand through the partially opened doorway. "I'm Detective Stephens. Ma'am, I'm sorry, but we have an order from a judge. If you'll step aside and let us get started, we'll be out of here as soon as we can."

He looked like one of those detectives on the TV shows Donna liked to watch. His suit was wrinkled like he'd been wearing it all day in the Florida heat. His tie was slightly loosened, and he'd undone the top button of his shirt to give his neck some breathing room. It was still warm and muggy even at this time of night, and his face bore the anticipation of relief at getting inside into the air conditioning.

"I don't know what you could possibly be looking for," Donna told him through the partially opened doorway.

"We have reason to believe there could be evidence related to a crime." The detective pushed slightly on the door. He entered the apartment, followed by the two uniformed policemen.

So, Jay wasn't off the hook.

"I need to make a call." Donna scurried to the kitchen for her purse hanging over the back of one of the chairs. It had not gone unnoticed that the detective had followed her.

Her heart was racing as she dialed the phone and hurried away to try to get some privacy. "C'mon, pick up, pick up," she whispered tersely into the phone while keeping an eye on the detective.

"What's up?" Jay answered just before it would have gone to voicemail.

"What's up?" Donna asked incredulously, her voice high and taut. "What's up is that the damn police are here searching the apartment. Where are you?"

"Out with my brother. Leaving right now." Jay's voice was stern. "Keep an eye on them, Donna."

There was a set of rapid knocks on the front door, and the detective was back in the living room to answer it. Donna hurried to the opposite corner of the room near the television. "Someone else is here," she whispered into the phone.

"Who is it now?" Jay asked over the pinging of the seatbelt warning as he got into his car.

"A man and a woman. Shirts say Crime Investigation. They both have cameras. Big bags over their shoulders."

"Watch them. Try to figure out what they're looking for. I'll be home in ten minutes."

"Just hurry up," Donna hissed through clenched teeth.

The uniformed police officers seemed to be there only if something got out of control. They stood by the front door talking to the detective while the crime scene investigators split up—one into the bedroom, the other into the kitchen.

Donna peered through the open bedroom door and watched as the woman rifled through drawers, their closet. She then focused on Jay's dresser, taking pictures, pulling out T-shirts, spreading them out on the bed. What the hell could she be looking for?

Donna shuffled to the big window that looked down on the parking lot. Damn him for leaving her with this mess. When she turned, the detective was staring.

"My fiancé is on his way home," she said. "He should be here in a few minutes."

"That's fine," Detective Stephens said with a curt nod. "We don't necessarily need him to be here, but I'm sure it will make you more comfortable."

An awful thought settled over Donna, making her pulse race. Maybe it wasn't Jay they suspected. Maybe it was her. What if—

Detective Stephens interrupted her thoughts. "Before we leave, we'll need to get your fingerprints and a DNA sample."

Donna licked her lips nervously. "Mine?" She cleared her throat and tried to sound casual. "Am I in some sort of trouble?"

He gave her a pointed look. "Well, there's two of you that live here. We just need to be able to identify any prints or DNA we might find—if it comes to that."

Donna wanted to tread carefully, but she also wanted to know her rights. "Do I have to?"

The detective shrugged with a small smile that suggested he'd get what he wanted one way or another. "You can decline. It just means we'd need to get a separate warrant for it. Your fiancé gave us his when we questioned him at the station." Detective Stephens looked her firmly in the eye. "*He* said he had nothing to hide."

"Well, I don't have anything to hide either." Donna swallowed down the lump in her throat. She wasn't sure if she felt better or worse that Jay had agreed. They had probably told him the same thing about getting a warrant if he refused. "Can we do it now?"

She didn't know why, but she wanted to have it done before Jay came barreling through the door. Her stomach twisted, and she was afraid her dinner might come up.

"Sure." There was that cocky smile again as he called out to the woman in the bedroom. "Hey, Sherridan, can you do the fingerprints and swab when you have a second?"

The woman came out and handed the detective two brown bags that had been sealed with tape.

Donna caught her breath and swayed unsteadily on her feet. They'd found something. Detective Stephens grabbed the bags before she could see what was written on them.

She followed Sherridan, who poked her head into the kitchen. "Hey, Bert, are you good if we use the table for fingerprints?"

"Yup, I'm almost done in here."

Donna slid into one of the kitchen chairs and glanced around. Her face felt damp, and she fanned herself with her hand. The cabinets under the sink were wide open, and the silverware drawers had been yanked out. Bert was at the counter, placing official-looking tape on a large brown bag to seal it shut. Donna's eyes scanned the countertop, and she let out a soft yelp. The knife set was gone.

"You okay?" Sherridan asked as she laid out her supplies.

"Fine." Donna's heart thumped furiously in her chest. She was anything but fine.

Sherridan had swabbed DNA from the inside of Donna's cheek and was just placing a piece of clear tape over the finger-prints she had taken when Donna heard the front door fly open.

"Am I finished?" Donna was already rising from the table.

"You are. Just need to give these to the detective, and then I have to go back to the bedroom——"

Donna wasn't listening as she rushed to where Jay was standing with the detective. He towered over the man. Donna now understood why the uniformed officers were necessary.

"I need to see this search warrant," Jay was saying to the detective as Donna sidled up beside him.

"Absolutely." The detective snatched the warrant from the coffee table where he had placed it when they arrived. "This is your copy."

Jay's eyes scanned the paper as he scowled.

Donna leaned in and whispered in his ear. "Is it legit?"

"I'm no lawyer, but it seems like it to me."

The detective reached into the inside pocket of his jacket and pulled out a small notebook. He flipped a few pages and pulled the pen out of the spiral binding. "Just confirming, does anyone else live here besides the two of you?"

Donna glanced at Jay and then responded, "No."

"Have you allowed anyone to reside or stay here recently, even temporarily?"

Jay snorted and answered the detective in a clipped tone. "We're not running a bed and breakfast if that's what you mean."

The detective glanced up, his expression flat. "So, that's a no, right?"

"That's a no," Jay said as he set his jaw.

It had to be killing Jay to be polite when their apartment had been invaded. Donna glanced around. Bert had moved into the living room. He picked up her mother's quilt, shook it, and tossed it on the couch.

"Hey." Donna's voice broke as she turned. "My mother made that for me."

Jay's hand was on her arm as he warned her with his eyes

to stay put. She choked back tears. Her precious memory of her mother now sat crumpled on the couch.

"I have a few more questions, Mrs. Thomas."

"Ms. Thomas," she corrected him tersely. Donna knew her crimson face betrayed how furious she was. She swiped at her tears and gritted her teeth. "Go on."

"I noticed the mailboxes for this building are all together. Does anyone else besides the two of you have access to your mailbox?"

Her blue eyes blazed. "The mailman."

The detective's no-nonsense expression conveyed immediately that her sarcastic tone was not appreciated.

"Donna," Jay said, his tone firm as he seemed to be pleading for her to behave. He'd had run-ins with the law in the past. She knew he'd learned the hard way that disrespect of the law really didn't get you very far. "The sooner we answer his questions and let them do what they need to do, the quicker this is over."

Jay directed his gaze and his pointed words back to the detective. "After all, we have nothing to hide. We haven't done anything."

Donna let out a sigh of resignation. "We have one mailbox key. It hangs on the hook in the kitchen."

"Bert," Detective Stephens called out to the man photographing the living room. "You see it?"

"Yup, already took pictures."

He thought he was so smart, but Donna knew what he was getting at. "We only have one key, but everybody throws their junk mail out at the boxes. There's a trash can right there. I do it, too."

Detective Stephens nodded as he scribbled a note. "I see." He glanced up and fixed a steely gaze on Donna. "Do you pay the bills for the household?"

She swallowed hard under his intense stare. "Yeah …"

"Would you throw bills into the trash? Would you consider those junk mail?"

Damn Jay for not telling her more about the envelope they found. "Well, no."

"What about a new credit card or a bank statement? Would you consider those junk mail?"

Donna pressed her lips together. Her blue eyes grew cold as she returned his stare. "Of course not."

"Is your fiancé collecting unemployment at the moment?"

Donna shifted a concerned gaze to Jay. The detective glanced up from his notes, waiting for an answer.

"He was. I mean, he is, but he's about to go back to work. He's in construction. Sometimes—"

"So, if he got something related to his unemployment benefits, that would be considered important mail, I would think. Would you throw that away?"

"Well, no ..." She was like a mouse trapped in a maze. He had led her around and around until she was stuck in a corner with no escape.

Detective Stephens wrote something in his notebook, and then closed it and put it back in his jacket pocket.

Donna's face warmed. Anger boiled her insides. He'd backed her in a corner until he got the answer he wanted. Jay should have told her more about what they had. This wasn't her fault.

Jay shook his head as if he suddenly thought they might have reason to be worried. "Are you almost done here?" His worry turned to anger as he stared at the brown bags placed by the door. His face reddened as his fists clenched by his sides. "You're just *taking* stuff?"

"Don't worry, you'll get an itemized list of the evidence we're seizing before we go."

The detective's gaze landed on Jay's balled up fists. He

tapped the arm of one of the uniformed officers who gave a quick nod. Clearly, his job was now to keep an eye on Jay.

"Let me see where Sherridan's at in the bedroom, and I'll let you know how much longer we need."

As Detective Stephens walked away, Donna clutched Jay's forearm, her nails leaving indentations in his skin. "If they're taking things, they must think whatever's in those brown bags proves something, right?"

"They can't prove *anything*. I just can't figure out why they'd even be here." He hesitated. "Didn't you say one of those detectives has a brother that's a cop?"

"Well, yeah, but—"

"Maybe they're setting me up."

Donna frowned. "Why would they do that? They don't even know you."

Jay threw his hands up in the air. "Maybe they know something about the murder. Maybe they're in on it and need a fall guy."

Donna rolled her eyes. "Why would they want to kill anyone? That makes no sense."

Jay grabbed her by the shoulders. "Then who? Why are the police targeting me?"

Donna searched his eyes and shrugged helplessly. "I don't know."

Detective Stephens came back and handed a yellow piece of paper to Jay. "We're done here for now. Here's your copy of the property we're seizing."

"You're just leaving it like this?" Donna asked incredulously as she glanced around at the disarray in the apartment.

He gave her an amused shrug. "This is actually not bad. You should see some places when we're done." The detective lifted his chin in the direction of the two investigators. "You got everything you need?"

They both nodded and followed the detective out the front

door. The uniformed officers went right behind them and shut the door as they left.

Donna groaned. The whole scene seemed surreal, and now she'd have to put the place back together. She stared at the paper in Jay's hand. "What's it say? What'd they take?"

Jay was studying the paper and shaking his head. "I don't get it."

"Why? Tell me what they took."

Jay read from the paper. "They took two All-Star Construction T-shirts, one All-Star Construction baseball cap, a Nike sneaker, the wooden block and knife set from the kitchen counter, and a letter about my unemployment benefits."

Donna wrinkled her forehead. "Why would they take that stuff?"

"This is not good." Jay's eyes met Donna's, and she could see the fear etched on his face. "This is not good at all."

CHAPTER THIRTY-TWO

Jules stood at the kitchen counter, willing the coffee to brew faster.

"What do we do about Donna?" Becky asked. She knelt down next to Gene's dog bed. He rolled over to present his stomach for a scratch, which she happily obliged. "I haven't heard from her. Have you?"

Jules shook her head. "No, nothing. I guess we play dumb. If Jonas hadn't told us they were serving the search warrant last night, we wouldn't know. We'll have to see if she says anything." She opened the small cupboard, and her hand paused at the shelf with the mugs. "You want coffee?"

Becky nodded. "Definitely." She leaned back on her palms next to Gene. "What could they have been looking for? Do you think Jay really did it? Murdered Robert?"

Jules spooned sugar into both cups on the counter and then filled them from the pot. "They must have some reason to think he did. Jonas said they needed a probable cause affidavit to bring to the judge to get the warrant."

She reached into the refrigerator, grabbed the creamer, and poured a bit into each mug before returning it to the fridge.

Becky got up off the floor and grabbed her coffee from Jules. "Oh, so maybe there's something in there that explains it? Can't Jonas get a copy?"

"Apparently, they're very protective of their case, even to someone else in law enforcement." Jules took a sip and then strode to her desk. "The only reason they even told him about the search warrant is because they were already at the apartment getting ready to serve it. It's not like he had time to warn anybody. I guess they don't take chances, especially with a murder investigation."

Becky sat in the chair in front of Jules's desk. "I get it. What if he knew me, and I turned out to be the murder suspect? If they told him something, he could warn me so I could skip town. So, I guess I'm in the clear."

"Maybe your alibi receipts did the trick. They definitely seem focused on Jay. Jonas said the cops have to file the affidavit with the court clerk within ten days. Could be sooner. But as soon as they do, it's posted for public release. That's usually when the media gets hold of it, so we'll be able to see it, too."

Becky scrunched up her face. "Poor Donna. Seems a bad time now for a long-awaited reunion with her aunts. What do we do?"

Jules raised one shoulder. "Maybe it isn't the greatest time, but again, we don't know anything about the search, right? I think we need to tell her. Remember, this isn't what she hired us for. It's our responsibility to turn the information about her mother's family over to her. It's up to her to decide what to do with it."

Becky bit her bottom lip and finally nodded. "You're right, but she might be having a rough morning after the search last night. It could have been a late night."

Becky got up, made her way back to her own desk, and opened her laptop. "I'll just send her an email."

She dictated as she typed. "*Hey, Donna, your first set of DNA results came in, and we found someone unexpected. It's not your half-sister, but we think you'll be interested. Give us a call when you have a chance.*" She glanced up from her keyboard. "Sound okay?"

"Sounds good to me."

Becky hit the send button and swiveled in her chair so she could face Jules, a serious expression on her face. "Listen, Bryan's starting to think we might be a little over our head with this one. Between you getting followed and Robert being murdered. And now, what if Jay really is a suspect?" Becky bit on her nail and shrugged. "I'm not sure Bryan's wrong."

Jules put down her coffee cup and let out a weary sigh. "I know. Tim's worried, too."

"I told Bryan we'd concentrate on finding Donna's sister so we can close the case. Forget about the real Robert or worrying about who got the life insurance policy."

Jules nodded. "I agree. We're close. We're pretty sure we have the right Molly. We just need to figure out her married name and where she lives. Why don't you go back to building her family tree and looking for any obituaries that might help? I'll start searching old newspapers. Use all the family names and see if I get a hit on anything."

Jules pulled open her desk drawer, but her gaze landed on the white business-sized envelope with the flash drive Donna's father had left. She tossed it on the desk. "You have to wonder what could possibly be on here."

"The flash drive? The odds of us ever figuring out the password are between slim and none."

Jules rubbed her chin. "I don't know about that."

"What do you mean?"

"I just think there's a lot of clues in those boxes he left for Donna. I can't believe he'd leave the flash drive with no possible way of figuring out the password. If he didn't want Donna to have whatever's on here, he could have just thrown it out." Jules pulled the drive from the envelope and turned toward Becky. "Here, catch."

Becky caught it and scowled. "What am I going to do with it?"

"Get creative. Think like a dying man who wants someone to eventually figure it out. Keep a list of everything you try."

Becky shrugged. "Okay, here goes nothing."

After about thirty minutes, Becky groaned. I've tried everything I can think of. I feel like there's something obvious I'm missing."

Jules looked up from her computer. "What have you tried?"

"I've tried Ava's name and birthday, Donna's name and birthday. Their wedding date. The day she died. They had no pets that Donna mentioned." Becky rubbed her temples. "Do you think it's written down on something in those boxes?"

"I guess we could have missed it in one of those datebooks. Do you have this year's book?"

"I'm pretty sure I do. I remember seeing a ton of doctor appointments. Not much in the way of court dates." Becky stood and stretched. "The books are in my trunk. Keep thinking, and I'll run out and look for it. Want me to take Gene out with me?"

"I'm sure he would love that." Jules picked up his leash from her desk and handed it to Becky.

Becky turned to the dog who had opened one hopeful eye at the sound of his leash rattling. "C'mon, wanna go potty?"

Gene got up, shook himself, and trotted to the front door of the office. Becky clipped the leash to his collar and headed outside.

Jules thought about locking the front door while Becky was outside but then chastised herself. It wouldn't be more than a few minutes.

She wandered over to Becky's desk to consult the list of passwords she'd already tried. Jules added a few to the list, and after sitting in Becky's chair and testing them with no success, she drew a line through each. Maybe Becky was right that they'd never figure it out, but part of her still believed that the answers they needed were somewhere in the things Jerry had left behind.

Gene bounded back into the office and headed directly to his water bowl.

Becky was behind him, cradling her phone to her ear and clutching Jerry's datebook. "Hey, Donna, hang on, I just walked back into the office, and I want to put you on speaker so you can talk to Jules, too." Becky looked confused that Jules was at her desk but slipped into her guest chair and hit the speaker button.

"Hi, Donna," Jules said into the phone.

"Hey. I got Becky's email," Donna said flatly. "Disappointed the match wasn't my half-sister. Did my dad have another kid I don't know about that wants to be cut in?"

"No," Becky said. "It's actually not on your father's side. It's on your mother's side." There was silence on the line. "Donna, you still there?"

"Yeah. I guess I'm nervous." She let out a deep breath, and her voice was steadier when she spoke again. "Okay, what did you find? Or I guess should I ask, *who* did you find?"

"You got a match for 1875 cMs of DNA," Becky said. "That's about the same amount we thought you'd need to match your half-sister, but it also—"

Jules waved her hand in a get-to-the-point gesture. There was no way Donna cared about the minute details.

Becky nodded and mouthed *okay*. "Sorry, I'm sure you don't need all the details right now. Your match was J Salter. We found out it was your Aunt Jone, your mother's sister."

"My Aunt Jone?" Donna's voice broke. "She's my mother's younger sister. Did you—did you talk to her?"

"I did," Jules said. "She's very excited."

"I can't believe this. Did Jone say anything about my Aunt Kathy, my cousins, my uncles?"

Jules leaned in closer to the phone. "They're all fine. I know you were worried, but they're all fine, and they can't wait to see you. Your Aunt Kathy lives in Fairfield, about twenty minutes away."

Donna let out a sob. "I can't believe that. This whole time she's been that close to me? What about my Aunt Jone? Does she live nearby, too?"

"She lives in Tennessee, but say the word, and she's ready to get on a plane," Jules said. "Your mother's sisters have been looking for you for years."

"Really?" Donna's voice cracked.

Jules smiled at Becky before she responded. "Really."

There was a beep on the line. Call waiting. Becky lifted her phone from the desk and glanced at the ID. She turned the phone around so Jules could see. It was Darla.

"Interesting," Jules whispered. "Maybe she found out where Molly is."

"Hey, Donna, it's Becky now. I have another call to answer, but Jules will text you all their information from her phone. Okay? Let us know how it goes."

"Okay, I still can't believe this. Thank you."

As Jules waited, she hung up the first call with Donna and then answered on speakerphone. "Hi, this is Becky."

"Hi, Becky, it's Darla. The friend of Molly's that you had lunch with at the pizza place."

Becky laughed. "Of course, I know who you are. Did you have any luck finding out where Molly is or the guy she married?"

"No, but I've been asking around. No one seems to know. I did remember something else. Not sure if it's important or not, but I figured it couldn't hurt to let you know."

Becky glanced at Jules and crossed her fingers. "We appreciate it. What did you remember?"

"That day I saw Molly at the mall with the kids. She told me she was moving to North Florida, and there was a woman she kept talking about. She was great to Molly and Ally, sort of like an older sister. This woman—she was the reason Molly moved. I finally remembered her name."

Jules held her breath while she waited for Darla to say more.

"Her name—the woman's name was Ella."

CHAPTER THIRTY-THREE

BECKY PULLED the datebook from next to her in the chair and tossed it on her desk. "Well, that was a juicy little nugget. So, his secretary knew Molly and her daughter. Do you think Jerry had any idea?"

"I don't know what to think," Jules said. "In his letter, he didn't seem to know what happened to her or where she was now. I was actually thinking about her the other day. Remember, in the letter, he said *I told Ella to stop putting her through*? I just figured even if we reached out to her and she remembered anything, it wouldn't be Molly's married name. This changes everything."

"We need to call her. Go see her. She must live somewhere nearby if she worked at Jerry's office in Deerfield." Becky really hoped Ella had kept in touch with Molly. They could have this case solved by tonight if she did. Bryan would love that.

Jules held up her hand. "Okay, slow down for one second. Let me text the information about Katherine and Jone to Donna before I forget." Jules went back to her own desk and grabbed her phone.

"Yeah, let's talk about that call for a second," Becky said as Jules started typing.

Jules held up her index finger. "Give me one second, so I don't mess this up. Okay … sent." She brought her gaze back up. "Donna seemed really emotional, right?"

"Yeah, I'm happy for her. But she didn't say anything about the search last night."

"We really didn't give her a chance. We went right into the stuff about her aunt, and then you hung up to talk to Darla."

Becky dipped her head thoughtfully. "I guess that's true, but her tone was pretty serious when the call first started."

Jules shrugged. "I guess thinking your fiancé could get arrested at any minute would do that to you."

"Even if she goes to see her aunt, she should be safe. If Jay really is behind this, he'll know they're not related to the inheritance."

"Okay, let's talk about Ella," Jules said, changing the subject. "How do we find out her last name?"

Becky pressed her lips together and then eked out an exclamation when she remembered something. "Jerry's office."

Jules bobbed her head as she recalled it, too. "The notepad. Do you remember what it said her last name was? It was embossed at the top." She tapped two fingers against her lips.

Becky closed her eyes and tried to visualize the pad on the desk. She could picture the font, a fancy script. Were there two words after her first name? She forced her brain to drill in, look closer, remember how it looked. Her eyes flew open.

"McBride. It was Ella McBride."

"I think you're right. Okay, she worked for Donna's dad for a long time, so she's gotta be what, in her sixties?"

"Unless she started really young."

"Okay, fifties to sixties. Let's start looking. Ella can't live too far from where Jerry had his office. Let's start with a twenty-mile radius from that address." Jules pulled up the office building's GPS from her phone and copied the address to a piece of paper. She handed it to Becky. "Let's both look."

Becky grabbed the piece of paper and went back to her laptop. "Anything?" she asked after a few minutes.

"Not yet. You?"

"There's an Eleanor McBride about twenty minutes from the office. Oh, wait, she's seventy-two." Becky glanced up. "Probably too old, right?"

"I guess it's possible, but you'd think the poor woman would have wanted to retire way before this year. Flag her as a possibility."

"What else do you think Ella could be short for?" Becky asked. "There's a Gabriella McBride."

"Hang on. I think I found something. Ella McBride. Sixty-two. Also known as Eloise Jane McBride, Eloise Carver. Ella J. Carver." Jules looked up and smiled. "This has promise." She glanced back down at her screen. "Lives ..." Jules clicked a button and focused on the screen. "This has to be her. She lives five minutes from Jerry's old office." Jules recited the address. "Can you look it up on one of the realtor sites and see what it says?"

After a minute, Becky nodded at Jules. "The address checks out. Looks like the house was bought in the name of Steven McBride and transferred into Ella's name in 2001."

"Maybe the husband died. When did he buy the house?"

Becky consulted the screen. "Looks like 1989."

"So, she's been in that house for over thirty years. Sounds promising. Does she have a phone number listed?"

Several clicks later, Becky pulled up her contact information. "Three of them."

Jules grinned. "Well, let's get this show on the road and try them."

After two disconnected numbers, Jules had Ella's son on the

line. He confirmed his mother had worked for Jerry for almost thirty years.

"I'm sure she knows Donna then," Jules said to him. "Jerry's daughter. She's hired us to look for someone, and we think your mom might be able to help."

"Can you hang on a minute?" Ella's son asked.

While they waited, Becky nervously bit her lip. "This is going to be it. I can feel it."

Jules gave her a warning with a shake of the head. "Don't get ahead of yourself. Ella may have no idea where Molly is now."

Becky admonished her with a stern stare. "How 'bout you be a glass half full person today?"

"I want to——"

"Hi, I'm back," Ella's son said. "Do you live near Deerfield?"

Jules and Becky exchanged an excited glance. "We do," Jules said.

"My mom has a cast on her leg and isn't getting around too easily. She wants to know if you can come here. I can give you the address."

"Sure." Jules wrote it down even though it was still up on Becky's screen. "Thank you. We'll see you soon."

As they got in the car, Becky reached for her phone. "I need to call Bryan. I promised him if we went to meet anyone we didn't know, I would let him know where we're going."

Jules put the car in reverse. "Okay, can you hold on that for a little bit? I need you to help me make sure no one is following us first."

"Oh, right." Becky swiveled in her seat and scanned the parking lot as Jules pulled out. "I don't see anyone leaving the lot with us." Becky kept watching for several traffic lights. "Still nothing."

"Look several cars back. See any silver cars?"

"Nope. A few SUVs and a pickup." Becky craned her neck. "The car behind that looks like a red sedan. Not a single car that's silver."

Jules blew out a deep breath. "Okay, I feel better. We need to figure this out. I can't keep worrying about someone following me every time I leave the office."

"I get it." Becky patted her on the shoulder. "Being paranoid is my department. You're supposed to be the reasonable one."

"I was until that guy wouldn't stop chasing me the other night. Now, I'm taking no chances. Go ahead, call Bryan."

"Hey, babe," Becky said when he picked up the phone. "I'm checking in like I promised."

"Good girl. Where are you off to?" Bryan asked.

"It looks like Jerry's secretary, Ella, actually knew Donna's half-sister and her mother, Molly."

"Wow, really? You're heading there to see if she knows where they are now?"

"Exactly. We haven't talked to Ella directly, but her son said she wanted us to come over. She lives in Deerfield, not far from Jerry's old office."

"Jules with you?"

Becky glanced over at Jules in the driver's seat. "Yup, we're together. And I've been checking to make sure no one is following us. We're good."

"Okay, text me the address where you're going and call me when you leave." He paused. "I know I sound crazy. I hear myself."

Becky shook her head even though she knew he couldn't see her. "It's okay. We want to be safe, too. Hopefully, Ella knows where Donna's sister is, and the case can be closed. Then we'll go back to adoptions where no one is getting followed or killed."

"I would certainly feel better if you did. Make sure you text me the name and address. See you later," he said pointedly.

Becky hung up the call with a half-shrug. "Hey, there was a time I was zip-tied to a chair that I only wished someone knew where I was."

Jules reached out and patted Becky's arm. "I know. The man loves you, and he went through hell. We both did. I don't have a problem if he knows where we are. If Tim finds out it's an option, he'll be on me to report in, too."

Becky texted Ella's name and address to Bryan and frowned. "I just had a thought. Do you think Ella could be involved in this somehow?"

Jules took her eyes off the road to shoot Becky a look. "The woman with a broken leg? Doubtful. Besides, it's a man that's on our trail."

"Right, but we know Ella has a son. Maybe he thought his mother should have inherited money from Jerry. I mean, she did work for him for thirty years. Maybe we're walking into a trap."

Jules rolled her eyes. "There's nothing in the will that says Ella gets anything if anyone winds up dead. Especially if it's us. I think we're safe."

Becky shifted in her seat. "You're right. I guess I just suspect everyone these days."

Jules gave Becky a look that said she wasn't worried about Ella and her son. "I think we both know who's responsible. When we find Donna's sister, we need to figure out how we're going to tell her so that Jay doesn't find out."

Jules made the final turn onto Ella's street and parked at the curb in front of the house with the perfectly manicured lawn. She held up her crossed fingers. "Let's hope this is the break we need."

Ella's son let them in and led them through the house to a sunroom where Ella sat with her leg propped up on a pillow. A thick white cast went up to her knee. "Sorry, I couldn't greet you myself. I'm not getting around too easily these days."

"We appreciate you seeing us," Jules said. "I know we didn't say much on the phone, but it's probably better we chatted in person."

"You told me enough." Ella gestured to the couch across from her. "Come in and sit down. I'll tell you everything."

CHAPTER THIRTY-FOUR

ELLA ADJUSTED the cushion behind her as if she was getting comfortable to tell her story. "I worked for Jerry for almost thirty years. He was driven, I'll give him that. Went into court and fought like a tiger for his clients. But when he wasn't working, he had such an underlying sadness about him."

"Were you working for him when his wife and son died?" Jules asked.

"I had just started for him when Donna was born." Ella gazed off with a wistful expression. "He was so happy. Pictures all over his office. Couldn't stop talking about her. He and Ava were a nice couple. No petty fights. He worked a lot of hours, but she understood that's what it took for him to become successful."

"We read about what happened," Becky said, her tone somber. "It was so sad."

"It was ..." Ella leaned her head back and took a moment. "Horrific. That's the only word to describe it. He second-guessed himself all the time. Had he made the right decisions? It changed him."

"Did he ever tell Donna what actually happened?" Jules

already knew the answer but was curious about what Ella knew.

She shook her head. "No. He thought she was too young at the time. As she got older, well, he just didn't want to think about it. He was afraid Donna would blame him for not doing more. Not telling her the truth."

Becky leaned forward. "And we saw he sued the hospital."

"He did. He knew he didn't really have a case. It wasn't anybody's fault—just a bad draw in the genetic deck of cards. The hospital settled for a modest amount. Mostly to make the case go away."

"Is that what made him want to go into Personal Injury law?"

Ella gave a slow nod. "He found his passion for helping people. He was never one of those firms you saw on the billboards—ambulance chasers. He took on big cases. He never agreed to represent anyone he felt wasn't doing it for the right reasons."

"He left behind a box of his files for Donna. He had some big wins," Jules said.

Ella dipped her head. "Yes, he did. The courtroom is where he got his greatest satisfaction. And he was rewarded for it."

Jules shifted slightly in her seat. "We had some questions about some things in his will."

"For the longest time, I used to have Jerry's will in my desk drawer. About four months ago, he told me to toss it. Said he was going to see Norman to change it." Ella scowled, and her concerned gaze bounced between Jules and Becky. "He didn't cut Donna out, did he?"

Jules was quick to reassure her. "No. But he did write a letter to her, and he—he put some stipulations on her inheritance."

Ella's forehead creased. "What kind of stipulations?"

Becky reached for her purse. She pulled out a copy of the letter and handed it to her.

Ella rooted around on the couch for her reading glasses. Reading silently, she flinched at one point until she finally laid the letter in her lap.

Shaking her head, she said, "I had no idea he'd done this. How is Donna handling it?"

"She's angry, as you can imagine," Becky said. "I guess you know he wasn't a very hands-on dad, and now he has another daughter she didn't even know about."

Ella squeezed her eyes shut for a moment. "He never came out of his depression about Ava and the baby. He was really no good to anyone except his clients. So many times, I tried to talk to him about it." Her face sagged as if she was disappointed she couldn't have done more when she had the chance. "Donna deserved better."

Becky exchanged a glance with Jules. "She said you were very kind to her. Invited her for holidays and dinners."

There was a faraway look in Ella's eyes. "How could I not?"

Jules cleared her throat softly. "In the letter, it says that Jerry asked you to stop putting through Molly's calls. Someone told us she moved to North Florida." Jules pinned her gaze on Ella. "You helped her." It was a statement, not a question.

"I did," Ella said firmly, in a way that told Jules she had no regrets about it.

"We've been looking but haven't been able to find Molly or Ally. Sounds like Molly got married and moved away. Do you have any idea where she went?" Jules held her breath as she waited on Ella's response.

"I do," Ella said slowly. "I wrote a check to Molly every month for years."

Jules and Becky wore matching expressions of surprise.

"You—you gave her money?" Jules asked.

"Jerry had no idea. I did all the bookkeeping. I set her up as an LLC, so he would never know."

Jules thought about the bag of checks they had found and the Post-it with the question mark on it. "M&A Enterprises?"

Ella wore a proud smile as if remembering how clever she'd been. "Right."

Jules rolled her eyes. How did they not figure that out?

Ella shifted on the couch to get more comfortable as she started to explain. "Molly did call Jerry at the office for a while. At first, I thought maybe she was chasing him because she wanted to date him. I didn't think much of it when he told me to stop putting her through."

"So, when did you find out who she was?" Becky asked.

"Molly brought Alexandra to see him when she was almost three years old."

"Alexandra?" Jules asked as she shot a look at Becky. No wonder they couldn't find her.

"Yes, that was her name, but Molly called her Ally. They came to the office. Molly must have waited until Jerry left to grab lunch. I heard them talking outside my window, and when I took a peek, I saw the little girl."

Ella closed her eyes for a moment as she went back in time. "She was the spitting image of Donna at that age. Her hair was blond, but she had the same mess of curls and those crystal blue eyes." She opened her eyes, but her expression changed. "I heard Jerry call Molly a liar, but I knew she was telling the truth. I watched him get in his car, and when he drove away, I ran out after her. I told her I would try to talk some sense into Jerry." Ella met Jules's curious stare and shrugged. "He did listen to me sometimes."

"Not this time?" Becky asked, even though they already knew the answer.

Ella gave a disappointed shake of her head. "Nope. Wouldn't even discuss it. As far as he was concerned, the subject matter was closed. I'll never forget his last words on the topic." Ella jabbed her index finger into the couch. "'That little girl deserves better than me.'"

Jules glanced at Becky to see if they were both thinking the same thing. Jerry didn't really abandon Ally. It was more like he tried to save her from having him as a dad.

Ella adjusted the pillow under her leg. "I called Molly. Told her that if we tested the little girl and she was Jerry's, I would support that child for him whether he liked it or not."

Jules wanted to laugh as it became quite clear who ran the show in that office.

"Jerry knocked a coffee mug off his desk one day and cut his finger picking up the pieces," Ella said. "I helped him clean it up and saved the tissues. We took them with the little girl and had them tested. Not that I had any doubt, but before I started giving away his money, I had to know for sure." Ella confirmed what they already suspected was true. "Ally was Jerry's daughter."

"Molly didn't mind you wanted her to do the test?" Becky asked.

"No. I think she was just happy someone believed her. We became friendly. She used to bring Alexandra to my church for Easter, Christmas. I invited them for holidays and family dinners. Molly knew they were always welcome at my house."

Jules cocked her head to the side. "Were these the same holidays Donna was at?"

Ella smiled as if she was pleased the connection had finally been made. "Yes, for a few years. Donna obviously didn't know they were sisters, but, oh, how she adored that little girl. Used to try to fix up her hair." Ella laughed. "I remember her saying, 'I have these terrible curls, too. I know just how to fix them for you.' When she finished, Alexandra's head was covered in bows and ribbons and barrettes. Alexandra loved the attention."

Becky shook her head in disbelief. "Wow. I can't believe Donna's met her. This could change everything. Obviously, she isn't exactly happy about sharing her inheritance. But maybe now—"

"You said it was only a few years," Jules cut in. "Did something happen to Molly and Ally?"

"Molly met a nice man who doted on Alexandra and he asked her to marry him. They lived nearby for a couple of years, and then his job moved them to Atlanta. I continued to send her check every month, but after a few years, she called me and said David—that was her husband's name—was doing well and wanted to adopt Ally. She wasn't comfortable taking Jerry's money anymore." Ella rubbed the back of her neck. "She used to send Christmas cards, but then I lost track of her."

"This David she married—what was her married name?" Jules asked.

"Yosco. She became Molly Yosco."

Jules's wheels were spinning. She'd be much easier to find now that they had her married name. It was an unusual last name, and they had an idea where she might live. This could be easy. "Ella, do you know how old Molly was when she had Ally?"

"She was just twenty-four when she met him, so I guess she was almost twenty-five when Ally was born. I was shocked when she told me that." Ella shook her head as if she could still feel the disappointment when she'd first found out. "I mean, what was Jerry thinking?"

"I still can't believe Ally and Donna knew each other," Jules said. "And Jerry never knew you befriended her?"

"Definitely not in the beginning. If Donna ever went home and mentioned it, I don't think he would have made the connection. Jerry only knew her as Ally. We always called her Alex or Alexandra at my house. Just in case."

"I love that you made a way for them to spend time together," Becky said. "It's funny that they bonded as sisters even though they never knew."

"I did what I did for those two little girls," Ella said firmly. "I made my peace with Jerry. He threw himself into work so he wouldn't have time to think about the past. Winning was the only redemption he had. When he lost his last case, it almost broke him." Ella stared off, lost in thought for a moment. "He had promised this family so much, and then he couldn't deliver. It crushed him. He really cared about the family, and he knew they'd been counting on him."

Jules crossed her legs and leaned back on the couch as she considered this. The way Ella told it, Jerry seemed to have cared about his clients more than his own daughter.

"Was that when he found out about the cancer?" Becky asked.

"It was actually the second time. They'd found lung cancer about three or four years ago. He'd beaten that." Ella let out a deep breath. "This time it was in his pancreas. Jerry knew when he took the case—he just didn't want to admit he couldn't handle it. When they lost, he knew he had no choice. He officially retired after that, and essentially, so did I. But before we parted ways, we had a long talk about the way he had lived his life."

"You mean Donna and Ally?" Becky asked.

Ella slowly nodded as if remembering their conversation. "For years, I had a copy of that test Molly and I had done. It was in my desk drawer, but when I packed up everything, it was gone. I have no idea if he saw it, but—" She shrugged knowingly. "It couldn't have just disappeared."

Maybe this explained why Jerry was so sure about Ally being his. Jules tilted her head as she asked, "So, you think he knew?"

"I do," Ella said with a nod. "He expressed deep regret

about both Donna and the daughter he never acknowledged. A few months later, he was gone. But obviously not before he changed his will."

"Even then, you never told him you befriended Molly and supported them all those years?" Becky asked.

Ella shook her head. "He already had enough guilt about it. His daughter didn't need to meet him for the first time when he was dying. Besides, I don't even know where she is anymore."

Jules glanced over and watched Becky's shoulders sag. This wasn't the slam dunk they hoped for, but they had enough. They could find her. "Maybe your conversation *is* what spurred the change in his will. Donna also thinks there was a life insurance policy, but she isn't named in it. Do you have any idea who the beneficiary was?"

Ella ran her fingers through her hair. "The policy showed up in the mail about a week before he passed. A letter, too, same as Donna. Jerry said he wanted to make sure I would be able to retire comfortably. He actually thanked me," she said softly.

Ella hesitated and shifted on the couch. "He told me he had taken care of Donna in his will." She rubbed her finger against her lips thoughtfully. "Maybe he did it this way so I wouldn't see how he changed it." She placed her palm on her chest. "It was me. I was the sole beneficiary."

CHAPTER THIRTY-FIVE

As MUCH AS she wanted to stay and figure out where Molly was now, Becky knew she had to honor the commitment she'd made. Molly and Ally would have to wait. She just hoped she could convince Jules.

After they got out of the car in the office parking lot, she turned to Jules. "Can we wait on doing anything on this until tomorrow?"

Jules flinched in surprise. "You're kidding, right?"

Becky felt an odd sense of guilt. She hated keeping things from Jules, but she had no choice on this one. "No. I have—I have an appointment I have to go to."

"Another one?"

As soon as the words were out, Jules looked like she regretted them. All these mysterious appointments had to be making her wonder what was going on.

Jules then nodded with a small smile. "Sure, no problem. I'll hold off, and we can work on it tomorrow when we come in."

"Thanks, I appreciate it." Becky hurried up the stairs to the office to pack up her laptop as she was already late.

Jules packed up hers as well. "I guess if you're leaving, I'll go home, too. Maybe Tim can have dinner tonight."

"Um, that sounds great." Becky gave her one last look and hoped her plans weren't written all over her face. "Okay, I gotta run." She scampered down the stairs and out to her car.

After she slid into the driver's seat, she called Bryan. "Hey, babe, we're back from Ella's house. Everything's fine. I'm heading to you now."

"We'll be late. Weren't we supposed to be the first ones there?"

Becky put the car in reverse. "Don't worry. It'll all be fine."

She pulled out of the parking lot and gave her rearview mirror a quick peek. The last thing she needed was someone tailing her. She'd feel better once Bryan was with her.

As she squealed into his parking lot, he was waiting out front. "Easy, NASCAR driver," he called out when she rolled down her window. "You want to drive, or you want me to?"

"You drive," Becky said. "I'll pull in next to you."

He approached her car just as she popped the trunk and gestured inside. "All the stuff is in that box. Can you transfer it to your car?"

"The cooler, too?" he asked.

"Oh, yeah, bring the cooler. We need to stop and get ice." She caught the look he gave her. "Did I know we'd have the chance to go see Jerry's secretary today of all days?" Becky asked defensively as she glanced at the time on her phone. "It should only take about twenty minutes to get there."

Bryan rolled his eyes as he dropped the cooler in his trunk and shut it.

"Okay, twenty-five since we need to get ice," she said as they got in the car.

"And gas," he added.

"Are you kidding? You should have let me drive." Breathe,

Becky told herself. This would all work out the way they planned.

"So, did the secretary give you anything useful? Did she tell you where Molly is?" Bryan asked as he started up the car.

"She actually hasn't talked to her in a long time, but she told us her married name and where she moved to when she left Florida. But get this, she supported Molly and Ally for years with Jerry's money."

Bryan glanced over. "He never knew?"

Becky shook her head. "She doesn't think so, and if he did, he never said a word or admitted he knew. But not only did she support them with his money, she befriended them. Invited them over for dinners and holidays."

"She sounds like a nice woman."

"It's more than that, Bryan. She was a nice woman because she *also* took care of Donna when her father was too preoccupied to be a good dad. She invited *Donna* for dinners and holidays, too."

It took him a moment to make the connection. "Wait—so did Donna know her sister?"

"She did," Becky said with a grin. "Ella said Donna loved playing mom to the little girl. Can you imagine? The whole time that was her half-sister, and she never knew."

"You said Donna was bitter about having to find her. Maybe this will be a good thing for her."

"I'm really hoping. Money changes the way people look at things, but maybe she'll decide having a sister is worth giving up some of the money." Becky reached out to him, and he took one hand off the steering wheel to hold hers. "I really hope tonight goes off without any problems."

Thirty minutes later, they pulled into the designated spot.

"There," Becky pointed off into the distance. "I think that's where we need to go." She grabbed her phone and made a call. "Yup, this is it," she confirmed after hanging up. "Let's grab the stuff from the trunk. We should be able to bring all our stuff in one trip. Let's just hope everything else is here."

They made their way down to the group. "I know, I know, we're late. It's my fault." She glanced around and covered her mouth with her hand. "This is exactly how I pictured it." She turned to Bryan. "Can you handle the rest of the stuff? I need to call Jules."

He nodded. "Go ahead."

Becky walked away and dialed Jules's number.

"Hey." Jules's voice registered surprise. "Are you done with your appointment?"

"I had to make a stop." Becky paused for a moment. "Jules, I found Ally."

"What? Where? You said we were going to work on this tomorrow," she said in an accusatory tone.

Becky hoped Jules wasn't angry. "You need to come meet me. Bryan insisted on coming with me. He didn't think it was safe for us to meet her by ourselves. Get Tim to bring you."

Jules let out a puff of frustrated air. "Tim went to play basketball with some buddies. I can come by myself."

"Jules, no. Don't take a chance. What about Jonas? Call him. Maybe he can come with you. Then he can make sure you're not followed."

"I'll call him, but if he's not around, I'm coming by myself." Jules's voice was firm.

Becky didn't argue. She knew Jonas was waiting on Jules's call.

"Don't leave from where you are. I can't believe you found Ally. When I get there, I plan to give you hell for finding her without me." Becky winced but knew Jules's aggravation would only be temporary. "Tell me exactly where you are."

Becky recited an address in the area but didn't give her specifics. Jonas knew where they would be. When she hung up with Jules, Becky texted him. *Get ready. She's calling you.*

As she walked back down to Bryan, Becky wished she had thought to bring a change of clothes. The day had been crazy, and it was about to get even crazier.

Becky nodded as she approached the group. "She should be on her way shortly."

CHAPTER THIRTY-SIX

WHILE SHE WAITED for Jonas to get there, Jules changed into a pair of jeans and grabbed a light sweater. It was October, after all, and it could be breezy. Her mind was swirling. How could Becky have found Ally in the short time since she left? She told Jules she had an appointment, and now she and Bryan were both with Ally? Had she just diverted from the IVF appointment?

Jules's phone buzzed with a text from Jonas. *Pulling in now.* She shuffled down the narrow staircase to the main floor and grabbed her purse off the back of the kitchen chair.

"Hey," Jules said as she slid into his passenger seat. "I have no idea what Becky did tonight to find Ally, but thanks for taking me. She's got Bryan with her and was adamant I needed someone to come with me. Tim was already at the rec center playing basketball."

Jonas waved dismissively and pulled out of Jules's guest spot. "I agree with Becky. With all the stuff that's gone on, I feel better going with you."

After a glance around the parking lot, Jules's shoulders

relaxed. Not a silver car in sight. "Any new updates on Robert's case?" she asked.

Jonas shook his head. "Nothing anyone will tell me. I keep looking for the probable cause affidavit, but they haven't filed it. It hasn't been ten days yet."

"What do you think's going to happen?"

"Depends on what they found. If they found something that linked Jay to the crime, they're probably getting ready to arrest him. If nothing panned out, then they'll probably move on to someone else."

Jules was silent for a moment as she mulled over the possibility that there could be an arrest. The panic she felt at being followed, the worry every time they left the office—could Jay have been behind it? Doubt had also started to creep in about Donna.

"What do you think?" Jonas asked. "Do you think he could have done it?"

Jules shrugged. "I can't really say. I've never even met him. I do agree there's motive, but in all fairness, the same could be true for Donna. Maybe even more so. For all we know, they could be in it together."

"That's an interesting theory."

"Maybe she hired us just so we could lead her and Jay to Ally and Robert." Jules let out a sigh, in it all the confusion she felt trying to figure out what was really going on. "Or maybe she didn't know anything, and Jay has a plan to get rid of her after they're married and she has the money."

"If they figure out he killed Robert, he won't get the chance to marry or kill Donna," Jonas said. "He'll be in prison for a very long time."

They drove quietly for a few minutes. This whole case had her brain going in circles.

Finally, Jonas broke the silence. "You never told me. How was your lunch with Mom?"

The corners of Jules's mouth turned up, grateful for the change of topic. "It was wonderful. I thought it might be awkward, but it felt so comfortable. We have a lot in common."

"Including your looks. Did it shock you how much Mom looks like you?"

Jules's eyes widened. "I'd seen pictures, but in person, I couldn't believe it." She paused and pressed her lips together. "She also gave me my birth father's name."

Jonas's head turned swiftly in her direction. "Really? She didn't tell me that."

"Yeah, she said it was time for me to make my own decision about what I wanted to do with it. Looks like I have a few more half-siblings."

"Hey, now," Jonas said dramatically. "Don't go replacing me."

Jules reached for his arm to reassure him. "Never. I can't believe six months ago I didn't even know you existed. It's crazy, right?"

"A good crazy, although you and Becky and this case are making me a little nutty. But I'm glad you and Mom are good." He glanced over. "If you decide to find your birth father, you know I'll be right there to support you."

Jules shrugged. "I'm not sure I'm ready. My parents … I just wish they'd be happy for me. I would love to introduce them to Barb. I want them all in my life. Is that too much to ask?"

Jonas reached over and put his hand over hers. "It'll happen. Probably sooner than you expect." He glanced over at the GPS. "Okay, I think this is it. We're here."

Jules's forehead wrinkled in confusion as she looked around. "Here? You're sure? There's not even a restaurant or anything."

Jonas pointed up ahead. "Isn't that Bryan's car?" He pulled

into the spot next to it. "They have to be here somewhere. I'll shoot him a text."

He typed into his phone and hit send. His phone beeped with a response, and Jonas nodded. "Yup. We're in the right place. Follow me."

Jules sidled up next to him. "Seriously? We're afraid someone's stalking us, so let's meet the person we need most on a dark road. I find it hard to believe there wasn't a better option."

She wrapped her hand around Jonas's arm, and he led her behind the empty building onto a darkened path. Trees lined both sides, the moon helping eerie shadows splash against the walkway. She tipped her head up, and the smell of smoke was in the air, so faint she thought maybe she imagined it.

Something rustled in the trees, and she gripped Jonas's arm tighter. As they walked, the hush in the air gave way to the sound of waves crashing. Jules glanced back toward the road they had just left. "Are you *sure* this is where we're supposed to be going? This feels like it leads to the beach."

"You worry too much." Jonas glanced over and studied her concerned face. "I'm a cop. Don't you think I can protect you?"

"Of course, I do. It's just—"

The walkway dropped them at the sand, a sliver of the moon lighting up the beach and shimmering off the water. Jules caught her breath. A small bonfire glowed against the darkened sky, tiny sparks floating like fireflies into the night air. Hundreds of little white lights had been strung between poles stuck in the sand to create an area around the fire. There were a few small tables, tiki torches stuck into the sand.

Jonas lifted her hand off his arm and gave her a gentle push. She swung around, but he had retreated, expecting her to walk on without him.

Wary of what she was walking into, Jules squinted into the darkness, but there was no sign of Becky or Ally. Or anyone for that matter. Maybe they were making sure she and Jonas hadn't been followed. But why the elaborate setup?

She cautiously walked forward, her breathing slow and shallow in nervous anticipation. Waiting for something or someone to tell her what was going on.

Then, out of nowhere, he appeared, barefoot and strolling toward her, a satisfied smile filling his face. Jules bit her bottom lip, and in that instant, her eyes welled up. This had nothing to do with Ally. Becky had gone out of her way to ensure Jules didn't suspect the real reason for her nighttime visit to the beach.

Tim approached her and leaned over, his lips brushing against hers in a soft kiss that made her stomach tingle as if it was filled with tiny butterflies.

"Hi, honey." He offered his arm for her to hold.

Jules glanced down and, without a care, she kicked her expensive sandals off into the sand. Arm in arm, they walked down the beach toward the bonfire. As they got closer, what had been darkness when she arrived, grew clearer.

Faces shrouded in the shadows came forward to be illuminated by the glow of all those white lights. As her gaze flitted around, the lump in her throat grew. Not only were her parents there, but Jonas had made his way to the group, and he and his fiancée Erin now stood beside Barb. Becky and Bryan held hands, her best friend looking like she could break out in happy tears at any moment. Tim's parents looked on, pride etched on their faces. Even Gene was in attendance, a plaid bowtie attached to his collar. Tim's father had a firm grip on his leash, so he couldn't bound up to her and ruin the moment. This was what fairytales were made of.

Tears dripped from her eyes, warm at first, and then cool as the night air blew against them on her cheeks. She didn't care. There was no way she'd let go of Tim to wipe them away. Seeing everyone together was a moment that would be seared in her memory forever.

Tim led her to a spot surrounded by tiki torches. The outline of a large heart had been made in the sand using red stones that seemed to glow. He led her to stand inside. With the waves crashing in the background, he got down in front of her on bended knee.

He took her hands in his. "Jules, I knew from the moment I met you that you were my forever. I know the road to get here wasn't without a bump or two, but what matters is that we found our way back to each other. When I saw you through that window at Riley's, I thought I was imagining it. My eyes seeing what my heart wanted. I love you, and I don't ever want to be without you."

His eyes sparkled with mischief. "Gene and I both need you, right, buddy?" Tim turned and gave a quick clap of his hands. Gene barked on cue. "Can you believe I taught him that?" Tim whispered.

Jules laughed, and her eyes welled up again as new happy tears threatened to fall. She felt like the luckiest girl in the world.

Tim let go of her hands and reached into his jacket pocket to withdraw a small black velvet box. His eyes were loving and wet as he anchored his gaze on her. "You're my dream come true, my soulmate, my best friend." He opened the box and removed the ring. "Jules, will you marry me?"

Her hand flew up to cover her mouth. The ring his fingers were wrapped around sparkled brilliantly under the golden glow of the tiki torches. Jules had dreamed of this moment, never daring to let herself believe it could really happen.

"Yes, absolutely, yes!"

Tim slipped the ring on her finger and stood up. "Good

thing you said yes. I'm not sure how much longer I could have knelt down there." He spoke softly into her ear while she wrapped her arms around him.

There was a time she thought she'd never get her happy ever after. Just the thought of trusting someone with her heart had filled her with anxiety. But now, as Jules looked into the eyes of the man who would be her husband, she knew she had changed. She believed in him and the life they could have together.

"Do you have any idea how much I love you?" she asked before he leaned down and kissed her.

There was applause, and Gene barked as if the group had given him his cue.

"See, Gene's happy, too," Tim said. He kissed Jules again and took her hand. "Hungry? We have lots of food."

People scurried, and food and drinks appeared. A cooler with champagne. A couple of small grills. Sticks and marsh-mallows. Jules shook her head as she took it all in.

"I can't believe you pulled this off."

"You have your best friend to thank for most of this. Go talk to her, and I'll help Bryan get the grills ready."

"Hmm," Jules muttered as Becky poured champagne into a glass. "You found Ally, huh?"

Becky cringed. "I know. I'm sorry I had to lie. It was my job to get you here any way I could." She lifted Jules's left hand. "I knew once you saw that ring, you'd forgive pretty much anything."

Jules held out her hand to admire it. "It's so beautiful. I'm shocked Tim managed to pick out exactly what I wanted." Her lips formed a knowing smile. "I feel like he might have had some help."

Becky handed Jules a glass of champagne. "I'll never tell."

Jules took a sip and leaned in toward Becky. "I can't believe my parents *and* Barb and Jonas are here. All together in one place. Did you make that happen?"

Becky glanced in their direction. "That I might have done. Your parents love you. I think they just needed to hear from someone else how important this is to you."

Jules pulled Becky into a hug and tried not to spill her champagne. "You're probably the one person who knows just *how* important. Tim knows a little, but you've always understood."

"I'll tell you more about it tomorrow, but before you got here, they were chatting. I even saw your mom laugh at something Barb said." Becky poured another glass of champagne and held it out. "Here, take one for Tim. Go mingle."

Jules came up behind Tim, who was helping Bryan with one of the grills. "I brought you some bubbly."

He reached for the champagne and clinked his glass against hers before giving her a kiss. "I think you should go talk to your parents. You have Becky to thank for the audience here tonight."

Jules sipped her champagne and nodded. "I know. She told me. Aside from this gorgeous ring and my amazing husband-to-be, nothing could have made me happier." She kissed Tim again and then made her way to where her parents stood.

She hugged her mom tightly. "I can't even tell how much it means to me that you're here. That everyone's here."

"Jules, we just love you so much," her father said, and Jules knew Becky had made them understand just how important them meeting her birth mother was to her.

Her mom nodded. "We spent a good deal of time chatting with Barb while we were waiting for you. She's really quite lovely."

Jules worked to keep her expression neutral, but her heart swelled with joy. "And did you meet Jonas?"

"Not yet."

Jules called over to Jonas, and he and his fiancée trudged through the sand.

"Welcome to the club," Erin said with a congratulatory hug. "I'll be happy to pass along all my wedding planning information. Only forty-two days."

"I can't wait," Jules said with a genuine smile. "Now I won't even have to mortify Tim by diving for the bouquet."

Jules made introductions to her parents, and as they all chatted, her gaze wandered to take in all the people she loved. She dreamed for so long about what it would feel like when it was her turn. She didn't want this night to end.

Tim's dad let Gene loose, and the dog seized his chance to greet Jules. She leaned over. "Hey, buddy. We're getting married, did you know that?"

Becky came up behind her. "Your dad and Jonas are really hitting it off," she said, her voice low so only Jules could hear.

"Can you believe it? Next thing you know, they'll be golfing together." Jules pulled Becky into an embrace, hoping it would convey the heartfelt appreciation she intended. "I know you put so much into this night. It's been … magical. I can't even put into words what it felt like to see both my parents and Barb here." She pulled back and chuckled. "Imagine that, me speechless."

"You deserve it all. I'm so happy——" Becky was interrupted by muffled ringing. "Uh, your purse is calling."

"Who could be calling?" Jules asked as she reached for her phone. "It's late, and everyone I love is here." Just as she pulled it out, the ringing stopped. She shrugged it off. "Oh, well."

This was her night. Anything else could wait. The phone then beeped in her hand with a text message.

"Somebody is really trying to track you down," Becky said.

Jules rolled her eyes, but as she scanned the message, she stiffened. Maybe the doubt she'd felt was warranted.

"Who's it from?"

Jules dropped the phone back into her purse and closed her eyes for a moment. "It was Donna."

She massaged her temple and then met Becky's questioning gaze.

"She and Jay are at the police station. She thinks they're both about to be arrested for Robert's murder."

CHAPTER THIRTY-SEVEN

Donna shifted in her seat, an unforgiving metal chair with only a thin layer of padding. No doubt it was worn that way by the parade of criminals that sat there before her. Or maybe they just didn't want her to be comfortable. That was probably the point.

They'd left her alone in this dank, windowless room. She knew from the TV shows she watched they were probably somehow studying her right now. She wouldn't sing, or do handstands, or cry—nothing to see here.

While she hoped her bravado shined through, her insides quivered. They had her here about a *murder*. They'd separated her and Jay as if they thought one of them might turn on the other.

The door opened, and a man entered. Donna couldn't help but notice the gun jutting from underneath his jacket as he took a seat around the small table.

He extended his hand. "Sorry you had to wait. I'm Detective Feeley. I appreciate you coming in so we could ask you some questions about a case we're investigating. I'm just going to read you your rights before we get started."

Donna felt her pulse quicken. "Am I under arrest?"

The detective shook his head and smiled. "No, nothing like that. It's a formality mostly that you are okay with talking to us. That you understand you are free to leave at any time if you didn't want to answer questions."

"Oh."

As he read her rights, Donna pressed her lips together. It sounded like she could refuse to talk to them. But wouldn't that make her look guilty?

"Do you understand these rights?"

Donna hesitated and then nodded. "Yes."

"And you're willing to talk to us?"

What choice did she have? They'd obviously found something during the search of the apartment.

"Yes," she said again. She'd say as little as possible until she found out what evidence they thought they had.

"Okay, so we have a few questions about your father's will. Was someone named Robert Taylor listed as a beneficiary?"

"Yes." Donna realized they still thought the murder and her father's estate were connected.

The detective leaned back in his chair as if this was just a casual conversation. "And did you know him or know why your father had left part of his estate to him?"

Donna shook her head. "I didn't know who he was, and I had no idea why my father listed him as a beneficiary. I've never even heard his name mentioned before."

"Did you hire a detective agency—" The detective leaned forward to consult his notes. "Did you hire Investigation Duo to locate him for you?"

"Not exactly." Maybe Jay was right. Had Becky and Jules set them up for some reason?

"Okay." He nodded. "Tell me about that."

"I hired them to find my half-sister. I didn't even know I had one, but my dad left her part of his estate." Donna rolled her eyes. "He stipulated I have to find her before my share of the money is released. *That's* why I hired the detectives. I just happened to mention that I would also like to know who Robert Taylor is. He was named in the will, but I have no idea who he is or why my father left him so much money."

"Okay." The detective made a note. "But you didn't *have* to find Robert to get your portion?"

"No. He was merely a curiosity."

"A curiosity. Okay. And have you found your sister yet?"

Donna corrected him. "*Half*-sister. No, not yet."

Detective Feeley opened the folder that sat in front of him. "I have a copy of your father's will here."

Donna flinched. She couldn't help it.

"Once a will is filed with the probate court, it's public record," Detective Feeley said. "Anyone can access it. Did you know that?"

Donna shook her head. "No, not really." Maybe Becky and Jules didn't have anything to do with this, after all.

"So, if I'm reading this correctly—" The detective pulled a pair of reading glasses from his jacket pocket and flipped through the pages. "If something were to happen to your half-sister before she got her money, her share would be split between you and Robert Taylor." He took off his glasses and laid them on the table. "Is that right?"

Donna shrugged casually. "If that's what it says, then yeah, I guess so. But we haven't even found her yet. I'm sure she's alive and kicking."

"Perhaps she is." The detective leaned back in his chair and clasped his hands behind his head. "So, what if something happened to both your half-sister *and* Mr. Taylor?"

Donna's forehead wrinkled. "What do you mean?"

"I mean, you get your sister's portion—"

"Half-sister."

"Okay, your half-sister's portion. If something happens to her, you'd split her portion with this guy Robert—"

"We already covered that." Donna crossed her legs and flicked her foot impatiently.

He nodded. "Right. We did cover that. But what if something happens to her *and* Robert Taylor? Where would that leave you?"

"Robert would already have his money. It would go to his family," Donna said matter-of-factly.

"Right. But what about your sister's share?" Detective Feely pinned an expectant gaze on her. "If your sister couldn't claim it, and Robert was deceased? Then what?"

Donna shrugged, her palms dampening. "I'm not sure it covers that."

"Oh, but it does." He sat up straight, flipped through the pages, and pushed the will across the small table toward her. "The highlighted section."

Donna's eyes scanned the yellow, highlighted words. She swallowed hard. "I didn't even know this was in here. My half-sister is younger than me. I'm sure she's not deceased."

"Not yet," Detective Feeley muttered.

Donna heard his comment but chose to ignore it. No one knew at this point whether her sister was alive or not. Not even her.

"So, are you saying the man killed was definitely the Robert Taylor in the will?" she asked.

He shook his head. "I'm not saying that at all, but we believe someone *thought* he was."

"And you're saying you think it was Jay?"

"He's definitely one option. Seems your sister's in for a pretty nice chunk of change." His attention was laser-focused on her. "People have killed for much less. If you got her portion as well as your own, you'd have two-thirds of your father's money." He cocked his head to the side, but his gaze on her didn't drift. He barely blinked. "I'm sure you thought you were entitled to *all* his money."

Donna felt her face grow hot. "I knew—I mean, yes, I thought—we didn't have any other family to leave it to. That I knew of anyway." A realization struck her, and her mouth dropped open. "Wait a minute, you think it was me? I had motive because of the will? And the money?"

The detective shrugged, but it was clear he thought her disbelief was an act. "It's possible. Your husband-to-be might have an interest in helping you get that money, so you could both share in your newly found wealth." With his elbow on the table, he rested his chin in his hand. "Let me ask you something. Do *you* have a will, Donna?"

She narrowed her eyes as she glared at him. "No, I don't. I've never had anything worth leaving to anyone. At this point, I still don't."

He leaned back and crossed his arms against his chest. "How's your relationship with Jay, Donna? Any problems?"

Her face grew hot. "Who doesn't have problems? He hates my ex-husband. Has a brother back in his life that's a pain in my ass." Donna jutted out her chin and gave the detective a hard stare. "But Jay was there for me when I was trying to rebuild my life after I got divorced. When my father's health took a turn for the worse, he wanted me to know I would always be taken care of." She pointed at the ring on her finger. "He proposed, and we're getting married. We *love* each other."

The detective nodded, and Donna could have sworn the corners of his mouth turned up slightly, almost as if he thought her naïve to believe in Jay. "Let me give you a little information about the order of probate. If you die without a will, your assets are distributed in the following order." He demonstrated using the sides of his hands in the air. "Spouse, child, parent, sibling. So, even without a will, your husband would inherit everything you have if something happened to you. Are you still sure you want to marry him?"

Donna caught her breath but tried to rebound. Her mind was reeling. Did Jay realize what the detective had just told her?

"So, you're saying ..." Donna folded her arms on the table and leaned in. "You think Jay is plotting to kill, or has already found and killed, my half-sister. And he also murdered this guy Robert because he thought he had the right person. All because he wants me to inherit as much money as possible so he can then marry me, kill me, and keep it all for himself?"

Detective Feeley stared her straight in the eye without blinking. "Like I said, I've seen people kill for much less."

Exasperated, Donna threw up her hands. "Do you have proof of any of this?"

The detective opened the folder he had on the desk, sifted through the contents, and then placed a photo of Jay's sneaker in front of her. There was an arrow on the photo pointing toward a small red splotch that had been circled.

"Looks like blood to me," he said with a knowing stare at Donna. "We're testing that right now to see if it might belong to Robert Taylor."

She pressed her lips together but said nothing.

The detective flipped to another photo. It was the envelope Jay had mentioned the first time they questioned him. The picture showed the front with Jay's name and address and the return address from Florida Unemployment. Beside the first photo, the detective placed a second picture—an image of the back of the envelope. An address had been scrawled on the back. Part of it was now partially covered in what appeared to be a smear of blood, but it was clear the photographs were of both sides of the same envelope.

"Do you recognize the handwriting?" he asked.

Donna stared at the eight-by-ten photo. It did look familiar, but it could have been written by anyone. There didn't seem to be anything particularly distinctive about the writing that she could see. It was mostly numbers. 1101 N 40 St/305. It was the address of her dad's office building. She assumed Robert Taylor was in suite 305.

She shrugged. "I'm not sure. I mean, it's not like Jay leaves me notes all the time. He's not exactly an old-school romantic. Most times, it's a text message to bring home beer."

The detective nodded. "Right, I can see that. I don't write letters to my wife either." He pulled out a copy of the letter from Florida Unemployment and slid it toward her. "Did you know Jay's unemployment benefits were about to end?"

"I did, but he's going back to work. He does construction. They called him about a huge job—a new office complex. They just finished clearing the land, so any day now—"

"So, you've seen this letter?" the detective cut her off.

It had been taken from the apartment, so it didn't seem to matter if she admitted she had seen it. "Yeah, I have," she said matter-of-factly.

He pointed to the top of the page. "And it's dated October second. You agree?"

It was written in black and white. Of course, she agreed. She let out a sigh that said his question was ridiculous. "Yes, it's pretty clearly typed at the top of the page."

Detective Feeley put the paper aside and picked up the photo of the front of the envelope. He handed it to her. "Can you see the postmark on the envelope?"

She squinted and bit the inside of her cheek to keep from groaning out loud. It was clear where this was going. "I can see it."

"Okay, so you can see it was mailed October third, right?"
She glared at him. "Yes."

"Okay, so good chance that letter," the detective gestured at the letter on the desk, "was in this envelope." He tapped the photo with two fingers.

"I guess." Donna cleared her throat. She could feel the walls caving in around her, and she didn't know how to stop it.

Detective Feeley pulled out another large photo and placed it in front of her. "These are the T-shirts we took from your apartment. Would you be able to confirm these are Jay's? He worked for All-Star Construction, right?"

Donna took a deep breath. Clearly, they were Jay's. They'd been taken from their apartment. "He did. He's about to go back to work for them again soon."

The detective nodded. "Right, the new office complex. Okay." He pulled out another picture and placed it on top of the first. "So, an All-Star Construction baseball hat? That would be his, too?"

"Yeah, they had a softball league. Jay played." She shrugged. "He was mostly just in it for the beer after the games." This still didn't prove anything.

"We have some guys here like that, too." He produced another picture. "This is the T-shirt we found with the murder weapon."

Donna leaned in. She bit her bottom lip as she studied the picture. It was the same T-shirt as the others they had taken, but this one was covered in what appeared to be blood. She brought her gaze back up, determined to not show how rattled she was. "I get that it looks like the same shirt, but do you know how many guys work for them?"

"I actually do have that number somewhere in my folder. But for now, let's just talk about what came from your apartment." The detective rustled some papers in his folder and pulled out a picture of their knife set with the wooden block.

He placed it in the middle of the table and pointed at the picture with his index finger. "This is the knife set we took from your apartment. Notice the big knife at the top is missing. We searched your entire kitchen, all the silverware drawers, the dishwasher, everywhere, and there was no sign of it." He pulled out a second picture and placed it beside the first.

Donna flinched. A bloody knife rested against a white piece of cloth, making the blood look to be an even deeper, darker red in contrast. She said nothing, but her mind was racing.

He nodded as if he knew her silence meant he was making progress. "This is the murder weapon. Perfect match, right?"

She threw up her hands. "I got that knife set at Walmart. C'mon, you know how many of those they must sell? I have no idea what happened to the missing knife. Jay probably used it to cut down weeds or flowers or something outside. He never puts stuff back where it belongs. Anything's possible. Just because we have the same set doesn't mean this particular knife is ours."

He nodded as if he already considered the same possibility. "You're right. It is a very common knife set. But here's the part that doesn't seem like just a coincidence." He pulled the photo of the bloody T-shirt and placed it next to the photograph of the bloody knife. "It was found wrapped in this T-shirt. The same T-shirt we've already established is for the company Jay worked for and is going back to. We know he had other All-Star Construction T-shirts, *exactly* like this one, and the baseball hat for the same company, in the apartment you both share."

Donna didn't want to admit it, but he was getting to her. Could Jay really have been planning to kill her to get her money?

"So, you're saying all this has to mean Jay killed this man. There's no other explanation?"

He tilted his head to the side. "Not necessarily."

Donna let out a breath, relieved they had considered another suspect. Her shoulders relaxed slightly. "Okay, so you admit—"

He didn't let her finish. The detective pinned her with a

determined stare. Gone was the friendly man who had greeted her when she first got there. "We know the envelope from unemployment, found near the murder scene, is from your apartment. The T-shirt and knife found together in the trash can outside the murder scene? Again, they match items in your household. The knife came from your apartment because it has Jay's fingerprints on it. He also can't seem to get anyone to provide him an alibi for the time of the murder."

"So that's it? He did it? I thought you said there could be another answer?"

"That's right, I did." The detective gathered the photographs spread out on the table, put them back into the folder, and then glanced up at her. "We did find another person's fingerprints on the knife."

The detective placed his palms on the small table. He pushed himself out of his seat and leaned over until his face was about a foot from hers. Donna could see his nostrils flare as he gave her a hard stare through eyes narrowed into slits.

"The other fingerprints on the murder weapon? Those belonged to you, Donna."

CHAPTER THIRTY-EIGHT

"Stop, you're blinding me with that rock." Becky giggled and held her hand up to cover her eyes.

Jules sat on the edge of Becky's desk. She waved her left hand while she beamed. "It is a rock, isn't it? A ridiculously beautiful rock that says the most perfect man in the world wants me to be his forever."

Becky had never seen her best friend so happy. "Imagine a year ago, it wouldn't have mattered how gorgeous the ring was. You would have still taken off in the other direction running."

Jules's expression turned serious as she acknowledged Becky's comment. "You're right. I was terrified to want this, and then have it all fall apart. I tried to explain it to Tim. You know, I had—still have—some abandonment issues. But it's helped a lot to find Barb and know she didn't really want to give me up. Tim's been so patient with me." Her smile was back and seemed to radiate from her heart to her lips. "That's how I know he's my Mr. Right."

"And now we get to plan a wedding," Becky said with a grin.

"We *so* get to plan a wedding." Jules held out her hand to

admire her ring again. "The biggest thing I was worried about was my parents and Barb. Whatever you said to get them all there last night—"

"They all love you," Becky said firmly. "And if the way they were last night is any indication, this will all be fine."

"They *did* seem to be getting along. My mother called Barb *lovely*." Jules emphasized the word in disbelief. "It really was an incredible night. Thank you so much for everything you did."

"It was my pleasure." Becky smiled, and then a deep crease formed between her brows as she remembered the message from Donna. "What do we do about that text?"

Jules hopped down off the desk. "Now that we have Molly's married name, Ally should be a cinch to find. We could have this wrapped up today, but if Donna's in jail—"

"Do you really think she could have had something to do with it?" Becky asked as she unzipped her cooler bag and pulled out a yogurt.

"If they both got arrested, then the police must think they're in it together." Jules peered at Becky's breakfast. "Got anything in there for me?"

Becky shot her a look. "You mean in my new replacement lunch cooler?" She opened it up and pulled out a protein bar. "You want this?"

"Yes, please." Jules reached for the bar. "I'm starving."

"I really hope Donna's not involved," Becky said as she stuck a spoon in her yogurt cup. "I know she hasn't always been the greatest client, but I felt like I was just starting to understand her."

Jules pulled back the wrapper on her bar and took a bite. "Well, let's see what we can find out today about Ally. We'll hold off telling her anything until we know for sure Donna's not involved. I wonder if she can still collect her inheritance if she's in jail."

Becky considered it and shrugged. "Not sure. It seems her father thought of every scenario but that one."

Jules sat behind her desk and opened her laptop. "Okay, come sit here so we can look together."

Becky rolled her chair next to Jules as she started typing. "So, Ella said Molly's married name was Yosco, right? Her husband's name was—"

"David," Becky said. "David Yosco. Do you think the last name has an E on the end or just ends in O?"

"I'll check both. Should I look in Atlanta first?"

"I would since that's the last place Ella knew she lived."

Jules twirled a long strand of hair around her finger as she stared at the screen. "I'm not seeing anything with the name spelled with an E at the end. Let me try the other spelling."

Becky rested her elbows on the desk while she watched Jules type. The anxiety of being this close to finding Ally was palpable.

"Oh, I think I have something," Jules said as she pulled up another screen. This has to be her. Molly Yosco. Age forty-nine. Lives in Lithia Springs, GA. Known relatives ..." Jules clicked another button. "David Yosco, Alexandra Yosco, Michael Yosco. Michael's nineteen. Looks like Molly had a son, too." Jules glanced up and cocked her head to one side. "Ally's last name is Yosco, which goes with what Ella said about Molly's husband legally adopting her." Jules continued reading. "Other known relatives, Francis Middlebrooks and Bret Middlebrooks." She turned to face Becky. "Molly's mother and brother. We're in the right place."

"Click on Ally's name." Becky's pulse quickened. They were so close.

Jules clicked on Alexandra Yosco, and it brought her to Ally's information.

Becky pointed at the screen. "Look. Also known as

Alexandra White and Ally White. She must be married. She lives in Dunwoody, Georgia. Are there any phone numbers?"

Jules hit the back button. "A few we can try and some social media accounts. Let's see what she has on Instagram." When the screen opened back up, it was filled with tiny images.

Becky squinted. "Open her profile picture so I can see."

"I can't make it any bigger. Hang on." Jules clicked on another photo. "This must be her and her husband."

Becky's eyes widened. "Now I see what Ella meant. She still looks like a blond version of Donna."

"She really does." Jules sat back in her chair and tapped her finger against her lips. "I'm assuming you think we should call Ally directly. Not go through Molly."

"Of course. Why wouldn't we?"

Jules gazed off for a moment as she seemed to be considering something. "I'm just wondering what Molly told Ally about her dad. Maybe she thinks this guy David is her biological father. She does have his last name." Jules scrunched up her face. "We'd be bursting that bubble pretty abruptly."

Becky let out a deep breath. "I see what you're saying. But at this point, I think our priority is to do what Donna hired us for. To find Ally."

Jules dipped her head in agreement. "Right. And we can still do that through Molly. I'm just thinking about Lucy. It pretty much shook her to her core to find out her dad wasn't her biological father. Ally's going to have to take that DNA test to prove *Jerry's* her biological father ..."

"Oh," Becky said, as the realization of what Jules was trying to say hit her. "So, you think Molly should soften the blow if Ally doesn't already know Jerry is her biological father?"

"I just think if it were me, I'd rather find out the truth from my mother than from two strangers," Jules said softly. "No matter how much money was at stake. This is someone's life, not a business transaction."

Jules was looking at this from a different angle, but Becky could see her point. This could change Ally's whole life, her perspective of who she was, her relationship with her parents.

"I'm on board with calling Molly first," she said. Do we have a phone number for her?"

With a few keystrokes, they had her number. Molly was helpful and accommodating.

Thirty minutes later, they were on the phone with the elusive half-sister Donna had worried they might never find.

CHAPTER THIRTY-NINE

"IT WAS NEVER a secret that David wasn't my biological father. He adopted me officially when I was nine," Ally explained. "I couldn't have asked for a better dad. My mother got a great guy when she married him. She told me what you went through to find her. And me. You're quite the detectives."

"We had some good clues along the way," Jules said with a sideward glance at Becky. Could they have found her without some of the information Jerry had left for Donna? She wasn't sure.

"My mother told me I had a half-sister a long time ago," Ally said. "A couple of years ago, when I had my daughter, it started to hit me. Not only do I have a sister I don't know, but my daughter has an aunt. I started to wonder what she was like and whether I could find her."

"Did you look for her?" Jules asked.

"About six months ago, I did a DNA test."

Jules's mouth fell open. "You did? With what company?"

When she told them, Becky and Jules groaned out loud in unison.

"What's the matter?" Ally asked, confused.

"Jerry tested too but at only one company," Becky explained. "It wasn't the same company as you, so we never would have found you on there. But we had Donna send in tests to several companies. She hasn't gotten her results from the one you tested with. I guess we would have found you the easy way when those results came in."

"Not that we didn't enjoy the challenge of finding you the old-fashioned way," Jules added with an eye roll in Becky's direction.

"Did you ever try to figure out your matches or use them to try to find Jerry?" Becky asked.

Ally took in a deep breath. "Honestly, I never really wanted to find him. I mean, after all, he never wanted to acknowledge me, and besides, I already had a great dad. I would never do anything to hurt him." She paused. "I guess that might be hard to understand."

Jules thought of her birth father. "Not for me. I understand completely."

"But the idea that I had a sister—I couldn't stop thinking about her. I have a younger brother, but ever since I was a little girl, I've always wanted a big sister. Someone who wanted to do girl things, you know?"

Ally would be shocked when she discovered she had already met her sister. Jules didn't think it was fair to tell Ally before they broke the news to Donna.

"Jerry also left his DNA with a company whose results are used for legal purposes," Jules said. "Let us make some calls. You can probably give a sample at an office near you. When they confirm you're a match, which we all feel confident will happen, we can make plans for you to fly down. There are some papers you'll have to sign with the lawyer before he can release your share of the inheritance."

"When I come down, will I get to meet my sister?" Ally

asked, not even commenting on the inheritance or what she needed to do to get it.

Jules didn't want to tell Ally that Donna had been arrested for murder unless they were sure. With a glance at Becky, she crossed her fingers in the air and said, "That's the plan. But first, we've got to get the DNA test done. Let us make some calls, and we'll call you back about that."

"Okay, let me give you another number. My mom gave you my cell phone number at work. My personal cell number is probably better." Ally recited the number, and Jules wrote it down.

After she disconnected the call, Becky tapped her phone against her lips thoughtfully. "I have mixed feelings about all of this."

Jules crossed her arms over her chest and frowned. "What do you mean?"

"I mean, I'm happy we solved the case. Sure, Ally needs the DNA test, but we both know she'll be a match." Becky let out a deep sigh. "I just can't say I feel like celebrating. This came at a huge cost, Jules. A man's *dead*. Maybe at the hands of Donna's fiancé. Maybe she was even involved. And we *still* don't know who the real Robert Taylor is or why Jerry left him so much money."

Jules nodded thoughtfully. "Let's take one step at a time. Why don't you call the DNA company and see what you can find out? Ask if Ally can take her test in Georgia. I'll call Jerry's attorney and see if we can have the DNA lab send the results directly to him."

Becky went to work back at her own desk.

"Hey, is the lawyer's phone number in the file?" Jules called over to her. "I remember his business card being stapled to the front of the folder."

"Which we don't have anymore," Becky reminded her.

"Crap. I remember his name was Norman. Do you remember his last name?"

"I remember he had an esquire at the end," Becky said with a smirk.

Jules rolled her eyes and groaned. "You're a big help. Was there anything in those boxes of Jerry's that mentioned his lawyer?"

"Not that I remember, but we never went through all the file folders."

Jules pulled herself out of her chair and shuffled to the supply closet. She dragged out the box with the file folders. "Do you think Donna's ever going to want to read about all these cases?"

"Not sure, but maybe Ally will be curious and want to find out more about Jerry."

"I still think he gave her all these folders for a reason," Jules said as she sat on the floor next to the box. "Almost everything else in these boxes had some sort of meaning. It's like he wanted her to figure it all out, understand more about him."

"If he was really leaving a trail of breadcrumbs, he should have left the password to the flash drive," Becky said with a trace of sarcasm.

Jules reached into the box. "We're missing something to figure that out. I know we are."

"I have an idea." Becky rooted around in her computer bag, pulled the flash drive out of a small pocket, and inserted it into the USB port of her laptop. "I haven't tried everyone's name. That might be obvious if he thinks we've come this far. When the password box blinked, Becky typed in AvaDonna-JeromeAlly and hit enter. "Well, that didn't work."

"Try just the kids and leave Ava off."

Becky typed again. "Nope. Do you think Robert fits in here somewhere?"

"Try it. And maybe use just everyone's initials as an option."

Becky tried every combination she could think of, but none of them worked. She groaned loudly. "I give up."

"So frustrating. I still think Jerry would have used something that would be easy to figure out once we had all the pieces. There wasn't anything in his datebook for the year he died. Maybe there's a clue in one of these folders." As Jules rifled through them, there was a loud knock at the door.

Becky glanced down at her. "Is Tim dropping off Gene?"

"I don't think so. I'll go see who it is." Jules let out a groan as she pulled herself off the floor. "Remind me not to sit down here again."

She staggered to the front door, peeking out the window before turning the lock to open it. "Hey, what are you doing here?" She reached up and gave Jonas a hug.

"I met Erin for lunch nearby, so I figured I'd see if you were in the office. I have news."

"We have news, too." Becky stood and gave him a hug when he entered their office.

Jonas slid into the chair in front of her desk. "Okay, you go first."

"We found Donna's half-sister," Jules said with a grin.

"Alive and kicking?"

"Yup. Alive and kicking."

"That's awesome. Good work. You two are starting to get really good at this investigation stuff."

"We still have to close the case," Becky said. "Get Ally's DNA tested and get her here so she can get her money. She wants to know if she's going to meet Donna."

Jules cringed. "After the text Donna sent me at my engagement party, we don't even know if Ally will be able to meet her sister. She might be in jail."

"That's what I stopped by to tell you. They arrested Donna's fiancé."

"But not Donna?" Jules asked.

"Nope. She had an alibi for the time of the murder. Jay didn't implicate her, and there's no proof she knew anything about it."

Jules exchanged a look with Becky. "So, Jay admitted he killed Robert?"

Jonas's expression seemed to say most murderers didn't admit it. "He's still claiming he didn't do it. But he's also not saying Donna was involved. If they find something down the line that proves otherwise, they could still come back for her, but as of now, she's a free woman."

Becky moved to stand next to Jules. "Could they be wrong?" she asked. "Maybe they have the wrong guy. If he's not confessing—"

Jonas leaned back in his chair. "They filed the probable cause warrant and the arrest report. Looks like they found compelling evidence at the murder scene that matched evidence taken from Donna's apartment, including the knife set the murder weapon came from." His glance traveled between Becky and Jules. "If Donna has an alibi, then that just leaves the other person who lives there."

"I feel bad for her," Becky said.

"So, that's it?" Jules asked. "They stop looking for any more evidence?"

Jonas shook his head. "Not necessarily. They could still be testing something they found at the crime scene or even still working to find evidence that places him near the crime scene. They want an iron-clad case. But unless there's a major development with new evidence that points away from Jay, he could be in trouble."

"It just goes to show money doesn't always solve your problems," Becky said. "Sometimes it just makes new ones."

"Looks that way," Jonas said. "What about the other rich sister? What did she think about inheriting that much money from a father she never knew?"

Jules had been surprised at Ally's reaction. She had never even asked how much she stood to inherit. "To be honest, she seemed more excited about having a sister than about the money."

Becky nodded. "That was the impression I got, too."

Jonas grimaced. "I thought you said Donna didn't want anything to do with her."

"She didn't." Jules offered a coy smile. "But we found out from Jerry's secretary that Donna and Ally have actually met before."

Jonas shot up an eyebrow. "Really?"

Jules recounted the story that Ella had told them. "If it wasn't for his secretary, I'm not sure we'd have found her."

"Yet," Becky added.

"Oh, right." Jules kept forgetting about the test since they had already found her. "Turns out Ally did a DNA test about six months ago. We just haven't gotten Donna's results from that site yet. But when they show up, it'll be a match."

"You hope," Jonas said with a mischievous smile.

Jules swatted him playfully on the shoulder. "Don't even say that. Can you imagine if there's a surprise we don't know about?" She hoped it would have a happy ending, and they'd have each other and their money. "So, what about Jay? Can Donna get him out on bail?"

Jonas gave his head a shake. "First-degree murder? That's pretty much a non-bondable offense. He'll go before the judge, today probably, but he won't be granted bail."

Jules pressed her lips together as she digested this news. "At least we know Ally will be safe when she comes into town."

Becky nodded in agreement. "And then we just have to hope Donna wants a relationship with her sister after all."

"There's also her aunts." Jules exhaled a puff of air as she remembered the night she tried to go to Kathy's and had to call Jonas. "After being followed by Jay, I called them when I got home that night. They can't wait to see Donna."

"No more silver cars following you around?" When Jules shook her head, Jonas patted his palms on his thighs and stood. "Seems like you girls have this all under control. No more frantic calls about being stalked or people missing and murdered. It should be smooth sailing from here on out." He gave them a stern stare. "Maybe the next case can be a little tamer, please. A little more DNA in front of the computer and a lot less threat of murders and car chases? I'm relieved this one is coming to an end, and I'm sure Tim and Bryan are, too."

"Oh, I'm sure they will be," Becky said with a smile. "We haven't even told them we found Ally yet."

"Okay, well, I'll leave you to it."

"Hey, before you go, can you help me?" Jules gestured at the file box on the floor next to the closet. "I wanted to put that box on my desk, so it's easier to go through, but it's heavy."

Jonas pretended to flex his muscles. "That little thing?" He lifted it easily and placed it on Jules's desk.

Jules grinned. "Having a brother is pretty awesome."

He let out a laugh. "I knew you were only after me for my super strength. I gotta go. I guess you don't have to worry anymore about locking the office door." He glanced over at the empty dog bed. "But it's not like you have Gene, the attack dog here, so maybe you should still think about it."

"Kelly," Becky said after he left.

"What?"

"Kelly. That was Norman's last name. I just remembered."

Jules sat down at her desk and googled the name. "Well, you're right. I found him."

An hour later, they had everything set up for Ally's DNA test.

"You asked them to rush the results, right?" Jules asked.

"I did. There's an extra fee, but I paid for it. Hopefully, it won't be more than a couple of days."

"You emailed all the details to Ally? The address she needs to go to, all the instructions?" Jules didn't want anything to go wrong. They were so close to closing this case.

"It's all done. She has the last appointment of the day today. The lab will send the results directly to Norman with a copy to us. Do you think we should try to call Donna? Or should we wait until it's confirmed?"

Even with Jay in jail, Jules wasn't sure she was in a hurry to tell Donna anything yet. "Let's give her a day or two to deal with Jay's arrest. Maybe by then, we'll have the results."

"What about what Jonas said?"

"Which part?" Jules asked.

"What if they don't turn out to be a match?"

"Well, I think we feel pretty confident Ally will match Jerry."

"But what about Donna?" Becky asked. "Can you imagine if they didn't turn out to be half-sisters? Ally was his rightful daughter, and Donna wasn't? Would that affect Donna's portion of the inheritance?"

Jules wrinkled her nose as she considered it and then shook her head. "There wasn't anything in the will that said Donna had to prove she was Jerry's daughter."

"But still. I can't imagine how that would make her feel."

Jules nodded. "Maybe Ava had secrets. I really hope not, but we both know, anything's possible."

CHAPTER FORTY

DONNA PUSHED OPEN the glass doors and stepped into the sunshine. She was more confused than ever. Jay was stuck in jail with a public defender, but the defense lawyer she'd just left needed a huge retainer. Donna had worn the black dress, the one she'd worn to Norman's office. Her outfit said money, but their checking account and non-existent savings said otherwise.

Even if she got her inheritance soon, she debated whether she should use it to help Jay. Her mind kept drifting back to the detective's question. *How's your relationship with Jay, Donna?* They were fine, weren't they? Jay had called from jail yesterday, pleading with her to believe him. She didn't know what to think.

When her father had gotten sick, Jay had insisted on getting married. Even though Donna's relationship with her father was strained, the idea of him actually dying over-whelmed her. She'd have no one, she told Jay. "You'll always have me," he'd promised, and then he proposed.

It seemed romantic at the time, but now Donna worried it was all part of his master plan. Jay knew her father was dying, knew he had a lot of money. Donna sighed heavily and frowned when she glanced up. Lost in thought, she'd headed in the wrong direction from where she had parked.

She swung around to go the other way.

"Hey, Donna," a man's voice called from behind her.

She spun around and stifled a groan. Nick. Just what she didn't need right now. She already had her hands full with Jay's brother, who wouldn't leave her alone and kept asking questions she didn't know how to answer.

"I thought that was you," he said as he jogged to catch up with her.

His eyes scanned her from head to toe. She'd never been able to afford a dress like this when she was married to him. Hell, she really couldn't afford it now.

"Hey, everything okay?" he asked.

Was it that obvious? He had never noticed a single mood she had when they were married. Was the new sober Nick just more in tune? She studied him looking for a clue of some sort.

Nick pointed at the building she'd just come from. "The lawyer's office. I saw you walk out. Just making sure you're okay."

"Oh." So much for his meter reader on her emotions. "Yeah, everything's fine." No way would she tell him Jay was in jail. Her eyes traveled down the rest of the street, trying to figure out where he could be coming from. "What are you doing in this part of town?"

He pointed at a church farther down the road on the other side of the street. "AA meeting. I work down on Clover, so I usually just walk to this one. Gets me some fresh air to clear my head." He glanced down at the phone in his hand. "Oh, I gotta go. Don't want to be late getting back. My boss understands to a point, but I try not to push my luck, you know?" He dipped his head and smiled warmly at her. "Take care, Donna."

"You too, Nick." She watched as he went back in the other direction toward Clover Street, and then she headed to her car.

After she slipped into the driver's seat, she sat for a moment, remembering what Jay had said after he saw her with Nick at the gas station. *If I catch him near you again, I swear I'll kill him.* Donna had dismissed it at the time. Just Jay's macho ego as he beat his chest possessively over her. It didn't mean anything. Or did it?

Nick was fine. Granted, he hadn't come back again or given Jay any reason to make good on his threat. But still. Jay's words reverberated in her head. *I'll kill him.* Had Jay, at some point, had the same idea about her?

Donna started the car and glanced at the clock on the dashboard. She had twenty minutes to get to the restaurant where she was meeting her aunts. She'd made plans before she knew any of this was going to happen, but with Jay behind bars, she needed the distraction more than ever. She needed her family.

Donna hadn't seen her aunts since she was a little girl. A short while later, as she glanced around the restaurant, she was grateful they recognized her immediately. Both aunts stood and waved her over to the booth they were sitting in.

Donna's pulse raced as she made her way to them. Family that was happy to see her was unfamiliar territory. What if she was a disappointment?

The two women leaped out of the booth as she approached and wrapped her in a group hug. When Donna pulled back, they were both crying.

"Sit, sit," Aunt Kathy said as she gestured toward the seat.

Donna took in a deep breath as she slid into the bench on the other side of the table. She didn't remember her mother, but she could tell from the pictures she had seen that her Aunt Kathy, with her dark hair and striking features, bore a strong resemblance to her mom. Jone had blond hair teased high on top and into a bob that framed her warm face and genuine smile.

"The men wanted to come," Kathy said as her gaze fixed on Donna. "And of course, all your cousins can't wait to see you, but we didn't want to overwhelm you right off the bat. Besides, we wanted you all to ourselves for a little while."

Jone nodded and then shook her head in disbelief. "I just still can't believe we're sitting here with you." She turned to Kathy. "And you said that DNA test was silly. Who's silly now?"

"I didn't say it was *silly*."

It was clear from how the two sisters bantered back and forth that they loved each other dearly. Donna thought about her half-sister. For a fleeting moment, she considered if maybe they could find this kind of relationship.

"Even though we told our guys they couldn't come, you could have brought your fiancé," Jone said. "Jules told us you're about to get married. His name's Jay, right?"

Donna nodded slowly. How in the world could she fill them in on the status of her life? After all these years, she finally had her aunts back. How could she tell them only a mere three days ago, she herself was suspected of murder and now Jay was in jail?

Jone narrowed her eyes as if she was trying to decode Donna's somber expression. "You know what, let's get some lunch ordered, and then we'll catch up about everything that's going on in your world." She lifted her hand in the air, and within a few minutes, they'd given their order and had drinks sitting in front of them.

Kathy held up her glass. "I know this is only soda, but I feel like we want to say something. A toast of sorts." She waited for Donna and Jone to pick up their glasses and then began. "Donna, we've missed you more than you'll ever know. You're a piece of our sister and a piece of us. We're your family, and we don't ever plan to lose you again."

Jone chimed in as well. "We can't go back in time. But from now on, we plan to be there for you, no matter what. Aunt love is unconditional. You need help, you come to us. Advice? We're your sounding board. And if you need love, we have plenty for you."

They all clinked glasses with a chorus of cheers.

Donna lowered her glass, her shaking hand making it sway in the air until she settled it safely on the table. She thought she had her emotions under control, but a sudden sob erupted from deep in her throat.

"Oh, honey." Jone came around to Donna's side of the table and hugged her. "I thought this might be a bit over-whelming."

Kathy pushed a napkin across the table. Jone reached for it and handed it to Donna.

Donna dabbed her eyes and sniffled. "I'm okay. It's just—it's just—everything."

Their lunches arrived. In between bites of a burger, Donna recounted her childhood, told them how her dad was always working and not very involved in her life. She even told them about Nick.

"I was looking for someone, anyone, to take care of me. I was far too young and naïve. He drank too much. Spent money we didn't have at the bars. I didn't know what a good marriage was supposed to look like, so I had nothing to compare it against. It took me seven years to figure out I deserved better." She didn't mention that Nick had finally gotten his act together while her life with Jay was now a disaster.

"Good for you. So, you got a good one this time around?" Kathy asked as she wiped her mouth and laid her napkin on her plate.

Donna took in a deep breath and blew it out as she contemplated how much to tell them. "Actually, I have no idea."

When her aunts looked at her with concern, Donna knew she could tell them anything. She filled them in on the stipulations her father had put in place to get her money and the mystery man who got a large chunk even though Donna had no idea who he was.

"And then a man with the same name was murdered."

Jone's eyes widened as she sipped her soda. "Was it the guy from the will?"

"No one will tell me for sure. He worked in the same building as my dad, but why my father would leave him so much money—I have no idea." Donna shrugged. "That's if he's even the right guy." She shifted uncomfortably in her seat as she prepared to tell them everything. "There was some stuff at the murder scene. The police—they came and searched our apartment."

Donna's gaze drifted to check if her aunts flinched at all. They didn't, so she continued. "A few days ago, the police actually suspected I might be involved. If I hadn't needed to deliver the rent check at the time that man was murdered—" Her voice broke. "I was saved by a surveillance camera at the rental office and my downstairs neighbor walking that yappy dog of hers." Donna stared down at her half-eaten burger. "They found what they thought was evidence. In our apartment." She brought her gaze back up and forced herself to tell them. "They arrested Jay. He's in jail."

"Oh, Donna, that's just terrible," Jone said, pushing her plate to the side and focusing on Donna. "But why would Jay kill this man you didn't even know?"

Donna explained in detail how the will had been written. She confided her fear that her half-sister might be in danger and the nagging doubt there might have been a bigger plan for Jay to keep her inheritance for himself. "I don't *want* to believe he planned to kill me. I find it hard to believe he would have murdered anyone." She placed her elbow on the table and let her head fall into the palm of her hand. "I also don't know how to explain away any of it."

"Have you found out anything about your half-sister?" Kathy asked gently.

"Jules and Becky—I hired them to find her, but they haven't said they've found her yet. And with Jay and I both under suspicion ..." Donna's shoulders sagged with her sigh. "I'm not sure I'd blame them if they didn't want to tell me anything. But if she was in danger because of Jay, well, he's not getting out of jail anytime soon." Donna tilted her head, and her face turned serious. "Do you think my father thought the money would make Jay show his true colors? Maybe this whole inheritance is his way of sticking it to me even after he died."

"You poor thing," Jone said without answering the question. "That's a lot for one woman to shoulder, but we're here now. You lean on us, and we'll hold you up." She glanced at Kathy. "Let's get the check. We have somewhere we want to take you."

They insisted Donna go with them in Kathy's car, promising to take her back to the restaurant when they were done.

"We chose that restaurant for a reason." Kathy glanced over at her sister. "Jone and I have shed our fair share of tears there." When the car turned the corner, Donna glanced out the back, and it became clear they were taking her to the cemetery.

"Whenever I come to town, I come to see them." Jone turned to face Donna in the back seat. "You know she's buried with your little brother, right?"

"I know now. Jules and Becky found the information in some boxes my father left."

Kathy wove her way through the cemetery until she finally pulled the car to a stop. "We have to walk the rest of the way."

She turned to Jone. "I'll pop the trunk. Can you get the flowers?"

Donna followed the two women through the beautifully manicured property. Her stomach churned at the mix of emotions coursing through her.

"Here we are," Kathy said finally. "The Campbell family plot."

Sunlight streamed through the trees that provided shade from the Florida heat. The grass was Crayola green and so perfect it almost didn't look real. Headstones stood at attention, ready to tell their stories of lives and loss. Of living and dying. Of being part of a family. Donna felt a sense of calmness envelop her.

Kathy and Jone stopped in front of a beautiful marble headstone. "We'll introduce you to your ancestors, but first, we want to share you with your mother and brother." Kathy put her hand on Donna's shoulder.

Donna didn't care if her expensive dress got dirty. She knelt in front of Ava's grave, the grass under her knees, and ran her hand over the engravings. *LOVING WIFE, MOTHER, SISTER, DAUGHTER* was inscribed under Ava's name. Next to her name on the other side of the headstone, it said *OUR ANGEL, SWEET BABY JAMES, Jerome James McDermott III.*

Donna's eyes welled up. His date of birth and date of death were a mere three days apart. She glanced back at her aunts, confusion etched on her face. "James? I thought my brother's name was going to be Jerome, like my dad's."

"Your mother knew your father wanted him to carry on the name. But she always planned to call him James," Kathy said softly. "When she was pregnant, that's what she always called him. My sweet baby James."

The headstone looked well cared for and placed on the top and around the base were hundreds and hundreds of small rocks. Jone handed Donna the bouquet. There was a holder in front of the grave where Donna inserted the flowers.

After she got to her feet, she smoothed down the front of her dress and turned to her aunts. "I don't understand—"

"The rocks?" Kathy asked, her lips turning up at the edges.
"Yeah."

"Every time I came to visit my sister's grave, there were fresh flowers in the holder. Mold never grew on the headstone, and the pile of rocks grew year after year." She put her arm around Donna. "It was your dad. He came once a week, every week, until he died. I knew something must have happened. The flowers just stopped."

"Every time he came to see them, he added a stone," Jone said. "He must have wanted to be buried near her. If he had just reached out ..."

Donna turned back toward the headstone. All those rocks. At that moment, she understood. Her father hadn't been negligent. Not really. He'd just been a broken man who had no idea how to exist after losing his wife and son.

CHAPTER FORTY-ONE

BECKY HEARD the shouting by the front door of the office before she saw who it was. With a quick glance at Jules, she frowned and got up from her desk. Jules followed.

"Yes, I know his first appearance is in an hour," Donna said into her phone as she slammed their office door behind her.

A few seconds later. "No, I'm *not* going to be there."

Donna looked up to see Becky and Jules staring at her. She held up a finger. It was clear from the growing flush on her cheeks that the call was making her madder by the minute.

"Kevin, if you want to go so bad, *you* go. It's not like he was thinking about killing *you*." Then a moment later, she added, "Well, I don't know he *wasn't*." Donna gritted her teeth and shook her head. "I have to go." She disconnected the call, and a deep growl erupted from her throat.

"Everything okay?" Jules asked, which was silly because it was clear everything was not okay.

"Jay's brother. He's driving me crazy."

"Come on in. Want some coffee or water?" Becky asked.

"I'll take some water," Donna said as she headed toward

their office. "It's hot out there. You would think it would have cooled off by now."

Donna dropped into the chair in front of Becky's desk. She reached out for the bottle of water Becky handed her, and after she took a sip, she held the cold bottle to her cheek. Her color was slowly returning to normal. She let out a deep breath.

"They arrested Jay yesterday for Robert's murder."

Becky nodded as she slid into her chair on the other side of the desk. "We were a little worried after the text message you sent the other night."

"Sorry about that." Donna placed the water bottle on the desk. "I was a little premature. They released us both after they questioned us, but only because they needed to confirm my alibi for the time of the murder." She pursed her lips and offered a small shrug. "I guess they figured it had to be one of us. When my alibi checked out, they came to the apartment and arrested Jay."

Becky watched Donna's face for a tell of whether she thought Jay was guilty. Donna gave nothing away, at least nothing she could read.

"And how do you feel about that?"

Donna looked down at her hands in her lap. When she brought her gaze back up, her eyes were filled with tears. "I don't know how to feel. Is Jay rough around the edges? Maybe. Bar fights? He's had a few. But a *murderer*?" She shook her head. "I just can't believe he'd kill anyone. And why? My inheritance alone would have been plenty of money for us. More than either one of us has ever seen, that's for sure."

"Money makes people do crazy things," Jules said as she rolled her chair over near Becky's desk and then sat down.

"The police think—" Donna swallowed hard. "They think maybe Jay wanted me to inherit as much money as possible. Then, he'd kill me off after we got married so he could have it all."

Becky's eyes widened. "Oh, Donna. Do you believe that?"

"He swears it's not true." Donna's voice shook. "I don't know what to believe. I thought he loved me, but—" She picked up the water bottle and took a long swig.

Her voice was steadier when she continued. "Maybe it was all an act. Maybe Jay had this plan since the day he asked me to marry him. My father had been diagnosed. He might have figured he'd marry me so he could cash in. He wanted the wedding to happen as soon as possible."

"Do you think—could there be another explanation?" Jules asked softly.

"About him being Robert's murderer?" Donna took a moment and leaned her head back to consider the question. She slowly shook her head. "I don't think so. There's too much evidence. I mean, they have blood on his sneaker. But planning to kill me, too? That's where I'm struggling. I mean, there's no proof of that."

"Do you think maybe he did it so you *both* would have more money? He just didn't want to tell you?" Jules gently pointed out the obvious. "Of course, he wouldn't be able to kill *just* Robert. He'd have to find your half-sister, too, or the plan would be a bust."

"I considered that." Donna wrapped both hands around the water bottle and fiddled nervously with it, the crackling of the thin plastic seeming to help her anxiety. "You know, Jay's brother, Kevin, just came back into his life. He's been in and out of trouble with the law. Not murder. Just petty stuff. But maybe he convinced Jay he should hatch a plan to get the money. I swear, every time I see him, Kevin's talking about the inheritance like it's part his."

Becky leaned forward. "Maybe he was part of it? Did he have an alibi?"

Donna shifted in her seat. "I actually asked him about it, and he said he was at the gym that morning. I mentioned

Kevin to the police. Just in case he was lying." She shrugged. "They said his alibi checked out. They have his membership card scanned in and the guy behind the desk confirmed he was there."

"That doesn't mean he didn't know about it," Jules pointed out.

"I guess, but Jay hasn't said his brother was involved. How can he? Jay's still saying he's innocent and doesn't have any idea who killed Robert. And Kevin genuinely seemed shocked about Jay being arrested." Donna let out a frustrated moan. "Or I'm being scammed. It wouldn't be the first time."

"It sounded like you didn't want to go see him in court," Becky said. "You look nice. Were you thinking about going and then changed your mind?"

Donna glanced down at the black dress she was still wearing. The day had been a whirlwind. "I went to meet with a defense attorney this morning. Right now, Jay has a public defender." She ran her fingers through her hair. "It's a lot of money to get him a real lawyer, but—I still don't know if I believe him. Not that I even have the money yet. And then, I went and met my aunts for lunch."

"Your aunts? Plural? Is Jone in town?" Jules's eyes brightened.

"She flew in last night. I met them both for lunch." Donna managed a meek smile. "It was really wonderful. It's like I have —it's like I have a family." Her voice caught ever so slightly. "I told them about everything. Even Jay being in jail."

"What did they think about that?" Becky asked softly.

Donna lifted one shoulder. "They don't know him, so I'm sure they don't know what to think. They just want to be there to support me."

Becky exchanged a glance with Jules. Something good had come out of this case. Donna had her mother's family back.

"Yeah, it's ironic, right?" Donna said with a soft grunt. "If my dad hadn't made me find my half-sister, I wouldn't have done those DNA tests. I might never have known my mom's family has been wanting to find me all these years."

"I wonder if your dad considered that possibility." Becky wanted so much to believe that Donna's dad had wanted to right the wrongs he had caused her.

"Maybe." Donna's gaze drifted to Jules. "They took me to the cemetery," she said in a soft voice. "Where my mom and brother are buried."

"Oh, good," Jules said. "I know you were nervous about that. But see, your aunts are both fine, and I'm sure it was nice they went with you."

There was a small smile on Donna's face as she nodded. "It was actually beautiful. Peaceful. Serene. My ancestors are all buried there. It was really emotional to see all those headstones and know—I mean, that's *my* family history." She reached for her phone. "Is it weird I took pictures?"

Becky shook her head. "Not at all."

Donna pulled up a photo and handed Becky her phone. Jules scooted over closer so she could see as well.

Becky let out an appreciative sigh. "It's beautiful. I love the overhang of the big trees. They seem to be protecting everyone." She handed the phone back to Donna.

"The sun coming through the trees was unbelievable." Donna scrolled to another picture. "This is my mother's headstone. My mother and my brother." She handed the phone to Jules this time.

Becky peered over to see. "Oh, Donna, what a loving tribute, and those flowers are gorgeous. Based on the paperwork we found, your father ordered this stone. And your brother— my sweet baby James. Was that what they were going to call him? Not Jerome?"

Donna's voice was bittersweet. "It was. My aunts told me

that's how my mom always referred to him when she was pregnant. My sweet baby James."

Jules blew up the picture with her fingers and squinted at the screen. "Are those—"

"Rocks?" Donna finished Jules's question with a smile. "They are."

Jules studied the picture. "There must be thousands of them."

"I learned a lot today at the cemetery. My dad put those there. My Aunt Kathy said he came every week to visit their grave until he died. Always left a stone and brought new flowers. My Aunt Kathy knew something must have happened to him when the fresh flowers stopped."

Becky furrowed her brow as she tried to make sense of it. "But couldn't your aunts have found you through him if they knew he was coming to the cemetery?"

"They could have. I think my aunts weren't sure how he would react. They decided they would wait until I was eighteen, but then I got married and changed my name."

"But he was still going to visit. I'm surprised they didn't finally just ask him where you were." Jules frowned as she laid Donna's phone on the desk in front of her.

Donna let out a breath. "They explained it, and I think I understand. They felt like his time at the cemetery was sacred. They forgave him a long time ago for what happened, but they never felt like he forgave himself. He *needed* to be able to visit the cemetery. They didn't want to do anything that might make him feel like he couldn't keep coming. You know, like he was being watched."

"He went every week for what—over twenty-five years?" Becky shook her head in disbelief.

Donna nodded slowly. "Do I wish I had my mother's family all this time? Of course. But today I saw my dad through different eyes. How broken he must have been to spend more time at the cemetery than he spent with me some weeks." She shrugged as if she was okay with what she was about to say. "Maybe I was a painful reminder of what he'd lost."

"Or maybe he was scared to love you," Jules said softly. "Worried something might happen to you, too."

"I guess that's possible. My dad took my mom's family away from me when I was young, but in a weird way, he gave them back to me when he died. I don't remember what it's like to have family. It's … nice. Really nice. They're planning a party. So, I can reconnect with my uncles, all my cousins. It's a little overwhelming, but I'm looking forward to it."

Becky offered Donna a hesitant smile. "It's like a new beginning."

"I may need one too. If Jay's guilty, I never want to see him again." The look in Donna's eyes softened. "But if he's innocent—if he really didn't do this, I want him to have the best lawyer money can buy. For that, I need my inheritance. Any updates?"

Jules and Becky exchanged a glance. Jules gave a quick nod, which meant she was okay with telling Donna the news.

"We found Ally, Donna. We found your half-sister."

Donna's gaze drifted between Becky and Jules like she didn't believe they were telling the truth. "Really? Are you sure it's her? When did you find her?"

"Just a few hours before you walked through the door today," Jules said.

Donna held her hand to her forehead. "Did she finally show up on one of the DNA tests?"

Becky smiled. "Actually, no. Or I should say, not yet."

Donna's brow wrinkled in confusion. "So, how did you find her?"

Becky turned to Jules, lifted her hand, and high-fived her. "Good old-fashioned detective work. But she actually did take a DNA test. About six months ago. Just not at the site your father tested, and we haven't gotten your results back from that site yet." Becky didn't mention to Donna that something unexpected could still show up. They'd cross that bridge if they came to it, and Becky prayed they wouldn't.

"So now what happens?" Donna's gaze flew excitedly between Jules and Becky. "When can Norman release my money?"

Jules held up her hand. "She still has to take the DNA test with the lab."

"That's the test for paternity that's legal," Becky explained. "She has an appointment to take the test at a lab in Georgia and—"

"She lives in Georgia?"

Becky nodded. "Yes. She's married with a little girl."

"Okay, so she'll take the test, and we'll be able to close the case."

Becky waited a moment to see if Donna would ask any more questions about her sister. When she didn't, Becky continued, "The lab in Georgia is affiliated with the lab in Florida that has your dad's sample. When they confirm the results, they'll send a copy to us and a copy directly to your father's attorney. Then you and Ally can make arrangements to meet and collect your money."

Donna frowned. "Meet? Why do we have to meet?"

Becky glanced nervously at Jules. "Well, we thought—"

"Does this Ally want to meet *me?*"

"She does," Jules said firmly as Becky nodded.

Donna pressed her lips together as she seemed to consider it. "Then I guess it would be okay. Did she ask about my dad?" Donna rolled her eyes. "Her dad too, I guess."

Becky glanced over at Jules and chose her words carefully. "She might have questions about your dad at some point, but she seems much more excited at the idea of having a sister."

"Actually, I'm only a half—" Donna stopped herself. "Really, she's excited?"

"She did her DNA test to find *you*, not your father," Jules said pointedly. "Her stepfather adopted her, but her mom told her the truth about everything, including you."

"We hope you'll give her a chance," Becky said. "We think you'll be pleasantly surprised." She and Jules had agreed not to mention yet that Donna had already met Ally at Ella's. Just in case something unexpected happened at the lab.

Donna hesitated and then slowly bobbed her head. "Okay. When is she coming?"

"First, we need the DNA results, and then we'll make a plan," Jules said. "We asked the lab for a rush, but it could still take a few days, and then she'll have to make travel arrangements."

"So, I could potentially have my money within a week." Donna rose from the chair. "I guess I have a week to decide if I think Jay was plotting to kill me and whether I want to save his butt." She picked up her water bottle from Becky's desk. "Keep me posted."

After Donna left, Jules went back to her own desk. "Shoot. I should have asked Donna if she wanted these files." She scowled at the box in the middle of her desk. "Now that I had Jonas put it here, it's right in the way."

"I still think Ally might want them eventually. Hopefully, not at the same time Donna decides she wants them. I would hate for that to be their first fight."

Jules sifted through the files. "He had a lot of cases. Some of these names I even recognize. He worked on the Penn case. Remember the guy who got his hand stuck in the grinder at the meatpacking plant?"

Becky cringed. "Oh, I do remember that. Not that I want to. I almost stopped eating burgers after that happened."

"Jerry proved the machine was defective. Judgment for 1.2 million."

"If every one of these folders has a payout like that, it's no wonder they're fighting over so much money."

"No kidding." Jules reinserted the folder into the box and kept thumbing through the files. "I wonder if they're in chronological ord—" Her eyes widened as she whipped a folder out of the box. "Seriously?"

"What?"

Jules opened the folder and scanned the contents intently.

Becky jumped out of her chair. "Jules, what is it?"

"It's Jerry's last case." Jules met Becky's questioning gaze. "The one Ella said crushed him because he lost. Remember, she said he promised the family so much and couldn't deliver?"

"Right. I remember. So, what was the case about?"

"It's more like *who* was the case about." Jules held up the folder and turned it around so Becky could see the label.

"You've *got* to be kidding," Becky said with a groan as she read the name on the file.

Jules grinned. "Will the real Robert Taylor please stand up? Or should I say, Bobby Taylor? He was Jerry's last client, the case he lost that crushed him."

CHAPTER FORTY-TWO

"I CAN'T BELIEVE this file has been right under our noses the whole time," Jules said incredulously. "I *told* you Jerry left clues about everything."

Jules wasn't prepared for Becky's somber expression. "What's the matter?" she asked as she tossed the file on her desk so they could go through it in detail. "This is good news. We found the answer we needed."

Becky sank into her seat. "I just wish we found it sooner. Maybe the other Robert Taylor would still be alive."

Jules nodded as she pulled up her chair and opened the folder. "I know. But let's see what this says and see if we can figure out why Jerry left him so much money."

Becky swiveled in her chair to face Jules. "We know why. Jerry lost the case and felt like he owed him."

Jules started reading. "Robert was suing a company called Outdoor Adventure and Entertainment, Inc. It looks like he took his family to an outdoor course that had a zipline."

Becky put her hand over her mouth. "Don't say it."

"He fell right after he started the decline. The safety clip failed." Jules looked up, her face drained of color. "He ended up paralyzed."

Becky's shoulders sagged. "Oh, how awful."

"He was thirty-nine years old. They were suing for future wages, medical expenses, pain and suffering—"

"Did Jerry win *anything* for him?"

Jules flipped through the pages. "It looks like they gave him something to cover the hospital bills, but it was nominal considering what they were asking for."

"So, he probably can't work anymore. How is he supposed to support his family?"

"I guess that's where the inheritance comes in," Jules said with a shrug. "Jerry wanted to help them."

Becky tapped her index finger against her lips. "Remember the picture?"

"Which picture?"

"The family picture with Jerry's father. In the wheelchair."

Jules's mouth formed a circle. "Oh, you're right. His dad was paralyzed. What did Donna say—some sort of work accident, right?"

"Right. Donna also said her dad had to go to work to help support the family," Becky said. "He was what—twelve? Does Bobby have kids?"

"It didn't say."

"Does it say where Robert lives?"

Jules flipped through the file, pulled a Post-it off one of the pages, and handed it to Becky. "It seems he has a new address." She rubbed her hands together and reached for her purse. "I'm ready whenever you are."

* * *

As Jules and Becky pulled up to the old sprawling ranch home, it was clear they had finally found the right person. Newly installed ramps led to the front door, and there was a wheel-chair accessible van in the driveway.

Jules gestured at the bikes leaned up against the garage door. "Looks like he does have kids."

Becky bit on her bottom lip as Jules rang the doorbell. A few moments later, a woman answered the door as she wiped her hands with a dishrag. Warm brown eyes set in mocha-colored skin stared at them cautiously. "Hello. Can I help you?"

Jules quickly explained who they were, and the woman's face erupted in a warm smile. "Come in, come in. I was just making supper. Are you two hungry?" She bellowed into a room off to the right. "Bobby, come out here. There's some ladies you need to meet."

"Ignore the boxes. We've only been here a couple of months. Some days, it feels like I'll never get it all unpacked." She gestured toward a couch. "Have a seat. Sometimes it takes my husband a little bit to get going."

Jules elbowed Becky as three young faces peered out at them from the doorway. Mrs. Taylor's eyes followed Jules's, and then she called out. "Don't be rude. It's not nice to stare. Come say hello."

The children wandered in and stood in front of Jules and Becky. "This is Vince, Maurice, and Tory." One by one, they stepped forward and offered their hands.

"Wow," Jules said to Vince. "You have a firm handshake." He was tall and already built like a boy who loved sports.

The older boy smiled. "I'm almost twelve. My daddy always says shake like you mean it."

Jules smiled and rubbed her hand. "Well, you certainly did mean it. It's nice to meet you."

At that moment, Robert made his way into the living room, the furniture arranged to leave a wide path for his wheelchair. He was a handsome man with dark skin and muscular biceps that stretched the short sleeves of his Bucs T-shirt.

"Kids, is your homework finished?"

Tory turned to Becky and rolled her eyes with an air of exasperation. "I'm only in kindergarten. Mine is *so* easy."

"Tory, go on now," Bobby said firmly. "I have a surprise for all of you after supper, but only if your homework's done."

The two younger ones squealed, and they all headed back to what appeared to be the kitchen table.

Bobby winked at Jules and Becky. "Sometimes a little bribery goes a long way, but I did make some of their favorite cookies today while they were at school." He glanced over at his wife, looking for an introduction to their guests.

"Bobby, honey, these two ladies were hired to help Jerry's daughter find you."

He rolled toward them, a broad grin on his face. "Oh, it's so nice to meet you. Is Donna coming, too? We were waiting a bit, and then we wanted to invite her over for a barbeque." He shook hands vigorously with each of them.

Jules settled back onto the couch. "We've had a hard time finding you. We wanted to make sure you were the right person before we told Donna."

Robert's brow creased with confusion as he glanced over at his wife and then back at Jules. "Jerry didn't leave our number for Donna?"

"Not that we've found."

"I can only imagine she must have been mighty confused when she saw Jerry's will. Believe you me, we were shocked." Bobby glanced at his wife for confirmation, and she nodded. "Jerry sent us a letter right before he died to let us know he was leaving us some money."

"Next thing you know, there's a lawyer looking for us," his wife continued. "We had no idea he'd been so insanely generous."

Bobby pressed his lips together as he shook his head. "Such a good man. It's a shame what that cancer did to him. He didn't need to leave us anything. We were already grateful he sold the house to us at such a fair price."

"This was Jerry's house?" Becky asked, confusion sliding across her face.

Melissa nodded. "We were in a two-story house before— before the accident. Obviously, Bobby couldn't get around. We started looking and then Jerry told us he was planning to sell his."

"Why do I need all this space for one person," Bobby said in a gruff voice as he mimicked Jerry. "But really, he knew he didn't have much time left." His face grew serious. "He even had all the ramps installed before we moved in."

A series of beeps came from the kitchen. Bobby's wife rose from her seat. "I'm sorry, that's my dinner." Her eyes bounced between Jules and Becky. "Please, won't you stay? Bobby's brother, Sheldon, eats with us most nights, but he got stuck at work. He's a big man with a big appetite so I'm always prepared. There's plenty."

Becky's head dipped with a quick nod as she turned toward Jules. "I need to call Bryan, but it's okay with me."

"I need to call my fiancé, too, but we would love to stay for dinner, Mrs. Taylor," Jules said.

With a flick of her wrist, Bobby's wife waved off any formalities. "Oh, please, with that Mrs. Taylor nonsense. Call me Melissa."

"Okay, Melissa," Jules agreed with a smile. "Whatever you're making smells amazing."

"Beef stew and homemade cornbread. Excuse me before it's dry, overcooked cornbread." Melissa hurried off, and a moment later, the beeping ceased.

"I'm so glad you're both staying. It will give us a chance to chat. If you'll excuse me, I'll go help Melissa get things ready." Bobby grinned. "You know what they say. Happy wife, happy life. Make your calls and come in whenever you're ready." He gestured in the direction the kids and his wife had gone. "We'll be just through there." He maneuvered his wheelchair around the couch and rolled toward the kitchen.

Jules widened her eyes as she grabbed her phone. "I can understand why Jerry wanted to help them. What a nice family."

"I know. I guess I probably should have checked in with Bryan before we came here, but with Jay in jail, I figure I'm off the hook from now on."

Jules called Tim, got his voicemail, and left a message. She waited for Becky to finish her call so they could go in together.

"You won't even believe the day we had," Becky said into the phone. "We found Ally *and* the real Robert Taylor. We're at his house now. Which is actually Jerry's old house."

By the look on her friend's face, Jules knew Becky was getting a scolding for not calling before they got there.

"I know, but that's the other news." Becky lowered her voice so as not to be overheard by anyone in the kitchen. "Donna's fiancé was arrested for the murder of the other Robert Taylor." A moment. "Nope, Donna wasn't. She had an alibi. Listen, I'll fill you in when I get home, but I wanted to let you know we're staying for dinner." She rolled her eyes. "Okay, I will."

Becky hung up. "Do you still have this address on the GPS in your phone? I have to text it to Bryan."

"You told him Jay was arrested. He's still worried?" Jules turned her phone around so Becky could read the address on the screen.

"I guess so, but it's simple enough to give him peace of mind." She typed in the address and hit send. "I guess I under-stand. He was never like this before, but he did almost watch me get killed. We both have our own issues to deal with after what happened."

When they made their way into the kitchen, homework had been removed, and the large table was set for seven.

Tory hurried over and took Becky's hand. "We had to add an extra chair. Will you sit next to me?"

Becky gazed down at the little girl and hoped her voice didn't betray how being childless still hurt like hell. "I would be honored."

"You can sit next to me," Maurice told Jules as he sidled up close to her. "But don't call me Maurice," he whispered. "All my friends in third grade call me Moe."

"You got it, Moe," Jules said as she slid into the chair next to him.

"Vince, please pour the milk for your brother and sister," Melissa said as she ladled beef stew into bowls. "And then help me put these bowls on the table."

Once everyone was settled, Melissa bustled over with a large plate of cornbread and slipped into her seat. "I hope it's okay," she said as she reached her hands out to Bobby and Moe on either side of her. "We always say grace before supper."

As they all held hands around the table, Bobby closed his eyes and spoke. "Lord, we thank you for this meal, for blessing this day and our family. We thank you for bringing Jules and Becky to our table and for the blessing of having Donna soon become part of our family as well. We thank you for our health and the love that binds us together and guides us each and every day. Amen."

There was a chorus of amens. Jules was afraid that when she opened her eyes, everyone would see they were wet with tears. Love and gratitude after all they had been through. She sniffled quietly and blinked hard a few times.

"We can't tell you how many times Jerry sat at this table

with us," Bobby said as he buttered his cornbread. "That man loved Melissa's cooking."

"This cornbread *is* delicious," Becky said as she took a bite. If you're willing to share the recipe, my husband would love it. Of course, he does most of the cooking, so I'll be passing the recipe along, but still——" She laughed.

"It's Bobby's grandmother's recipe, but I'm happy to share." Melissa buttered a piece for Tory and put it on her plate. "It was Jerry's favorite, too."

"So, Jerry spent a lot of time with your family?" Jules asked as she sipped her sweet tea.

"As much as he could until he got too sick," Bobby said. "At first, he wanted to come over to talk about the case." He gestured at his wife. "Somehow, Melissa *always* convinced him to stay for supper."

"It didn't take much." Melissa snorted, but then her face grew serious. "I always thought he really didn't have any other place else to be."

"He felt terrible when we didn't win what he thought we should. After the case ended, he thought he wouldn't be welcome here anymore, which was just silly." Bobby brought a heaping spoonful of stew to his mouth. "We all loved having him here."

Tory bit into her cornbread. "I loved Uncle Jerry. I'm sad he died."

Vince nodded. "We were all sad. When I wanted to try out for the football team, he would throw the ball over and over to me." His eyes welled up. "He was really proud of me when I made the team."

Jules and Becky exchanged a glance. This was a side of Jerry they hadn't heard about.

"We had a lot of late-night talks in the old house, Jerry and me," Melissa said with a sigh that seemed to hold disappointment they hadn't met earlier in life. "He had a whole pile of regrets. Used to say he wished he could do things over again. Sadly, we don't always get that chance."

Bobby reached for another piece of cornbread. "We used to tell him all the time to bring Donna over and introduce her to the family."

Melissa sipped her tea. "He never did. Just said he wasn't sure she'd understand. He thought she'd be angry that our kids had a relationship with him. It sounded like he wasn't the kind of dad to her he wished he could have been."

"He didn't tell Donna he sold us the house," Bobby said. It was a statement not a question.

Jules shook her head. "I don't think so. Otherwise the name would have clicked earlier when she saw it in the will."

"I hope she'll want to come here. That it won't feel uncomfortable. Jerry didn't want the house to go to strangers." Melissa's voice softened. "He said he wanted to see it finally filled with happiness."

"Did he tell you about his wife and son?" Jules asked softly.

"Not at first," Melissa said as her gaze drifted to Bobby. "He broke down one night and finally told us. It explained so much."

"Did you know Uncle Jerry?" Tory asked Becky as she scooped up the last bit of beef stew in her bowl and shoved the spoon in her mouth.

Becky turned to Tory and slowly shook her head. "We didn't. We know his daughter Donna, but we never got to meet Jerry."

"That's too bad," Tory said, her lower lip trembling. "I miss him a lot."

"We all do, pumpkin," Bobby said as he reached over and rubbed the little girl's arm. "But we're going to meet Donna soon, and I'll bet she'll love your momma's cooking just as much as her daddy did."

"He really was part of the family," Melissa said, her expression sincere. "We never expected him to leave us any money, much less the amount he did. I hope Donna isn't angry about it. If she is, we can—"

"Please don't say you'll give it back," Jules said firmly. "He wanted you to have it. Did you know Jerry's dad was paralyzed in an accident? He was in a wheelchair, too."

Melissa and Robert exchanged shocked glances that indicated they clearly had no idea. Bobby shook his head. "No, he never told us that. I wonder if that explains—"

"Jerry took a great interest when we found out there might be an experimental surgery we could get for Bobby," Melissa cut in. "It could help him walk again eventually. Of course, we didn't have the money, and insurance wouldn't cover it. But now—" Melissa left the thought unfinished, but it was clear Jerry's money might give Bobby the ability to walk someday.

When they finished dinner, Bobby brought out the cookies he had made for the kids, and they were happy to share with Jules and Becky.

As they got ready to say their goodbyes, Tory reached up for Becky's hand. She fluttered the lashes that framed her hopeful brown eyes. "Will you come back? Do you have a little girl? Can you bring her for me to play with?"

Becky knelt down to hug her. "I would love to come back. I don't have a little girl yet, but you can bet when the time comes, I'll tell her all about you, and she'll definitely want to come play."

Becky and Jules hugged the boys and Melissa goodbye.

A wide electric grin crossed Bobby's face. "Listen, girls, I may be lower to the ground now, but I'm not settlin' for a handshake on the way out." Jules laughed and leaned down to embrace him. "Please tell Donna we're going to call her," Bobby whispered into Jules's ear. "She's part of our family now, too. It was important to Jerry."

"Y'all come back soon," Melissa said as she waved from the door. "You're both welcome here anytime."

After they closed the car doors, Becky turned to Jules. "It seems like they want to welcome Donna with open arms. Do you think that's what Jerry wanted most of all? I mean, he gave them the money. And the house. How crazy is that? Maybe it was out of guilt—"

Jules hadn't started the car. She had pulled her phone from her bag and was just staring blankly at it.

"Jules, are you listening?"

As Jules stared at the screen of her phone, her stomach churned. "I'm listening ..." she said half-heartedly, even though she really wasn't.

Becky's frown turned to concern. "Did Tim call back? Is everything okay?"

Jules slowly nodded. "Yes, Tim's fine. He brought Gene to my condo to wait for me to get home." She brought her eyes up to meet Becky's. "But that's not the only message I had. There's a text, too. From Lucy."

"The mystery cousin? What's it say?"

Jules handed Becky her phone.

Becky read the message out loud. "I found my birth father. I found yours, too. He wants to meet you. Call me."

CHAPTER FORTY-THREE

"So, what did you decide to do about your biological father?" Becky asked when it seemed clear Jules wasn't going to bring it up.

"I'm not sure yet. I talked to Tim about it last night when I got back from Bobby's."

"What does he think?"

"He thinks I should at least call Lucy and see what she has to say. Then based on whatever she tells me, I can decide. You know what's weird? If I had found him before Barb, I would have been jumping up and down, but now—"

"He told Lucy he wants to meet you. That has to mean something." Becky knew Jules had strong feelings that he had known all about her but didn't want to be involved.

"I know." Jules pushed back her chair from the desk. "Want coffee?"

Becky wasn't fooled by her best friend's sudden need for caffeine. She was buying time.

"Nah. Another cup and I'll bounce off the walls. Will you just bring me a bottle of water?" She watched as Jules moved in slow motion in their little kitchenette.

"If you don't want to talk about it, we don't have to," Becky said when Jules finally came back to her desk.

Jules shrugged and handed Becky the water. "I guess if I'm so hesitant, maybe I'm not ready."

Becky put the bottle down on the desk and reached out to grab Jules's hand before she walked away. "And that's okay. You don't have to do anything you don't want to do."

Jules backed up and sat on the edge of Becky's desk. "I should at least call Lucy, right?"

Becky dipped her head. "When you're ready."

Jules sipped her coffee and then changed the subject. "What about Bobby? We need to tell Donna we found him."

Becky winced as she considered Donna's reaction. "How do you think she'll feel knowing how good her father was to those kids?"

"It was only a short amount of time. Jerry knew he was dying, and after he lost the case, he retired, so he had a lot more free time."

Becky gave Jules a hard stare. "Still."

Jules leaned back on her palms. "We just need to frame it up carefully. Donna was bitter. Maybe he thought it would be too hard to make amends at the end."

"He was probably right. I just hope Donna gives the Taylors a chance."

"She seemed to have a change of heart about Ally." Jules hopped off the desk and grabbed her phone. "Let's give her a call."

Donna didn't even say hello when she answered. "Did the paternity test come in?"

"We haven't gotten anything back from the lab yet," Jules said. "But after you left yesterday, we figured out something else."

"Oh yeah, what's that?"

"We figured out who Robert Taylor is. The one named in your father's will."

"So, not the man who was murdered?" Donna seemed to be holding her breath.

"No."

Donna exhaled loudly on the other end. "So maybe the man who was killed has nothing to do with the will. Maybe it's not related to me at all. Jay *could* be innocent."

Jules threw Becky a look of concern that made it clear she thought Donna was still in denial. "Most likely his murder was a case of mistaken identity," Jules said as gently as possible. "He worked in the same building as your father—I mean, *we* thought he was the right person."

Donna let out a soft groan. "I know. I'm grasping at straws. The knife that killed him came from my apartment and they found blood on Jay's sneaker. I need to accept it, but—" A sob caught in her throat. "It's hard when Jay keeps calling me— telling me he didn't do it. Why won't he just admit it? At least to me?" She started crying.

"I'm so sorry," Becky said, and her heart broke for Donna. The betrayal had to be so painful. Maybe this wasn't a good time to tell her about the Taylors.

"They record all the calls from jail, Donna. I'm sure Jay knows that," Jules said.

They heard Donna sniffle and then blow her nose. "You think he can't admit it because they're listening?"

"I'm just saying it's possible. I wouldn't expect Jay would do anything but profess his innocence if he knows the call is being taped."

There was silence on the line, and then Donna said reluctantly, "I guess that's true."

"We know you didn't go to his appearance. Have you been to visit him?" Becky asked.

"I've thought about it. His brother is trying to convince me I should stand by him. He thinks the truth will come out."

"Well, you know Jay better than anyone," Becky said softly. "Maybe you should go see him yourself."

"That's what's killing me. Maybe I don't know him as well as I thought I did." Donna groaned. "Tell me about Robert. The one who *wasn't* murdered."

"Are you sure you're up to it?" Becky asked. "We can always do it another day."

"Why wait? I'm always up to hearing about someone who got my father to leave them so much of his money."

Becky cleared her throat. "Robert Taylor, or rather Bobby Taylor, was a client of your father's."

"A client?"

"Yes, more precisely, he was your dad's last case before he retired."

"Did he lose the case?" Donna asked pointedly.

"Pretty much. How did you know?"

"Because my dad would never have retired if he hadn't lost a case. I'm guessing he wasn't up to par because of the cancer, but he would never have admitted it. So, he felt guilty. That's why he left him the money. Because he lost."

Becky was starting to wish they were having this conversation in person. "That might not be the only reason."

"What else could it be?"

"Bobby—he's paralyzed," Becky said. "He fell from a zipline because the safety latch broke. That's why he was suing."

Donna was silent for a moment. "My grandfather—my dad's father— was paralyzed, too. He had a hard life. My dad was only twelve, but he had to go to work to help out. Does Bobby have kids?"

"Three. Two boys and a girl."

"So, he left them the money so they wouldn't have to

struggle like he did," Donna said matter-of-factly. "He knew he was dying and decided to be charitable. I guess I can't be mad. It's not like there's more family I didn't know about."

"We went to see him. Jules and me. We had dinner with them."

"Dinner?" Donna sounded confused as if she had misunderstood. "You both had dinner with Bobby Taylor and his family?"

"We went to see him, and they invited us to stay," Becky said. "It seems your father spent a lot of time there, even after the case was over. He was very close to the entire family." She wasn't sure how to tell her about the house.

Jules must have sensed her hesitation and offered a shrug that seemed to say she'd bite the bullet for both of them. "When we went there, they told us—"

"Told you what?"

"Your father sold his house to the Taylors."

There was silence on the line that went on longer than expected.

"Donna, they very much want to meet you," Becky said finally.

She let out a snort. "What for? Wasn't the house and the money enough?"

Becky and Jules traded glances. This wasn't going the way they'd hoped.

"Where'd they move from?" Donna asked.

"They didn't say."

"So, this is why he didn't leave me the house. His own daughter. How much did he sell it to them for?"

"I'm—I'm really not sure," Becky said uncomfortably.

"It doesn't matter. I'm sure it's all on the internet somewhere."

"They're really a wonderful family," Jules added in an obvious attempt to redirect the conversation. "They welcomed your dad, and they want to welcome you. They're going to call you. Invite you over for a barbeque."

"A barbeque?" Donna asked sharply. "At my old house. That seems odd."

"It won't be once you meet them. Trust us, they're very welcoming."

"If they're so nice, I guess it's a good thing no one killed this one, huh? I'll think about it. Let me know when you get news about the paternity test. I'll need all of Ally's information when she makes her plans to fly in."

"And Jay?" Becky asked.

"I'll think about going to see him. Maybe he'll give me answers if I'm sitting right in front of him."

After they disconnected the call, Becky turned to Jules. "So last night in bed, Bryan said something interesting."

Jules smiled. "In bed? Are you sure you want to share his sweet nothings?"

Becky swatted at her playfully. "This was before. I mean, my ovaries were *killing* me when I left that sweet little Tory."

"I had a feeling they might be."

Becky opened her mouth to say something but then closed it. She'd learned that lesson a long time ago.

Jules was staring at her expectantly. "So, what did Bryan say?"

"Oh, right. He said he had a feeling something wasn't right about this case. That we should be careful and not assume anyone is telling the truth."

Jules tilted her head as she considered it. "Why do you think he said that?"

Becky didn't know that he had a legitimate reason. "Just a feeling he had."

Jules got up and headed to the kitchen. She shot Becky a look over her shoulder. "Maybe it's to keep you checking in, so he knows where you are at all times."

"Bryan wouldn't do that. He seemed serious. And worried." Becky continued to speak as Jules returned crunching an apple. "This morning, before I left for work, he did something to my phone so it would always share its location with him. You know, in case I forget to check in."

Jules bit into her apple while she considered this. "Hopefully, that will ease his mind a little. This will all be over soon. We'll get Ally's results and plan her trip here. They'll each get their money, and the case will be closed."

Jules set down her apple and flipped open her laptop. "I wonder—well, that's a relief." She spun the computer around so Becky could see the screen. "Donna's results are in at the site where Ally tested. They're a match. Right in the range of half-sisters. At least we know there won't be any surprises when the paternity test comes in."

Becky let out a deep breath. "That's good news." She wondered again about Bryan's gut feeling and his warning. *Trust no one.* Her mind replayed the call they'd just had. What was it Donna had said? *I'll need all Ally's information when she makes her plans to fly in.*

Maybe they did still need to be careful. Suddenly her heart did a backflip in her chest. They'd just told Donna where Robert Taylor and his family lived. What if she was the one lying to them?

CHAPTER FORTY-FOUR

"You're early," Becky said when Donna walked into the office. She gave Donna a hopeful look. "You must be ready to meet your sister."

Donna shrugged, but her lips held a small smile. "I suppose I am."

"Hope you're hungry. The food at Geraca's is amazing."

"Why can't I just take my own car to the restaurant?" Donna asked with a scowl. "I can meet you there."

Becky was just about to dismiss her suggestion when Donna's phone rang.

Donna glanced at the ID. A deep crease formed between her eyebrows as she answered, "Jay?"

Becky and Jules exchanged a curious glance.

"So, they're just letting you go?" Donna slid into a chair, the back of her hand against her forehead while she listened. "Uh, huh," she muttered once and then again. "Okay, then we can talk later," Donna said finally before hanging up.

Donna pinched her lips together and turned her gaze to Jules and Becky. "Jay's out of jail. His brother just picked him up."

"Out of jail? That's great," Becky said. "Isn't it? That must mean he didn't murder Robert."

Donna nodded slowly. "There was unidentified DNA at the murder scene. Blood. Mixed with Robert Taylor's blood." Donna pointed at her hand while she gazed off. "Jay had a Band-Aid on his finger. Said he cut it on a piece of glass. I thought—I was sure—" She ran her hand over her face and then met their eyes with a dazed look. "It wasn't his. It wasn't Jay's DNA at the murder scene."

Jules lifted her eyebrows. "So, whose DNA was it?"

Donna shook her head hesitantly as if she was still in shock Jay had been released. "They don't know yet. I guess that takes longer to figure out. They just know it wasn't his."

"So, that's it?" Becky asked. "It's over?"

"For now, I guess," Donna said with a shrug. "Apparently, they also found a surveillance camera near the job site he said he was at that backed up his alibi. The blood on the sneaker they took from our apartment wasn't Robert's. It was Jay's. From when he cut his finger, just like he said. I suppose there's still the matter of his fingerprints on the knife and the rest of the evidence they thought pointed to him. He said they could still reinstate the charges if they find evidence that he was involved somehow."

"But how could his fingerprints be on the knife and someone else's blood be at the crime scene?" Becky asked. "Wouldn't the person who killed Rob have cut themself on the murder weapon?"

"According to Robert Taylor's wife, her husband always carried a pocket-knife. They didn't find it on the body, so the police think he pulled it out during the struggle and cut whoever killed him. They never found it."

Jules scowled. "But they conveniently found the murder weapon. The whole thing seems fishy."

Donna nodded. "I guess that's what the police think now, too."

"Did you want to go home?" Becky asked hesitantly. "Or do you still want to go meet your sister?"

Donna pushed herself up from the chair. "I told Jay we'd talk later. I'm ready to go meet my sister, and I'm definitely ready to get my money. What I'm not quite sure about is getting married anytime soon."

Becky nodded with a soft laugh. "That's probably the best plan for right now." She checked the time on her phone and glanced at Jules. "We probably need to go."

In the parking lot, Donna looked over at her car longingly.

"Just come with us. Jules will bring you back later," Becky said. She still had an uneasy feeling. If Jay hadn't killed Robert, who had? There was still no proof Donna didn't know what was going on.

They just settled into the car when Jules's phone started ringing.

"It's Ally. She must have just landed." Jules answered the call on hands-free. "Hey, Ally, are you on the ground?"

"I am. My mom decided to come and bring my daughter, but they're coming on a later flight, so I'll just need to tell them where to go when they land. We all want to meet Donna."

"That's great. She's looking forward to meeting you, too." Jules glanced into the back seat and gave Donna a pointed look.

Ally's voice came through the speaker. "I was perfectly fine taking an Uber to meet you, but thanks so much for sending the car service. It is easier, I guess."

Becky threw a frantic gaze at Jules. "Car service?" she asked.

"Yeah, it was actually pretty cool to see my name and have someone waiting for me." Ally giggled. "I feel like I'm famous."

"He had your name on one of those cards they hold up?" Jules asked.

"Right. The driver said you sent him to get me at the airport. I'm in the car now, and he's putting my bag in the trunk. It shouldn't take me too long to get to the restaurant, right?"

Becky's heart thumped wildly. "She needs to get out of there," she whispered to Jules.

Jules tried to keep her voice measured and calm. "Ally, I'm going to tell you to do something, and I need you to trust me. Is he still putting your bag in the trunk?"

"No. We're getting ready to go, so I should be there—"

"Ally, listen to me." Jules's tone was urgent now. "I need you to open the car door and *run*. Go back into the airport. Get away from—" The call disconnected.

"Call her back," Becky screamed in a panic.

Jules hastily redialed the number, but it went right to voice-mail. She groaned loudly. "No answer."

Becky's hand flew to her throat. She couldn't breathe. "We should have told her to leave her bag and run the minute she called. Jules, why didn't we just tell her to run?"

Donna leaned forward and stuck her head between the two front seats. "What the hell's the matter with you two? There's probably just bad reception at the airport."

Becky whipped her head in Donna's direction. "We didn't send anyone to pick her up. Someone's *taking* your sister, and who knows what might happen to her." Becky gave her an intense stare. "If you know anything, you *have* to tell us."

"Know anything? Like what?" Donna asked, indignant.

"Who the hell would be trying to get your sister?" Jules asked sharply.

"You really think I had something to do with this?"

Jules threw up her hands. "We don't know what to think

anymore, but Ally's in serious danger if we don't figure this out."

Becky grabbed Jules's arm. "She has another phone. Remember, we called her on that number first? Maybe she has both phones with her." Becky hastily scrolled through all the numbers on her phone and finally looked up. "Did we call her from your phone or mine?"

She bit on her lip as she scrolled through a long list of numbers and tried to remember when they had first called her. Finally, she glanced up again, defeated. "I know I wrote it down. It has to be in the office."

Jules slammed the car into park, and the three of them raced toward the stairs to their office.

Becky inserted her key and pushed open the door. She ran to her desk and rifled through the stack of papers.

She let out a frustrated moan and raked her fingers through her hair. "What would I have done with it?"

"Take a deep breath," Jules said. "Let's think about the day we talked to her. We called Molly first. Maybe you wrote the number on the papers we printed with Molly's information."

Becky jabbed the air with her finger. "Right. That's exactly what I did." She shuffled through papers in her inbox. "I found it." Becky started to dial the number.

Donna ran over and ripped the phone out of her hand. "Don't," she insisted. "Think about it. Don't you watch any of those scary movies? The bad guy's chasing the girl, so she goes into the closet to call someone to help her. When the guy who's looking for her gets close, she hangs up so he won't hear her, but the dumb person on the other end always calls right back. The ringing phone gives her away so he can find her."

Jules pressed her lips together and eyed Becky. "She might have a point."

"He probably grabbed the phone Ally just called on,"

Donna said. "The last thing you want to do is alert him she might have another one."

Becky held her head in her hands. "So, we just need to pray she has it, and somehow she can call us? I can't just sit here and do *nothing*." She spun around. "Jules, call Jonas. Ask him what we should do."

Becky turned back to Donna. "Do you have any idea who'd want to hurt Ally?" As Donna started to shake her head, Becky grabbed her shoulders. "Maybe Jay *didn't* kill Robert. Maybe whoever has Ally did. She could be in real trouble, Donna. Do you have *any* idea who it could be?"

Donna frantically shook her head. "I don't. I swear."

Becky rubbed her eyes, and then her gaze landed on Jules. "Anything from Jonas?"

Jules put the phone down on the desk and pressed the speaker button.

"So, you have no idea who might have picked her up, no inkling of a car, a description, anything?" Jonas asked.

Jules shook her head, even though she knew he couldn't see her. "No, nothing. We have no idea who it is or where he'll take her." Jules swallowed past the lump in her throat. "Jonas, he might not take her anywhere. He might just pull over and ..." She didn't finish the thought.

"Okay, give me her cell number and let me see if I can get someone to see where it pinged last. If this guy didn't turn it off at the airport, we might have some luck."

"Give him the other number, too," Becky said. She ran back to her desk for the piece of paper it was written on and thrust it in front of Jules.

Jules nodded and took the paper. "We think she might have two phones. We're hoping he doesn't know about the second one, so maybe he wouldn't have shut it off." Jules read off both numbers. "Please let us know if you find out anything."

Becky leaned against Jules's desk and put her face in her

hands. "This is our fault," she said as she started to cry. "Bryan was right. We shouldn't have been so trusting. Why didn't we go to the airport and pick her up ourselves? We would have been there."

Donna sunk into a chair. "You thought it was Jay," she said quietly. "You thought if the boogeyman was in jail, then who could hurt her?" She met Becky's eyes. "But the police confirmed Jay didn't kill Robert, so it can't be him."

"Is it just a big coincidence that he's out of jail and someone grabbed her?" Jules asked, her tone accusatory. "I hate to say it, but he has to be involved in this somehow."

"You said Jay's brother picked him up. Does he drive a silver car?" Becky asked.

Donna pressed her lips together. "He usually drives with Jay. I only saw his car once, but it was dark out." She shrugged helplessly. "I don't know if it was silver."

"Beck, we don't know the guy in the silver car picked up Ally," Jules said.

"It has to be him. Nothing else makes sense."

"But even so, Jay's brother would have nothing to gain." Jules turned to Donna. "And didn't you say he had an alibi for the time of Robert's murder?"

"He did. The police said it checked out."

Beck groaned. "Is there any way he could have lied? Maybe he's not in it with Jay, but he figures if Jay gets the money, he can get his brother to will it to him."

Jules looked skeptical. "Beck, that's a lot of dead people before the brother sees a cent. Plus, he needs Donna and Jay to get married."

"I know, but I don't know who else would benefit by taking Ally." Becky groaned. "I feel helpless just sitting here, but I don't have any idea what else to do."

"And what do we do when Ally's mother and daughter show up, and we have no idea where she is?" Jules asked.

Becky bent at the waist and let out a moan. "It can't end like this. It just can't."

Donna's eyes welled up with tears. "I was actually starting to think it might be nice to have a sister. I can't be this close and then not even get to meet her."

"You actually have met her." Becky pulled over a chair and sat next to Donna.

Donna wiped at her eyes. "What?"

"We went to talk to Ella."

"My father's secretary? What did she tell you?" Donna shook her head. "I've never met Ally, I swear."

Becky leaned forward in her chair. "Molly came to your father's office with Ally when she was a toddler. Ella followed her into the parking lot. She offered to help support Molly if your father wouldn't. But first, she did a paternity test to make sure Ally was really his."

Donna looked at Becky expectedly. "And?"

"She was."

Donna let out a breath. "So, Ella sent them her own money?"

Becky shook her head. "She set Molly up as a corporation and paid her with the company money."

Donna let out a snort. "Oh, that's brilliant. I always did love her. She never let my father get away with anything. But I never—"

Becky anchored her gaze on Donna. "Ella's house. She used to invite you over. Dinners. Holidays."

Donna narrowed her eyes ever so slightly. "Right, but—"

"Ally's real name is Alexandra," Becky said softly. "You called her Alex."

The air escaped Donna in one loud whoosh. "I loved that little girl. She was my sister? And my father never knew?"

Becky shrugged. "We don't think he knew Ella befriended

Molly. Ella did think maybe he saw the paternity test at some point. She had it in her drawer, but it disappeared."

"I can't believe—" Donna was interrupted by a ringing phone.

"Whose is it?" Becky asked as her gaze flew around the office.

"It's yours."

Becky scrambled for the phone, glanced at the ID, and put it on speaker. "Ally?"

The voice on the other end sounded petrified. "Becky, I'm scared. The guy who picked me up from the airport—he grabbed my other phone and brought me somewhere. I don't understand what's happening. I have no idea where he took me. I'm in a shed of some sort."

"Ally, I'm so sorry. We didn't send that man to pick you up, but we're going to find him. Please hang on. We'll find you." Even as Becky said the words, she prayed they were true. If they didn't know who had her, how would they ever save her in time?

Donna sat silently, her chin on her clasped hands as if she was praying.

"I think I hear him. I need to hang up before he realizes I have another phone." Ally's voice broke. "Please hurry."

"Jules, call Jonas," Becky said, her tone urgent. "The other phone is definitely on. Tell him to ping that one."

Donna narrowed her eyes and then jolted upright. She shook her head, jumped to her feet, and without a word, took off toward the office's front door.

CHAPTER FORTY-FIVE

"Donna, wait," Jules yelled. With a panicked gaze at Becky, she sprang from her seat and went after her. "We'll call the police," she called out. "We need to let them handle this."

The sound of the front door slamming confirmed Donna had no plans to wait.

"What do we do?" Becky asked frantically.

"Grab your stuff. We need to follow her."

"Oh, Bryan's gonna kill me." Becky grabbed her purse and followed Jules out the door.

"There." Becky pointed toward the exit as she yanked the car door closed. "That's her car."

"Hang on." Jules put the car in reverse, the tires squealing when she punched the gas. She raced toward the exit, but Donna had already left the lot and pulled out into traffic. Jules glanced to the left and peeled out onto the road. "Do you see her car anymore?"

Becky scanned the lanes ahead. "There. Up there, in front of the red pickup."

Jules cursed loudly as an older woman drove next to her at precisely the same speed. She called these people creepers. She couldn't get around her, and there was a car directly in front of her. Jules was stuck.

"C'mon, c'mon, get out of the way," she shouted.

Finally, Jules fixed a hard stare on the driver next to her and leaned on the horn. The older woman glanced over in her direction. Jules pointed at the road in front of her car and mouthed *emergency*.

The woman scowled.

"Please." Jules was screaming, hoping the woman would understand even if she couldn't hear the urgency in Jules's voice. Finally, the woman rolled her eyes and slowed her car. Jules swiftly changed lanes to get in front of her.

Jules gave Becky a quick glance. "Do you still see her?"

"I think Donna made it through the light."

Jules pounded on the steering wheel as the light turned red, and they were forced to stop. If Donna had sailed through, they'd never find her now. As she sat impatiently waiting, the older woman pulled up behind her. Jules glanced in the rearview mirror to see the old woman holding her hands up, seeming to mock her that she hadn't gotten very far.

Jules gritted her teeth. "I swear, if I wasn't in a hurry—"

Becky grabbed her arm. "Jules, go, it's green."

Jules punched the gas, and her car shot off the line, leaving the old woman lagging far behind. "Any sign of her?"

Becky sat up in her seat and scanned the road. "No," she moaned. "Oh, wait, wait. I think that's her. Speed up."

Jules glanced down at the speedometer. "If I go any faster, we're going to get pulled over or cause a wreck."

"I know, I know. She's just past the bank up there, in the right lane. She's heading for the highway."

"Going in what direction?"

"I don't know!"

"Keep watching her." Jules weaved in and out of other

cars. Finally, she got in the far right lane with no one in front of her.

"She's getting off," Becky said impatiently. "We need to catch her."

The speedometer hit seventy and then eighty and then close to ninety. If Jules took the exit at this speed, they would crash for sure. "I'm going as fast as I can." Adrenaline had her heart racing.

"If she gets around the curve, we won't be able to see which way she's heading." Becky sat up in her seat. "Take the exit. She's getting off."

Jules lifted her foot only slightly off the gas and held her breath as they took the exit. She gripped the steering wheel while Becky strained to see as far up the road as she could.

Just as Jules headed into the curve, Becky screamed, "South. She went south."

"Okay." Jules could afford to get a little control over the car now. She followed the highway sign and merged. Once she was safely on the road, she brought her speed back up. "Do you see her?"

Becky nodded. "I can see her. She's just *flying*."

"Then hold on because so are we."

"Should I try to call her?" Becky asked as she held on to the handle above her door.

Jules focused on the road. "If we lose her, we'll try that. Right now, I need you to keep an eye on her car."

Becky raised up off her seat to look above the cars in front of them. "She's getting over to the right lane. She might be getting off."

Jules changed lanes, but now she was stuck behind someone. She veered back to the left and went around them, skidding back into the right lane.

"I can't even imagine how much road rage I've caused today," Jules said as she exhaled a puff of air.

"Too bad. Okay, I was right. Donna's getting off." Becky pointed at the highway sign up ahead. "Get off at the next exit."

As they pulled up to the light, it was red.

"Damn." Jules pounded her fist against the steering wheel. "Any idea if she made a left or a right?"

"I can't see that far." Becky groaned. They were stuck behind two other cars. "Maybe I should call her now." She reached for her phone and dialed. "Voicemail. Why would Donna not tell us where she's going?" Becky held her head in her hands and then turned to face Jules. "Maybe she *is* in on it." The light changed to green. "We have a fifty-fifty chance. Make a—make a right."

Jules yanked the wheel to the right and immediately made her way around the other cars.

"I see her." Becky pointed up the road. "She's stuck at the next light by the McDonald's." She gave Jules a hard stare. "When it changes, you need to make it through, too."

"Oh, I will." Jules sped up, and just as the light turned to green, she was several cars behind Donna heading through it. She nodded at Becky. "Good call on making the right."

"I can't breathe." Becky's hands were on her chest.

"Just keep your eye on the prize," Jules said firmly. Donna was still a little way up the road ahead of them.

"Are you kidding me?" Jules let out a loud groan as a land-scaping truck pulling a trailer eased out in front of her. She slammed on the brakes to avoid hitting him. "Don't take your eyes off her, Beck. Let me figure out how to get around this moron. I mean, seriously, he's doing twenty-five in a forty-five."

Becky got up on her knees to peer over the truck. "I can still see her. We're not going to lose her."

Jules beeped her horn at the truck, but it did no good. Workers were sitting in the back of the pickup truck, curiously watching her as she gestured wildly at them.

"I can't take it anymore," Jules moaned as the truck came to a stop at a set of railroad tracks. "Nobody's coming. Just *go*," she wailed even though she knew the driver couldn't hear her.

"It's okay. Donna just slowed down," Becky said as she took in their surroundings.

Jules pressed her lips together. The truck lumbered to a slow start, almost as if it was dawdling on purpose to frustrate her.

"I've never wanted to ram my car into somebody as much as I do right now," Jules said through gritted teeth. "Those guys in the back would go flying. They're not even supposed to be in the bed of the truck."

Becky patted her on the arm. "We've got her. I know exactly where she's going."

CHAPTER FORTY-SIX

DONNA SLIPPED OUT of the car and shut the door gently so as not to make any noise. Her pulse raced as she ducked down and ran toward the neighbor's property. The houses were divided by a fence, but the shed was in the backyard behind a closed gate.

Donna crept along the fence line on the neighbor's property, stopping when the wooden structure was directly on the other side. The fence was old and rotting, but the boards weren't flush. She peered through the space between the slats and then turned to place her ear at the opening, straining to hear anything. The only thing she heard was her own heartbeat thumping in her ears.

Donna made her way farther down the fence until she was in the area behind the shed. One of the slats had rotted through where the top nail had previously held it in place. The wood had curled back in the Florida heat. She pulled gently and cringed when it made a cracking sound as it broke off in her hand. She paused a moment, ready to take off if the noise had alerted him to her presence.

When nothing happened, she peeked through the opening

she had made. There was a slat on his side she'd need to push out of the way if she had any hope of slipping through. Donna knew she had to enter the yard behind the shed so she'd be hidden. She reached through the fence, pushed on the wooden slat, and let out a breath of relief when it gave way easily. One hard push and it would crack.

She held her breath. In one quick movement, Donna lifted her foot and gave a swift kick. It gave way, and she froze, hesitating to make sure the piece of wood falling from the fence hadn't been noticed. She threw a glance at the house behind her. The last thing she needed was the neighbors screaming about her busting up their decrepit fence.

When she didn't hear anything, she held her breath and squeezed between the remaining slats. Grunting, she pushed her way through and stifled a moan when her shirt caught on a splinter of wood. She tugged at the hem of her shirt until the material ripped, setting her free to step through to the other side. She rubbed her arm where the wood had scraped it raw as perspiration dripped down her face.

Donna ducked down and made her way around the side of the shed. There were no windows, so she couldn't see inside. Ally had to be here. She just had to be. Donna crouched close to the ground and crawled around to the front.

The lock was still in place. That had to mean Ally was locked inside. With a furtive glance toward the house, Donna prayed the code for the lock was the same. She rolled to each of the four numbers, stealing glances toward the back door. When they were all in place, she closed her eyes and tugged.

Relief flooded through her when the metal of the lock lifted, and she put her hand on her chest. Her heart thumped so hard against her ribs, she wondered if she might pass out. The sun beating down on her wasn't helping.

Gingerly, she lifted the lock out of place and held it in her hand while she pulled back the latch it had kept shut. With one last look toward the back door of the house, she gently opened the shed and slipped inside.

"Ally," she whispered into the darkness.

A muffled grunt responded.

"It's Donna. I'm here to get you out of here." She pulled her phone from her back pocket and switched on the flashlight. She shone it around until she found Ally curled up on the floor with her hands tied and her mouth gagged.

"Oh my god, it is you." Donna rushed to Ally's side and struggled with the gag until she was able to move it out of her mouth.

Ally licked her lips and swallowed hard. "Donna?"

When she nodded, Ally smiled meekly. "My mother was right. We do look alike."

"We have plenty of time for a reunion later. Let's get you out of here first. Can you turn around so I can see if I can get your hands untied?"

Ally scooted on the floor until her hands faced Donna. "I think he zip tied them."

Donna leaned down to check. "Such an asshole," she mumbled.

"Do you know the guy who took me? Why me? I don't understand any of this."

"I'm not sure I understand why either, but hang on." Donna used the flashlight to look around the shed. "There's a toolbox around here somewhere. At least there used to be."

She aimed the light toward the shelves against the wall until she found the metal box she was looking for. Lifting it carefully so as not to make any noise, she strained under the weight of it but finally set it down on the floor next to Ally.

After Donna lifted the lid, she rummaged around it as quietly as she could until she found a pair of clippers.

Donna knelt down. "He's got this tight." She slid the clippers under the plastic that was binding Ally's hands together. "I'm trying not to hurt you."

"Do whatever you need to do. Just get me out of here," Ally pleaded.

With one precise clip, her hands were freed. As the plastic fell away, Ally rubbed her wrists.

"Okay, let's go. Do you need help getting up?" Donna asked.

Ally nodded slowly. "Maybe. I've been sitting too long like this. I think I've lost feeling in my legs."

Donna helped Ally to her feet, holding her steady when she wobbled slightly. "Let me know when you have your bearings."

Ally met Donna's eyes and dipped her head.

"Okay, there's a small opening in the fence, which is how I got into the backyard. It will let us out into the neighbor's yard. My car is parked at the curb—the black Hyundai. Just run as fast as your legs will take you. You ready?"

Ally's voice sounded determined in the darkness. "I'm ready."

Donna made her way carefully through the darkened shed, with Ally right behind her holding onto her belt loop. The shed door creaked when Donna put her hand on it, years of rust betraying them as it announced their departure. She turned and spoke over her shoulder into the darkness. "Get ready to run."

Donna put her head down and swung the door open. The shed flooded with sunlight, and for a moment, she was blinded as her eyes adjusted from the darkness. She blinked hard, and as she looked up and took a step forward, strong hands shoved her backward until she and Ally tumbled over each other as they hit the floor.

"Well, damn, Donna, you've shown up early." The smile he gave her was wicked. "I wasn't ready to kill you just yet."

CHAPTER FORTY-SEVEN

He'd always been able to smell fear on her. Not this time. Donna wouldn't give him the satisfaction. Her gaze drifted to his hands. Empty. The fact that he didn't seem to have a weapon bolstered her bravado.

She stared up at him from the floor, her blue eyes blazing with contempt. "What do you think you're doing, asshole?" Her strong voice belied the trepidation that had her stomach twisting.

Nick's thin-lipped mouth turned into a sneer. "I upped my game on this one, don't you think? And by the way, just in case you bought that sob story I was peddlin', I'm not sorry about *shit*. And I certainly haven't given up drinking."

"Take your problems out on me, then. My sister has nothing to do with you."

Nick leaned up against the shed's doorframe, his worn work boots in Donna's line of sight. "Oh, but she does." He rubbed his chin thoughtfully. "You showing up here like this does change things a bit. You just had to butt your nose into my business, didn't you?"

"Your business? If you're smart, you'll let us go. Jay knows where we are."

He didn't, but Nick didn't have to know that. Donna scooted back along the floor, out of kicking distance.

"He'd like nothing more than to have a reason to kill you," she said through clenched teeth.

Nick snickered. "There's a couple things wrong with this little pretend scenario of yours. First of all, your savior Jay is in jail. I'm pretty sure they don't let a murderer out of jail to rescue anyone."

Donna glared at him. "Jay's not in jail anymore. They let him out because he's not a murderer, and you damn well know he's not." She glanced at the bandage on his right arm. "Did Robert Taylor get you with his pocketknife, Nick? Your blood at the crime scene was Jay's get out of jail free card."

Nick reached down and covered his arm. He studied Donna through eyes narrowed into slits. "I think you're full of it. There's no way they'd let him out. I mean, his fingerprints and DNA are on the murder weapon. Nice try. Nobody's coming to save you."

He glanced over Donna's head at Ally. "Since Robert's out of the picture, now I just have your pretty little sister to contend with."

Donna glanced back at her sister, who was crouched behind a lawnmower. She whipped her head back around. "You killed the wrong guy, you moron."

Nick scratched the side of his head. "Really? Well, *that* sets me behind schedule. If you know he was the wrong guy, then you must know where the right guy is." He shook his head and let out a dramatic sigh. "I may need to keep you both alive longer than I planned."

He nodded at Ally. "I saw the email. She's a perfect match to your dear old dad. So, jackpot, she gets the money." He winked at Donna. "Unless, of course, she's dead. But let me think, I probably need to kill the right Robert first, so his family doesn't try to stick their greedy hands in the pot. Once they're both out of the way, the rest of the money goes to you, my rich little minx. For as long as you're alive anyway."

"You're an idiot, Nick," Donna spewed as hatred flooded her features. "If you kill me, no one gets the money. It certainly wouldn't go to you."

Nick cocked his head as he seemed to consider this. "Too bad for Jay he didn't drag you down the aisle yet. As your husband, then he would have inherited everything." He sneered. "But you see, Donna, you wouldn't have been able to marry Jay. Not legally anyway." A cocky smirk filled his face. "You're still married to yours truly."

"Bullshit," Donna spit out through clenched teeth.

"You didn't really think I'd let you legally let me go with a rich daddy about to kick the bucket? Of course, I didn't quite count on him recovering from that first bout of cancer." Nick shrugged. "I guess good things come to those who wait."

Donna shot him a venomous look, her pulse racing. "You're full of it. We signed the papers."

"Uh, huh. You're right, we did. You so kindly offered to let me handle it all." He crossed his arms against his chest. "I still remember that night, the restaurant where we met. You were so grateful to be done with it all. Walk away and let me file the papers through my attorney." He leaned in over her, and she could smell his breath, a mixture of beer and weed. "I'll let you in on a little secret."

Donna gritted her teeth. "Let me guess. You didn't file them."

Nick shook his head. "'Fraid not, sweetheart. You see, I didn't really want to be divorced. I *tried* to tell you that, but you just wouldn't listen. Told my lawyer we reconciled." He tsked. "The court never even saw those papers."

Donna lunged for him. He spun her around and put his

forearm against her neck. "That wasn't very nice." He whispered in her ear, his breath hot and sticky on her cheek. "I remember when you used to be *real* nice to me." He pulled her tight against him and then reached between their bodies. He yanked her phone out of her back pocket. "You won't be needing this." He pushed her away from him, down into a pile of boxes.

Donna grabbed her throat as she expelled the air his grip had prevented. As she tried to sit up and catch her breath, she heard a loud whimper.

Nick's glance drifted in Ally's direction. "Well, look at you. Seems like someone took that gag out of your mouth." He knelt over her and yanked the cloth from around her neck.

As he leaned over, Donna saw the gun protruding from the back of his pants. A sly smile filled his face as he leered at Ally. "Maybe just one little kiss first."

Rage filled Donna's insides as he pressed his lips hard against Ally's. She squirmed in his grasp. Donna cringed and shook her head at Ally as she tried to mime behind his back that he had a gun.

"Oh, pretty girl." Nick smacked his lips. "I wish you and me had more time together. Alone time." He placed his boot on Ally's chest and retied the gag tight in her mouth.

He had a gun. It was now or never.

As he turned, Donna jumped on him. She grabbed for his face, his eyes. She would dig her thumbs into them until he never looked at anyone with that lecherous stare again. Then his fist connected with her jaw. He grabbed at her arms and sent her flying into the metal shelves. Some of the contents rained down on top of her as she crumpled to the floor.

Nick reached behind him, pulled the gun from his waistband, and pointed it at her.

"Listen, I'm not going to tell you again. Behave, or I'll have to kill you sooner rather than later."

Donna glared at him, her jaw throbbing. "Kill me, and you won't see a cent. If I die before I collect, the money goes to charity."

She didn't know if that was true, but it was all she had. Before he could respond, she heard a sound in the distance.

Nick whipped his head around and then stepped backward out of the shed. "Looks like we might have company." His gaze landed on the lock that had fallen from the shelf onto the floor next to Donna. He gestured with the gun. "Get that and toss it to me."

When Donna hesitated, he cocked the gun and pointed it at Ally. "Now is not the time to test me."

With her eyes focused on the gun, Donna slowly stood. She grabbed the lock and pitched it past the doorway of the shed into the yard.

His eyes burned into hers. "This ain't baseball, bitch."

Nick backed up with the gun trained on her until he reached the lock sitting in a clump of grass. Without taking his gaze off her, he knelt and picked it up. Within seconds, the shed door slammed shut, and he locked them both back into the darkness.

CHAPTER FORTY-EIGHT

"SHE WENT INTO A NEIGHBORHOOD," Becky said, almost standing in the passenger seat. "We must be close. We'll find her as soon as we can make that right. Get ready. It's coming up."

After the last of the trailer made its way past her turn, Jules pressed the gas and swung wide past the weathered development sign that said Hunter's Glen.

She peered through the windshield. "I guess I'll drive around until we see Donna's car. She has to be here somewhere. There doesn't seem to be any other way out."

Jules made her way around the neighborhood's perimeter and then started down each street. Up one and down the next.

"There she is." Becky pointed down the street at Donna's car parked at the curb.

There was a muffled ring coming from Jules's purse. "That's my phone. Maybe Donna's calling."

Becky reached into Jules's purse and pulled out her cell. "It's Jonas."

"Answer it."

"Jonas, it's Becky." She tapped the speaker button. "Ally

called us back, and after we hung up, Donna flew out of the office. We followed her, but we have no idea where we are. Some neighborhood off exit six called Hunter's Glen."

"You're there now?"

"Yeah, she gave us a run for our money, but we just pulled in and found her car."

"I called the sheriff's office since they cover the airport. They're going to have the phone company trace Ally's phone. If it's on, they'll bring the local unit in on a possible kidnapping."

"What if it's not on?"

"Call 911. It won't hurt to have another call into the police just in case the phone was turned off." His tone turned serious. "Listen, both of you. I hope you learned your lesson after last time. Do *not* try to be heroes. Don't go in. Don't get involved. Let the police handle it."

"Don't worry," Jules said into the phone as she pulled up behind Donna's car at the curb. The driver's seat was empty. "We'll wait, but it looks like we're too late to stop Donna."

As Jules hung up with Jonas, Becky's phone rang. She winced. "It's Bryan. I never called him on the way here. This isn't going to go well."

"Hey, babe." Becky knew her voice was hesitant, her guilt evident in just those two words.

Her husband didn't even say hello. "You know what's weird, Beck? Jonas called and told me about someone grabbing Ally from the airport. Of course, I didn't have a call from you, so I felt sure you must still be at the office. Lo and behold, I track your phone, and you seem to be in some neighborhood called Hunters Glen. Care to explain?"

Becky groaned and rolled her eyes in Jules's direction. "I know. I'm sorry. There just wasn't time. After Ally called, Donna ran out of the office, and we had to follow her. I navigated for Jules."

"You had to *what?*" he shouted. "I don't believe—"

"We had to figure out where she was going, so we could call the police," Becky explained desperately. "Jules is about to call 911 right now. Jonas also has the phone company tracing Ally's phone, but we had no way of knowing if she had it—"

"And where's Donna and Ally now?" Bryan asked tersely.

Becky hesitated, but she had to admit the truth. "We don't know. We found Donna's car, but she's not in it."

Bryan took a deep breath. "Seriously, Beck, get the hell out of there and come home. Now. Tell Jules I called Tim. He's not very happy with her either. This is insane. Don't you remember any of what we went through last time?"

"I do, and I'm sorry. You're right. I know you're worried about me." Becky turned to Jules. "Tim's pretty mad, too. They want us to leave." She bowed her head and ran her hand over her face. "We'll leave now. We're going. I promise."

As Becky disconnected the call and glanced up, her breath caught in her throat. She blinked hard and prayed it was her imagination. When she opened her eyes, he was still there. The man on the other side of the car had a gun, and it was pointed at Jules.

"Jules ..." Becky wasn't even sure her voice had been loud enough to hear. It was more like her best friend's name had been expelled in a gasp of air. "Jules," she said again, only slightly louder.

"Don't worry, I'm calling 911 now. And then I guess I need to call Tim. Why would Bryan—"

Becky gripped Jules's arm, jerking back the hand that was trying to dial.

"Hey," Jules said with a slight air of annoyance. Her gaze lifted toward the passenger seat. "What?"

Becky nodded in the direction of the driver's side window. When Jules turned, she stared through the glass into the barrel of a gun.

The man stepped back from the car door, the revolver still aimed at Jules. He rubbed his free hand against the stubble on his chin and leered at her. "Well, damn, you're just as pretty up close." His face turned dark, and an iciness filled his eyes. "Now, get out."

Jules took in a stuttered breath and then slowly pushed open the car door.

"Throw your phone into the back seat," he demanded. He glanced over at Becky and gestured with the gun. "You too."

Becky and Jules both did as he said. Jules glanced over at Becky, widened her eyes, and stepped out of the car. When the man averted his eyes from Jules for a split second, Becky watched as she twisted off her engagement ring and tucked it down in the front pocket of her jeans.

They came around to her side of the car, Jules in front and the man behind her. He leaned down and pulled open the passenger side door. "You too. Let's go."

Becky slid out of the car. He slammed the door shut, then gestured with the gun. "Start walking. Did you really think you were going to drive up and save the day?" He shook his head. "Now, where the hell am I going to bury you two?"

He led them through the wooden gate and into a backyard. The man spun the dials on a combination lock holding the shed door closed.

When he swung it open, he pointed inside with the gun and called out, "I brought you some company."

As he shoved them inside, Becky squinted into the darkness as her foot hit something, and she stumbled. Hands reached out to steady her—Donna's hands. The door slammed behind them, and she could hear the metallic clink of the lock going back into place.

As her eyes adjusted to the darkness, Becky saw Ally sitting on the floor behind Donna. She let out a deep breath. "Oh, Ally, I'm so glad you're okay."

Jules was already fumbling with the gag in Ally's mouth, loosening it enough so she could remove it.

Ally licked her lips. "For now, I am."

"Why did you guys follow me?" Donna asked as she ran her hand through her hair. "The last thing I wanted was for you to be in this mess, too."

"We were worried about you." Becky gestured around the shed. "Rightfully so, it seems."

"How did you know where she was?" Jules asked.

"I used to live here. When Ally called, I heard the train whistle in the background." Donna shook her head and sighed. "I used to hate that damn train."

"You lived here?" Becky asked. Now she was perplexed. "So, who—"

"The asshole with the gun is my ex-husband, Nick. I never made the connection at first when she said she was in a shed." She shook her head apologetically. "He also drives a silver car."

Jules frowned. "Ex-husband? I don't understand. Why would he—"

"Apparently, we never got a legal divorce. Nick made sure of it. He knew I had no family, no one else. He figured my dad would leave his money to me. Then if something happened to me, accidentally or otherwise, my inheritance would go to my husband. Him."

Jules stood with her hands on her hips. "So, he was the one—"

"He killed Robert Taylor," Donna said with a slow nod. "He's been following you. I'm sure he's the one who broke into your office. It even sounded like he had access to your email." Donna leaned against the door. "He must have also broken into our apartment somehow to get the stuff to frame Jay." She gingerly touched her cheek. It felt raw and hot.

Becky strode up to Donna and tried to study her face in the darkness. "Are you okay? Did he hit you?"

"Nothing he hasn't done before," Donna said as she waved it off. "I'm fine, really. It's Ally I'm worried about. He came onto her. I was worried—"

Becky's eyes widened. "Oh, Ally—"

"I'm okay. But, man, he has terrible breath." She smiled meekly. "You should have seen Donna, though. She jumped him like she was some sort of ninja."

Donna clenched her teeth. "I wanted to kill him. I'm still mad I didn't get the chance." She groaned. "I can't believe I was gullible enough to believe he might have changed."

Becky touched Donna's arm. "But at least Jay's not a murderer. And he wasn't planning to kill you."

"There is that." Donna glanced at Ally, and her shoulders sagged. "I just feel terrible I dragged my little sister into this."

Despite the circumstances, Becky felt the corners of her mouth turn up. *My little sister.* Donna was coming around.

Jules let out a puff of air and put her hands on her hips in her typical take-charge stance.

"We need to figure out how we're getting out of here." Her gaze bounced between them. "There's four of us. I get that he has a gun, but between us, we have to figure out a way to take him down. No offense, Donna, but he doesn't seem like the sharpest tool in the shed."

Donna cringed. "No offense taken, but are you really making shed jokes right now?"

Jules groaned and threw up her hands. "You're right. I'm sorry. So, Jonas called the sheriff's office that handles the airport and reported you as a kidnapping. They should be able to get the phone company to trace your phone. I was also about to call 911 when—"

"He showed up at the car with a gun," Becky said. "He made us leave our phones in the back seat."

"He took mine, too," Donna said as she wiped the sweat from her top lip. "Damn, it's hot in here."

Jules turned to Ally. "What about your phone? The one you called us back from. Is it still turned on?"

Ally shook her head. "If I was smart, I would have called 911 first. He found it after I called you." She pointed toward the lawnmower. "I think it's over there somewhere. He stomped on it with his boot."

"Crap," Jules said. "Maybe there's a possibility they can still find the last place it pinged before it went dead."

"Or maybe no one's coming to save us," Ally said with a whimper.

Donna wove her way between Jules and Becky to get to her sister. She put her arm around her shoulders. "Don't worry. We'll figure this out. He may be an idiot, but he's not a killer."

"What about that guy Robert?" Ally asked, her brow furrowed. "It sounded like he killed him."

Donna bit her lip. "Shit. He used to just be a two-bit con man. What the hell happened that turned him into a murderer?"

There was a rustling at the door, and when it swung open, a man stood there, but this time it wasn't Nick.

Becky's breath hitched in her throat as she exchanged a confused look with Jules.

Donna's eyes went wide.

The man shook his head in disgust. "I didn't want to believe that was your car parked outside. Why couldn't you just stay out of this, Donna? It wasn't supposed to go down like this."

She skewered him with a furious stare. "You," she said accusingly. "How could you do this?"

The man shrugged, almost apologetically. "I'm not involved the way you think."

"Then, what the *hell* are you doing here?" Donna growled.
"I live here."

"You live here? With Nick? How the hell did that happen?"

And then Donna's mouth went slack. "It was you. You took the stuff from the apartment. *You* framed Jay. Where is he, Kevin? What did you do with him?"

Donna lunged at Kevin, but he pushed her backward.

"Easy," he said, his arms still out in front of him in case she came at him again. "I dropped him at home. It wasn't anything personal, Donna. Nick offered to cut me in, and all I needed to do was grab a few things from the apartment. I mean, I knew they'd let Jay go eventually. Nick just wanted him locked up until you got your money. Just to make sure you two wouldn't try to get married and find out you weren't legally divorced."

"Nick has plans to kill me, you idiot!" Donna screamed.

Kevin shook his head nervously. "No, he doesn't. He told me since you're still married, he'd just divorce you, and he'd get half the money in the settlement."

Donna let out a loud groan. "How could you have fallen for that?" She glanced back at Ally. "He killed Robert Taylor. And why do you think he grabbed my sister? Even if he could get the inheritance in a divorce settlement, which would never happen, why would he settle for half when he could kill me and get it all?"

Jules nudged Donna. "Could we fight about this later?"

Donna nodded. "Right. Move the hell out of the way, Kevin. We're out of here."

Kevin hesitated and then stepped back away from the doorway to let them pass.

Donna turned back to Jules and Ally. "Just make a run for it through the gate to my car. I still have my keys."

They all nodded, but before they could move, a loud shot rang out. Becky grabbed Jules and shuddered as Jay's brother crumpled to the grass.

Ally's piercing scream hung in the air around them.

"Not so quick." Nick now had the gun pointed at Donna. He fixed a steely gaze on Ally, who was hiding behind her sister. "I should have killed you right off and left you on the side of the road. That's on me, I guess." He raised his eyebrows. "I hoped we'd have a little alone time together before we had to say goodbye, but then the circus had to show up."

Donna pulled Ally closer to her. "Leave her alone, Nick."

He grabbed Donna's arm and yanked her away from Ally. Nick held her with one hand and whipped his other hand across her face. "You had to go and ruin everything."

Donna winced but gritted her teeth. Filled with loathing, she stared him down.

Becky wanted to run to her, make sure she was okay, but her feet were frozen to the floor in fear.

"Now I'm gonna have cars here for people who are dead. How's that gonna look, Donna?" His angry gaze drifted between the four of them. "It's time for us all to go on a little road trip."

"Nick, don't be stupid," Donna said as she backed up out of punching range. "You'll never get away with this. They'll lock you up and throw away the key."

He cocked his head as an evil sneer filled his face. "Now there's an idea for the four of you. Not to mention, now I gotta figure out what to do with that one." He gestured with the gun toward where Kevin lay bleeding in the grass outside the shed.

"C'mon, you don't want to do this," Donna pleaded. "Just let us go. We won't tell anyone about any of this, and I'll even sign over my inheritance to you. You'll still have the money, and you can go start a new life somewhere."

"Have you forgotten about our little accountant friend? And poor Kevin. Stroke of luck meeting him at the gym, huh. I figured there couldn't be two guys with the last name Kittsmiller that weren't related." He glared at her. "Did you really think I didn't know all about your new boyfriend after you left me?" He shrugged. "At this point, Donna, I don't have nothin' to lose."

His gaze shifted between Jules and Donna, and his lips curved into an evil smile. "Now, whose car has the bigger trunk?"

Becky swallowed hard and felt her eyes well up. Bryan had been right. Why hadn't she listened? Her insides felt queasy that she had done this to her husband again.

"Who wants to test them out for size?" Nick lunged for Becky, his fingers digging into her arm as he dragged her out the doorway.

The last thing Becky heard was Jules's scream as he slammed and locked the door behind them.

CHAPTER FORTY-NINE

Jules yanked on the door, convinced if she pulled hard enough, she could break the cheap lock. Finally, as sweat dripped down her face, she wilted into a heap on the floor of the shed.

After a moment, she turned to Donna. "You know him better than any of us." Jules swallowed hard. "Is he going to hurt her?"

Donna hesitated and then shrugged helplessly. "I don't know. Nick was always a con man, a drunk, but never a killer. I don't know what happened to change him ..."

"Money happened," Jules said. "Greed."

"Do you think that guy outside is dead?" Ally asked softly.

Donna shrugged again. "I hope not. Jay's going to want some answers from his brother."

Jules patted her pocket to make sure her engagement ring was still safe. She'd waited a long time for that ring, and she'd be damned if she'd let this lowlife steal it. They were going to get out of here. There was no other choice.

"We need to figure out something quick," Jules said. "Becky must be terrified."

Ally was staring down at the floor. She looked up, and her blue eyes brimmed with a small bit of hope. "Maybe they pinged my phone, and the police are coming."

Jules wiped the sweat from her forehead. "That would be great, but we need to take matters into our own hands just in case they aren't. Donna, he needs to keep you alive until he gets his money, but Becky and I …" Dread enveloped her. "He doesn't have a single reason to let Becky and I live."

"Stop. We're getting out of here. Let me think for a second." Donna glanced around. "This place is full of old junk. There has to be something we can use against him."

Donna rooted around in the back corner of the shed. There was a loud thump followed by cursing. "Ow. I wish there was some light in here."

Jules heard stuff being shoved around and dragged until finally Donna let out a squeal.

"What is it?" Ally asked.

Donna huffed as she dragged a large, heavy black bag out into the open floor space.

"Way back when, Nick thought he could meet a higher class of people to scam on the golf course." She stood the bag upright. "He stole these clubs from someone's trunk while they ate lunch at the club." She let out a snort. "He never played once." Donna pulled one of the clubs out of the bag, dusted off the cobwebs, and smiled. "Perfect weapons."

Jules nodded slowly. "I like it, but what if he sees us before we can strike and starts shooting? One of us could still get hit."

Donna dipped her head and inserted the club back into the bag. "You're right." She brought her gaze back up and met Ally's eyes, then Jules's. "This is my fault. Let me take the risk." She glanced around the shed until she spotted something and started tugging at boxes. "Help me over here."

"What is this?" Ally asked as they all pulled at a large piece of corrugated steel.

Donna let go and kicked at stuff on the floor. "Help me move some of the stuff out of the way. Otherwise, we'll never get it out."

Jules hastily relocated boxes and bags of junk to the other side of the shed.

Finally, Donna and Ally dragged the piece of sheet metal carefully out from against the wall.

"Careful," Jules said to Ally. "The edges are sharp. Don't cut yourself."

Donna glanced back toward the wall. "There should be a couple of pieces. He had some idea of reinforcing the walls in here. Who knows why? Of course, he never did it. Let's pull them all out, and you both can hide behind them. Use them like a shield in case he starts shooting."

Ally bit her bottom lip and swiped at the sweat dripping down her cheek. "Do you think they'll stop a bullet?"

"I hope so," Donna said as she examined the clubs and pulled out the one with the most oversized head. "At least until I can pretend his neck is a golf tee and his head the ball."

"You're sure you won't choke?" Jules asked, concern etched on her face. "That would leave you vulnerable if you couldn't go through with it at the last minute."

"He kidnapped my sister, grabbed your best friend, and had Jay sitting in jail." Donna shook her head swiftly, her face a mask of determination. "I *won't* choke. Trust me."

After they had carefully dragged all the sheet metal out, Ally felt her way around and got behind it.

Donna had built herself a perch out of boxes to the right of the door. "If I'm higher, I'll have the element of surprise on my side."

"Are you sure it's sturdy?" Jules asked as she pushed against the pile.

Donna planted her feet. She wobbled slightly, but not so much that the pile was in danger of collapsing. "It'll do."

Jules reached into the golf bag. "Are you sure you don't want me to get a club? Perch on the other side. You know, two against one."

Jules could make out Donna shaking her head in the darkness. "This is my fault," she said in a shaky voice. "All of it. I know I hired you, but getting shot at is above and beyond the call of duty, Jules. This is—"

A shot rang out, startling Donna. She lost her footing, and Jules reached up to steady her.

Jules felt bile rise in her throat. "Oh my god, do you think that was—"

"Get back there with Ally," Donna hissed into the darkness. "Now."

Jules scrambled back behind the metal and huddled next to Ally. Two more shots. She bowed her head and pulled Ally down until they were crouched as close to the floor as they could get. Jules's hair, matted against her head with sweat, had fallen in her face so she couldn't see.

A series of shots rang out in succession. "That's a different gun," Jules said to Ally. "Maybe it's the police."

"Or maybe he has more than one gun," Ally whispered nervously.

The next shot sounded like it came from the front of the shed. The bullet stirred the air above their heads with a whoosh and seemed to echo off the steel as it exited through the wall behind them.

Ally let out a yelp. "Jules, he's shooting at us. He's trying to kill us."

"Stay down." Donna's tone was urgent. "That one came through the shed."

In the silence that followed, Jules heard the pulsing sound of her heart thumping wildly in her chest. Ally reached out for her, and Jules grabbed her hand and squeezed. Her breathing was shallow with anticipation and dread about what would come next.

Jules heard a sound. Someone was fumbling with the lock on the shed.

"Maybe it's the police," Ally whispered in the darkness.

And then they heard him.

"You want me?" Nick yelled. He sounded like he was right outside.

Jules leaned into Ally. "He's screaming at someone. The police must be here."

She heard metal on metal as the lock was pulled off, and the latch slammed open.

Ally moaned. "He's coming in here. If the police are here, why aren't they stopping him?"

Above their heads, sunlight flooded the shed as the door was kicked open with a vengeance. Hate filled Nick's voice. "You called the cops. I told you I ain't got nothing to—"

A shot rang out. Jules huddled closer to Ally. From behind the steel panels, they had no idea what was happening. Jules held her breath as she bowed her head next to Ally's and waited. Had Nick shot Donna? Were they next?

"You bitch." Nick's voice was raspy and broken.

In an instant, she heard Donna's zealous wail and the sound of force cracking into a hard object. Muffled voices followed—men's voices.

"Over here," someone shouted.

"Donna, what's going on?" Jules asked loudly as she gripped Ally's arm. She wasn't letting her move until she knew the coast was clear.

Jules heard Donna exhale loudly. "You can come out. They have him."

They? That had to mean the police. "What about Becky?" Jules asked as she scrambled around the stacked metal.

An officer wearing SWAT gear leaned in through the

doorway of the shed and called out, "Ally, are you in here? Are you okay?"

"I am," she said, making her way out into the light streaming into the shed. "There's three of us."

Jules pushed her hair out of her face and followed Ally. She held her hand up to Donna to help her down off the boxes. The SWAT officer led them out of the shed and directed them around Nick. His body laid awkwardly just a few feet from the shed where he had fallen backward after being hit. Blood had spattered against the front of the shed, and a river of red had pooled into the grass beside his right leg.

Jules peered around the SWAT team, who had Nick surrounded. The hair on the side of his head where Donna had hit him looked wet and sticky.

Donna stared down at him. "Is he—"

"Dead?" The officer finished the question for her. "It's not a good sign if they're not racing him out of here to the medics. Nice shot, by the way. You golf out in the real world?"

Donna shook her head and kept her eyes on Nick. "Nope. Just prepared. We didn't know you were out there. We heard the shots, and then a bullet went through the shed."

The officer nodded. "That was him. He shot first, and we returned, but then he headed toward the shed and fired. We were just hoping you were all low to the ground when his shot went through. We held fire when he opened the door until we could get a shot that didn't endanger anyone else. There was already another guy down."

Donna glanced around the yard. Kevin was gone.

The officer nodded. "They have him in the rig. They're working on him." He pulled Donna's arm gently. "C'mon, let's get you out of here."

When they reached an open space of grass out of the way, he focused on Donna's cheek, red and raw from where Nick had hit her. "That looks like it hurts. The medics can check you out."

Donna touched her face. "I'm okay, really. Wasn't the first time he hit me, but it's definitely the last."

The officer's gaze drifted between the three women. "Which one of you is Becky? Your husband called this in. He was pretty freaked out."

Jules's eyes widened. "You haven't found Becky?"

She took off running through the open gate. As she sprinted across the front yard, Bryan, Tim, and Jonas stood across the street. Obviously, they had been told to stay out of the way. The police were already putting up yellow crime tape around the property.

Jules screamed as she ran toward her car, "Pop the trunk! Becky—"

Tim took off toward her vehicle. He yanked the car door open, reached in, and pulled the lever that unlocked the trunk. Jules made it to his side, gasping for breath, and peered over his shoulder as he threw open the trunk. There was no sign of Becky.

Donna reached into her pocket and threw a set of keys to the police officer. "That's my car in front of hers."

The police officer hit the key fob's button, and the trunk opened just as Jules and Tim came around.

Nothing.

"What did he do with her? Where the hell is she?" Jules knew she was shrieking, but her stomach twisted as she remembered that first shot.

Jules spun around toward the house and put her hands on the side of her face. "He said he was going to put her in the trunk," she said to Tim. Jules took off and raced back across the grass toward the driveway. "Open the garage," she yelled. "Someone open the garage."

An officer reached down for the handle, but the door

wouldn't budge. "Go inside," he called out to another officer. "See if there's a way to open it electronically."

The front door slammed behind the cop as he hurried into the house. A few moments later, the garage door started to move.

Jules watched the door lift and moaned when she realized the silver car in the garage was running. She would give anything to be wrong. "Check the trunk. Hurry!"

One of the officers smashed their flashlight into the driver's side window, reached in and unlocked the door. He pulled the keys from the ignition and twisted the lever for the trunk. As it slowly opened, Jules let out a piercing scream. Her best friend lay nestled inside, bound and motionless.

"Get the medics," the officer yelled as he pulled Becky's body from the trunk and carried her away from the car to lay her on the grass. The SWAT medics hustled in and surrounded her.

"That's my wife," Bryan shouted at the officer who tried to keep him from getting to Becky.

"Let the guys help her," he said kindly but firmly.

Jules reached for Bryan and stood between him and Tim as they watched them work on Becky.

Bryan shook his head. "How—"

"She's going to be okay." Jules squeezed his hand. "Becky's tough."

"How is she?" Donna asked as she and Ally caught up with them.

Jules set her jaw to keep from crying. "They're working on her, but she's going to be fine. She *has* to be fine."

"She's breathing," one of the medics said finally as he leaned back on his heels.

Bryan and Jules raced to Becky's side. "Can we untie her hands?" he asked.

One of the medics produced a pair of medical scissors from their bag and clipped the material, freeing Becky's hands.

Bryan knelt and grabbed her hand. "How do you feel?"

Becky opened her eyes slowly and moistened her lips. "My head hurts." She tried to sit up and then laid back down. "Feel a little woozy."

One of the SWAT officers leaned in and glanced at Jules and Bryan. "Give her some breathing room." He directed his attention to one of the medics. "Broken window in the garage."

The medic dipped his head in acknowledgment. "You're very lucky," he said as his gaze bounced from Becky to Bryan.

The officer tapped the medic on the shoulder. "The rescue unit should be here. Transfer care for her, and you should be good to go."

"Okay. The other guy still in the backyard?"

"Yeah. We're just waiting on him to be pronounced. Bullet managed to hit him in the femoral artery. He bled out quick."

Jules glanced behind her to see if Donna had heard the news. She leaned into Bryan. "Be right back."

She made her way to Donna and Ally. It was clear from the stunned look on Donna's face she had heard what the officer said.

She rubbed Donna's arm. "You okay? The bullet was what killed him." Jules spoke gently. "And even if it had been the blow to the head, it was self-defense. He was going to shoot you, maybe even all of us."

Donna leaned forward and gestured for Ally and Jules to lean in until they were huddled together. "After what he did to Ally and to Jay ..." Donna glanced over their heads to where Bryan sat on the grass. "And look what he did to Becky. Even to Kevin. For that poor accountant who didn't deserve to die—"

"And Susan in Orlando who was killed," Jules added.

Donna looked at her quizzically. "You'll fill me in on that later, but okay, for Susan, too." She lowered her voice to a whisper. "I'm not sorry at all that he's dead. For everything he did, for the evil human being he turned out to be, I hope that the last thing he saw was my club heading straight for him." Donna clenched her jaw as she shook her head. "I only have one regret. I just wish my impressive golf swing had been what killed that son of a bitch."

CHAPTER FIFTY

BRYAN HAD WANTED Becky to rest after the hospital released her. She'd had lots of time to think while the doctors monitored her, and although Donna's case was over, there was one more thing she needed to do.

"Hey, buddy," Becky said as Gene came trotting over, tail wagging furiously, to welcome her as she pushed open the front door to their office. He sat obediently in front of her, his brown eyes betraying how desperately he wanted his good behavior to be rewarded. Becky obliged.

"Hey, when did they let you out of the hospital?" Jules asked as Becky strolled in with Gene still glued to her side.

"First thing this morning. I just couldn't hang around the house anymore."

Jules studied her. "You look much better than you did yesterday, but you didn't need to come in at all. I'm just boxing all Donna's stuff to send to her."

"There's something I want to check—"

"I can't get over how much they look alike," Jules said as she taped up the box with Jerry's files. "And they laugh *exactly* the same."

"I'm just glad they're both laughing."

"I can't even believe everything that happened yesterday." Jules looked up from the box and pushed her hair off her face. "You're feeling okay?"

Becky nodded. "Oxygen is a wonderful thing. The doctor said I was really lucky."

She didn't mention the blood work at the hospital also confirmed what she'd already suspected. Despite some short-lived hope this month, she wasn't pregnant. She was relieved she hadn't said anything to anyone yet. After the carbon monoxide exposure, she knew it was for the best and was glad Bryan didn't also have their baby to worry about yesterday.

"Good thing that garage window was broken," Jules said. "You had me really scared."

"Me too. If you hadn't found me when you did ..." Becky didn't finish the thought, but they both knew it could have been much worse.

"I'm just thankful you're okay. Nick's dead, and it wasn't Donna's fault. Even Kevin's going to make it, though I guess he'll have charges of some sort against him, not to mention Jay to deal with. It's over."

Becky sank down into the chair beside Jules. "Bryan begged me last night to go back to the boutique."

"I know, Tim and I talked about it last night, too." Jules wagged her finger in the air as she mimicked him. "Why can't you go back to taking pictures for a living. It was so much safer."

"But did you see Donna and Ally yesterday? I'm a sucker for a happy ending. And Jules, we did that. Think about all the people she has in her life now." Becky scrunched up her face. "What about Jay?"

"Donna wants to take it slow. She's in no rush to get married, but she's relieved he didn't have anything to do with all of this." Jules gave a small shrug. "She still loves him. It's not like Jay had any idea his brother even knew Donna's ex-husband."

Becky nodded and nudged one of the other boxes with her foot. "Is there anything else in the other boxes she or Ally might want? Can we condense them into one?"

Jules put down the tape gun and peered into the box. "I still think Jerry knew what he was doing when he left this stuff for her. It's our fault we didn't go through the case files to find Bobby." She started pulling out the contents. "I'm sure Donna doesn't need all these canceled checks." She reached for the book they'd found. "I remember when Christopher Reeve was in that accident. Superman paralyzed. It didn't seem like it could be real."

Becky thoughtfully nodded. "Maybe Jerry had this book because of his dad. Or maybe he bought it because of Robert."

Jules flipped open the cover. "Well, here's the answer." She handed the book to Becky.

Becky read the message. *Jerry, I'm still me, too, and no chair is going to change that. Just because we lost the case doesn't give me a reason to be bitter. I intend to be grateful for every day I have with my beautiful family. We now consider you an honorary member. Warmly, Bobby.*

Becky flipped through the book, and a piece of paper fell out.

"What's that?" Jules asked.

Becky rolled her eyes and flipped the paper around. "Bobby's address and phone number."

"Of course. Remember how surprised he was that Jerry hadn't left his information for Donna? Let's save the book for her. And the datebooks. Let's make sure we add those, too."

"I'll have to bring—"

Jules's phone rang, and she reached for it on the floor beside her. "Hey, Donna. She's okay. She's actually here in the office." A pause. "I know. Let me put you on speaker."

"Hey, Donna, are you with Ally?" Becky asked.

"I am, but Becky, I am *so* sorry about what happened. Are you okay?"

"I am, don't worry. What time are you going to see Norman?"

"We're on our way now."

"Hey, guys," Ally piped up in the distance.

"Hi, Ally," Becky and Jules said in unison.

"Did your mom and daughter make it in okay yesterday?" Becky asked.

Ally groaned. "My daughter wasn't feeling well, so my husband took her to the doctor and rebooked them for today. Of course, my mom was pretty freaked out when she kept calling and couldn't get through to tell me. I'm actually glad she didn't know everything that was going on. It was bad enough I had to live it."

"We're all glad it's over," Donna said. "They should be landing any minute. They're meeting us at Norman's office."

"Do you all want to meet up for dinner later?" Jules asked.

"Ally's mom wants to go see Ella, so we're going to do that after we see Norman. But afterward, my aunt and uncle are throwing a bit of a party so I can see all my cousins. She said I could invite the Taylors, too, so they're coming, and of course, Ally and her mom and daughter. And Jay's meeting me there."

"That's more than a bit of a party," Becky said with a smile.

"Please come," Donna said. "None of this would have happened without the two of you. Bring your husbands. Well, Jules, you bring the man who gave you that beautiful ring."

Jules held out her hand, happy her engagement ring was back on her finger where it belonged. "I would love to. I'll ask Tim, and if Becky's up to it—"

"I'm up to it. Bryan and I would love to come."

"Great. I'll text you the address, and we'll see you later. Around five?"

Jules disconnected the call, and her text message pinged seconds later. "When we started this case, did you ever imagine this is the way it would end? I mean, not the murder, obviously. But Donna—she's so happy."

Becky's eyes welled up. "I told you." She placed her palm over her heart. "The happy endings just get me."

Gene lifted himself off his bed and trotted toward the door in the front as someone opened it.

Jules wrinkled her nose. "I wonder who that could be. He's very friendly," she called out as she followed him.

A moment later, she returned with their visitor.

"Dr. Summers?" Becky asked as she stood, surprise on her face.

"You remember me?"

"It was only six months ago. Besides, you don't get into a car accident, think you're losing your mind, and not remember your neurologist. Obviously, you've met Jules. She's my partner."

"We did meet. At the door. And Gene, too." He glanced over at the dog, who was waiting to see if there would be any more attention coming his way. "Gene and I are now old buddies." He smiled and turned his gaze to Becky. "You're feeling okay these days, I presume?"

Becky shot Jules a look and then answered. "I'm fine." Yesterday, she might not have said the same thing, but there was really no need to go into that.

"I saw the newspaper article about your agency. I'm impressed."

Becky laughed. "It's not impressive just yet, but we did just solve a big case."

"That's actually why I'm here. I'm hoping you can help a patient of mine."

Becky gestured at the chair in front of her desk. "We might. What's going on?"

Dr. Summers lowered himself into the chair. "Brittany—actually that's probably not her real name—had an accident. We don't know exactly what happened, but she ended up in the hospital. She suffered some pretty significant memory loss. Physically, she's healing, but nothing's come back."

Jules's eyebrows raised. "She has amnesia?"

Dr. Summers nodded. "Pretty much. She can't remember what happened, and the ID she had on her doesn't seem to be hers. The police haven't been able to figure anything out about who she really is."

Becky pressed her lips together. "We could have her do a DNA test, see if we can figure out who she is through her matches—"

"That's precisely what I was thinking," Dr. Summers said. "Can I give her your information? Tell her to call and set up an appointment to come see you?"

They had their next case. "Of course," Becky said as she shook his hand.

"I guess we won't be sitting idle long," Jules said after he left. "Let's finish up with these boxes and get out of here. I need to get a hold of Tim and tell him about tonight."

"We can load them into my car, and then Bryan can put them into Donna's car at the party."

"There's not much except the file box, and we can merge everything else into this smaller one." Jules placed the book inside, added Jerry's framed diplomas and certificates, a few awards he had won. "I guess it's not our place to get rid of the canceled checks. That's on them." Jules tossed the bag into the box. "That's really everything that's left. Just bring the date-books tonight, and we'll add those, too."

"That's not everything."

Jules cocked her head. "What else is there?"

Becky pulled the flash drive out of her desk drawer. "I was thinking about this yesterday at the hospital."

Jules shrugged. "But we never found the password."

"Remember what you said originally? Jerry would have had no reason to leave it if he didn't think the password could be figured out."

Jules nodded as she came around to Becky's side and leaned her elbows on the desk. "You think you figured it out? We pretty much tried everything we could think of."

"Not everything. I remembered something Donna told us." Becky inserted the drive into the USB port of her computer and waited until the box requesting the password popped up. "I'm thinking he included everyone important in the password —Ava, Donna, her brother, Ally."

"We tried that."

Becky held up her index finger. "But we thought the son's name was Jerome. Remember, Donna said they were actually going to call him James."

"Oh, right. Try it."

Becky typed it in but got an error message. "Damn. I really thought that was it."

"Add Robert to the end. Wait—" Jules held up her hand. "Use Bobby instead."

Becky typed all the names, held her breath, and hit enter. The files popped up on the screen, and a smile lit up her face. "You're a genius."

Jules bowed. "Well, thank you, but we're brilliant together."

"There's a copy of the will," Becky said as she pointed at the screen. "And these look like the letters he wrote. Here's the one he wrote to Bobby."

"And Ella."

"Looks like there's one for Ally. And two for Donna." Becky glanced at Jules. "Maybe one was the first one we read, and the other is for today?" She clicked the mouse to open the first file, and it was the letter they had read in their initial meeting.

"Open the other Donna file," Jules said as she nudged her.

Becky double-clicked on the icon, and the letter popped up on the screen.

They both read silently until Becky finally glanced up, her eyes wet. "I hope this helps. Maybe Donna will realize, despite everything, her father really did love her. He just didn't prove it the way she expected."

EPILOGUE

As SHE SAT in Norman's waiting room next to her sister, Donna felt completely different than she had the last time. Gone was the pretentious outfit, the anxiety, Jay telling her to sit down and stop pacing.

Last time, the money had been the most important thing. She'd been angry at the idea of a sister and furious she had to share her inheritance. As Donna glanced over at Ally, she now felt calm and in control.

The same blond secretary as last time came out to get them. This time she smiled as she greeted them both and told them to follow her back to Norman's office.

"You must be Alexandra," Norman said as he rose from his leather chair.

"Everyone calls me Ally." She extended her hand.

Norman shook Donna's hand next. "Donna." He took in the bruises on her face, visible even through the layer of makeup she had used. "Everything okay?"

Donna nodded and glanced at her sister. "Better than okay. I'm wonderful."

Norman bobbed his head as a small smile played out on his

face. "I can't get over how alike you two look. Except for the hair."

Donna elbowed Ally and laughed. "She only wishes she got the cool redhead gene."

Norman gestured at the heavy chairs facing his desk. "Well, have a seat. I'm sure you're eager to get this over with and put it behind you." He lowered himself back into his chair and opened the folder in front of him. "I have some papers for you both to sign, but I have something else for each of you first."

Donna stared back curiously. What other surprises did her father have in store for them?

Norman handed Ally an envelope. "Your father—Jerry, he wrote you a letter."

As Ally took the envelope from his hand, she looked quizzically at Donna.

Donna shrugged. "It's okay. Apparently, he was fond of writing down his thoughts toward the end."

"There's another letter for you, too, Donna." Norman retrieved a second envelope and held it out in her direction. He returned his attention to his desk and shuffled through a pile of papers. "Go ahead and read them, and I'll get the papers ready for you both to sign."

Donna slipped her finger under the flap to unseal it, and after a quick glance toward Ally, she pulled out the paper with her father's words.

Dear Donna,

If you're reading this, I hope it's because you've found your sister. My greatest wish is that she's sitting right next to you. I hope you haven't held my shortcomings against her. She was an innocent child, just like you were.

I'm sure you were surprised, and no doubt bitter, when you were told about the contents of my will. I understand. I never gave you anything, but it should have been time for you to inherit all I had. You probably felt I owed you, and you'd be right. But while money often feels like the easy answer, there are things it can't buy—priceless things. More than anything, that's what I wanted to leave behind for you.

When you met Bobby and his family, I hoped you'd understand why I sold them the house and included them in my will. It wasn't merely that I lost his case. He reminded me of what my father could have been if his disability had not turned him mean and abusive. I wanted Bobby and his family to have an easier life than I had, and if there is a way he can walk again, I want to make sure he has that chance.

The Taylors are wonderful people who took me in and made me part of their family. Over and over, they told me to include you. But I was scared. I didn't want them to see me through your eyes. Disappointed and resentful. I love those children, but I didn't want that to make you angry they had what I was never able to give to you. To them, I was Jerry the lawyer, the guy who threw footballs and did puzzles.

You may not recognize me in the stories they tell, but I did find happiness there, and I want the same for you. Try to see me through their eyes, so you'll know I wasn't a bad person. I felt shame for making you an only child without a mother and for taking your mom's family from you when you needed them most. I knew it was wrong every time I sent Ella to do what I should have done as a father. That guilt paralyzed me. I'm sorry I wasn't a stronger man. I wasn't the dad you deserved, and I realized and regretted that every day of my life.

I considered leaving the house to you but realized sometimes the past is best left as a place you visit only briefly. When it is filled with the Taylor's love and laughter, perhaps you will have a flicker of a memory of when your mother filled those rooms with such joy. But I hope you can release the rest of it. Without the constant reminder of living there, I hope you will be able to build your future in a place you choose, a place that feels like your home. Your new beginning.

Attached to this letter are phone numbers for your aunts. Reach out to them. Tell them I'm sorry they had to wait so long to be part of your life. You have uncles and cousins who will be thrilled to reunite with you. They'll fill you with beautiful stories about your mom and share how much she loved you.

They'll be able to tell you about the past when your mother and I were happy. Sometimes you only get one great love. Your mother was mine. I can only hope you've found in someone what we found in each other. Taped to the back of our wedding photo, you'll find your mother's rings. I'm sorry I couldn't bear to part with them sooner. Wear them if they bring you peace or turn them into something you can wear every day to keep her memory close to you. You were the center of your mother's entire universe. She would want you to have them.

In the boxes I left for you, you will find the cemetery information where your mother and brother are buried. It's a peaceful, beautiful spot, and I found much solace in my time there. I'm not afraid to die. My greatest wish is that your mother and James will be there to greet me. I pray there will be forgiveness for me, as I'm sure she knows what a broken man I was without her. I hope you and your sister can do the same.

I know I don't deserve that you'll miss me when I'm gone. But I hope when you feel the warmth of the sun on your face, you'll know that I am watching over you and smiling that my girls have found each other. When I changed my will, my wish was that you'd finally have what I could never give you. I knew, more than any amount of money, what you really needed was a family. Revel in them and know I really did love you.

Dad

Donna folded the letter in her lap, and without a word, she reached over and squeezed her sister's hand. Ally's eyes were wet when she glanced over, but she nodded.

After they finished the paperwork, Norman called his secretary to walk them out.

"There's someone in the lobby waiting for you," she said over her shoulder as she led them back to the reception area.

A smile erupted on Ally's face as they pushed open the glass doors. "You made it." Ally made introductions. "Mom, this is Donna."

Molly extended her hand, but Donna leaned in and wrapped her arms around her. "I'm so happy to meet you. I couldn't be any happier to have Ally as my sister." Donna whispered in her ear. "I'm sorry this didn't happen sooner, but we'll all make up for lost time."

When she pulled back, Ally picked up the little girl shyly hiding behind her grandmother's leg. She balanced the toddler on her hip and held her small hand as she made the introduction. "Kristy, this is your Aunt Donna."

"Aunt Donna," the little girl parroted back.

Donna's eyes welled up. "I can't believe I have a niece. One who has the prettiest red curls I ever did see." Donna leaned in close to her but loudly whispered so Ally could hear. "Lucky you. You got the cool redhead gene."

She placed a kiss on the little girl's cheek, marveling at how soft it was against her lips. "Don't you worry, Kristy. I'll show you how to manage those curls. We'll get some bows and ribbons and get you all dolled up." She gave Ally a sidewards glance. "Ask your Mommy. Someday she'll tell you all about how I used to fix her hair, too."

"Speaking of Ella's house, let's go see her," Ally said. "And then we all have a big party to go to." She headed out of the lobby with Kristy in her arms. Donna fell into step next to her.

"And you're going to fill me in on exactly what happened yesterday, right?" Molly said as she pushed the empty stroller behind them.

Ally swung around to face her mom. "My sister saved my life. That's what happened."

As the group made it out of the building, Donna paused when they got to the parking lot. She brought her gaze up to the picture-perfect blue sky, and when a breeze blew her hair away from her face, she shut her eyes. Her cheeks grew hot and turned pink in the warmth of the sun. Contentment settled over her like a gentle hug.

Thank you, Dad, Donna said silently and then opened her eyes. Her father was right. There were some things no amount of money could buy. She looked over at Ally and Kristy, and a smile tugged at her lips.

Her father couldn't change the past, but he had changed her future. And in the end, he had loved her enough to leave her the perfect inheritance.

ALSO BY LIANE CARMEN

Thank you for reading *The Dark Inheritance*.

If you've enjoyed this book, a review or rating would be much appreciated. Reviews and referrals help other readers discover the Investigation Duo Series.

Book #1: *Where the Truth Hides*

Book #2: *The Dark Inheritance*

Book #3: *Memory Hunter* (coming in 2021)

When Brittany appears at the hospital, she's alone and in bad shape. Slowly, she begins to heal from her physical injuries, but she's locked away the memories of who she is and what's happened to her. She has keys to an apartment and identification, but neither belongs to her.

Brittany comes to Jules and Becky in hopes they can use her DNA to determine who she really is. While they wait for her results, the detectives dig into the identity she's using in hopes it might explain her past. It becomes clear she's in hiding—from something or someone. When a mysterious man seems to recognize Brittany, they know they need to protect her until they can figure out how he fits in.

As they unravel the man's agenda, they realize too late there's even more at stake than they imagined. When they're distracted by a big event, Brittany goes missing. Becky panics, especially when she realizes Jules is nowhere to be found either.

ACKNOWLEDGMENTS

First, I want to thank every person who read and enjoyed *Where the Truth Hides*. Your positive comments and reviews were the fuel that powered me to finish *The Dark Inheritance* earlier than I expected. You told me you felt like Becky and Jules were friends. I feel the same. I'm thrilled this is a series, so I can continue their story to see where it takes all of us.

I'm grateful for **Jonas Saul**, who went from a favorite author to an editor and mentor. I've learned more about writing from him than anyone else. He's incredibly gracious with his time, even when he sends me my final edited manuscript, and I respond a few days later that I made "just a few plot changes." Someday I will remember when to use blond vs. blonde and if not, my characters will all just be brunettes and redheads.

For all the advice **Lieutenant Steve Feeley, BSO** gave me, I made him a detective in this book. His police background was invaluable and his patience endless as I continually grilled him, "but COULD it happen that way?" I did ask if he needed an intern or had an in with the DNA department of the crime lab. I'm still waiting.

Poor Bryan's never going to let Becky out of his sight again. **Sean Maxwell** was right there with his paramedic training to tell me just how to handle Becky's time in the car trunk to ensure she came out of it without *too* many problems (though I did have to rewrite a chapter when he convinced me she would absolutely, positively have to spend time being monitored in the hospital).

When you have questions about a will and an inheritance, you go to a probate attorney. Lucky for me, **Regina Drennan** couldn't wait to jump in to help me, even going so far as to write an actual will for Jerry so I could reference it. Her legal skills went much deeper than my fictional story could accommodate, and I know she was glad none of this was for a real client. I was honored to allow her naming rights for Donna's dad which she used to honor her father and grandfather.

David Lubetkin, MD is my go-to doctor resource on anything pregnancy-related. Ava's troubles and her early delivery issues were courtesy of his obstetrics expertise and experience.

Stacy Ostrau is the Jules to my Becky. I loved that in this book I was able to give her Gene, a golden retriever of her own, and a proposal that made even me tear up. Girl, we've got a wedding to write!

For **Peyton Regaldo**, **Brenda Staton**, **Brittany Schroeder**, **Claire Cone**, **Stacey Halpin**, **Woody Kamena** and everyone who agreed to read this book ahead of the curve to provide feedback, I'm so appreciative.

To all the people who volunteered to let me use their names in this book (and a few who didn't), I thank you. Sometimes that's the most fun of all when I'm writing. If your name appears, chances are it's because I wanted a way to celebrate you. Unless, of course, you happen to find yourself murdered, and then you should probably ask yourself what it is exactly you've done to annoy me. Hmm.

ABOUT THE AUTHOR

Photo by Bill Ziady

Liane Carmen is the author of the Investigation Duo Series. After using DNA testing to solve her own family mystery, she became passionate about helping others and writing stories about buried secrets. She takes it up a notch for Jules and Becky, whose cases lead them down a much darker and dangerous path than her own.

Her DVR is filled with shows from the ID channel, which she tries to reassure her boyfriend are merely "book research." Her goal is to write novels that keep mystery lovers guessing, and if her Google searches ever come into question, she'd be grateful if her readers could vouch for her.

She loves to read in her spare time and is also a genealogy buff who's been known to lose large blocks of time researching her family tree. She lives in Florida with her teenaged son and a houseful of pets, all of whom are always hungry.

For more information and to subscribe to her newsletter, visit her website at www.lianecarmen.com.
Email: lianecarmen@icloud.com

facebook.com/LianeCarmenAuthor

twitter.com/liane_carmen

instagram.com/liane_carmen_author